MW01282101

Arms Race

ERIC SWAN THRILLER #6

DOM TESTA

Arms Race: Eric Swan thriller #6

By Dom Testa

Published by Profound Impact Group, LLC

PO Box 506

Alpharetta, GA 30009

Reach us at EricSwan.com

ISBN: 978-1-942151-71-5

Cover art by Damonza

More Eric Swan
from Dom Testa

Power Trip: Eric Swan Thriller #1

Swan takes on diabolical twins determined to bring down the power grid. If he fails, the country will slip into a dark age of chaos and anarchy.

Poison Control: Eric Swan Thriller #2

A treacherous madman is intent on poisoning the water supply. Swan must outsmart this rogue scholar before he can release his apocalyptic toxin.

God Maker: Eric Swan Thriller #3

Agent One has resurfaced, and he's kidnapped the mother of Q2's investment technology. Swan must not only battle this psychotic killer, but come to grips with his own fears.

Field Agent: Eric Swan Thriller #4

Swan's on the hunt for a tech billionaire who's out to control the world's food supply. But there's a sinister element to the plan with terrifying consequences.

Quiet War: Eric Swan Thriller #5

The world's most destructive hacker, a shadowy figure known only as *Ceti*, is on the brink of toppling the world's economy. How can Swan prevent international chaos when people see the madman as a hero?

Join the Swaniverse.
Get cool stuff.

With each new tale you'll learn a little more about Q2's super spy, Eric Swan.

You might also want to know how it all began. Join the Swaniverse and I'll send you Swan's ***Origin*** story as a thank you.

Plus, you'll be the first to learn of each new adventure *before* they're published. Just let me know where to find you.

Two ways to make it happen. Scan this QR code with your phone's camera and it'll take you to the Swaniverse page to sign up.

Or log on to EricSwan.com.

Thanks, and happy reading.
Dom Testa

CONTENTS

Chapter 1	1
Chapter 2	11
Chapter 3	21
Chapter 4	33
Chapter 5	45
Chapter 6	53
Chapter 7	63
Chapter 8	73
Chapter 9	83
Chapter 10	95
Chapter 11	107
Chapter 12	119
Chapter 13	133
Chapter 14	143
Chapter 15	155
Chapter 16	167
Chapter 17	179
Chapter 18	189
Chapter 19	201
Chapter 20	211
Chapter 21	221
Chapter 22	231
Chapter 23	243
Chapter 24	251
Chapter 25	261
Chapter 26	273
Chapter 27	285
Chapter 28	297
Chapter 29	305
Chapter 30	319

Chapter 31   333
Chapter 32   347

More Eric Swan adventures from Dom Testa   361

CHAPTER ONE

The view was magnificent. From a height of more than 60 stories above the street, one could see for miles up and down the coast, as well as miles out to sea. It was stunning, breathtaking, and all the other usual adjectives you'll find peppering brochures. The Four Seasons Miami was a glittering palace of glass and granite during the day and a beacon of wealth shining for all to see at night. I personally preferred the view right now, well after midnight, the quarter moon competing with lights from the city, mixed with the lights bobbing on the water, a testament to dozens of boats enjoying the balmy, early summer night. Between the hotel accommodations and the lavish, private condos that made up all 70 floors, hundreds of people might be relishing the same view I took in at the moment.

The difference was that they were *inside* the building, not suctioned to the outside.

With a free hand, I finished the keto chocolate bar I'd enjoyed while watching a spectacular yacht, one of those 280-foot beauties, motoring to the north. From this distance, I couldn't hear the churning of its engines, but I assumed it produced the type of low rumble that would act as a sort of brown noise, perfect to sleep by. I wondered what kind of crook was cozied up in the boat's stateroom and if he'd be amused to know that his ride was being admired by a man dangling outside a skyscraper, munching on a chocolate treat.

The conditions were ideal, with the wind calmer than usual. It whipped my hair a bit, but not enough to concern me. I unzipped a jacket pocket and stuffed the keto bar wrapper inside. Out of habit, I tapped the other side of the jacket and felt the comforting shape of my trusty Glock within. If all went well, I wouldn't need it.

I glanced upward at the cable connecting me to the roof, my primary means of support and propulsion. The suction pads were merely for convenience. They kept me from swaying while I waited for the target inside to pass out. Hopefully it wouldn't be much longer. He'd consumed copious amounts of whiskey during dinner and at the casino; how he'd managed to stay conscious this long was beyond me. Probably a case of acclimation. He was known for his love of drink, and a lifetime of excess allowed him to handle the booze longer than usual while simultaneously destroying his liver.

Remarkably dumb behavior from one of the world's smartest people.

His name was Sung-Ho Gwan, originally from North Korea before being smuggled out by a crack Russian team lusting for his brain power. Gwan outsmarted his kidnappers, however, and slipped away after a year. Since that time, he'd used his brilliant mind to not only stay undercover, but also to sell his services to high bidders.

Those services involved the formulation of chemical weapons able to devastate a population. Gwan's devices had been used a few times in isolated attacks, generally by shadowy but well-funded, subversive groups. The results were hideous. Gwan, in the meantime, made bank, all the while evading capture.

Now he was in Miami, and he was drunk again.

You might think, *He's an international terrorist; why not just bust in and arrest him?*

It's a good question. The answer was complicated.

Sure, we could waltz in and place him under arrest. But, for one thing, he hadn't contributed to an attack on US soil. Yet.

More importantly—and the reason *I* was involved—Gwan was currently at the center of a strange coalition of small foreign groups. These five factions hated each other, but they also shared common enemies, one of which was the United States. They'd just as soon cut each other's throats, but Gwan gave them an opportunity to pool their resources to go after America.

It was my boss, Quanta, the head of the secret group known simply as Q2, who'd come up with a brilliant plan. Well, brilliant on her part because she wasn't the one dangling 650 feet above the pavement. But still, if we pulled it off, we'd not only eliminate the mass murderer named Gwan, but we'd also pit all five of the evil factions against each other.

It was simple in theory: I break in, take the mad scientist, and leave clues that it was perpetrated by a couple of the factions working with each other and against the other three.

In practice, it wasn't so simple. Gwan occupied the lavish, rented residence alone, but a rotating team of armed thugs, representing the various groups sponsoring him, were stationed in the hallway outside the condo's door. Additionally, one protector was assigned to the living area of the suite. So getting inside in a traditional way was out of the question without raising hell and showing up all over the surveillance systems of the Four Seasons. The best we could do was plant a listening device in the bedroom of the suite.

No, not for pervy reasons. Stay with me.

That left but one avenue for an incursion: breaking in from outside. Thus, my Spider-Man routine. The hotel would be generously compensated on the q.t., more than enough to repair the inevitable damages, and the American population could go unsus-pectingly—and safely—through their days.

Naturally, after devising the plan, Quanta turned to her most experienced agent to do the dirty work. So now it was Swan versus Gwan.

A voice crackled in my earpiece. "Eric?"

"Yep," I said, worrying over a remnant of the chocolate bar with my tongue. "What's up, Agent Brosh?"

"Target is snoring like a freight train." See? That's why we had the bug in the room.

Then she added, "No wonder he's single."

I grinned. "All right. Let me unstick myself and you can lower me the rest of the way."

A minute later, I dangled outside Gwan's bedroom window, which stretched floor to ceiling. I reached into a zippered pocket on my workout pants and pulled out the glass cutter. Carefully tracing a line about three feet by three feet that began parallel to the floor of the bedroom, I sliced through the first layer. After attaching four suction pads to the corners, all connected to a separate guideline, I finished cutting through and slipped the glass cutter back into my pocket. With a gentle tug, the square section separated from the rest of the pane.

"Glass removed," I murmured into the small microphone beneath my chin. "Let me pack the sides and you can take it away."

I stuck a substance similar to bubble wrap around the perimeter of the piece so it wouldn't bang against the building and shatter. Then, giving the okay, I watched as Agent Brosh and her partner cautiously pulled the section up to the roof and out of the way.

I listened at the gaping opening to the room, but all I heard was the drunk snoring Brosh had described. She was right; it was pretty obnoxious. I chuckled as I pulled myself into the room. Standing up, I disconnected the safety harness and quietly laid it on the floor. Tiptoeing to the door, I put my ear against it. There was no sound at all: no music, no TV, no conversation. The hired goon in the living area was either asleep—which I doubted—or, more likely, scrolling through his phone. He shouldn't be a problem.

Moving back into the room, I glided over to where Gwan was stretched out on the bed. He lay diagonally on top of the comforter, clad only in underwear. Nice underwear, to be sure, but I wished that he'd at least have thrown on a T-shirt or something. I unzipped another pocket to remove the tranquilizer gun. At the sound, which was next to nothing, Gwan stirred. He made a comical grunt which could've been an attempt at a word, and I froze. But he was still asleep, his eyes closed.

Taking one more look over my shoulder at the door, I placed a gloved hand over Gwan's mouth and fired the tranquilizer at his midsection. The faint sound—some say it's similar to a cat sneezing—was nothing. Gwan's eyes popped open briefly and seemed to try to make sense of the variety of sensations overtaking him, but he quickly drifted off again. His eyes remained open halfway, which was creepy. I couldn't work like that, so I pulled them closed.

With a heave, I lifted him off the bed, thankful the man was on the smaller side. With him over my shoulder, I made my way back to the breach in the window and set him down. The next two minutes were spent securing my harness to him, then double-checking each connection.

Couldn't have 140 pounds of Korean scientist slamming into the street from 63 floors up, now could we?

"Package ready for pickup," I whispered into the mic, maneuvering his body out the opening.

I stood back and watched through the surviving portion of the window as he gradually rose out of sight. While they hoisted him away, I got to work arranging the bogus clues that would implicate a couple of the faction members. Ideally, they'd look like remnants accidentally left behind by clumsy kidnappers: a ski mask with the appropriate foreign tag on it and a cell phone, chock-full of contacts and messages conveniently created by the smarty-pants on Q2's second floor. One message, in the appropriate language, even said, "He's asleep. Easy."

Okay, so it was a little too obvious and maybe even amateurish. But we weren't exactly dealing with rational, reasonable people here. They were already a breath away from turning on each other; the "evidence" didn't need to be top-rate.

I looked out the hole in the window just as the harness, now empty, came back into view.

And that's when I heard the tapping.

It came from the bedroom door and had to be the bodyguard from the living room. What the hell he could possibly want from his boss's bedroom at nearly two o'clock in the morning wasn't important. What *was* important was that he was standing out there, knocking. Perhaps he was under orders to check in every so often, whether summoned or not.

I instinctively reached for the Glock, but a firefight would only alert the muscle who waited out in the hallway. It would also sound the alarm for a lot of people who would make their way to the rooftop before the FBI could pirate away the valuable treasure.

In a flash, another idea occurred to me. I rushed back to the bed, yanked down the covers, jumped in, then pulled the comforter back up over my head. I'd no sooner finished that move than I heard the door open and a deep voice call out in what sounded like a Greek accent.

I did my best impression of a snore.

Let me just say right now, impressions of snores are lame, have always been lame, and always *will* be lame. It's not something most people can fake without sounding more ridiculous than a *Tom and Jerry* cartoon.

But then again, Gwan was also known to be a lush, so maybe

my silly snoring wouldn't raise an eyebrow. Perhaps the guard simply wanted to get something out of a closet and would quietly get in and out. Plus, it was dark enough in the room that, unless he was looking for it, he might not even notice the nine-square-foot hole at the bottom of the far window.

A boy can dream.

I heard the lamp click on beside the bed, Then, with a *whoosh*, the cover was snatched away and I was looking up into the face of a very confused man. A very *large*, confused man.

I stared back up at him and said, "Please, Mom, five more minutes."

It bought me all of two seconds. After that, two meaty paws reached for me. I rolled to my left across the bed. The problem was, the blanket still covered the lower half of my body, making it hard to scramble effectively. Before I could extricate myself, he had a powerful grip on my right arm and dragged me back toward him.

As silly as it sounds, my goal was to have the quietest fight of all time. I had to somehow disable this beast without alerting the other goons out in the hall. Granted, in this massive suite, the bedroom was tucked out of the way and not necessarily close to the hallway door. But I couldn't take the chance. *One* guy I might be able to handle; three would be problematic.

Although handling this one dude didn't seem all that easy. He was not only big and strong, he was fast. Before I knew what had hit me, he—well, he hit me.

Don't let movies fool you. Getting punched is no picnic. It hurts. A heavyweight boxer once described it in the simplest terms ever. He said, "I can tell you right now, it don't feel good." And those guys wear padded gloves.

It also, unlike the Hollywood versions, leaves a mark. And it can easily take you out of the action in a flash. If you've ever seen an honest to goodness bar fight, they rarely last more than one or two punches.

At least the guy had me untangled, which gave me a little room to operate. I gave him a decent head butt, which normally would incapacitate an opponent. With him, the appearance of his own blood seemed to energize him.

"Shit," I muttered as his eyes widened and a cruel smile spread across his face. I jumped backward, landing back on the bed, then tumbled over to the far side. With his speed, he was immediately around the bed. The only thing handy to grab—don't laugh—was one of the pillows. I snatched it and swung it at him.

Yes, Eric Swan, super spy and all-American hero, was in the midst of a pillow fight. This would definitely *not* find its way into my report.

But it at least produced one positive result. The beast threw a hand up to ward off the cushy weapon, which took his eyes off me. As soon as he lowered the hand, I fired a solid kick into his chin, which jolted him back a step. I followed that with a round-house kick to the side of his head. But he still wouldn't go down. Instead, his left hand shot out and clutched my throat. Before I could knock it away, he'd lifted me off my feet and, with strength pulled straight out of a Marvel movie, the monster slung me toward the window.

Actually, directly at the gaping hole in the window. The hole *I'd* made.

If I hadn't quickly recovered and stretched out an arm to stop myself, it would've been a clean shot through the breach, like a perfect roll in Skeeball when it plops through the 50-point hole without touching the sides. The next stop would've been the pavement.

But I couldn't process all that in the moment. Big Boy was back on top of me, knocking my hand away from the glass and shoving my head out the hole in the window. It dawned on me: *Holy shit. That wasn't some lucky shot. The son of a bitch is actually trying to push me through the opening.*

He was strong enough to do it, too, especially because I had no leverage on the floor. I slipped a little farther out, to the point I felt cool night air blowing across my face. He wore a truly wicked smile, made all the more grisly when combined with the blood dripping from his forehead onto his lower lip, courtesy of my head butt. He shoved me out another few inches. Just a bit more and gravity would do the rest.

Trying to loosen his grip on me was pointless in my position. With his bulk manhandling me, it was impossible to reach the Glock strapped under my jacket. I still didn't want to fire a shot anyway, if I could help it. Although, given the choice of taking on two or three more hired killers or plummeting 650 feet to my death, I'd probably choose Option A.

Oh, wait. I did have another choice. Doing my best to drag my heels and slow down my movement, I scrambled with my right hand into the zippered pants pocket. While I did this, he grunted and shoved me another two inches, so now my shoulders hung outside. Finally, after fumbling for a moment, my fingers closed around the glass cutter and I yanked it out.

With one quick stabbing movement, I rammed the blade into the back of his neck.

His mouth shot open with a bizarre, soundless roar, like a scene from a silent movie. His body tensed and his grasp on me slackened. I yanked out the blade and jammed it in again. This time, he let out a gurgle and some blood sprayed from his mouth. Naturally, all over my face.

That's another way Hollywood deceives you. They never show you just how disgustingly gross a spy's job can be.

And yet, with all that, the brute still wouldn't die. He fell off me to the side, but was reaching back, trying to stem the tide of blood, and climbing back to his feet. I pulled myself back into the room and got up just as he tried to do battle one more time.

"You have got to be kidding me," I said to him, trying to wipe his blood off my face but mostly just smearing it.

He lunged. I sidestepped, reached down for the blanket on

the bed, and pulled it up and over his head, twisting it as he struggled to rip it off. Even with the two deep wounds in his neck, he actually got in a lucky punch to my side, knocking the wind out of me a bit. But I held on, spinning and twisting a little more. He let out a muffled roar.

"Shh," I said. "Don't wake the neighbors."

And with that, I reached down, grabbed the clock radio off the nightstand, ripped it out of the wall, and smashed it down on top of the blanketed head with every ounce of strength I could muster. This stopped him short, and I saw his knees buckle. A second bash put him down on the floor, still covered from the shoulders up with the blanket. A sizable pool of blood oozed around him.

I sat down on the edge of the bed to catch my breath and put my hand up against the side of my face where I'd been struck. I winced and, just for spite, kicked the dying goon in the stomach.

Childish? Yes.

I tugged the loose bed sheet over to me and tried wiping the gore from my throbbing face.

This was not at all what I'd expected on this job.

"Hey Eric," came the voice of Brosh in my ear. "What the hell are you doing down there? Getting a drink for the road?"

I had to chuckle. But then I looked toward the bedroom door and raised an eyebrow. These fancy suites *did* have bars in them.

CHAPTER TWO

The request I'd made was straightforward and direct: "Please don't hit me on the left side of my face. It's still tender."

And yet Quanta either didn't care, or she took sadistic pride in the amount of pain she could inflict during our routine workouts. I'd left the military with a significant knowledge of martial arts and hand-to-hand combat, enough to imbue anyone with a healthy dose of confidence. But it was as if I'd never had a single lesson when I first squared off against the Asian woman who was all of five feet two inches tall. Over time, I'd managed to absorb the lessons she'd imparted. Absorbed them not just intellectually, but physically, too.

It made me a better fighter. It's why I never felt a shred of fear against the behemoth who'd clubbed me inside the Miami hotel room. Once Quanta had kicked your ass for years, you'd at least be competitive with almost any fighter in the world.

At least, that's what I told myself.

It's another reason I inwardly looked forward to the punishment. Following these sessions, I'd almost always walk away with a new move or some insight into quality defense. The lessons took place in the idyllic garden outside her home in a Washington, DC, suburb.

When she'd put me on my butt for a third time in less than two minutes, she walked off toward her house, leaving me to brush off. I trudged in behind her, stretching my jaw open and closed like a fish out of water. She'd spend the next 10 minutes meditating, so I busied myself with an ice pack and sports scores.

"A job well done in Miami," Quanta said upon her return, joining me at the round table in her nook. It was rare to get praise, so I kept any smartass replies to myself. She added, "Did you enjoy the extra day on the beach?"

"I'd forgotten what it's like to do nothing for 24 hours. And yes, thank you. Since I came within one good shove of splattering the sidewalk the night before, a day of sun and sand was rejuvenating. But since it could've easily been 48 hours, I'm assuming you hustled me back for a reason other than to punch me in my sore face. Which I asked you politely not to do."

She ignored that. "You remember our discussion about the Arcetri?"

I nodded. "You wanted me to infiltrate them somehow. Have we figured out a way?"

"Not yet. But we're pretty sure this man is part of their little club."

She slid a tablet across the table to me. The screen was taken up by a photo of a man with the coldest, most dangerous eyes I'd ever seen. It took me a moment to catalog the rest of his face because the eyes were so dominant and frightening. Graying hair, still full for a man who appeared to have entered middle age; a sharp nose; and the kind of stubble some men wore perpetually, no matter how often they shaved.

"Name?"

"Ambrose Minor," she said. "Turned 60 a week ago and celebrated by setting fire to an office building in Huntsville, Alabama."

"Maybe the candles on his cake set it off."

She didn't smile. "It was a building owned by this man." She swiped to another photo. "Ty Hedrick. Aged 59. A business competitor. Or *was* a business competitor."

"I'm assuming that means Ty was in the building at the time."

"Along with his son and the son's girlfriend. Those two made it out. Hedrick Senior was not so fortunate."

"What kind of business are we talking about?"

"Death."

I looked up at my boss. She wasn't one to joke or to exaggerate for the sake of drama. I waited for her to explain, and she did.

"Ambrose Minor and Ty Hedrick have both been in the business of making and selling arms for a long time. Hedrick in Huntsville. Minor not far outside Charlotte, North Carolina. And we're not talking just small firearms, but everything from rifles to automatic weapons to flamethrowers and aircraft weaponry. If need be, they can accommodate requests of almost any size. Can and have, I should say.

"Both have established legitimate businesses that sell to the United States and its allies—much smaller than the household names we've all grown up with in that field—but no less influential. As what you might call *boutique* arms manufacturers, they're small and nimble enough to build relationships with the sorts of people we'd rather not see with advanced weapons. But they do the bulk of those deals under the table."

"And we couldn't just shut them down?"

"There's no real proof of these shadier transactions. And even if there were, they're not necessarily illegal. Just . . . troubling."

I flipped back to the image of Minor. "Why are we getting involved now? Couldn't be to investigate a murder."

Quanta sighed. "My instinct is that the police could investigate this fire for years and never tie it to Ambrose Minor. But it was certainly arson, and the timing is what makes some of us believe it was his doing. The way it happened one evening when Hedrick just happened to be there. There's been bad blood between the two for more than 20 years. One of my contacts in the Pentagon says he's frankly surprised one didn't kill the other a decade ago."

"All right. Two men who hate each other, selling weapons to other bad people, and one finally snuffs out his rival. I'm waiting for the big reveal."

She took back the tablet, found another page, and showed it to me.

"This is a message Ty Hedrick sent to one of his personal friends at the Pentagon. He sent it two days before he died in the fire. The friend, who swears she knew nothing about the subject matter and was merely following up on an earlier message, thought it might be relevant to the investigation."

I pulled the screen toward me and read the highlighted portion.

You're asking me if this is real or fiction. Let me answer it this way: If A.M. is as far along as he claims to be, you're looking at an exponential leap in human-machine weapon interfacing. I can tell you that we've attempted it—many have attempted it—but something has always gone wrong. And when it goes wrong, it's ugly.

As much as I hate the blustery bastard, if anyone could pull it off, it would be him.

Is it fiction? Well, if it's fiction today, it won't be tomorrow. And when tomorrow arrives, God help us all.

I looked up at Quanta, who was watching my face for a reaction. Neither of us spoke for a minute.

"Well," I finally said. "A human-machine interface.

Weaponized. Should I assume Hedrick was talking about a cyborg?"

Quanta took a long breath, considering the question. "I would say it probably stops short of the cyborgs we see in science fiction films. But in some respects, we've been cyborgs ever since the mass production of smartphones."

"I've heard this argument," I said. "And I think it's a bit of a stretch. Just because we walk around all day with our noses in our phones doesn't make us connected in a true cyborg way."

"No? The basic description of a cyborg—a mashup of 'cybernetic organism'—was originally described as an organism with enhanced abilities through the integration of artificial components. We don't have the devices physically implanted in our bodies yet—although an argument could be made that sophisticated prosthetic devices fit the requirement. But there are many examples of biomedical instruments interfacing with human bodies. Just because the people don't look like the Terminator doesn't mean they lack cybernetic qualities."

I stared back at her. "Well, when you put it that way—"

"Let's get back to the reason we're having this conversation. We've had our eye on Ambrose Minor for years. Until recently, it was because we wanted to keep tabs on who might be purchasing his weapons. Minor doesn't keep all his eggs in one basket, and that includes his manufacturing sites. Just last year, representatives from Ecuador discovered a small arms factory that was off the grid. They shut it down, but sources say it actually just relocated. That's not surprising. There have been rumors of others in the Philippines, Africa, and Eastern Europe. He's diversified not only his products, but also his resources and his clientele.

"Now, with the idea that he's developing a type of human-machine interface for the deployment of weapons—well, it's worth more than a quick glimpse into his operation. And with the murder of someone prepared to call him out, it tells us he's at least far enough along that this is serious. Serious enough for him to kill to keep it quiet."

I took a sip of the water and softly rubbed the cheek that was still tender. "How does the Arcetri play into this?"

"We had an FBI team travel to Huntsville to sit down with Hedrick's son, Bryson. He'd sifted through some of his father's notes in his home office the day after the fire, looking for an idea of who might've been responsible. On an old desk calendar, the word Arcetri was written under the initials AM, and then crossed out several times—but not enough to make it unreadable. We already know Hedrick referred to Minor as AM. Of course, the word Arcetri meant nothing to the son, Bryson, nor to the FBI team. But it certainly jumped out at me in the report."

"You think old man Hedrick was a member?"

She hesitated, then said, "Perhaps. Or perhaps the late Mr. Hedrick knew about the organization only because his chief rival was a member."

"Interesting theory."

"As clandestine as that group is, it doesn't make sense that someone randomly scribbled it on a calendar. I get the feeling Hedrick somehow heard about the Arcetri, had the impression that Minor was a member, and wanted to dig deeper into it."

I sat forward. "That could also explain why Minor had him killed. Those guys have a track record of killing anyone outside the association who starts poking around." I paused. "Should I assume I'm flying to Huntsville?"

She lifted her glass of water and saluted me with it. "This is why you're my top agent, Swan. You're so quick."

My flight was scheduled to leave in five hours, which wouldn't give me much time at home. That induced a tinge of guilt because I'd stayed in Miami an extra day. But I hadn't known then about the whole Minor-Hedrick drama. And damn it, downtime on a beach was something I hadn't experienced in—well, I couldn't remember the last time I'd done it. It wouldn't normally be considered selfish, but I had a pregnant wife at home.

Now, in my defense, Christina was the first to encourage me to stay in Florida. Although she was within a few weeks of delivering, she continued to work at the restaurant, where she reigned as one of the top chefs on the East Coast. Her schedule could be hectic, which meant I might not have seen her much, even if I'd been back in DC.

Complicating the ethical situation further, the child wasn't mine.

Don't get any ideas about my wife. She was acting as a surrogate for one of the restaurant employees and his wife. Not to get all gushy, but I considered it one of the most thoughtful, giving things a person could do.

I shoved all of that aside. I had perhaps an hour to spend with Christina and I wasn't going to muck it up with complicated feelings. If necessary, I could fall back on wallowing once I got on the plane.

As usual, I took the stairs to the seventh floor of the Stadler Building. The stairwell conveniently opened next to my unit, which meant I rarely saw my neighbors. That was for the best, especially since it cut down on awkward conversations and explanations in an elevator. Most people in the building assumed #700 was a corporate rental, which was the only way to explain why so many different people—at least by appearance—came and went.

Christina occupied the unit next to mine. It worked out better that way, allowing her to nest in her own space with her own designs, furniture, and fridge. Since I was away more often than I was home, it made sense. We'd installed a hidden sliding panel between the two condos, allowing us easy access back and forth.

This panel opened less than a minute after I'd walked in. I'd barely dropped my bag when I heard Christina say, "Not very tan for three days in Miami."

I turned and watched her set down a large, covered pot, then welcomed her into a big hug. "I can't explain it," I said. "This body just doesn't tan as well as some of the others. Genetics, maybe?"

She pulled back and gave an appraising look. "Yeah, you *are* mostly pale, aren't you? I hadn't noticed before. Are you hungry? I made some potato soup that's phenomenal."

"Everything you make is phenomenal. It's a little annoying, if I haven't told you that before. And yes, I'll eat all of it."

We moved into my dining area, where she set out a couple of bowls and silverware while I pulled a box of oyster crackers from the pantry. What followed couldn't actually be described as conventional conversation between a typical married couple, probably because we were far from that.

"I know I keep asking you this, but is that baby ever going to cross the finish line?"

She laughed. "Three weeks. Well, roughly. And wait 'til I tell you what Antonio asked me today."

I took another big spoonful of soup and raised my eyebrows.

"He asked me if I'd be interested in doing this again in two years."

I nearly spit out the soup. "He did not." She just smiled and nibbled on a cracker. "What did you tell him? This womb can only be rented once?"

"I didn't give him an answer. I just said I was totally flattered that they'd want me to do this again, and I'd have to think about it."

"Sure, it's flattering. I guess I never heard of anyone being a surrogate for the same couple multiple times." I reached for the crackers and eyed her. "You have a twinkle in your eye, Ms. Valdez."

"Oh," she said with a laugh. "It's just been a nice experience.

Mainly because I've never seen a couple happier or more excited about their child. Marissa—you remember how much she called me in those first few months? Really worked up, nervous, excited, all at the same time? Well, she's calmed down and has gotten comfortable with everything. She's turned into a good friend. She stopped by the restaurant last night to show me the latest pictures of the nursery, and I have to admit it's adorable."

I crushed a handful of crackers into the remnants of my soup. "Yeah. That's the twinkle I'm talking about." After a moment, I reached across the table and took her hand. "Babe, I think it's wonderful. I really do. I'm—I'm just sorry I'm not, you know—"

"I know. And you don't have to worry about that." She paused. "Now, if it was *our* kid, you wouldn't get off the hook jetting away every few days to play super spy. Even if you *are* saving the world."

"Not always the world. Sometimes just the country."

We eventually abandoned the dirty dishes and wandered into the living room to sit on the couch. She rested her head on my shoulder and we gazed out the large window at the park, content with the silence as the world paraded past.

Our talk about pregnancy and childbirth and happy couples, juxtaposed with the grim scene I'd just left behind in Florida, played on my mind. It often did. Sometimes I used my peaceful, joyous existence with Christina as a form of rationalization. To justify why I forged into confrontations with the most vile, wicked people on Earth. Why I continually walked through the valley of the shadow of death—and died, again and again.

Was it all really to protect the sanctity of the peace I knew with Christina? To protect that happiness for other families? To play the part of the hero?

Or was I wired to do it, regardless of the benefit?

I was pretty sure I knew the answer. And I didn't like it.

CHAPTER THREE

Huntsville has an interesting history, and not just in terms of the nation's Civil Rights Movement. While most people equate the tech industry with the Pacific Northwest, Silicon Valley, or Austin, Huntsville quietly became one of the top five tech hubs in the country. The aerospace industry flourished in northern Alabama, but so did computer tech, engineering, and companies working with military defense contracts. The historic city now boasted the state's largest population and by the start of the 21st century had flourished culturally, too.

Of course, I wasn't in town to visit any galleries.

It was a sultry evening and I had the air on full blast in my rental car, which had been conveniently waiting for me when I flew into Redstone Arsenal, just southwest of the city. As the hub for the US Space Command, Redstone had plenty of military craft going back and forth to DC, so it was easy to hitch a ride.

It had been years since I'd visited Huntsville, and I wondered if a certain oyster and shrimp restaurant was still going strong. Traffic was certainly busier, and, like many cities dealing with growth spurts, the trade-off was sharing the attraction with lots of other new folks. At one point, things slowed to a crawl on 565 and

I used the time to think back over the material I'd studied on the plane.

Bryson Hedrick, the son who'd survived the fire, was 32 years old and learning the ropes in his father's business. He'd started right after finishing his MBA at the University of Alabama. Worked in finance for a while, then shifted to research and development before becoming a vice president in the sales department. In other words, Papa Bear Hedrick had certainly been grooming his son to take over as CEO, with a solid background in most of the critical departments at Hedrick Sky Inc.

I didn't understand the "Sky" part of the company name, but I was sure someone in Huntsville would clue me in. Ty Hedrick had been well respected, someone who'd worked hard to build a business up from scratch, earning him the sort of capital that goes beyond financial restrictions.

And he'd built the kind of reputation that was often hard for a son to live up to. I never envied the progeny of self-made millionaires, and it was even tougher for the offspring of billionaires. If I was Bryson, I would've become a painter.

I finally reached the hotel within Cummings Research Park and went through the usual pleasantries at the front desk. I do love southern hospitality. My room overlooked a small lake and there were plenty of people frolicking around the pool. So no shortage of water distractions. There was a casual feel to everything, an easy vibe, an almost sleepy veneer that contrasted with the business buzz swirling around this part of town.

Normally, I'd need to wait for a Q2 courier to drop off a weapon and other spy goodies, but, thanks to my free ride with the soldiers, I had my Glock on me. Would I need it? Probably not. But stranger things—and people—had popped up in the past.

Quanta's assistant, Poole, arranged for me to have a quick meeting with Bryson Hedrick. He'd been told I was with the FBI, and that always opened doors.

At 7:15, I walked into a restaurant with the word "pub" in its name, but it clearly didn't understand the term. Still, it had a bar area and Hedrick was already there, with what looked like Scotch in front of him. I introduced myself, immediately offered my condolences for his tragic loss, and then suggested we move over to a high top where we wouldn't be overheard by the bartender or anyone else.

"I'm not exactly sure why you're here," Bryson said after we were seated. "Shouldn't you be in North Carolina, arresting Ambrose Minor?"

I didn't exactly smile, but installed a pleasant look on my face, meant to signify how patient I was. The young executive, already balding, bless his heart, and carrying a few more pounds than he probably liked, had angry eyes. He also sported a small bandage on his cheek that looked like it concealed stitches, and another on the back of his right hand.

"I don't blame you for saying that, Mr. Hedrick, and I certainly understand your frustration. I'd want immediate action, too, if I were you. The sad truth is, in order to make an arrest stick and to make a conviction likely, we have to do things in a methodical way. The old cliché: 'ducks in a row.' As much as it pisses you off—and it would do the same for anyone in your situation—can you imagine how furious you'd be if we rushed in without the right preparation and the perpetrator got off on a technicality? You'd be livid. Well, we would be, too. That's why we have to do things in a very slow and deliberate manner. If it seems like we don't care, please believe me that we're doing it this way *because* we care."

It was one of those speeches that almost always works. So I was taken aback when Hedrick actually leaned across the round table and, with eyes wide, said, "Bullshit."

I wiped a tiny bit of his spittle from my chin.

"Okay," I said. "Then how about this? You stay pissed off at me, and we can go about this in a confrontational way. It'll take twice as long and make the job of apprehending the perp that much harder. But at least you'll be able to express your outrage. Is that a better plan? I can do it either way."

He sat back and finished his Scotch in a gulp. He held the glass up to the bartender.

"I lost my father," he said with a growl. "Maybe you should apologize right now for talking to me that way."

It was my turn to sit back. I did so with an audible sigh. "All right. I apologize. I shouldn't have been direct with you." I pulled a $20 bill out of my pocket and put it on the table. Then I stood up. "This will cover one of your drinks. Take care, Mr. Hedrick. Again, I'm sorry for your loss. I'll let you know what I find."

I'd made one step toward the door when he reached out and grasped my bicep. "What the hell are you doing?"

"What does it look like I'm doing? I'm leaving you to drink and be angry. Please remove your hand."

He didn't. "This is more bullshit. Sit your ass down."

It was quite a show he was putting on. I didn't know if it was purely a reaction caused by grief, or if Bryson Hedrick was just a spoiled, rich kid who'd flowered into your common, ordinary, run-of-the-mill asshole and wasn't used to anyone defying him. Part of me wanted to snap the fingers on his hand like pretzel sticks, but I could only imagine the call I'd get from Quanta.

Now I did smile, and I did it while leaning in as close to his face as possible. Lowering my voice so only he could hear, I said, "Day before yesterday, I killed a man."

He squinted and pulled his face back a few inches, confused and repulsed. So I leaned in more to close the gap.

"That is *not* bullshit. I shoved a blade into the back of his neck. Twice. So listen closely, Bryson. I can be so *very* polite and professional, which is what I've been with you. Or I can give you significantly more bandages than you have right now. Remove your goddamned hand."

He made a show of slowly releasing it and bringing it back to his side.

"Good," I said. "Now, you can get your shit together and we can try this one more time if you like. Or I can leave and work this case without you. What's it gonna be? Because I've no time for drama. I'm pretty sure I'll be wading through enough of that as it is, once I get balls deep into this thing. I need calm, mature, and responsible cooperation from you. Can you do that? Without proving how oh-so-tough you are?"

The bartender arrived with another glass of booze, rescuing Hedrick from an embarrassing and awkward scene. As he lifted the glass to his lips, he used it to indicate my chair.

After a pause, I sat back down. The bartender looked at me and I ordered just water with lemon. I had no intention of drinking with Bryson Hedrick. Not yet.

"All right," he said. "We can start over."

I made myself comfortable in the high bar chair. "I'll be doing a deep dive into Hedrick Sky, but for now, give me a snapshot."

He turned the tumbler in his fingers, looking down at it. "My dad—" He paused, swallowing an emotional lump. "My dad inherited a business from *his* father, who died pretty young of a heart attack. My dad was in his mid-20s, just out of school. Hardware business. Real mom and pop stuff. Even had a small cafe in it. Anyway, Dad didn't really enjoy the hardware part of it. But he was an avid hunter and fisher, and kept a small gun shop as part of the hardware store. He noticed after a year or so that it brought in the bulk of his business.

"So, when he was 28, he sold off the hardware inventory, the building, and the cafe, and just kept the gun business. Moved to a new location. Put everything he had into it. But what made it work, besides being in a very hunter-friendly part of the country, was the huge list of contacts he made. Made and massaged." Hedrick grunted a half smile. "No one—and I mean *no one*—was better at building and maintaining relationships. All the manufacturers. All the distributors. He studied it. Learned every side of it. Learned what people wanted, what disappointed them. His first employee was a former Army Ranger who taught him even more."

My water arrived and I took a long drink. "All right. And that led to becoming a manufacturer himself."

"Yeah. By the time he was 30, he'd already hired two engineers and had some prototypes made. Not very good at first, but within a year they were damned good. He made rifles, a few handguns, and ammunition. Put out state-of-the-art gun sights and scopes. His engineers had their own connections with raw materials suppliers. It all kind of snowballed. When he had enough clout, he bought two other small companies. Hedrick Sky sort of became a boutique arms manufacturer. Which, I know, sounds odd. But a lot of people didn't want to work with the established names. They had—oh, I guess you could say those guys had a tarnished reputation. Hedrick Sky was new and innovative, and—"

When his voice faded off, I filled in the blank. "They didn't have any dirt. No skeletons in the closet."

He looked up at me. "Yeah. That's right. Nothing wrong with that."

I shook my head. "Nothing at all. It's a nice story. Young man knows what he wants, what he's good at. Makes strong connections. Delivers a good product." I shrugged. "What's not to like?" Then I tapped a finger on the table. "But someone didn't like it."

Another grunt from Hedrick. "Yeah."

"Tell me about the relationship between your father and Ambrose Minor."

His face clouded and I prepared for the next storm. But he took another sip and relaxed.

"Ambrose started out as a friend of my dad's. Or at least Dad thought he was. He acted like he was taking Dad under his wing, that sort of thing. Minor Arms had been around quite a few years; Ambrose had made some money in sales and used it to buy an existing arms company. I can't remember what they used to be called. Isn't important. What's important is that he's a killer. Dad isn't his first victim."

I scowled. "Oh? Who else has he killed?"

"Well—"

"Bryson, has he killed someone? Really?"

"He's *had* people killed. That's the same thing."

"And you have proof of this?"

"No. Do you have proof that Marilyn died by accident?"

He was getting dangerously close to the edge again. I had to guide him back.

But he did have a good point about Marilyn.

"All right. So you're convinced he's hurt people and maybe had some killed. But you say he and your father were friendly at first. What caused the rift? I'm told it's been quite the heated rivalry for decades."

His phone buzzed and he glanced at the screen. "It's my girlfriend. Okay if I get this?"

"I'd rather you not. Call her back."

He tapped a button. "Hi. I'm gonna have to call you back. I'm talking with the FBI right now." Pause. "I know." Pause. "Okay, I'll call you back."

"Back to the rift," I said.

Hedrick took a deep breath. "A little over 20 years ago, Ambrose reached out to Dad to see if he'd be interested in selling his business. Dad had just started getting some big orders, was closing a deal in Europe, and was starting to make a good name for himself. Still a smaller business, of course, but already with a good reputation.

"Well, the answer was an obvious *no*. Ambrose tried again a few months later, and even made an offer. It was insultingly low. When Dad respectfully declined, Ambrose did not take it well, to say the least. He claimed he would poison all of Dad's contacts and pretty much wreck the business. It was all so—so out of left field. I mean, nobody could've been nicer than Ty Hedrick. To swoop in, make an offer, and then threaten to destroy Dad's business because he didn't just roll over and sell his company for way below value? It was insane."

He finished off his second drink and raised the glass yet again. I wanted to suggest he take it easy, but we'd already gotten off to a rough start. Maybe we could get the girlfriend to come pick him up.

I said, "How was Minor Arms doing at this time? A bigger player, I assume."

"Yeah, they were successful. But only because they'd been around a while. They had contracts that often renewed only because the buyers didn't know better. So when Hedrick Sky began making waves, I'm sure Ambrose thought it would be easier to swallow us up than fix his own tired shop."

I'd played dumb when I asked Bryson to explain the feud. Some of the details were in the file Poole had sent to me, and I'd scanned it during the flight. Naturally, what I'd heard just now was slightly embellished. But then again, maybe the other accounts were skewed. What's the old saying? "There are three sides to every story: yours, theirs, and the truth." Or something like that.

"All right," I said. "Let's talk about recent history."

His face darkened again. "Seven years ago, there was a contract put up for bids. Venezuela. South America has seen a pretty remarkable arms race since the turn of the century. Tens of billions of dollars spent down there. It's a sizable share of our business, and this particular contract would've been the biggest in our history. Dad and I and two others spent weeks putting together a competitive bid. A lot of hard work, a lot of late nights. When it was time to present, we discovered the other two people on our little team—a man named Paul Kleeg and a woman named Shanna Wright—had falsified a lot of the inventory numbers. They'd basically sabotaged the bid, because it would all have to be done again and there was no time."

"Kleeg and Wright were plants?"

This earned a sarcastic smile. "Well, Mr. Swan, I don't have *proof*, which you're big on. But yeah, of course they were. Ticking time bombs. They infiltrated the company about three years earlier and were just waiting for the really big contract they could cripple. That's when things went from your basic bad blood to outright war. And Dad—"

Another wave of emotion swept over him. "Dad wasn't—he wasn't really wired for war. Which, I know, sounds ridiculous when you're talking about a man who sold weapons for a living. But like I told you, he was a good man who built long, steadfast relationships. He treated people fair. He was generous as hell, probably the most generous in the industry when it came to taking care of his people with benefits and bonuses. That's not just me boasting about my father. That's in the records, easy to find."

"He got along with everyone, you're saying, except Ambrose Minor."

"Yeah."

"Fair enough," I said. "Give me even more recent history. I want to know about the note your father wrote to his friend in the Pentagon. Tell me about human-machine weapon interfacing."

"Ah, the note." He exhaled a long, painful breath. "Okay. To begin with, everything I'm about to tell you is technically classified. But since it's all government research, I suppose I can tell you. Although I guess I've already screwed up by not asking to see some ID." He raised a questioning eyebrow.

"Don't push me, Bryson."

"Yeah, okay, okay." He settled in and spread his hands. "The whole business of warfare is nothing like it used to be. We have soldiers, we have tanks, we have planes, we have ships. We have all the same tools we've had for a hundred years. But those are almost for show now. I don't mean they're not important," he added quickly. "They are. But with technology, we've just added so much more. All those soldiers are learning a new way of doing battle, so that we're now at a point in history when computer skills are worth as much as learning how to pilot a fighter. And if that's an exaggeration now, it won't be in a few more years."

"Tom Cruise may punch you in the face for that."

He offered a weak smile. "Yeah. It's certainly not as sexy to defeat your enemy with a keyboard. But it's becoming more statistically viable, if that makes sense."

"Sure it does. Keep going."

"For years, governments—especially our own—have had a jones for taking the tech advances we've made and melding them into more natural tools for the soldier in the field. The more we could develop a tool with an almost innate feel for the user, like an extension of their own body—well, that's invaluable. Training is minimized, but, more importantly, mistakes are minimized. Practically eliminated."

He seemed to be searching for an example to explain it. Then he said, "Like, you know how we instinctively point our index finger like a gun? That's the kind of natural movement I'm talking about, but obviously much more complex. So then, if you take that outcome, you start reverse-engineering. We want a covert operative in enemy territory to be able to combine his own vision with enhanced vision. Without using goggles or something like that."

"Because goggles can get knocked off," I said. "Or run out of juice."

"Or not even be available," he said, nodding. "So, ideally, you'd have an agent or soldier who didn't need the tool. It would be built in."

My mind began running with the potential. I'd been one of those soldiers he described. I'd been in the field, in hostile territory, and knew how precarious my situation could be if something happened to my gear. I prided myself on my survival instinct—

yes, I know, ironic for a guy who's been killed over and over again. But that never happened while I wore a military uniform.

The point is, we took our tools into consideration when making plans. Mostly, we had to make contingencies if the gear either got left behind or failed to work. Because, honestly, if something could get fouled up, it would, sooner or later.

So imagine a soldier who carried a weapon, but was wired with all the other accessories. Not only would it mitigate tech failure, it would make a foot soldier more lithe, more nimble. Never underestimate the value of a quick army. Just ask the German generals after Patton moved his Third Army 100 miles in three days. In winter weather.

But just how much interfacing were we talking about?

"This is all very interesting," I said. "But everything you've told me so far I could've read about in *Popular Mechanics*."

He looked down at his drink and seemed to shake with a quiet laugh.

"Right. *Popular Mechanics*." He shook his head, then looked up at me. "Dad wrote that note because we think Ambrose Minor is getting close to a technological leap that will not only alter the course of human warfare, but set off a tidal wave of ethical debate."

I narrowed my eyes. "Because?"

"Because he's going beyond just making an interface for tools. He's begun actually experimenting with surgical implants."

He paused. "In the brain. He's trying to build a human-computer hybrid. And I've seen one of them."

CHAPTER FOUR

We made an appointment for the next day at Hedrick Sky. I left Bryson with a glass of water and he assured me his girlfriend would be joining him for a late dinner.

I had a lot to think about and needed to upload before getting some sleep. Although I hadn't learned much more than I knew before I landed in Huntsville, it was my interaction with young Master Hedrick that I wanted to preserve.

The uploading process itself was simple in one respect: It was not unlike backing up your hard drive. What made it complex was that we were dealing with the human mind, and no matter how advanced our computer systems became or how rapidly artificial intelligence accelerated, we were still a long way off from duplicating the staggering capabilities of the human brain.

I uploaded my consciousness, memories, and history as often as possible, and this feed was stored in a sophisticated hard drive. Well, I call it a hard drive because that's the closest approximation to the gear most of us are used to. This is several levels of complexity above that.

When I'm killed in the line of duty, a new body is secured for me, and the most recent upload is then downloaded into this new brain. The procedure, which we call the "investment process," is easily the most technologically advanced wonder in the history of science.

Developed by a woman I referred to as God Maker—she, by the way, detested that moniker—"investment" meant I could live over and over again, in a different shell, but still as Eric Swan. And yet, practically no one knew about it. It was the subject of considerable debate behind closed doors before the final decision came down. The public couldn't know about it, at least not yet, for fear it would cause upheaval. People would climb over each other for access and there would be fights over who should have the right to use it.

Only a small group of people knew the process existed, and they made the decision to reserve it for an elite squad of spies and covert specialists defending the country. The department, hidden within the US budget, was Q2. And you will never, ever find a secret so fiercely guarded.

There was also the little matter of donor bodies. There just would never be enough of them to make it practical for the masses. As for mine? They were prisoners who'd been sentenced to life behind bars with no chance for parole. We found volunteers who were in good shape and we made an offer: You could donate your body to science right now, and your family would get $2 million in cash, tax free. But there was no going back. If a convict agreed, it was a done deal.

They weren't even clear on what they were volunteering for. They only knew they'd be leaving a prison cell and they would say goodbye to their families and friends forever, never to be seen again. We weren't necessarily swimming in applicants, but it was more than you'd think. Many of these guys had no family, and they were willing to volunteer, rather than spend decades trapped in a cell.

The convict's own consciousness was uploaded into a hard drive, where it would remain indefinitely. There were plenty of times I thought about this arrangement, wondering whether the program was on steady ground ethically. But then I'd simply have to remember the countless times their sacrifice—and mine—had saved the lives of thousands, sometimes millions, of people.

Do the ends justify the means? I couldn't think about that right now.

In my hotel room, I pulled from my bag what looked like an ordinary stick of deodorant and a can of shaving cream. They camouflaged the equipment that would access my brain waves, encode them, and send them through the ether to the basement of Q2 headquarters. The last two steps of the process involved having a trashy tabloid magazine on hand and taking an abnormally sized pill—what older folks once called a horse pill—which assisted with the smooth transfer.

The tabloid was my own personal requirement. You couldn't sleep through the transfer, so you had to lie peacefully and relax. For me, that meant reading the delicious garbage served up by the celebrity world. It was my guilty pleasure. If you're shaking your head and wondering why, that makes two of us.

By the time I completed this particular upload, I knew who the country's latest reality star was sleeping with, and I was shocked at a certain royal for trashing her sister's poor choice of wardrobe at the movie premiere. Granted, her sister looked like a slob, but that was best handled behind the doors of Buckingham Palace, wasn't it?

Before going to bed, I checked in with Poole, who was thrilled to know she didn't need to chide me about uploading. Then I left a message for Christina. The usual sappy words.

Security at the gates of Hedrick Sky was impressive. While waiting for the guard at the front gate to phone in my name, affiliation, car description, license plate, and what I'd had for breakfast that morning, I glanced around the perimeter of the grounds. A

10-foot fence, topped with razor wire, would discourage the average interloper. I noticed a few small towers that ostensibly provided light for the grounds, but undoubtedly contained cameras and perhaps even motion detectors.

After finally getting the okay to pass through, I motored up to visitor parking, where a man at another small guard shack assigned me a space and the requisite tag to place on my dash. At the door, I had to look into a camera before the lock would open. This image was likely being compared to the one taken at the front gate.

If you had an invitation, it wasn't this difficult getting into the White House. I know; I've been there. I pocketed a teaspoon while I was there and felt like the biggest criminal kingpin in history until I accidentally left it in an Uber. Then I felt like the dumbest criminal kingpin.

Inside Hedrick Sky's lobby, another guard waited, but I was spared the strip search when a woman who appeared to be in her mid-30s met me, hand extended. She introduced herself as Mel Townsend and immediately asked the questions all assistants are required by law to ask.

"How was your flight? Are you enjoying Huntsville so far?"

"I'm a little disappointed, to be honest, Mel. I just found out this morning the tomato sauce company is *not* based here."

It took her a moment, but then I got the courtesy laugh. She probably didn't know what to say after such a horrible attempt at humor, so the rest of the walk to the executive office was quiet. I smiled to myself. I'm sometimes juvenile that way.

Bryson Hedrick was encamped in what must've been his father's office. It was good sized, but not ostentatious. The usual bookshelves took up a portion of the room, while large windows looked out over perfectly manicured grounds. The other walls showed off photos of Ty Hedrick posing with lots of rich and famous people, many of them politicians, and a few older celebrities.

I shook hands with Bryson, who eyed me with caution and perhaps a touch of fear. I had, after all, casually mentioned the prior evening that I killed people for a living. That tends to make people look at me in a different light.

"I imagine you'd like a quick tour of the place?" he asked when Mel had stepped out and closed the door.

I shook my head. "No, that's not necessary. I've poked around at a few weapons facilities. I'm not concerned with how your products are made, Bryson. What if we just sat down and you can finish your story from last night?"

"All right. Sure." He fell into a padded executive chair and seemed to appreciate the feeling of security that came from having a large desk between us.

"First," I said, "let's talk about what happened the night your father was killed. That wasn't here."

"No." He looked down at his hands in his lap. I took that as a sign he didn't want me to see him getting emotional. "It was at an office we keep closer to the airport. Dad owns that building, too." He paused again, then gave a mirthless laugh. "I guess I need to get used to saying he *owned* the building. Anyway, sometimes he would have quick meetings there. Some of his biggest suppliers rented office space in the building. Dad liked the fact that it made negotiations, well, friendlier. You know, both sides felt like they were on their home turf, sharing the same building. Vendors never had the feeling they were visiting some cold, corporate monolith."

"And you went with him to these meetings?"

He looked up. "The last couple of years, yeah. It was, uh, part of my training."

"All right. Who was he meeting with on the night of the fire?"

"Nobody. We were prepping for a meeting the next day and Dad wanted to drop off a few things. Gifts." He stopped and took a breath. "That's how he did business for 30 years. Do nice things for people, make them feel appreciated. So he died because he wanted to drop off some gift bags to give to prospective buyers. Probably $200 worth of stuff. And he died for that."

I let the silence linger for a few moments. Then: "Walk me through what happened. I know it's painful, and I'm sorry. I could read the police report again, but I prefer to hear it firsthand from you."

"Sure. I understand." He pushed back in his chair and crossed one leg over the other knee. "We'd gone to a quick dinner before heading over. Got there around 7:30. We were only in the building together for maybe 15 minutes. We dropped off the gift bags, then we looked at the materials my sales team had assembled. He had some questions. Made a few changes. That wasn't unusual; I mean, it was his company, he could change whatever he wanted. Then he said he had a call to make and would meet me back at the car."

"I understand your girlfriend was there, as well."

"Yes. Her name is Paige. She waited in the car the whole time. Wanted to call a friend. We weren't going to be long."

"Okay. So you left your father and went back outside. You waited with Paige. How long until the fire broke out?"

"I'm—I'm not really sure. But we waited quite a while. Probably about 30 minutes. Look, if Dad ever got busy with something, he'd get so focused that an hour or more could go by. We just sat there and talked. Paige was getting antsy. Said dinner wasn't sitting well with her and she just wanted to go home and go to bed. Eventually I tried calling Dad, but there was no answer. I waited a few minutes and tried again. I was just getting out to go back up and see what he was doing. And that's when I heard the alarm."

He fidgeted, uncrossing his legs, then crossing them the other way. "I didn't know what it was at first. Thought it might be a burglar alarm from the building next door. Took me a minute to realize. By that time, I heard sirens. So I stopped and looked up, and I saw really dark smoke coming out of the building on the upper floors. Dad's office was on the eighth floor, the top floor. I ran inside, but the elevators had been locked out. Took me a moment to find the stairs—I'd never used the stairs before. I ran up those as fast as I could, and when I came out on his floor, it was filled with smoke. I saw flames."

Now Bryson became overcome with emotion. He put a hand to his eyes, which had become red and watery. He sniffled, then blinked a few times before continuing.

"I tried yelling for Dad. I went to the office where I'd left him, but I couldn't see him. The smoke and flames were spreading fast. By now, I was panicking. I was also beginning to cough, inhaling a lot of smoke. I heard voices coming from the stairwell. It was the fire department. I opened the door and screamed down at them that my father was somewhere inside. They reached the eighth floor and told me to get out. I ignored them and kept looking. One of them caught me by the arm and pulled me toward the door. I—"

"You punched him," I said. "I read the report. Keep going."

He looked both sad and embarrassed. "I broke away and ran down the hall, but it was getting worse. I've seen fires in movies, but it's much more hellish in real life. I don't know if you've been close to one."

What could I say? I couldn't exactly tell him I'd been *killed* in one. That I'd infiltrated a group planning on killing thousands by lacing cocaine and meth with a synthetic agent worse than fentanyl, then mixing it into deliveries to saturate the streets of Los Angeles. Their plan was to kill 10,000 "druggie losers," as they called them. It was their solution for cleaning up the streets. I got close before the leader of the group got nervous and killed his team. That included me. Of course, it was during what I called the "lights out" time: the time frame between when I'd last uploaded and kicked the bucket. Those portions of my various lives were lost. I had to hear about or read about them later, usually in a gory report.

Now, I shook away this memory of a memory and said to Hedrick, "You were injured, obviously."

"Part of the ceiling collapsed on me and one of the firemen who tracked me down. He took the brunt of it. I—I feel like a complete ass for that. But I was desperate to find my father."

I nodded. I knew the rest of the story. Whatever fed the flames, it overpowered the building's sprinkler system. The top two floors went up too quickly for the firefighters to save much. That included Ty Hedrick. We were awaiting the official postmortem report, but his remains were found, exactly where Bryson had last seen him. When he'd run back into that room, his father had been on the floor, behind the table, probably unconscious. In his panic, Bryson had not looked there. Could he have saved his father's life? No one would ever know if the elder Hedrick had still been alive at that point. But I was sure his son would agonize over it for the rest of his own life.

"And you never saw anyone else in the building, at any time? Not even when you and your father first went in?"

He shook his head slowly. "Nobody. Not even janitorial staff. It was nearly eight o'clock on a Friday. The place was deserted."

"And the building's security?"

"It takes a key card to get in. No sign of forced entry to any of the doors. There are three of them that people can use. Two on the main level, one in the underground parking. We were parked on the street, since we didn't plan on staying—" A sudden sob choked off the rest of the sentence.

I let another minute go by before picking back up.

"Let's talk about the hybrid soldier. You told me you've seen it. I'm very curious about that."

He seemed relieved by the change in subject matter.

"We first heard about it from one of our vendors about six months ago. He said he'd been invited by Ambrose Minor to North Carolina to witness a video demonstration. Something they were experimenting with. A next-generation version of a soldier.

That's what the guy called it. Next Gen Soldier. Naturally, knowing Ambrose, we thought it would be just hype, some fancy name for a new camo outfit or something.

"So when the vendor said, 'No, it involves melding technology *into* a soldier,' Dad sat up and paid attention. I mean, we've all read about it in fiction and we've seen the movies. But this—" He made eye contact with me. "The concept of a soldier actually interfacing with military technology? That's our holy grail."

I scowled. "But why? It seems like it would take the business of weapons out of your hands. Isn't a development of this sort contrary to your business plan?"

He looked startled. "Contrary? No, Agent Swan. It opens up incredible opportunities." He leaned toward me. "Don't you see? Since the invention of gunpowder, there have been incremental advances in arms production. Sure, we've built bigger and more powerful guns and cannons and bombs. But all from the same mold; we've just been in a race to see who could give each of them a bigger bang. But this? You're talking about an entirely new method of fighting. This is man *as* the weapon."

It took me a moment, but then I began to understand. "It wouldn't undermine your business. It would open up a completely separate *branch* of your business."

"A branch that could eventually become the crux of the *entire* business," he added.

I studied his face. "Unless Ambrose Minor got there first and planted his flag. Because that would mean patents, which could—"

"Which potentially could shut us out until we found a way around them. And that could take years." He let out a long, heavy breath. "In a multibillion-dollar industry, it's not something to be taken lightly."

"Okay, I get it. So how did you see one of these Next Gen Soldiers?"

He hesitated. "Am I immune from prosecution if I tell you this?"

I almost laughed. "What? From prosecution? You *broke the law*?" I opened my eyes wide to punctuate the criminal act.

"Yes."

Now I gave a small chuckle. "Look, Bryson, I'm here to investigate this new technology. If you were trespassing somewhere and got a look at it, I really don't care. I'm interested in things a little more pressing than that. If you shoplifted a candy bar, I'll let that slide, too. So spill it."

He tapped a nervous finger on the desk. "I had some business in Charlotte, as it turned out. This vendor who'd told us about the technology was in town for the demo, and he was staying at a fancy hotel not far from Minor Arms. So I called him up, told him I'd love to buy him dinner at the hotel restaurant. After he was a couple drinks in, I excused myself and said I had to make an important call. And using a hotel master key card, I went up to his room and found the packet he'd gotten from Ambrose at the demo. It had a sketch and a rough listing of the skills this new soldier would have, um, installed, I guess you could say. I took pictures of all of it."

"I'm really impressed with those corporate espionage skills, Bryson. We might have to make you a junior spy. How'd you get the hotel key card?"

He shrugged. "It's easy to pay off housekeeping. A hundred bucks can get you almost anything. I gave her *five* hundred."

I laughed again. "Well, if this all turns out okay, I'll tell you a little secret about a gadget you can get for a lot less than that. It'll get you inside any hotel room."

"No thanks. My stomach was a mess that whole night. I can't imagine doing any of the things you do."

"I'm gonna need those photos you took."

He lifted a manilla envelope from the desk and handed it over. "Photos of the sketch and some rough specs. No details or information on *how* they're doing anything. But if they can deliver what they're promising—" His voice faded away, and he just shook his head. "It will literally change everything about traditional warfare. And more than that. If this technology fell into the wrong hands—"

"I'll give you a news flash," I said. "If this comes to fruition, it's not a matter of *if* some bad guys get it. They most definitely *will* get it. Nothing of this magnitude can stay under wraps." I added with another laugh, "If you can sneak into a fancy hotel suite for five hundred bucks, just imagine what people will do for a hundred million. Or more."

CHAPTER FIVE

Late that afternoon, I hitched a ride on another military flight out of the Army base and was back in Washington by eight o'clock. It would be a late night. Quanta met me at Q2 headquarters, an unmarked and unimpressive building no one would look at twice as they drove past. The people in those cars would be stunned to know what happened in that frumpy building.

We sat in a small conference room with Poole, my favorite foil. No matter how hard I tried to make her laugh, she simply was not wired that way. It never stopped me from trying.

I held up the envelope I'd received from Bryson Hedrick. "Poole, inside this are the kind of things that delight the weirdos on the second floor and give the rest of us nightmares."

She didn't quite know how to react to my usual slur when referring to the Q2 brain trust operating two floors below us. After a moment to process my statement, she responded with a respectful nod.

Quanta saved her any further puzzlement. "Before we get to those contents, tell me about the meeting with Bryson Hedrick. What did you take away regarding the death of his father?"

"Since we have no official report yet from the fire officials, we don't know how the blaze started. But everything screams murder. The timing is just too perfect. Ty Hedrick finds out about his biggest competitor having cracked the code regarding a hybrid human-machine soldier. Barely two weeks later, Hedrick is dead. Plus, the timing that night was too neat, as well. A deadly fire breaks out, after hours, and just minutes after Hedrick entered the building? We can assume it should've killed both of them, but Ty sent his son outside while he stayed to make a call."

"And no security?"

"Just keycard access. Which is far from real security. There are two other entrances besides the one Bryson parked near. Honestly, it wouldn't have been that tough of a job."

Quanta looked thoughtful. "But you said this was after hours. How would a killer have known they'd be there?"

Poole spoke up. "Could they have been followed?"

"Entirely plausible. The three of them—father, son, and son's girlfriend—had gone to dinner first. Someone could've tailed them the whole time, waiting for an opportunity."

"How long until we get autopsy results and a ruling from the fire department?" Quanta asked.

"The autopsy will be finished tomorrow. I'm told the fire report could be, too."

"All right," Quanta said. "Let's have a look at the soldier of the future."

I dumped the contents on the table. I'd made copies for each of them, as well as additional copies for the brainiacs on the second floor. I pushed two sets across the table to Quanta and Poole.

"I put the sketch on the top," I said. "It's the kind of artwork that would've made Stan Lee proud."

We all studied it in silence. It featured a man out of uniform in order to display the physical attributes. In several places, the drawing featured a cutaway image enlarged to reveal what was going on beneath the skin.

The entire body was well-muscled, naturally. The feet and ankles were definitely prosthetic, with drawings showing a complex set of hinges one had to assume allowed for more dynamic movements. It also eliminated those pesky sprained ankles.

The legs were toned and shaped like the fastest Olympic sprinters you've ever seen, although the knees were again artificial. The human knee is remarkable, while also one of the most vulnerable areas. Just ask your average athlete. Here, it seemed to be a titanium assortment of connections.

The torso was the most obviously human component, but that wasn't surprising. As far as we've come with organ replacement, it's still tough to beat the original parts we're born with. Data on the following pages listed enhancements that were protective in nature.

The arms were toned and strong, but the muscles were not overdone. Experiments had found the tipping point where fitness began interfering with flexibility and the need for precise movements. This hybrid reflected the perfect ratio and included artificially strengthened wrists to accommodate improved lifting abilities. An exploded diagram of the hands indicated a significant boost in grip strength, too.

The head is where this thing began crossing over into fantasy. Sophisticated cochlear implants provided superior hearing and, according to the description, could be adjusted by the user to target sounds in a specific range, both according to frequency and direction. Not unlike the way a cat will twist its ears to pinpoint a sound's origin. This was done internally.

The eyes required two enlarged drawings and the page of specs was crazy. The design promised vision that wouldn't *quite* equal that of an eagle's, but damned near it. Gathering data four times farther than a normal eye, these also had the ability to switch settings to see in ultraviolet light. It was like having built-in night-vision goggles, all of it to a stunning degree of clarity.

There was more. The average human brain wasn't designed to handle everything this hybrid sported. That's where the final piece of the cyborg puzzle slipped into place. The design specs hinted at the one thing that made everything work: a brain implant.

It was like adding a module or an external hard drive to your laptop. It was quite small and rested just under the skin at the base of the neck. A hard shell was stitched around it to provide protection.

I tapped the notes on this feature and said, "There are no details whatsoever about the brain implant. Just a rough description. That has to be the element they're most likely to guard. I'm sure they'll never release those specs. It's what makes their enhanced soldier more of that next generation they're touting." I turned to Quanta's assistant. "So what do you think, Poole? Should we put in an order now for my next body?"

She hadn't taken her eyes off the documents and for a moment it seemed she hadn't even heard what I'd said. I'd finally found something that legitimately fascinated her.

Finally, looking up, she said, "It's already incredible, just with what they've listed here. But I notice on page three that they refer to 'room for future enhancements.'"

"Yeah," I said. "I saw that, too. It's like the barista asking if you want them to leave room for cream. The designers know this is their base model. We haven't gotten to the model with leather seats yet."

But Quanta hadn't spoken. She'd flipped back and forth through the pages, quietly studying the sketch and the descriptions. Her face displayed the impassive look she wore whenever something really bothered her. I knew not to direct any snarky comments her way. I'd learned to read the room.

A minute later, with her eyes still on the specs, she addressed me. "It's fascinating and disturbing, all at the same time. But there's one thing that makes it even more disturbing."

Now she looked back at me. "Our people at the Pentagon were not invited to this demo meeting at Minor Arms. Word of it leaked out, of course, but there was never an official invitation. So if the demonstration was limited to only potential vendors, it means Ambrose Minor isn't necessarily creating this ultimate soldier to defend his country."

I nodded. "He's going to build it and offer it to the highest bidders. That may include the United States. But it may not."

She gave a long, slow exhale. "This puts us in an awkward position. Ambrose Minor is an American citizen, and he's free to run his business as he sees fit. At the same time, if he's making and selling a product that could unleash hell on our fighting forces around the world, we obviously will want to either procure it for ourselves or—"

She didn't finish. I knew where she was going and I understood why she'd left the thought hanging. She wanted to make sure I was on board with the suggestion without her having to say it. So, after a moment, I did. "Or we prevent it from being sold to anyone."

Poole looked back and forth between us. "But how would we do that? And *could* we do that?"

Quanta paused before answering. "We certainly *could*. That's not a concern. It's a question of how we get away with it. As I said, it's a very awkward position. Extremely delicate."

I waited the appropriate amount of time before asking the obvious question.

"When should I leave for Charlotte?"

My plane touched down the following morning at Charlotte Douglas Airport, and by 11 o'clock, I'd checked into my hotel. At 11:30, a Q2 courier stopped by to drop off my gear, including my go-to weapon, a Glock with four spare 19-round magazines, and some nifty little gadgets that could come in handy. They looked like ordinary business cards, but the Series-8 were on thick stock and somehow concealed a listening device. How the nerds on the second floor managed that, I have no idea. But as much as I respected their talents, they certainly weren't gods. They'd obviously failed miserably with Series-1 through 7.

My cover was the badge identifying me as a member of the FBI. I was scheduled to meet with someone from the actual Bureau at noon, so I prepared myself for the usual questions and my usual deflections. Federal agents often wanted to know where I was based and who I worked with, and other inquiries I couldn't really answer without bullshitting my way through. I'd gotten pretty good at that.

But, as it turned out, none of that was necessary.

When I strolled into the diner down the street at the appointed time, I stopped in my tracks, then laughed.

"Fife, you son of a bitch," I said. "Why didn't anyone tell me it would be you?"

The FBI man got out of the booth to shake my hand and seemed to enjoy the moment. "I told Quanta to let me surprise you. Anyway, it had to be me; we all know you're more likely to bungle a case when I'm not around. Plus, I was curious to see the latest incarnation of the great Eric Swan. Seems fit enough."

I did a small spin, letting him check out my latest body. "I won't lie: This one ain't half bad. And as you know, that doesn't happen all the time."

FBI agent Fife was tall and trim, and preferred a touch of pomade in his hair, which I always thought was quaint. The reason I could level with him was because at one point he'd worked at Q2—not as a field agent, more behind the scenes. And really, he still did. But Quanta had decided that we needed an inside person at each of the other major agencies, someone who knew our dirty little secrets. It helped to smooth things when we wanted interdepartmental cooperation but couldn't let them know exactly *what* they were dealing with. There was a woman—

whom I'd yet to meet—who'd infiltrated the CIA; we now had someone at Homeland Security; and we'd even secured a plant within the State Department. Fife was our contact inside the Bureau.

He and I had worked together more than once, and he was one of my favorite people in the spy game. As difficult as this assignment was shaping up, it was good to see a familiar and friendly face across the booth.

"As for your crack about me bungling things," I said, "let me remind you that I recently saved your sorry ass from being dropped from an airplane into Lake Michigan. Remember?"

He rubbed his jaw. "Are you sure that's how it happened, Swan? I mean, with all your uploads and downloads, maybe you're confused. Maybe it was me who saved *you*."

I laughed. "What an asshole. No gratitude at all."

A server stopped by and we ordered coffee and a cinnamon roll each. Another reason I appreciated Fife: He liked the same shitty junk food I did.

"I got the file late last night from Poole," he said. "So I arranged to have myself assigned to help you. Told them we'd served together in special ops."

I grunted. "Special ops? No offense, my friend, but you don't really have the build for that department. No doubt I would've been hauling you out of the jungle, too."

"My hero. Well, anyway, I was close by, finishing a job in Baltimore. So here I am. What's the plan?"

"Plan? You think I have a *plan*? I thought you knew me."

"Yeah, that's what I was afraid of. So let me rephrase it: What are we doing after we finish the cinnamon rolls?"

I looked out the window. It was a sunny day, although the winds were kicking up. Across the street, some guy was doing his best to parallel park, but he'd obviously flunked that part of driver's ed. The other motorists around him were not very patient and letting him know.

"I'm thinking the only way to play this is to go straight at Ambrose Minor. I can't think of a reason not to."

"Okay," Fife said. "Under what pretense?"

"I've been pondering that, too. The best approach would be direct. I want to make him squirm over Ty Hedrick's murder."

"Do we *know* it's murder?"

The server dropped off our coffees and promised that the rolls were coming out of the oven any second. When she walked off, Fife repeated his question.

"We do now," I said, dumping the contents of two little containers of faux cream into my mug. "Autopsy says Hedrick suffered a severe blow to the head. Someone bashed his skull in, then set the fire to burn him and his business to the ground. They either didn't count on his son being there at all, or maybe they didn't count on him getting out. Either way, he's alive to tell the tale."

Fife drank his coffee black. I probably should. He ran a finger through a drop that had spilled on the table. "The murder seems rather sloppy, wouldn't you say?"

"I would."

"Is it possible it's not connected with Minor or this new super-soldier project?"

I just gave him a flat look. "Yes. It's also possible that a ptero-dactyl might fly out of your ass."

He raised his hands, palms out. "All right. I had to ask. So now I'm curious how you're going to broach the subject with Minor."

I took a sip of my coffee, which was not very good. I should've gone with hot tea. Thirty seconds passed while I considered Fife's question. I looked back outside. The lousy parallel parking guy had finally completed the job after inching up and back about six times. I pushed the shitty coffee away and said, "Hell. I guess I'll just walk in and accuse him of murder."

CHAPTER SIX

During my misguided years spent chasing a college degree, I accepted a summer internship with an advertising agency. The managing director, a woman in her late 40s, had rocketed up the ladder in what was a very cutthroat industry, flying past men and women who'd toiled longer than she and who'd closed some big deals. She still earned promotion after promotion and passed up all the other chumps on her way to the corner office.

Her secret? She didn't win advertising awards; she designed advertising that actually sold products. What a concept.

On my first day at the office, coming in with the same preconceived notions about advertising that every layperson gathers from watching TV and listening to the radio, she took me on a sales call. I learned more in the first 15 minutes with her in that meeting than I had in an entire semester in a college classroom.

This was my biggest takeaway: Before even discussing the company's ad budget or prospective campaigns, she took the business owner out into their own showroom and pointed out everything they should change. As she told the owner, "You can spend a million dollars on your advertising and I'd be happy to make that commission. But if the customer walks in and gets a completely wrong feel—or if they're unsure what your business is all about—your money just went down the drain. Fix your product before you try to sell it. And your product most definitely includes your showroom, which is your public face."

Driving back to our office, she'd asked me if I had any questions about the sales call.

"Yeah," I'd said. "Everything you told that guy made complete sense. Why do no other advertising agencies do this?"

She lit a cigarette and cracked a window. "Because they're one of two things: Either they're lazy and greedy and want to grab a quick commission, or they're just stupid." She blew a lungful of smoke out the window, then looked at me. "Maybe both."

She sold that company two years later and retired to Panama. I never forgot her lesson about first impressions.

It struck me the moment I walked into the lobby of Minor Arms. It was as if Ambrose Minor had been on that same sales call with me. These were corporate offices, not a retail store, and yet the spacious room, open and bright with loads of natural sunlight, told you everything you'd need to know about the company. There were gorgeous display cases set up at different heights and angles, all showing off Minor's steady evolution in the field of weaponry. Large screens ran a loop of various videos showcasing their biggest hits, all without sound, which would've been off-putting when people were trying to talk. The images alone produced a powerful message.

There were cutouts of America's fighting forces, brandishing Minor products. A wall of advanced firearms not only displayed the guns, but also had beautiful engravings detailing the first actual use of each in the field. This included a quote from a distinguished military commander, offering thanks to Ambrose Minor and his team for providing the country's fighting men and women with top-of-the-line gear.

The room was comfortable, too, with pleasant, soft music,

remarkably expensive couches and chairs, and a buffet of beverages and snacks, all kept fresh and sparkling clean.

I found myself gazing at one particular wall display on the far side of the room. I actually recognized one of the faces from a small combat team I'd spent time with. "I'll be damned," I muttered under my breath. His name was Bream, and he'd been like family for the months we served together. I'd recently learned that Bream had perished in a firefight after being ambushed in a country where that wasn't unheard of. I gave a small salute to his smiling image on the wall.

"Did you serve?"

I turned to see who'd spoken in the Eastern European accent. It was a woman, nearly six feet tall with long, dark hair. She was impeccably dressed in a smart gray business suit with a crisp white shirt, and she carried herself with the kind of composure and self-assurance you wished could be bottled. She studied me with a quiet look of interest.

"I did," I said. "I appreciate you honoring the services like this."

She nodded and glanced at some of the large photos on the walls. "They're the people who make sure it's safe for me to get up every day and come to work. The least we can do is to represent their work and their sacrifice in a respectful and gracious manner."

She'd uttered these same words before, probably many times. But that was okay. They came out sincere, anyway.

"You are Agent Swan?"

"Yes. You are . . .?"

With a warm smile, she extended a hand. "Antoinette Lazarov. I'm with Mr. Minor's executive team. Would you please come with me?"

She led the way out of the lobby and down a hallway adorned with photos, plaques, and reproductions of magazine articles spotlighting Minor Arms. Each person who passed gave a pleasant acknowledgement. I felt like an honored guest, which isn't the way I'm usually greeted. And I didn't expect the good will to last too much longer.

Up a small staircase and through a security-laden door, we entered the inner sanctum. While just as professional and spotless, the atmosphere took on a decidedly serious feel. There weren't as many people visible, and the majority of them kept their heads down over their desks. At the end of a short hallway, we turned into a small office, comfortably appointed with a stylish desk and three guest chairs. I took the one in the middle.

After settling into her own chair behind the desk, Antoinette said, "How can I help you today, Agent Swan?"

I dropped one of my Series-8 business cards in front of her. "My appointment was with Mr. Ambrose Minor. Will he be joining us?"

"Mr. Minor was called away this afternoon. An emergency meeting. I'd be happy to answer any questions you might have."

I gave a thin smile. "What part of the world are you from, Ms. Lazarov?"

"I prefer Antoinette. I was born and raised in Bulgaria. Have you been?"

"I've been all around the perimeter. Greece, Turkey, Serbia, Romania. Somehow I missed your lovely country. Maybe someday. As for those questions you can help with: How did Mr. Minor take the news about one of his leading competitors being murdered?"

She barely reacted. Just a slight eyebrow raise. "You mean Ty Hedrick? I thought he died in a tragic fire."

"That finished him off. Someone made sure he was down and out by the time the flames took him."

"I see." She paused. "Mr. Minor has not publicly commented on the tragedy."

"But that's not what I asked. Did Ambrose Minor send somebody to Huntsville to meet with Mr. Hedrick?"

Now she offered the beginning of a frown. Not a complete scowl; I think she was trying to convey disappointment. "Agent Swan, this is a surprising line of questions. But I can tell you Mr. Minor sent nobody to Alabama to meet with Mr. Hedrick. And to answer your original question, Mr. Minor is saddened and deeply troubled that one of his oldest friends in the industry has passed. He will be sending an appropriate display of his condolences to the family for the memorial service."

"I'm sure that will mean a lot to the grieving widow. But listen, you work closely with Ambrose; tell me, Antoinette, has he ever discussed with you his failed attempts to buy out his chief competitor?"

She hesitated. "I know there were discussions many years ago, but certainly nothing recently. I was not employed by Minor Arms at that time."

"But you know Ambrose was furious about being rejected. And now, with his movement toward the Next Gen Soldier, it would help him greatly if he shook up the competition a bit, wouldn't you agree?"

Now she narrowed her eyes. "I'm not surprised you know about Next Gen, Agent Swan. It's not like it's a state secret. But I am appalled at the insinuations you're making."

"What insinuations are those?"

"That there could be any sort of connection between a business proposal 20 years ago and the deplorable passing of a great man, Ty Hedrick, today. I've read a good deal of detective novels, Agent Swan. I believe this is referred to as a fishing expedition, is it not? What I don't understand is what could possibly have motivated you to come here with these offensive questions."

"I guess you could toss me out of the building."

She smiled again, but it was forced. "And have you label us as *uncooperative*? No. I will answer your questions to the best of my ability, regardless of their merit. Or lack thereof."

She was good—and marvelously composed in the role she played. I decided to press just a bit more.

"When would Mr. Minor be free to visit with me about both the passing of Ty Hedrick and his plans for the Next Gen program?"

"Mr. Minor is under no obligation to speak to anyone about proprietary programs developed by Minor Arms. No laws have been broken. If and when he is ready to share his ideas, I'm sure he will contact the appropriate departments within your government."

"*Your* government? So you're not a U.S. citizen?"

"No. I maintain my Bulgarian citizenship. As for when Mr. Minor might be available to visit personally with you, I'm not sure he'll be free anytime soon. But you're welcome to check back later."

I shrugged. "All right. I'll check back later." I stood up and pointed at the card I'd set on her desktop. "You can reach me at that number. You'll have to leave a voicemail, but I always call back right away."

She nodded toward the doorway, where a young man had suddenly appeared. "This is Gavin. He'll show you back to the lobby. Thank you, Mr. Swan."

I smiled and walked out.

"Smooth," said Fife. We sat in his hotel room, each with a bottle of cold beer in our hands. We'd just finished listening back to the recording made from the Series-8 business card. "You utterly charmed her."

"Hey, I told you I was going to be direct."

"What kind of results do you expect from your full-steam-ahead tactic?"

"Ambrose Minor will call me within—" I glanced at the time on my phone. "—within 18 hours. I'm predicting tomorrow morning around 10. He'd like to call now, but to demonstrate that he's unconcerned by the FBI, he'll wait until tomorrow."

Fife chuckled. "I'm tempted to put 20 bucks on that, but you're just lucky enough to be right. Okay, let's assume he calls. What then?"

"Then I meet with him, but on neutral ground. People are much too smug when they're on their home turf. Too comfortable."

"And I can't join you for this meeting, either?"

I took a sip of my beer and shook my head. "Nope. At some point I might need you to play a part other than as a friendly neighborhood FBI agent. So let's keep you under wraps. At least for now."

"All right. Anything else we should discuss?"

"As a matter of fact, yes. One of the things intriguing me about this case is the possible connection with the Arcetri. You remember those assholes, I'm sure."

His eyes grew wide. "The lunatic scientist group? No shit. Where do they fit in with this drama?"

I told him how Ty Hedrick had scribbled that word on a desk calendar, beside the initials AM.

He looked thoughtful for a moment. "Well, now that you mention it, all of this Next Gen Soldier stuff could very well have an Arcetri link. I know I keep asking you what your plan is, but I'm especially curious how you'll track down a group that's practically invisible."

He wasn't exaggerating. I'd crossed paths with individual disciples of the organization, but never could pin down how they functioned. Or *if* they even functioned as a group. Of the few I'd encountered, most were now dead, not all by my hand. As for what the Arcetri *were*, I'd gradually settled on this description: a group of butt-hurt scientists who felt that revenge was a dish best served with a slide rule. Or something like that.

For hundreds of years, governments, religions, and, to a

certain extent, society in general had scoffed at the work and the results of men and women devoted to science. Many had been killed for their beliefs and their steadfast refusal to rescind their proclamations. Many more had been spared their lives, but were tortured and shunned by the public. One of those who'd been humiliated was the Italian polymath, Galileo. Some have dubbed him the father of science.

His findings ran contrary to the teachings of the church, and in the 17th century, that was a dangerous card to play. Although able to escape execution, he nonetheless was banished under house arrest. Perhaps one of the greatest scientific minds of all time, and he was condemned for trying to enlighten and educate people. Some modern scientists looked upon Galileo as a martyr who represented all victims of the ignorant.

And the home where the Italian genius was kept incarcerated? A hilly area around Florence, Italy, called Arcetri.

It became a brand for the disenchanted and the downright pissed off. No longer would they get slapped down by the ignorant masses—or the corrupt, near-sighted politicians—and turn the other cheek. Or go off and sulk. They would strike back. They would use their superior intellect to turn the tools of science against the bumbling populace that couldn't see what science had proven.

Couldn't see, or *wouldn't* see.

Since I'd first heard of the Arcetri, they'd been involved in horrific plots that nearly resulted in a staggering number of deaths. I'd apprehended one scientist in particular, a man who was within minutes of poisoning the water supply of a city in Arizona. His name was Steffan Parks.

Confined to a cell at the supermax facility in Colorado, Parks had struck a deal with me on another case. He shared information in exchange for a transfer to a more "comfortable" place to ride out his sentence. It had taken time, but I'd upheld my promise, and he now sat in a cell in the state prison in—ironically, given his association with the Arcetri—Florence, Arizona.

Would I be able to gather anything else from this madman?

Did I have anything to lose?

I mentioned Parks to Fife, to gauge his reaction. The FBI agent had accompanied me during my last visit with the scientist.

"Yeah," Fife said. "I suppose you could try to siphon a little more intel out of him. But how many times can you do that? You've already coddled him right out of Colorado. Pretty soon, he's going to be asking to be transferred to an ocean-front home in Malibu. I mean, what's in it for him?"

Fife was right. You can only go to the well so many times.

"Do me a favor," I said. "I need something else on Parks, something personal I can use as leverage."

He laughed. "He's in prison. Finding other naughty things he's done won't make any difference."

"I'm not talking about his naughty deeds. But there are people important to him, I'm sure."

"Well, that's just evil."

I shrugged. "In some cases, the only way to fight evil is with evil. Since I've already used the carrot, it's time to break out the stick. In fact, the more sticks at my disposal, the better. Besides, the threat alone will probably be enough. He's not Al Capone; he's a disgraced scientist. Anyway, you're good at poking around. See what you can find. I'd ask Poole, but she's much too nice of a person."

"Oh, thanks."

CHAPTER SEVEN

It didn't take Fife long to find something. I knew it wouldn't. The guy was a bloodhound. He could come across as laid-back and almost disinterested, but that was simply to confuse the unsuspecting. Once he put his nose to the trail, he could find almost anything.

By the following morning, I'd learned that Steffan Parks had a brother living well in Las Vegas, working in the casino industry. A bean counter with enough seniority to be paid not only a handsome salary but also a quarterly bonus based on the profitability of the gaming house. According to Fife's intel, Alton Parks had banked a cool $350,000 the previous year, and that was just the amount reported to Uncle Sam. Chances were good he saw another six figures in unreported gifts. The monetary kind.

Fife dryly observed, "People like Parks are creative enough with the books to save the casinos much more than a measly half mil. And if anyone knows how to show gratitude, it's a casino owner."

As for my prediction regarding Ambrose Minor, I'd been within an hour. He called at 10:45.

"Agent Swan," he boomed, one of those voices that's twice as loud as it needed to be. I pulled the phone back a few inches from my head.

"Mr. Minor," I said, amused.

"Swan," he said again. "One of my favorite constellations in the northern sky. Cygnus, the swan. Beautiful. And here on Earth, the most elegant of creatures. Intelligent and loyal, too. Although some people are fooled by the swan's graceful appearance, thinking the animal is meek. That's not the case; it's one of the more aggressive members of the water fowl community. But I'm sure you know all of that."

"My eighth-grade teacher thought it would be fun to make everyone do a report on the origin of their name."

"And what did you take away from that assignment?"

"That swans have remarkable memories, and they never forget someone who was kind to them. Or cruel."

He laughed. That, too, carried a few too many decibels. "I will be most kind to you, Agent Swan. Although Ms. Lazarov was troubled by your conversation with her yesterday. It sounds as if you and I should connect and clear up any misunderstandings. When would be a good time for you to stop by again?"

"Yes, I look forward to chatting with you, Mr. Minor, and I appreciate the opportunity. Rather than your office, why don't you recommend one of your favorite restaurants, and the government can pick up the tab."

Another strident laugh, no doubt forced. "Oh, I will never turn down a free meal on the government of the US of A. Lord knows my taxes should've earned me quite a few steak dinners over the years."

"Yes, I'm sure. Does tonight work for you?"

"Suits me just fine. I'll have Ms. Lazarov make a reservation for seven, and she'll send you the details. Oh, this place requires a jacket, but not necessarily a tie. If you don't have a jacket, the restaurant will certainly provide one."

"I'll bet I can dig up an old Members Only jacket at the very least."

"Well—"

"Just kidding, Mr. Minor. I'll see you at seven."

We hung up, and I massaged my poor, mangled ear.

Next, I made a video call to Quanta, where I spent 10 minutes catching her up on the meeting with Antoinette Lazarov and my brief conversation with the starstruck Ambrose Minor. I could tell from her tone of voice and the look on her face that she wasn't enamored with my tactics, but that was par for the course. Our tenuous relationship through the years teetered back and forth between friendly and furious, and my style of play had never thrilled her. But as long as I—mostly—delivered positive results, she looked upon it as the cost of doing business. In return, I appreciated her strong governance of my work without resorting to an iron fist.

"What is Agent Fife doing?" she asked.

"Research, so far. He, um, looked up some information for me on a certain prisoner in Arizona."

There was a pause. "You think Steffan Parks will help you again? He won't even know who you are."

I sighed. "I know. This will be the second time I'll have to tell him I've been sent by Eric Swan."

That's one of the problems with my constant changing of bodies. Parks knew Eric Swan with a completely different look. The problem was, *that* guy was several guys ago.

"But it doesn't matter," I added. "I think he'll ultimately give me what I want. I have some leverage."

"All right," she sighed. "I probably don't need to know what that is. But hear me, Swan: Don't step in it with Minor. It's still early in this investigation. Move cautiously."

I grinned. "Cautious gets you killed, boss."

She responded without a trace of mirth. "You manage to do that regardless of your pace. One other thing. Upload tonight after your dinner meeting. No excuses."

.   .   .

It wouldn't have been difficult to find a tie for dinner, but I chose to go with the more casual look. I found a nice sport coat at the men's store two blocks from the hotel and arrived 20 minutes early so I could position myself at the bar and watch the grand entrance of Ambrose Minor.

He'd had the same idea. I found him sitting at the bar with what looked like a vodka martini before him. He stood up to greet me with his thundering voice.

"I like a man who's early for meetings," he said, clasping my hand in a manner that matched the volume of his voice. "Nice jacket."

"What, this old thing?" I nodded to his cocktail. "I hope that's just your first. I'd hate to have to catch up too quickly."

The laugh could've been genuine, but I doubted it. After clapping me heavily on the shoulder, he turned to the bartender.

"Alex, would you freshen this and have it sent to our table? And my friend, Mr. Swan, will have . . .?"

"An old-fashioned. Two cherries, please."

The hostess delivered us to a corner table, away from the bulk of the other clientele. I smirked on the inside, wondering if it was Minor's request or if the restaurant did it intentionally to protect their diners from the noise. Not a minute later, our drinks were set in front of us.

"I hope it's okay with you," Minor said, smoothing the white tablecloth with the side of his hand. "I've asked Antoinette to join us in a while. She's so intimately involved with the business, and I've found it saves time. You know, eliminates the need for me to remember everything that transpires. And, if I have a few too many of these—" He held up his martini and winked. "—I might actually *mis*remember a thing or two. She's good at keeping me—well, accurate."

I gave the requisite polite smile. For some reason, my mind latched onto the casual reference to Antoinette's "intimate involvement" and wondered where that intimacy began and ended.

"So," he said, warming to his primary interest. "Talk to me about the reason for your visit to Minor Arms."

I procrastinated by taking a drink of the excellent old-fashioned. For a drink that's technically created with a precise formula, 10 bartenders will make it 10 different ways. All will be good; some are exceptional.

"Your old friend, Ty Hedrick, met with a violent death. We're assisting in the investigation."

"That much I gathered, Agent Swan. I'm naturally curious why that investigation involves the F-B-I." He punctuated each letter with special emphasis. "And why it involves *me*. I haven't been to Alabama in many years. *Lovely* state." Now the emphasis on the adjective was borderline sarcastic.

"You can call me Eric. I can't go into specifics of the case. But I'm sure you appreciate that when a major figure in the international weapons industry is killed under suspicious circumstances, it will pique our interest." I gave him a small salute with my drink. "We would have the same interest if anything like that ever happened to you, Mr. Minor."

His smile faltered. That little shot was clearly not appreciated. But he recovered quickly and lifted his own drink. "Nice to know one is suitably important to rate such . . . attention."

The game was now officially on, and I couldn't have been happier. While most people shied away from conflict, the juvenile delinquent in me relished it. And this conflict was the best kind. The man sitting across from me gave every indication that he, too, got a buzz from the battle. Between my research on Ambrose Minor and my first five minutes in his company, I could smell the corruption. It oozed from him. Whether or not he'd been involved in the death of his chief competitor, he clearly would profit from it. That wasn't a crime in itself; clubbing Ty Hedrick and setting him on fire certainly was.

"How was your relationship with the recently deceased?" I asked. "I've heard from others, but I'd like to know how *you* would define it. Would you characterize it as a friendly competition?"

For the first time, Minor seemed unsure how to respond. He couldn't say they were pals; he'd know that I knew better. To his credit, he finally gave a shrug.

"Ty and I began on very friendly terms. You could say I helped steer him through some difficult times when he was young and inexperienced. It's a cutthroat industry. Well, many are. But the degree of nastiness, I've found, increases exponentially with each 10 billion dollars of sales. At our level, it can be brutal."

I nodded. "Deadly, you might even say."

His look turned decidedly darker. "All right. Yes, I've seen some horrific things. Most of them in the past. It used to be more like the Wild West, which is appropriate, I suppose. Today, there's much more regulation and much more, uh, decorum."

I kept up the assault. "You tried to buy out Ty Hedrick. And he shut you down. More than once, isn't that correct?"

"Your facts are correct, but you lack context."

"By all means, color it in."

It was his turn to slow down the pace by taking a sip from his drink. He also looked over my shoulder at something, then pushed back his chair and stood. I guessed that our other dinner guest had arrived, so I also got to my feet.

Antoinette breezed up to our table. She'd passed up the hostess, who trailed by a few feet, looking unsure if she should continue to follow or simply go back to her station. The tall Bulgarian, between her appearance and the way she carried herself, was the most intimidating person in the restaurant.

She gave a quick nod to her boss, then shook my hand. The grip was tighter than I recalled from the day before.

"Agent Swan," she said, a flat expression on her face.

"Ms. Lazarov." We maintained eye contact longer than was generally comfortable. I refused to be the first to break it.

With the hint of a smirk, she finally withdrew her hand. Minor had pulled out a chair between us. She settled gracefully into it and requested straight bourbon on ice from the flustered hostess.

Minor saw no need to catch her up on anything. He fell right back into our conversation, content to let his assistant get up to speed on her own.

"You're right. I did make an offer to buy Hedrick Sky. A very generous offer, I should add. There was no attempt to steal anything. I respected what he'd begun to build. He said no to the offer. End of story. There were no hard feelings."

I narrowed my eyes. "None? You weren't perturbed by the stop sign? I find that hard to believe. A man of your determination."

He gave a low chuckle. "Let me share some of my history with you, Eric. I got into the business young, but I had the focused work ethic of an experienced veteran. That's what made me different from every other young fool trying to get their start in business. I worked my ass off. No weekends off. No vacations. Little time for a personal life. I was social when it helped, and I could schmooze people when necessary. But I also could be tough when the situation demanded it. As I said, it's a hard industry with a lot of hard people.

"During those early years, as I grew and acquired more clients, everyone could see that the future looked bright for Minor Arms. We created a name for ourselves and I like to think our reputation was golden. Because of all this, I kept expecting someone to swoop in and make me an offer." He laughed again. "I honestly believed I could build a solid business quickly, then turn it for a nice profit and retire before 40. But it never happened. No suitors. No one banging down my door, offering to buy my business. No one offering me that early retirement."

I sat quietly and listened. Antoinette's drink arrived and she let it sit in front of her, untouched.

Minor leaned forward. "But while I was surprised, Eric, when no one came calling, I soon realized something. Something that has defined my approach to business and to life ever since. To put it simply, I learned I was here not to be the one who is devoured, but to be the one who devours. If fate had wanted me out of the industry, living on a beach, there would've been offers. There *should've* been, in fact. Should've been a line of people with checkbooks in hand. But it was as if the universe wanted me to do this. *Needed* me.

"So, after a time, I accepted that there would be no early retirement—which wouldn't have suited me, anyway. Who was I kidding? I was meant to thrive and grow. To absorb those who lacked the constitution to push ahead. To dominate."

He sat back now, and for the first time his voice calmed. "I've bought other companies. Hell, I quietly bought another just last year. I've built a business that could sustain itself for the next hundred years. One little competitor like Ty Hedrick would never cost me a single night's sleep. So no, Agent Swan; I wasn't perturbed by his reluctance to sell. I respected him. He reminded me of *me*."

It was the right answer. It might've satisfied almost anyone else listening to the speech.

I didn't believe a word of it.

Well, except the part about him enjoying the process of devouring his competitors. That was evident, just looking into his volcanic eyes. Hard, staring wolf eyes. Eyes that said he not only enjoyed it, but he also thrived on it. Ambrose Minor was a hunter.

I glanced to my right. Antoinette still had not uttered a word, nor had she made a move for the drink. She was a most curious specimen. Yesterday, she'd been an eloquent speaker. Tonight, with her boss taking the lead, she was like a silent vulture, circling over the soon-to-be victim, ready to swoop in from above and pick off any remains left by the wolf. Besides, Minor was clearly the type to suck up all the air.

The two of them, Ambrose and Antoinette, were a tag-team nightmare: the loud carnivore and the stealthy scavenger. A creepy sensation worked its way up my spine, because I couldn't tell which one worried me the most. They both gave off a powerful danger pheromone.

Minor did the smoothing motion again with the edge of his hand. "Antoinette tells me you're also curious about one of our projects."

"Yes, the Next Gen Soldier. I'd love to hear more about that."

He gave a faint smile and raised one eyebrow. "What more could I reveal that you haven't gleaned from the stolen file Bryson Hedrick shared with you?"

I kept my face emotionless. "What file is that?"

"The one he copied after breaking into a Charlotte hotel room. Which, as I understand it, qualifies as criminal trespassing. Or is that breaking and entering? I'll need to have our attorneys look into that before I can be sure." He grunted. "Please, you're not really going to play this game are you, Eric? Didn't I make it clear that my nature is to dominate? How do you think that's accomplished? Certainly not by being oblivious to the actions of my competitors, regardless of their size. I haven't worked this hard for this long without learning how to protect my investment."

We sat in silence, his eyes boring into mine. He'd scored the first hit, surprising me, and he knew it. In a confrontation of this sort, that first round can be crucial in setting the perceived pecking order, allowing one party to gain the high ground. But if Minor thought he would intimidate me, he had a lot to learn.

"To be blunt," I said, "how you dominate other companies in your industry is of no interest to me. I'm not with the Justice

Department and I'm bored by anti-trust arguments. As far as petty complaints like breaking and entering, well, you can take that up with young Hedrick, if you think it's worth the time and trouble. Something tells me it's not."

I leaned in toward him and matched the intensity of his eyes. "What I *am* concerned with, Mr. Minor, is a murder that could be connected to national security. That will always grab and keep my attention. Because, while I may have to follow a few more pesky rules than someone in private industry, I, too, am a hunter. And I, too, have been at it for a long time. But, as you can see, I'm still here."

We stayed like that for 10 seconds, eyeball to eyeball, neither flinching. It was somewhat childish, I admit. But the wolf metaphor was gone; we were clearly two bull elks, pawing the ground, and, to be honest, it was one of my favorite parts of the job. Seemed like he enjoyed it, too.

He blinked first. Sitting back in his seat, he took a healthy sip of his cocktail. Now his eyes were smiling. Either he enjoyed the banter and the accompanying blast of testosterone, or he'd simply decided I was a nuisance he couldn't wait to eliminate. I wondered whether he got off more on business wins or crushing people. Probably both, equally. He may not have perceived a difference between them.

"Well," he said, setting down his drink. "Now that we have huffed and puffed, why don't we settle back and enjoy a nice meal together. I'll be happy to tell you everything you want to know about our advances in military technology. Well, almost everything. You'll understand if I don't give away *all* our secrets, won't you?"

I returned a friendly smile and shot another quick glance at Antoinette. She still had not so much as touched her drink. She looked at me like I was an insect caught in a Venus flytrap and she was curious to see if I could struggle my way out.

I looked back at Minor. "How's the filet?"

CHAPTER EIGHT

It was late when I got back to my hotel room, but I'd promised Quanta I would upload. This time, instead of reading my favorite trashy magazines, I took the horse pill and sprawled onto the bed with nothing but my thoughts of the evening. I would sort through them while at the same time electronically filing them in Washington.

Ambrose Minor, with his intimidating voice and mannerisms, had told me as little as possible about the Next Gen Soldier. In fact, he was reluctant to even use the term; it was more of a nickname applied by others. In his words, we were discussing "an upgraded system of technological improvements with strong military applications." While the description was clunky, it was at least accurate.

"The idea itself is not revolutionary," he'd said over his meal of salmon and vegetables. "It may have been the subject of countless science fiction novels, but it has always been based on practical science. I know for a fact the Defense Department has pursued their own versions—although, if we're being honest, those have not produced the results anyone was hoping for. It wasn't until about seven years ago I realized what was holding up progress."

He dabbed at his mouth with a napkin. "People and companies have been trying to incorporate technology into a hybrid soldier, but they've gone about it backwards. Everyone has started with a wish list of the features they'd love for their hybrid fighting machine to have. Early designs were based upon an imaginative leap forward; perhaps they were influenced by those novels. I don't know. But what I do know is that the human body naturally has limitations. So, with every design, there were always going to be problems. And with each problem, there were also disastrous failures. You can't force the cybernetic design you have in your imagination into the frailties of a human frame."

I took a bite of my steak which, as advertised, was insanely good. I didn't want to jump in yet and break his momentum.

"These early blunders created a negative association with the concept, in general. For many of the engineers working on it, their attitude became, 'This is all just pure fantasy. We're wasting our time.' That sort of thing. So they gave up."

He gave a proud smile, and I knew I was supposed to inject something here. "Minor Arms filled the vacuum. Only you didn't begin with the image of a machine. You began with a drawing of a human body."

"That's precisely correct. We consulted with soldiers who'd logged significant time in battle, including many who'd suffered severe injuries. The insight we received in particular from soldiers wounded in battle put us miles ahead of where previous attempts had failed."

I nodded. "Other designers were working from a place of 'How do we keep them from getting hurt?' So you took men and women who'd already been hurt and reverse engineered the things that could've prevented it."

"You understand perfectly," he said. Then he turned to Antoinette. "Some of that early research was thanks to my intrepid assistant here."

I turned to her and raised an eyebrow. "Oh. My apologies, Ms. Lazarov. I didn't know you were a trained engineer."

She studied me for a moment. "I am not an engineer."

My look of confusion caused Minor to let out a low chuckle. "You misunderstand, Eric. Antoinette didn't work on the design for the hybrid soldier. She provided a test ground for it."

I shot a quick look at him, then back to the Bulgarian woman.

"Before joining my team, she was *Captain* Lazarov. A highly decorated soldier in the Bulgarian Land Forces before being loaned, I guess you could call it, to NATO forces. She's trained with the elite tactical units of at least three different European nations. You could ask her to name them, but I doubt she would. And, although a remarkable officer in the field, she unfortunately suffered injuries that temporarily ended her association with combat units."

"Temporarily?" I said.

"That's right. She could report back tomorrow if she wanted. But she's been invaluable to us at Minor Arms." Minor turned to his assistant. "Care to show Eric one of your special qualities?"

After a moment of hesitation, Antoinette brought a hand up to her face and covered her right eye. Then, with a twist, she brought her hand back down.

And set her eye on the table, next to my side dish of potatoes au gratin.

I must've stared at it for a long time. I finally heard Minor laughing again and looked up at Antoinette. She sat placidly, her hands folded neatly in her lap. The space where her right eye had been didn't look grotesque at all; it wasn't a bloody wound, but rather a socket where one might expect a piece of electronics to go. Because that's exactly what it was.

I noticed a tiny flash of blue light emanating from inside the cavity, but it was gone just as quickly. I had to assume it was part of the electrical connection between the artificial eye and her optic nerve. Antoinette, meanwhile, wasn't self-conscious or embarrassed one bit. She calmly looked at me with her remaining eye, as if waiting for me to tell her about the weather.

Looking back down at the orb on the table, I asked what I thought was a sensible question. "May I pick it up?"

"Of course," Minor said. When I hesitated, he reached over, picked up the eye, and tossed it to me. Officially one of the strangest things that had ever happened to me in a restaurant.

I tried to respectfully handle the property which, only moments earlier, had been tucked comfortably into the head of the woman sitting next to me. On one side—the side I'd seen before the big reveal—it looked like any other ordinary brown eye.

Turning it over revealed the magic side. Although it was obvious the hardware contained a dazzling array of features and improvements to the human eyeball, it filtered down to a stem, about half an inch long. This would plug into the socket to provide not only stability and control but also to act as a conduit for the electronics.

While I examined the medical wonder, Minor gave me an audio tour.

"The human eye is a remarkable tool. You could fairly say we take it for granted, never marveling like we should at the advantages it gives us when aligned with our complex brain. But, despite its incredible capabilities, it falls far short of the *potential* of the tool. Once you understand the astonishing differences in visual abilities between species, you discover we're nothing special in that regard. And I'm not just talking about acuity; yes, eagles and owls, for example, put us to shame when it comes to seeing clearly across vast distances. But that's barely scratching the surface of what this tool can accomplish."

He'd warmed to the topic. "Imagine having a wider field of vision than you currently have. Imagine being able to function capably in a dark room without the need of adaptive goggles. Think about the advantage you might get from seeing in ultraviolet, rather than just visible light. You're no doubt familiar with heat sensitivity; we have tools that can pick up the heat signature an enemy gives off. Now a soldier could track their prey without the need of extraneous gadgets. When you get right down to it, we are creatures who make decisions based on information gathered through our senses. What if those senses were tuned to a much greater degree? The amount of data we miss out on because of the limitations of the human eye is staggering. It's a case where we don't even know what we're missing."

He glanced at his assistant, then back to me. "Granted, our earliest attempts were somewhat primitive. More a design defect. But we've come a long way. Antoinette has one of our newer models."

I set down the artificial eye. "Sure. All of this is fantastic. But the human brain has evolved to handle exactly the data we receive from our eyes. Suddenly dumping an extraordinary amount of additional data would overwhelm us, would it not?"

"Yes!" His enthusiasm was genuine. "Very good, Eric. That is *exactly* right. And, again, that's where previous attempts made an error. A wish list of everything we could do to improve eyesight would be more than we could handle. But—" He picked up the eye. It seemed odd to be passing around part of Antoinette's body like this, but she didn't seem to mind at all. "If we select one or two particular adaptations and apply those, it becomes a matter of enhancing rather than overwhelming."

I looked at the electronic eye he was gazing upon. "Are you saying the eye can do all of these new functions, but the user manually selects the ones to apply? Or do you have separate eyes for separate functions?"

"Eric, you are the brightest student in the class. Another gold star for you." He handed the eye back to his assistant. "In a perfect world, the user would be able to switch from application to application. Like a menu setting. Ultraviolet view now. Then long-distance view. Perhaps the multi-cone selection later, which triples the number of colors the eye can distinguish. Night vision the next time."

Antoinette took her napkin, dipped a corner in her water glass, then set about casually polishing the eye. Then, after a quick inspection, she lifted it back into place and, a moment later, it was impossible to tell anything had ever happened.

Minor finished his answer. "Sadly, what I just described is more of a software issue with the human brain, and we're nowhere close to that capability. Yet. So instead, we have prepared a variety of different eyes for different scenarios."

I grinned. "You're kidding. Antoinette has a suite of eye choices, depending on the need?"

He looked surprised. "You find that funny? I think it's astonishing."

"No, don't get me wrong," I said. "It's incredible to be able to swap out parts. I'm just gonna have a hard time not thinking of Ms. Lazarov here as Mrs. Potato Head."

Neither of them found that the least bit funny. Antoinette may not have even gotten the reference. Did they have Mrs. Potato Head in Bulgaria? Sometimes the best I can do is to amuse myself. I salvaged the moment by finishing my drink and moving on.

"Other than the electronic eye, what else does our bionic woman have going for her?"

Minor shook his head. "Nothing. Her specialty is the eye. We're testing other components with other volunteers."

"Volunteers," I murmured. For the first time, I wondered if Ambrose Minor was forcing people to play the part of crash test dummies for his Next Gen experiments. He certainly wasn't above coercing individuals into doing his will. Granted, there were plenty of ex-military who'd suffered egregious wounds in battle, and many of them might be willing to try out new body parts.

Antoinette had been silent for the entire dinner. I wasn't sure what she was doing here, other than to listen and observe. Or perhaps her only role was to show me the eye. I decided to engage her.

"Did you lose your eye in an armed conflict somewhere? Or was it an accident?"

She laced her fingers together on the table in front of her and said, "I did not lose an eye."

I gave a small start. After a quick glance at Minor, who wore a faint smile, I looked back to Lazarov. "Wait. You *didn't* lose an eye? So you—you volunteered to have them pluck out one of your eyes in order to test drive this piece of machinery?"

Minor began to answer. "It was well tested before—"

"Hold on, please. I'd like the lady to answer." I leaned toward her. "You let them cut out a perfectly good eye in order to be a guinea pig for this experiment?"

Now she was the one who smiled. "You seem repulsed by the idea. You heard what Mr. Minor said. The equipment was tested over and over again. Why would I not want an upgrade?"

I just shook my head. Then, to Minor, I said, "And when it's not some special application, she has normal vision in that eye?"

He pursed his lips, shot a quick glance at Antoinette, then went through his smoothing technique again. "No. Not yet, anyway. For now, the device can only be used for whatever its primary purpose is. When it's not being used in that respect, it rests."

I grunted a disgusted laugh. "So she lost the use of one eye, except when she needs to find her socks in a dark bedroom. My god, Ambrose." I pushed my plate aside and said to Antoinette, "I hope you've been well compensated, Ms. Lazarov."

Her look was flat and cold. "You don't need to concern yourself over my well-being, Mr. Swan."

The server stopped by the table to clear away plates. I ordered a second drink, which was unusual for me. Minor asked only for a refill of water. Antoinette freakishly continued to ignore the alcohol she'd ordered.

"All right," I said. "Are you willing to tell me about the other soldiers who are test-driving your various Next Gen designs?"

"Not at this time. Perhaps soon. I just wanted to make sure you understood that all of this is still early days. There's no need for the United States government to feel anxious. When the time is ready, we'll be happy to treat them to a demonstration."

I didn't believe him. Even as the words spilled from his mouth, I knew Minor Arms would not be peddling its goods to the American military. For one thing, Minor would've already set up meetings with them in order to secure funds for the research and development phase. No company playing on the level would ever turn down a pile of cash. For Minor, the black market would be far more lucrative. And the cherry on top: These other buyers, most likely foreign governments and terrorist cells, would not meddle in his business. Once the Pentagon became a partner, they'd strong-arm several aspects of the program, steering its progress toward their own needs.

One dinner date with Ambrose Minor was all I needed to know he would never agree to that sort of relationship. As my uncle was fond of saying, "He wouldn't cotton to that." Somehow, Ty Hedrick had made Minor nervous, and I now understood it had nothing to do with a rebuffed purchase offer. That was a red herring. No, it had everything to do with the Next Gen Soldier. The result was a charred body and a competing business left rudderless.

As I stared across the table at him, I wondered how many other bodies littered the path Minor had taken to reach this point. Only a fool would think it began and ended with Hedrick. I shot another glance at Minor's mechanized marvel, Antoinette Lazarov, she of the bionic eye and a bizarre relationship with bourbon. In my opinion, there was no such thing as a *former* elite soldier. Why would Minor hire someone with such specialized fighting skills and use her simply as an office assistant?

The answer: He wouldn't. Especially not to simply test an electronic eye. A handy tool, certainly, but let's just say Ms. Lazarov was overqualified for the tasks listed on her business card. The chill I'd felt earlier intensified. If things followed the spiraling path I expected, there'd come a day when the Bulgarian captain and I would likely tangle.

Now, back in my room, nearing the end of the uploading process, I went back over the evening's conversation one more time. The only thing I'd neglected to bring up was the possible connection with the Arcetri. Even if he was involved, there was no chance of Minor copping to an affiliation. All I would've accomplished would be to put him on even higher alert, if that was possible. There was nothing to be gained from poking him about it. At least not yet. Not until I'd snooped around for more intel.

As I finished the upload, I knew there was only one way to get that intel.

It involved a trip to Arizona.

CHAPTER NINE

It was just after 1 p.m. and Phoenix was stifling. For the record, the next person who told me "it's a dry heat" would get punched in the throat.

The drive to the prison facility in Florence would take about an hour, and the AC would be on max the entire way. My personal playlist was on shuffle. At the moment, I was testing the capacity of the rental car's speakers with a grinding song by Stereophonics. It soothed me while my mind went through its version of an outline process.

My name was FBI agent Trevor Michael, and I had the badge to prove it. I'd been sent by Eric Swan. "You remember Swan," I would tell Steffan Parks. "He's the guy who got you out of super-max." Then I would hope to God his next demands would be much easier to accommodate in exchange for a little information.

Sometimes it just came down to a prisoner's mood that day. You know, like the rest of us.

I stopped about 10 minutes from the prison and got a milk-shake, which just sounded good. In the parking lot, sucking down the cold, chocolate goodness, I called Quanta.

"I read your report regarding the Next Gen developments,"

she said. "Agent Fife is doing an in-depth background check on Antoinette Lazarov?"

"Yeah. When I landed in Phoenix, he'd already left a message that said it's a 'strange file.' His words. But after spending an evening with the woman, it'll be hard for me to be surprised by anything else he turns up."

"While he's doing that," she said, "I'll have the second floor look for any other connection between Ty Hedrick and Ambrose Minor in the past 12 months. If, as you suggest, the murder had something to do with these bionic advances, they may find a digital trail for us to follow."

"All right. Good. I've also decided that just shooting the shit with Ambrose won't get it done. I want to get inside his biggest production facility. It's about an hour north of Charlotte. Fife's working on that, too. Says he knows a 'delightful way'—again, his words—of getting into a secure plant like that. I didn't ask; I can tell when he wants to surprise me."

"And you're meeting with Parks. Do you have a specific agenda for that?"

I adjusted one of the car's vents so it blew directly on me. "At some point, we have to track down the person who functions as something akin to a director. Or whatever they call it in their little society. We don't know their lingo. But I refuse to believe they have no organization whatsoever. Otherwise, what's the point of even having the damned club in the first place?"

She considered this. "You don't think Ambrose Minor is in this alone, is that right?"

"Oh, he may be. He's dastardly enough, and certainly has checked 'megalomaniac' on his questionnaire. But his utter disdain for working with his own government smacks of the Arcetri. And if there's an entire web of assholes working on this project, it would be nice to find A-Hole Number One. That might save us some trouble down the line with other assignments."

"Let me know what you—wait, what is that obnoxious sound?"

"It's the bottom of a chocolate shake. And yes, I'll call you when I'm done with Parks."

I'm intrigued by prison life. Not enough to want to call it home, but the social order is fascinating to me. Yeah, like you, I've seen plenty of prison movies, which creates the feeling that we know how it all works inside.

We don't. It's a completely different world. Trying to organize it in your mind using your own cushy life as a guide will fail you. There's an order of things, but it's hard to define. At your office, you may have a system of seniority based on time served. Inside these walls, seniority can be built around a number of factors; time served *can* be one, but it's not the only one. Sometimes seniority is determined with a fist. Sometimes it's predicated on who has the best connections, both inside and out. At some prisons, the guards play a part in which convict has the power; in other institutions, the guards couldn't give two shits.

All of this has a feel to it, so that each prison has a sort of atmosphere. I've been in many of them—as a visitor, thank you—and the first five minutes at each one are spent acclimating, getting to know the vibe. In the facility housing Steffan Parks, I felt a definite vibe of simmering violence. The guy maybe should've stayed where he was in Colorado.

Oh well. Whether or not Parks was treated kindly by his fellow guests was never going to keep me up at night. But I filed away that vibe as a guard escorted me to a visitation room. On the way, I struck up a conversation with the guard, gathering pertinent information about some of the top-rung folks who wore the prison orange. It might just come in handy during the little talk I was about to have.

After waiting 10 minutes, I heard the lock turn. The door

swung open and in walked Steffan Parks, handcuffed. When his own escort had him seated, the handcuffs were removed, and the guard left us alone.

Parks studied me, probably trying to figure out who the hell I was. Not that he looked overly concerned. After a while, inmates learn not to care too much about anything they have no control over.

I used the time to assess him, as well. Still gaunt, still bald, still sullen. But now his eyes displayed more of a hollow look. He'd aged several years in the last two. Even with the transfer out of supermax, time in the slammer was not being kind.

"I'm Agent Trevor Michael with the FBI, Mr. Parks."

"Good for you. What sort of deal do you want this time?"

I smiled. "Cutting straight to the chase. Are you sure you don't want another minute or two of small talk?"

"The next thing you're going to tell me is that you were sent by Eric Swan, and you'll remind me that Swan got me transferred. I'm just saving us time."

"You sound like there's something you're eager to get back to. A game show on TV? A round of dominos with a cellmate? Writing your memoir? What's it called? Wait, let me guess. *Don't Drink The Water*."

He let out a sigh. "If you're trying to win me over in order to help you with something, Agent Michael, you're doing a shitty job."

"Forgive me. I never got around to reading Dale Carnegie."

He looked around the room, clearly bored. There was nothing to see. "So, again: What do you want?"

I waited quietly until his eyes made their way back to me. "Like Swan, I'm curious about the Arcetri."

He gave a groan and sat back in his chair. "What is *with* you people? Give it up already."

"Oh, but I can't. Maybe you thought your little after-school club would shrivel up and die after you got put away. But, sadly, they're still playing tricks on people. Or trying to."

"Then, with your remarkable talents as a lawman, you should be able to hunt them down and show them who's boss. You don't need me."

I shrugged. "One would think. But I was told your agreement with Agent Swan was that, in exchange for your transfer, you'd help anytime we came calling. It certainly wasn't a one-and-done arrangement."

He crossed his arms. "You're assuming I have an encyclopedia of knowledge about this alleged group. And besides, it seems far-fetched to think the busy people within the Bureau of Prisons would go through all the trouble and paperwork to pack me back off to Colorado just because you whined about me not telling you enough. I've told Swan everything I know. There. I've cooperated. So, are we done?"

The sigh that slipped out of me was genuine. Dancing with inmates could be so tiring. It always came down to shoving. Not physically, though it was tempting.

"No, Steffan, we're not done yet. You're back to pretending that you have some sort of power here. When, in reality, I've got power for days. To be specific, I've got an unholy trinity of power punches I can deploy. Let me lay them out for you."

I held up one finger. "Don't kid yourself. There's really no paperwork necessary to ship your ass back to Colorado. It's a call. Some underpaid, overworked office assistant can fill in the forms while you're actually en route. You're not so important that we need to bother the Bureau. All it takes is one report of your violent behavior and threats, and that will start the ball rolling."

"Right," he grunted with a laugh. "What violent behavior and threats?"

"The ones I'll have three other incarcerated dickheads around here swear to. They'll be happy to get a nice treat or two."

He scowled but kept his mouth shut.

"Second, there's the matter of your brother. Alton, right?"

His face went blank, and the eyes got even colder, but he still didn't speak.

"Seems his bookkeeping at that casino has been a little off. Columns that are supposed to balance are not balancing. Well, they are after he gets done with them. But a little postmortem on the ledger will show different."

Parks shook his head. "What a crock. You're threatening to tell the IRS or something? Have him arrested for a math error? He can beat that."

I rubbed my forehead and winced. "You are totally misunderstanding the situation in Vegas, my friend. Of course, you're a science nerd, not a career criminal, so there's a certain amount of naiveté involved. You see, I have no intention of telling the government anything about your brother's bookkeeping." I looked up at him. "But I think you know who's ultimately on the top rung of that organization. And they're the kind of people who don't forgive and forget someone skimming off the top."

"Bullshit!" he roared. "You wouldn't do that."

I adopted my most incredulous look. "Why not? I don't know your dumb brother. If he's buried in a shallow grave out in the Nevada desert, it won't ruin my appetite."

He went back to the crossed-arm look. After a long pause, he said, "You wouldn't do that. That's no different than murder."

"Says the man who tried to murder 10,000 people."

"You're in law enforcement."

"Desperate times, desperate measures, as they say. And perfectly happy to do both of those things I've mentioned. But you haven't even heard my favorite yet. That one involves Julio Molina."

The name didn't mean shit to me. I wouldn't know Julio if he walked up and tried to sell me a magazine subscription. But the guard who'd escorted me to this room had graciously informed me that Julio Molina was the biggest badass within the prison walls.

Originally sentenced for murder and attempted murder, he'd been in and out of solitary for a number of beatings and other rude behavior in the exercise yard. Parks would certainly know who he was. Everyone in every prison knows the name of the guy you never cross.

Parks didn't utter a word. Just kept his eyes locked on me.

"Julio may or may not know why you're in here, Steffan. I doubt you two are in a knitting circle together. And even if he knows you tried to poison the water supply of a town, he probably doesn't know *which* town. He doesn't know it's Sun City. That's just a detail." I leaned toward him. "You're a really bright guy, Steffan. You must see where this is going."

He still didn't answer.

"Okay. You wanna sit there all tight-lipped? I'll fill in the blanks. Julio's grandmother—his *grandmother*, for chrissakes—is a resident of—can you guess? Come on, guess. Make this fun for both of us."

If Parks could've spit at me, I had no doubt he would've. But I was sure his mouth had gone bone dry and his balls were at this moment curling up inside his abdomen.

It was my turn to look around the room, as innocent as I could be. Without looking at him, I said, "How would Julio Molina feel about some guy trying to murder Grandma in one of the most horrific ways imaginable? I saw the reports of what that toxin of yours would do to a person. Ugh. Gives me the shivers just thinking about it."

Then I turned back to him, and my voice turned ice cold. "I want two things, Steffan. I want to walk out of here knowing that you'll never again play this chicken-shit game of clamming up when any of us need information. *Any* of us. Eric Swan. Me. Glinda the Good Witch. *Anyone*.

"And two, I want the name of the person who oversees the Arcetri. I want the name and I want to know where to find them. You have one minute before I make a call to burn your brother to the ground and then stroll over to Julio and clue him in about how you hate his grandmother."

I leaned back. Parks fidgeted for a few moments, but we both knew he'd spill.

"I don't know his name," he finally said.

With a long sigh, I began to stand up.

"No," he said, both hands out toward me. "I'm not saying I won't help you. I'm saying that I don't know the guy's real name."

I sat back down. "What does that even mean, Steffan? Do you guys have fictional names, like comic book villains? Am I supposed to go on the hunt for Beaker Man? Don't test my patience, asshole."

He shook his head. "I've only seen him twice. Once at a conference in Palo Alto, once at my house in New Mexico. He wasn't at either place very long. Just enough to size up people. At least that's what it seemed like to me."

"Size up how?"

Parks shrugged. "I don't know. Like he wanted to see how serious people were."

"Serious. You mean, serious enough to kill?"

He didn't answer, but his nervous eyes said yes.

"All right," I said. "So he was at two places with other scientists, and nobody knew his name? How did people refer to him? Doctor?"

"No. He's not a doctor. He's not even a scientist. And nobody really called him anything. He was just—"

"Whoa, hold on a minute. You said he's *not* a scientist? The guy who's prodding scientists to fight back and to lash out and murder people. He's not one of you?" I gave him a quizzical look. "Then what the hell is he doing with you knuckleheads?"

Parks slumped in his chair. Now that he was talking, all the bluster had gone out of him. I imagined it might even feel good for him to finally blow out the carbon. Really, he would be incarcerated for a long, long time. What did he have to lose?

Unless this was all part of an act. But I didn't think so.

He answered in a voice barely above a mumble. "I don't know what his story is. Like I said, I don't even know his name. He went by a phony name, just so we'd have someone to reference. He called himself Vincenzo."

"What's the significance of that?"

"Vincenzo Viviani. One of Galileo's assistants. Some called him a disciple."

"Cute. You guys really took this covert club thing all the way. Next you'll tell me you had a secret handshake."

"Yeah. Anyway, this guy was like a—"

I waited for him to put a label on it.

"Almost like he was a labor organizer." He looked up at me. "I know it sounds ridiculous. But that's the feel I got. Like he was some high-priced, highly educated manipulator who understood the nasty undercurrent in the world of science and knew how to rally the troops. But quietly."

This wasn't what I expected. My vision of the Arcetri had been a handful of pissed off scientists, realizing what they had in common—their anger—and one of them bashfully stating that they're mad as hell and not gonna take it anymore. The others nodding in agreement. A trickle of disappointment turning into a torrent of rage. But all of it initiated by the women and men who'd been scorned and ridiculed.

The notion that it was an *outsider*? Someone who recognized what these brilliant people had in common, then herded them into a collective rabble that would strike back?

This did not track. The only way it made sense was if this mysterious organizer had his own reasons. Someone who stood to benefit. Otherwise, why bother?

A minute went by where neither Parks nor I uttered a word.

"Tell me something," I finally said. "When you decided on your revenge, what part did this stranger play?"

He shifted in his chair. "You could say he worked like a consultant. I had the scientific knowledge. I knew how to create the formula and how it could best be distributed. Vincenzo would be no help with that. But he talked to me about how to transport the poison. How to get inside the facilities. Even how to find help."

"And you only saw him twice? Then how did he provide all this information?"

"It was condensed. Shared via a portable hard drive that contained what I needed to learn. Then I destroyed it. If he needed to get in touch, he'd call me at the office, like any other routine call. From burner phones, I imagine. But it wasn't overly complicated. The bulk of the plan was mine. He acted like a coach."

I shook my head. "Why didn't this come out at your trial? You may have been able to plead for a reduced sentence if you'd turned state's evidence and helped to bring this guy in."

A pained smile played across his face. "Agent Michael, you don't understand. For one thing, I don't *want* this man put away. I want him to succeed. We all do. I may have failed, but the next person may not.

"Besides," he added, "there are two other very good reasons why I didn't talk. One, there wasn't anything I could really say to catch him. No name, other than a useless code name that I'm quite confident he never used anywhere else. No way of contacting him. What good would that be? And two, he's—" He took a heavy breath. "Well, this is not a mild-mannered guy we're talking about. He's . . . quite dangerous."

I raised an eyebrow. "Oh. You're saying he'd have people killed?"

"Uh, yeah, you could say that. He's killed people. Some he's done himself, but mostly he has people who do the nasty deeds for him."

"How do you know this?"

He chewed his lip for a second. "He, uh, killed a woman who was at the meeting at my house. She stood up and said she wanted no part of it. Said she would contact the police if we didn't call the whole thing off. This organizer very calmly told her she was free to go, and we would consider her warning." He paused. "I got a call from her business partner the next day. They'd found her mangled car at the bottom of a ravine. We all got the message."

Without thinking, I got to my feet and began pacing. It was a habit of mine when thoughts began cascading. Just the act of walking helped me sort things out. At the moment, too many ideas jostled for attention. The fact that, after all this time, we were learning that the force behind the Arcetri was not a scientist himself, but an organized killer—

I came to a sudden stop. My heart began thumping, fueled by a sudden burst of adrenaline.

Turning to face Parks, I said, "Steffan, describe Vincenzo."

He appeared to recall a visual file in his head. "Uh, medium height. Medium weight."

"Great. So far that's really helpful."

"He had short-cropped dark hair. His eyes were very dark, too. Obviously a lot of melanin, because they were ultra-brown. Uh, thin lips."

"Much better, Steffan. What about his voice?"

"His voice?"

"Yeah. High-pitched? Baritone?"

"Calm. I can only describe it as calm. It never modulated too high or too low. And he never raised his voice. Like he was a robot."

The more he described the person, the faster my pulse raced. Though still far from a positive identification, subtle pieces fell into place, forming an image of someone in my mind.

Someone I'd hunted for a long time.

CHAPTER TEN

It was probably 15 degrees hotter on my way back to Sky Harbor International than it had been when I left in the rental car that morning. And I didn't care. The cauldron that was Arizona was the last thing on my mind. The assignment had now taken on an entirely new component. Suddenly, it was personal.

Before sending him back to his cell, I'd cleared up one other thing with Steffan Parks. I now chewed on that discussion as I raced down the road, my music on but barely heard. I needed to be able to contact this guy who went by the name Vincenzo. Once Parks had been apprehended, his ability to contact the organizer had evaporated.

But if Ambrose Minor was working with him, that required an active conduit. One I could exploit.

"What was the protocol for contacting Vincenzo," I'd asked Parks. "How did that work?"

"First of all, you never contacted him. Ever. If he was going to work with you, he'd call and arrange another time when you could have 20 or 30 minutes uninterrupted. He'd hear you out, offer some feedback, then send you an external drive with further instructions and data. Like I said, that would then be destroyed.

Not that there was a single thing on there that could finger Vincenzo for anything. Plus, it could only make sense when viewed in context with the proposed exercise."

I'd nearly jumped on him for referring to mass murder as an "exercise." But I needed to keep him talking. I let it slide.

By this point, I understood the consultancy aspect of the arrangement. What I didn't get was the *why*. What would motivate Vincenzo to indulge a segment of society that wanted nothing more than revenge? It couldn't be financial, could it? He wasn't taking money from the scientists he aided. At least, not at first glance. So what was the endgame?

I mentally flipped through my history of this consultant's operations. They all had one thing in common: They created chaos. He was a villainous tornado, dropping out of the sky without warning and cutting a wide swath of destruction before disappearing back into the mist. He'd undoubtedly made a fortune from his talents, and money always played a part. But was that his *motivation*? It never had that feeling to me. It never smelled like a heist, like a scheme to make millions or billions and escape to a private beach.

His association with an army of angry lab coats had to somehow meld with his purpose. The only way it wouldn't fit would be if he was thoroughly insane—and my nemesis was not insane. He was a cold-blooded killer, a psychopath for sure. But he was not insane. Which meant his purpose was TBD.

And the identity of this mastermind behind the Arcetri, the shadowy figure the organization knew only as Vincenzo? I was confident I knew him by another name.

Beadle.

That wasn't his real name, either, but at this point I didn't care about his true identity, or his childhood background, his political affiliations, or if he preferred a window seat or the aisle. The only thing I cared about was finishing the business between us.

That meant killing him.

Not long ago, I had a golden opportunity. I had a gun pointed right between his eyes. All I needed to do was squeeze ever so gently and my long nightmare would be over. And what had I done in that moment? I'd relished it. I'd basked in that feeling of victory, the joy of finally coming face to face and *winning*.

That delay, which may have lasted all of three seconds, had allowed Beadle to wriggle off the hook. I'd buried a slug in his shoulder as he escaped, but that wasn't the goal. The goal was to end him. The way he'd ended my sister's life.

For the record, he'd killed me, too. More than once. During my assignments over the years, our paths had crossed. That was only natural, considering that Beadle was one of the most successful criminal minds of the past 20 years. He was damned near impossible to track down because he had no home. He flitted not only around the country, but across the globe. He took on jobs wherever the money was good and the assignment could challenge his obvious intellect. He had no family anyone knew of. He had no ties. He left no digital trail.

He was the ultimate criminal phantom.

I had no proof that Vincenzo was Beadle, but my own version of Spidey sense usually served me well. The Arcetri had placed their attacks in the hands of a man who was a specialist at planning and organizing. He was mysterious and impossible to reach. And he didn't hesitate to kill. Check, check, and check.

The physical description was close enough but proved nothing because Beadle changed his appearance like I change my socks.

It came back again to that one question: *Why?* Well, if I could go through back channels to find him, I might get the chance to find out.

I knew this much, though: Should Beadle and I come face-to-face again, there would be no hesitation.

. . .

We'd considered flying me back to DC, but Quanta decided I should return to Charlotte and push Ambrose Minor a little harder. I'd filled her in on the interesting chat with Steffan Parks. The only thing I *hadn't* shared at first was my suspicion concerning Vincenzo's identity. Sitting in the concourse, waiting to board, I'd initially thought it would be a mistake. I might have a big-ass problem with Beadle, but Quanta had a big-ass problem with my problem. It was just easier sometimes to selectively report and leave out the stuff that would get me yelled at. You know, like a child.

But, at the last minute, I realized something this important couldn't be kept from Q2's boss. So I told her what I was thinking.

The response was exactly what I expected. She sat quietly, digesting everything. That left me sitting patiently in a hard plastic chair, watching travelers trundle past with their roller bags and listening to monotonous announcements about gate changes. But I was glad it wasn't a video call. It was better imagining her scowl than seeing it.

When she finally broke the silence, she displayed that cool-headed ability to distill a matter down to its fundamental parts. Quanta never allowed emotion to interfere with her leadership responsibilities. It's what made her the perfect choice to head up Q2. "If Beadle is involved with the Arcetri and with Minor's plan to create hybrid soldiers, it could potentially be a break for us."

It was my turn to scowl. "How so?"

She measured her words carefully. "In the past, Beadle has been selective about the criminal minds he worked with. He could vet the prospect and choose to work with ones that offered a profile that was more . . . professional."

I saw where she was going. "So you're saying his potential partners in the Arcetri are much more likely to be dog-paddling in the amateur pool."

"It stands to reason. Their background is academic in nature, not criminal."

"Okay," I said. "I buy that. And it means more opportunities for mistakes."

"Which is why we'll send you back to Charlotte for now." She paused. "Be on your toes. Amateurs or not, if you're correct about all this, they're assembling quite a team of villains."

I inhaled a long breath and slowly let it out. Quanta was right. Their starting lineup might be composed of Ambrose Minor, supplying money and influence; Antoinette Lazarov, the elite tactical operative; a collection of mad scientists stirring the pot and cooking up a modern day devil's brigade; and Beadle, who was simply evil incarnate, coaching it all.

Sometimes I wondered if we had enough good guys to counterpunch the forces aligned against us.

Quanta couldn't let the discussion end without addressing the matter clearly bothering her. "Let's not pretend that injecting Beadle into this operation won't affect your performance."

It took everything I had to stifle a sigh. *It was her job to bring this up*, I told myself. *It's her responsibility*.

Carefully picking my way through my words, I said, "The effect you're describing will be to *heighten* my performance, not hinder it. Now that we suspect he's involved, it could very well provide some clarity about the things we encounter. It's additional information, and that can only be a positive."

There was no way in hell she bought my ad-libbed gobbledygook. It sounded like street corner psychology to my *own* ears. Whenever I tried a con on Quanta, the timbre of my voice shifted, a dead giveaway I'd fired up the bullshit machine. But I was pretty sure she appreciated the effort. And, like a parent who knows their child is spouting complete nonsense in an attempt to talk their way into something, she likely smiled on the inside. I could almost hear her inner monologue taking pity, saying, "*Poor thing*."

In an almost sadistic way, however, she remained silent. I knew I had to fill the space with something a little more tangible. More real.

"Look," I said. "Your concern is noted. And it's even justified —to a certain extent. But it's not like dealing with Beadle throws me entirely off my game."

"Are you forgetting Connecticut?"

From anyone else, it might've been considered a low blow. The last time I'd engaged with Beadle had been at a private compound on the shores of Long Island Sound, the now-infamous encounter where he'd escaped wounded, but alive. Quanta wasn't criticizing my failure to terminate the asshole; she was making a subtle reference to the six weeks it took for me to get over the incident with Beadle and the former Q2 agent who'd gone rogue. The two had teamed up to work quite a number on my soul. The indestructible Eric Swan had nearly crumbled.

Now, Quanta was doing her job. She was assessing the mental state of her top agent in the field. The possibility of my hurt feelings would have zero impact on decisions she made. Could I get the job done without my history with Beadle fuzzing up everything?

Perhaps I was too close to the situation to fairly offer an opinion. But I was clear-headed enough to know one of the cold, hard truths regarding our delicate human psyche: What we never want to believe is that clues to our future are littered throughout our past.

Beadle played a critical role in my past and it now appeared he could loom large in my near future. It would be disingenuous to suggest this new development would have no impact. It already had. Here I was, thinking about it.

And there would be much more of that to come.

It had been Christina who'd given me the most honest viewpoint on it: "The biggest mistake you can make with Beadle is believing you can make other people understand."

It was the kind of tenet I could count on from my wife. It made me explore the issue at hand in a fresh, new light, but it carried enough simple truth to apply across a spectrum of life's complications. For all of us.

I'd stopped trying to make Quanta understand. I gave Q2's shrink, Miller, slightly more access to my obsession, but only because he sincerely tried to help. Otherwise, I internalized the conflict and used it as a perverse form of fuel.

"No," I said to Quanta. "I'll never forget Connecticut. But it doesn't cripple me, if that's what you're wondering. *Still* wondering."

She was silent before saying, "Good work today with Parks. Even with all of your various identities, you have an interesting relationship with that man."

I caught the overhead announcement that my plane was now boarding. I ended the call with Quanta and dug my headphones out of my backpack. The music would cloak any chatter around me while I focused on everything I'd absorbed in the last 24 hours.

And if the boss wanted me to push a little harder, she'd get no argument from me.

Fife had been busy. He picked me up at the airport in Charlotte, and we promptly retired to a pub near my hotel to compare notes. It was late and, while there were a few patrons scattered around the high-top tables, we had the actual bar to ourselves. The woman schlepping drinks, who introduced herself as Tay, was a blueprint for bartender perfection: the exact right amount of talk to establish a friendly server/drinker relationship, a deft touch with the alcohol mixtures, and perceptive enough to know when her customers wanted to talk privately. She would be tipped well.

I went first. "Parks was his usual morose self. Not too different from when you saw him. The move might've put a couple of pounds back on him, but it didn't make him any more sociable."

"Oh, I'm sure you found a way to loosen his tongue."

"A triple shot of threats did the trick. Good thing he's not an actual hardened criminal."

Fife laughed. "They suck down threats like free beer at a frat party. So what was the big takeaway?"

I told him my suspicion regarding Beadle and the Arcetri.

Fife's response was barely a whisper. "No shit."

He didn't know details about my personal connection with the criminal mastermind, but everyone in the upper echelons of law enforcement knew about Beadle. He was the unicorn of villains, the one everybody wanted to find.

I picked up my cocktail and swirled it before taking a drink. "All right, your turn. What do you have to share? Have you got me into that arms factory yet?"

"Got half the work done this evening. The rest will be done in the morning. But forget about that for now. Look at this." He reached into a jacket pocket and pulled out a folded sheaf of papers. Placing them on the bar in front of me, he said, "Antoinette Lazarov. Born Dimitrovgrad, Bulgaria. Good athlete. Good student. But also a rabble-rouser. Troublemaker. Married young. Accused of killing her husband, but never convicted. Definitely *did* kill a man trying to rob her in a park, but no charges were filed because they ruled it self-defense."

Fife leaned close to me. "From what I read, she took the guy apart. And this was *before* she had training in the Bulgarian army."

I nodded. Sometimes you can tell about a person's ability to defend themselves just by looking in their eye. Given Antoinette's adaptations, the eye thing was problematic. But she still gave off the vibe.

"She was actually recruited into the Bulgarian Land Forces, and not long after that she received an invitation to their Special Forces. Apparently she was fearless to the point where she scared the shit out of her commanding officers. It was just easier to boot her upstairs to get her out of their hair."

"How did she end up with the NATO forces?"

Fife laughed. "On some training exercise, she surpassed not only the objective of her mission, but she penetrated into the opposing team's command center. Jacked up a few people who took offense. From what I could tell, the choice was either to court-martial her or loan her out to the big leagues."

I kept a placid look on my face during this accounting, but inside was a different story. My gut told me there would be a day of reckoning between me and Ms. Lazarov. I had the advantage at the moment because I could gather intel on her, while getting the dope on me would prove a little more difficult for Minor and Company. And based on Fife's report, it wasn't Antoinette's military experience or her track record of brutality that concerned me. It was the liquid nitrogen running through her veins at 320 degrees below zero. In all my years and all my battles, I'd found that military training could be defeated with superior training and execution.

Slicing through the demeanor of a true killer? That was the challenge. And I'd seen it in person. During our dinner, she'd displayed about as much emotion as my steak.

"Anything else?" I asked. "Other than the bionic woman?"

"Someone in our office tried to do some follow-up questioning with Paige Walters."

I paused. "Bryson Hedrick's girlfriend. She was in the car when everything went down."

"Yeah. Anyway, one of our Bureau agents in Huntsville went by her apartment. And she's gone."

My drink was halfway to my mouth and stopped there. "Gone? Gone how?"

"Moved out. Roommate told the agent she packed everything she could take in two suitcases, said she'd send someone later to get everything else, and took off. When the agent asked where she'd gone, the roommate said, and I quote, 'hopefully to hell.'"

"Pissed."

"Understatement."

"Did she move in with Bryson?"

He shook his head. "No."

"Huh" was all I could think to say at the moment. I finished bringing the cocktail to my lips, thinking. A moment later, I turned to Fife. "None of us have really questioned Paige Walters. But her report to the police said she waited outside while the two Hedricks went into that building. Bryson claims she was on the phone with a friend. So was there a reason she didn't want to go in?"

Fife gave a wry smile. "Your suspicious mind went the same place mine did."

"I mean, think about it. Somebody knew they were there, when by all accounts they shouldn't have been. It was a last-minute decision by Ty Hedrick to stop by and prep for the next day's meeting. He and his son go inside—"

"—while Paige waits in the safety of the car. On the phone."

"So was she really talking with a girlfriend?"

"And now," said Fife, "she's gone. Didn't even wait around to move her stuff. Just grabbed two bags and split."

It was a stunning development and one I hadn't even considered. I couldn't really kick myself, though; *nobody's* mind had gone there. She was an innocent bystander, someone traumatized by the death of her boyfriend's father, just minutes after dining with him.

Only maybe Paige Walters wasn't traumatized one bit.

I pulled out my phone and called Poole, who answered a little slowly for her. This time it took two and a half rings.

"It's late, Poole. Please tell me you're not at the office."

"No, I am out."

"Oh." I pulled the phone away and made a surprised face at Fife. "Well, I'm sorry to interrupt."

"No need to be sorry. What can I help with?"

I told her we suddenly were very interested in Paige Walters. We'd need to sic the second floor on her right away, if they hadn't already compiled a dossier. I also wanted to know where she'd gone when she left her apartment. To a hotel? To someone else's house? Out of town?

"And let's get a copy of her phone records the night of the murder," I added. "I'd like to see who she was talking to while Ty and Bryson Hedrick were inside that building."

"I will get on that right away," Poole said.

"Great. Thank you. Uh—" I tried to sound upbeat. "All right. It doesn't have to be immediately. Have a good time tonight."

We ended the call, and I shook my head with a smile.

"What's so funny?" Fife asked.

"I'm not sure, but I think Poole was on a date."

Fife laughed. "Good for her. She deserves to get out and have some fun. She works too hard. Usually doing shit for you."

"Can't argue with that. I just never thought about . . . that." I chuckled and finished my drink.

My recent past included an ambush in a hotel room. That only has to happen once before you become overly cautious, especially after having been away longer than usual. Not to mention that my trusty Glock was locked inside the room's safe and not in my hand. I slipped the door open—although modern hotel room doors refuse to be opened silently—and reached in to flick on a light. Then, pushing the door open a little more, I scanned the interior. Anyone watching through their peephole across the hall would've enjoyed the Paranoid Show.

The room was clean and quiet. That didn't necessarily mean it was safe.

I crept into the bathroom, checked the closet, and even peered under the bed. Sure, I felt a little stupid. But hearing the lowdown on Lazarov, along with the startling Paige Walters news, was enough to give my caution a turbo boost. It's a given in the espionage world that an adversary who feels pursued or cornered will strike like a viper. Well, I'd let Ambrose Minor know he was, at the very least, being investigated, if not actually pursued. The goal had been to force a reaction; it was best to be prepared for one.

Feeling comfortable with my surroundings, I bolted the door and retrieved my gun from the safe. Then I unloaded my bag, grabbed my uploading tools, popped the big pill, and sent my memories off to Washington.

CHAPTER ELEVEN

Exhaustion can paradoxically keep you from falling asleep, which is one of nature's cruel jokes. But it also can bring on the slumber of the dead. It was after nine o'clock the next morning when I finally surfaced.

I was greeted with a message from Poole. She'd attached a file on Paige Walters. I felt guilty that she might've cut short her date in order to process my request, but it thrilled me to have the file so quickly. And hey, nobody working for Q2 could ever expect a normal life. Or, in my case, lives.

Picking up my tablet, I stretched out on the bed and skimmed through the relatively short document of background information first, then went back for a more intensive read. It's not like I'd expected to find something that jumped off the page, but there was nothing to even raise an eyebrow.

Thirty-two years old. Born and raised in the Huntsville area. Daughter of an accountant father and pharmacist mother, solid upper-middle-class family. Graduated from Auburn with a degree in business administration, so she'd even stayed in-state for school. Then back to Huntsville to take a job as a market research analyst, hopping from one job to another—presumably working her way up the salary ladder—and currently employed by a regional retail chain with seven stores. Never married. No children. No arrests. Four traffic infractions, all for excessive speed. Good credit score.

In other words, borderline boring, in a good way. Nothing to indicate a shady life, and certainly nothing that would catch the eye of Minor or Beadle.

But, I reminded myself, everything changed when she met and began dating Bryson Hedrick. That alone would make her approachable in the eyes of a scheming competitor. Approachable and maybe pliable?

Sometimes the easiest people to turn were the ones who, like Paige, had always been a straight arrow. Other than a lead foot, what had she ever really done that veered from the path of righteousness? Raised by a virtuous Southern family, educated at good schools, pledging the perfect sorority, doing all the things she'd maybe felt were expected of her, even down to dating the heir to a thriving Huntsville business.

I looked closely at the photo of my subject. She wore the smile of someone taught at an early age how to slip on that smile like a pair of Crocs. Shoulder-length blond hair, blue eyes, a small nose, and teeth courtesy of Huntsville's best orthodontist, no doubt. Could it be that Paige had longed for something a little more exciting than a life of work-home-occasional entertaining? Did a future of minivans, office Christmas parties, and battling HOAs frighten her to the point where an opportunity to step outside her prescribed life—even an opportunity of dubious moral substance—seemed like the escape she'd inwardly longed for?

I rested the tablet on my chest and looked up at the ceiling. Automatically making this connection was tempting, but the truth was, you could build a story like this from almost any background. Troubled life? Clearly she wanted an escape. Idyllic life? Clearly she *needed* an escape. It was too easy to assign criminal motivations to any upbringing: good, bad, or boring. What I'd learned from the file, however, was that I needed a sit-down session with Ms. Walters. I would learn a lot more from her eyes and her words than I ever would from a cold, digital summation.

First, we'd have to find her.

I picked up the tablet again. Poole's message included a post-script that Paige had not used her credit card in the past 36 hours. The Bureau had determined she was not at her parents' house, which meant she likely was staying with another friend. Or paying for everything with cash. Eventually, she'd have to surface.

The last item in the Paige Walters report involved the phone call she'd made the night of the fire. The one she'd made while waiting in the car. I'd counted on that being a clue we could follow.

But there was only one problem. Phone records showed Paige had not made a phone call that evening. None. The only texts she'd made just prior to the murder came during dinner, and those were part of an innocent thread with two other friends. Once the shit hit the fan at the office building, she'd sent a flurry of texts to family and friends, all either expressing a sense of shock and bewilderment or simply letting people know she was okay.

In other words, the disappearance didn't align with the theory that she'd been the mole who'd directed the killer to Ty Hedrick. Unless she'd done all of it with a burner phone. Which made sense. But her excuse for remaining in the car had ostensibly been to call a friend. No one would use a burner phone for that. And surely they'd expect the authorities to check the phone records; wouldn't she at least place one call to cover her ass?

Something didn't ring true with her story.

Again, was I creating scenarios to fill in the holes in the investigation? Or were they legitimate possibilities?

A little voice told me she'd made up the story about calling a friend simply to keep from traipsing along with the Hedrick boys. She may have just wanted to sit there and scroll through social media. Or flip through dating sites, looking for someone a tad more exciting than Bryson. Which wouldn't be hard.

Where were you, Paige?

After catching the last few minutes of the dismal free breakfast in the lobby, I sat on the hotel's veranda and placed a call to Bryson Hedrick. I was told he wasn't available to come to the phone, so I dropped the FBI reference. That always works.

"Oh, Agent Swan," he said, pretending to be surprised. "What can I do for you?"

"I want to talk about your girlfriend. Let's start with the most obvious question. Where is she?"

He paused and must've been wondering how much I knew. Then, with a sigh, he said, "I don't know where she is. She moved out of her apartment. That's all I know."

"You didn't have a formal breakup?"

"What? No. I tried calling her last night and her roommate told me she'd packed up and left."

"Come on, Bryson. What's going on?"

His voice took on an angry edge. "What is this? I don't know what's going on. One day she's fine, we're talking about where we're going to dinner on Friday, and the next day she's disappeared. Why are you asking me like I'm hiding something?"

"I don't know, Bryson. Most girlfriends don't witness a murder and then run off without telling their boyfriend where they're going. I just want you to know that concealing information from me won't look good when we eventually find out anyway."

"What is this shit? I'm not concealing anything. I called her this morning and her roommate said she was gone. So you know as much as me, Swan."

I took a slightly more relaxed tone. "Think for a moment. Any ideas at all where she might go? A favorite hotel or resort? A friend she always relied on? A family member other than her parents? Anything that might help us find her?"

"I'm confused," he said. "Why are you so desperate to locate her? You haven't even mentioned her until now."

"Nothing unusual. There were only two people who were there that night and one of them—the one I haven't spoken with yet—mysteriously vanished. It's routine. Well, it *was* routine until she fled. I just need to hear her story."

"Well, I have no idea where she is. It's not like we've been dating for years. I mean, I have strong feelings for her. Probably more than she has for me. But I don't know any other family members besides her parents—I've only met them once—and I've already called her friends that I know. Nobody's heard from her."

"Did you have a fight?"

"That's none of your business."

"News flash, Bryson. The minute your father was murdered, it became my business. Now quit playing tough and just answer my goddamned questions. Did you two have a fight? Or did she bolt with no warning whatsoever?"

He let a long breath escape his lips. "We didn't actually fight. I just asked her why she's been so distant since everything happened, and she went off on me. Told me I was being insensitive or something like that. I told her I was the one who'd lost a father, and she said something else that I don't remember now, except it was angry. Like I didn't appreciate how traumatic the whole thing was for her, too. Anyway, she blurted all that out and then hung up."

"When was this?"

"Day before yesterday. Early evening."

I thought about that. She had the fight with Bryson, then within an hour or two she packed up and left. Seemed like quite an overreaction to an argument with your boyfriend, but we never know what other pressures people are dealing with.

Like pressures from Ambrose Minor, perhaps?

"All right," I said. "Let me know the minute you hear anything. And I mean anything."

We hung up, and I texted Fife, who said he was finishing up some work and could meet me after lunch. Then he added:

You'll be happy.

He pulled up just after one o'clock. Climbing into his car, I handed him a cup of hotel coffee.

"Having a hard time waking up?" he asked, a bemused smile on his face.

"Slept a hard eight hours. I mean really deep. Must've needed it. Anyway, this is my third cup, and I didn't want you to just watch me."

"How considerate. So what's new?"

I gave him the bullet points on Paige and shared my conversation with Bryson.

"You know," he said, blowing on his hot coffee, "did you ever stop to think she's sick of the guy and this just provided her with an excuse to bolt?"

"Definitely crossed my mind. *I* think the guy's a tool, so why wouldn't *she*?" I sipped my coffee. "But then, why not just break up with him? Why so dramatic? I mean, packing your bags, abandoning your roommate, and disappearing without a trace? I've had my share of relationships go wrong, but no one ever went to *that* extreme to break up with me."

"Who would ever want to dump you?"

"Funny. So tell me what's been keeping you extra busy? Your plan to get me into Minor Arms, I hope."

"As a matter of fact—" He handed me a medium-sized manilla envelope. "Your credentials, Mr. Charles."

I set my coffee into a cup holder and took the package. "Mr. Charles? This has to be from the second floor."

A puzzled smile spread across his face. "Well, yeah. How did you know that without looking?"

"Because it's become a joke for them. Every fake name they give me is always two first names. When I went to see Steffan Parks, I was Trevor Michael." I opened the envelope and pulled out a laminated security pass. "Yep. Raymond Charles. Never fails."

Fife grinned. "Your name is Ray Charles? I'm sorry, but that's funny."

I responded with a sarcastic smirk, then studied the pass. It was an official identity card, showing that Raymond Charles was employed by Minor Arms. It not only looked good, it seemed identical to the ones I'd seen during my visit with Antoinette at the corporate offices. Also in the packet: a thick, rectangular white card, the kind used to open security doors. Embossed on it, I made out the letters *MA*.

"Well, isn't this the shit? How did you manage this?"

Fife grinned. "I had one of their plant managers picked up late yesterday afternoon on his way home and brought in for questioning. A guy named Masterson."

"For what?"

"Suspected corporate espionage. Told him Ambrose Minor was convinced somebody at one of his plants was leaking classified information. Masterson nearly lost his mind until I told him *he* wasn't a suspect—at least not yet—but that we'd need him to answer some questions about his team. How well he knew them, how long they'd worked there, things like that."

"Okay. How does that produce these goodies in the packet?"

"Hold on, I'm getting to that. When he shows up at the Bureau, we make him dump everything into a small box: keys, wallet, ID card, phone, everything. Security reasons, we say. Can't bring anything back into our secure area. We even make him kick his shoes off, just for show. Then we have him place it all in a locker, which he locks and keeps the key. You know, for peace of mind."

I chuckled. "Of course, you guys have another key."

"Probably several. Anyway, while he's in the interrogation room, two of the folks from Q2's second floor go through everything he's placed in the box. They're taking photos, weighing things, scanning the security card, doing things with gadgets I couldn't begin to understand. We kept Masterson in that little room for over two hours, which was plenty of time for all of his things to be completely deconstructed.

"Then, the stuff went back into the box, back into the locker, and when Masterson came out, he collected everything without a clue. We thanked him for his information and threatened—in a courteous way, of course—that discussing our little meeting with anyone would bring him right back in. And if that happened, he might not be going home for a long, long time. Compromising a serious investigation, national security concerns, all that stuff."

"Then the Q2 geeks went to work," I said, nodding. "That's what you were doing this morning, right? Waiting for them to finish manufacturing my new identity and all my toys."

"Hey, you not only work for Minor Arms, but you're in the system all the way. I think they even hacked their way into payroll to make sure you've got a healthy history. You're legit, baby."

I looked at the ID again. "That's fantastic. But what the hell have they done with my photo?"

"Oh, right," he said, reaching into the back seat and grabbing a small bag. "Here you go. Your new hair, facial hair, and glasses. I think there's a mole in here somewhere, too. Yeah, here it is. You can see on the photo ID where it goes."

"Fife, I am impressed. And you know how much I enjoy playing dress-up."

"Hey, give me a challenge and I'll come through. Now we're off to test it out."

"What does that mean?"

"It means we're driving up to the plant, just to have you walk in, walk around, then walk back out. We need you to test all the security measures before you go back tonight to snoop around."

I laughed again and gestured through the windshield. "Onward, sir."

He plugged the address into his GPS and we pulled onto the road in his ostentatious rental sedan. The drive would take about 35 minutes.

It *should've* taken 35 minutes. Six minutes after merging onto I-77, Fife muttered, "What the hell?"

He was looking in his rearview mirror, so I turned around. The flashing lights on the motorcycle were directly behind us. "Way to go, Speed Racer," I said. "Trying to beat Paige Walters' record for tickets?"

"I was doing maybe seven miles an hour over the speed limit. Who gets pulled over for that?"

"They don't suffer lead-footed fools in North Carolina, son."

He flipped on his turn signal and coasted to a stop on the side of the road. The motorcycle cop just sat there for a few moments, probably checking to see if we were wanted in six states. Then he dismounted and walked up slowly, eyeing the car and us.

Fife rolled down his window and kept his hands in plain sight on the wheel. "Hello, officer," he said in a friendly tone. "Did I do something wrong?"

The cop, a sturdy-looking fellow in his 30s, sporting a pair of dark sunglasses, held his hand out. "Good morning, sir. May I see your license and registration, please?"

"It's a rental car," Fife said, but produced his FBI badge and driver's license. I retrieved the car's registration from the glove compartment and handed it over.

"Yes, sir," the cop said. "Just a moment, please, and I'll likely have you on your way."

He went back to his motorcycle. Fife and I sat quietly, just waiting to get back on the road. Every few seconds, I glanced through the rear window. I'd picked up my share of tickets over the years and it never failed to strike me how awkward the situation was for everyone involved. The driver felt irritated and generally embarrassed by the whole thing as cars whizzed by. You were on display as a big loser, and the other drivers were either laughing at you or grateful you were the one dragged to the side of the road and not them.

But it had to be an uncomfortable moment for the cop, too. They couldn't know what was waiting for them in that innocent-looking vehicle, so they essentially put their lives on the line each time they approached. And even though they were simply doing their job, it couldn't feel good knowing you were wrecking some-one's entire day simply because they'd been rushing to get to the office on time or to pick up a child from day care.

There were no real winners in traffic stops except the county coffers.

Only two minutes passed before the police officer began walking back, then detoured to my side of the car, where he seemed interested in something. After intently inspecting the car, he came back around and handed the badge and registration to Fife.

"You're good to go, Agent. I'm sorry for the inconvenience. Your rental car matches the description of a stolen vehicle used in a crime. We have to check, since they'll often swap plates from another stolen car. Thank you for your patience. Hope I didn't keep you from something critical this morning."

"No problem," Fife said, his voice flat. "I appreciate your courtesy. And good luck."

"Yes, sir. Also, just a heads up; your right rear tire is low. There's an exit two miles ahead. You're fine right now, but I'd stop there and air it up. Probably nothing major."

"Will do. Thank you again."

I stuffed the paperwork back into the glove compartment,

and Fife rolled up his window. He put the car in gear and we began rolling back up to speed to merge into traffic.

A moment later, Fife turned to me. "Something was odd about that traffic stop, Swan."

"Like what?"

"I watched him in the side mirror. He never called in anything with my badge. He just sat there for a moment, looking at it."

"Are you sure?"

"Pretty sure. And when he handed everything back, I looked for a name tag on his shirt. You know, to refer to him by name." He glanced at me. "There wasn't one."

I turned and looked through the back window. The cop was cutting across the median and hurrying the other direction. "He's taking off." I looked back at Fife. "What do you think he was really doing at the back of the car? Are we buying the tire story?"

We stared at each other. Then, Fife immediately braked and pulled over to the shoulder. He drove the car onto the grass, as far from the pavement as possible. Without a word, I gathered up all my new Minor Arms gear, and we both flew out of the car and sprinted about 50 feet away. Fife pulled out his phone. "I'm gonna call this in and see if the Charlotte Police—"

He never finished the sentence. With a percussive blast, the car exploded in flames. We were both knocked to the ground as shrapnel rained down around us.

CHAPTER TWELVE

The plan had been for me to push Ambrose Minor and see what happened.

What had happened was now a burning pile of metal on the side of Interstate 77.

My first call was to Poole, informing her I'd need a quick visit by Sanitation. They would handle the real police, who would arrive soon.

Things like this happened in our business. Bad guys shot people, stabbed people, and sometimes tried to blow them to smithereens. Law enforcement people were naturally curious about what the hell was going on, and we couldn't always tell them. In those situations, we called in Sanitation.

I had all the physical training I'd need to play spy. These guys, however, had all the negotiation and bullshit training necessary to clean up any messes I made in the field. Thus, the unofficial name we applied to them. To me, these special agents were an odd combination of CIA spooks, public relations experts, and Jedi mind trick artists. I knew nothing about these people personally; we didn't really chat, other than to exchange information. We'd basically been told not to get chummy. Sanitation simply rolled in, spoke quietly with the cops on the scene, and, before you knew it, things were smoothed over. They'd have a believable story in place for the media, if any arrived—and with a car in flames on the side of the highway, there very well could be. I never stuck around to find out how they explained everything to the police and press, but I could guarantee the story would *not* involve a government spy at war with a leading arms manufacturer.

In the meantime, Fife would use his FBI status to keep things on hold until the cavalry arrived.

The next call was to Quanta. She'd already heard from Poole, but she asked for details. When I finished explaining, she said, "You were fortunate."

"I'll be sure to pass along your compassion to Agent Fife. Well, at least we know we're on the right path. I was on my way out to Minor's nearby plant to test out my new bag of toys. Now I guess I'll just go tonight during their third shift."

"This attempt to kill you shows that Minor is sufficiently rattled. It also could mean the Next Gen Soldier program is closer to completion than we thought and he's trying to buy a little more time to get it to market. We need to see what that progress looks like and, just as important, see who Minor's potential clients are. There's a concern these enhanced soldiers will be used against American forces somewhere in the world as soon as they're available."

"All right. I'll poke around tonight and see what I can dig up." Something else occurred to me. "So, do we let Minor think he's taken me out?"

"I don't think we need to play that game. Maybe it's best to let him know how indestructible you are, Swan."

"Great. So he'll try harder next time. By the way, any word on Paige Walters?"

"No. She's fallen off the radar. We don't suspect foul play—at least not yet—so she's probably just hiding out somewhere. She'll turn up sooner or later. I'll let you know when she does."

Quanta hung up, and I walked over to where Fife squatted on his haunches, watching the traffic slow to a crawl. We'd nearly been killed, but at least we'd provided a few thousand people with an exciting video they could share all day on social media.

"So," I said, "just another day at the office, eh?"

He squinted up at me. "Hanging out with you is dangerous, pal. Remember, some of us don't get do-overs."

I laughed. "And this particular body happens to be one of the best I've had in a while. So me and my current convict appreciate your eagle eye today."

He stood up and removed his ID again as a police car and an ambulance rolled up to the inferno. Another siren meant a fire truck was close behind. Fife ambled over to meet the police officer—a legit cop this time. Until Sanitation arrived, I preferred to hang back and watch the fun.

And to plot my next move against that murderous asshole, Ambrose Minor.

I still felt behind on sleep, so I'd grabbed a nap in my hotel room after uploading. I didn't want to lose the day's experiences, that was for sure. Sadly, the car bomb had curtailed our attempt to test the efficacy of my new identity. I'd just have to trust that the crew on the second floor got it right the first time.

Honestly, they just about always did.

Now, just past 11 p.m, I sat in a new rental car a hundred yards from the entrance gate to the Minor Arms assembly plant. Wrappers from two fast-food tacos lay crumpled on the passenger floorboard, evidence of the glamorous life of a government agent on assignment. I slurped down another mouthful of soda, staring through the windshield. So far, I'd watched a stream of cars leaving, carrying the workers who'd finished their eight hours. The third-shift crew had mostly arrived between 10:30 and 11. From what I could tell, they all simply held up their lanyard to the guard who, at this time of night, probably gave zero shits who went in or out. He knew the hardcore security took place at the building's door.

Still, I waited. A few stragglers drove through, the same people who probably were late at least once or twice every week. Every company had them. But when I saw the guard turn suddenly and enter the little shack to pick up his phone, I fired up the car and hurried down the road to the gate. He was still engaged in his conversation as I slowed to a crawl and nonchalantly held up my lanyard. As expected, he gave it only a cursory glance before waving me past.

Hurdle number one, complete.

The employee lot was filled, even this late—the sign of a thriving business. To stay competitive globally, Minor kept his factory lines rolling 24 hours a day. I didn't know if his Next Gen program occupied this location, but I'd hopefully find out soon enough.

Shutting off the car, I gathered my small work bag from the passenger seat, then glanced at my image in the rearview mirror. The wig looked believable, the goatee looked ridiculous but passable, and my new mole adorned the space just to the right of my nose. All in all, it should be good enough to get me in the door. We had to assume they'd distributed a photo of Eric Swan throughout the company. But now I was Raymond Charles.

With my bag slung over a shoulder and the hard plastic security card in my pocket, I approached the employee entrance. I timed it so I came up right behind a woman who scuttled along in a hurry. She ran her card across the electronic beam and the door clicked open. I caught it before it closed all the way, but still tried my own card. The reader flashed a comforting green light. So far, so good.

Next up was another guard station. This might prove a bit trickier, but at least I had my flustered guide ahead of me. She was chattering to the older man who stood behind the desk, and if he wasn't fully enthralled with her story, he faked it pretty damned well. I heard him dish out a hearty laugh to a story that probably hadn't deserved one. She ran her card across another beam, then also held her lanyard up to yet another electronic eye. After three seconds, she got the green-light-go signal, wrapped up her story with her own laugh, and pushed through the door.

"Hello, sir," the guard said to me with a genuine smile and the world's scratchiest voice. "Are you new? I don't recognize you."

"Sorta new," I said, going through the same motions I'd seen the woman do. "I've been here with Ambrose a time or two." I leaned toward him, lowered my voice, and gave a conspiratorial wink. "To tell you the truth, I think he grew tired of escorting me."

My casual use of the first name made the guard straighten. "Oh, I see. Well, I'm Leonard, sir. If you need any help with anything, just call my extension. Two-two-four. And welcome."

"I'm Raymond," I said, returning his big smile. "And thank you. I'll let Ambrose know that his team is first-rate and friendly."

He beamed and gave a slight bow with his head.

Through the door, I encountered a short hallway before reaching a third point of security. This time, my card did nothing. I frowned at the device, wondering if I should go back and already take Leonard up on his offer of help. But, just then, the door opened and the same woman barreled out, nearly running into me.

"Oh, my god," she said, holding a hand up to her throat. "I'm so sorry."

"No worries," I said, glancing down at her lanyard, which identified her as Elaine. "Forget something?"

"My lunch. It's not so much that I'll get that hungry tonight, but I sure don't want it smelling up my car. You know how it is."

I chortled the appropriate agreement and went through the open door, leaving her to go rescue her car from a tuna fish sandwich or whatever it might be.

I was in a locker room of sorts, one that held coats, bags, and, soon, Elaine's lunch. A cacophony of factory sounds leaked from beyond the swinging doors on the far side of the room. I was entering the bowels of a Minor Arms assembly plant. Not knowing how the locker system worked, I kept my bag over my shoulder—which might look suspicious, but I was bound to stand out anyway if I wasn't standing at an actual work station.

We'd thought of this, though. Should anyone ask, my story was that I was from the compliance office. The beauty of this explanation was that no one in the history of the world had ever understood what compliance people actually did. They might never do *anything*, but nobody wants to question them for fear of being labeled out of compliance themselves. It was best to just smile and nod and let them do whatever the hell they were pretending to do.

Besides, in order for me to make sure everyone at Minor Arms was in compliance, I'd need to look around from time to time. That would explain my curious exploration of the facility, even late at night.

Under this guise, I wandered up and down one of the factory lines, politely greeting the workers who toiled away. The line was dedicated to a product I didn't recognize. That was unsettling. I'd been in special ops, for chrissakes; you'd think I'd know every article of war under the sun. But I'd also been out of the military for a few years now, and who knew what clever new gadgets had been dreamt up to kill the enemy?

Eventually, I figured out that it wasn't a finished product at all, but a component. Final assembly would take place on yet another line. Perhaps in another facility altogether. I felt a little better for my ignorance.

But the assembly line wasn't where I wanted to be. I wanted an office. I needed intel. Glancing up, I spied a series of windows. Somewhere up there—that was my destination.

It took a few minutes, but I found an elevator. Standing back,

I noticed another security panel. This could be a problem. So far, my card had worked at one door but not another. The big shots at Minor Arms might have an entirely different type of key card to access the upper floors, and if I was seen fumbling around—

Well, I was here to explore, not to fret.

I walked over and confidently flashed my security card across the electric eye. Accompanied by a soft ping, a small yellow light appeared above the elevator door. Ten seconds later, it opened. I walked in like I'd taken this ride every day of my life, and the door closed behind me.

But a new problem arose. There were no buttons in this elevator car. Imagine being in an elevator with no buttons. This one had a screen, which for now was blank. So I did what anyone would do in that situation: I touched the screen.

Nothing happened.

The screen mocked me with its silence. There's almost no more awkward feeling than to be standing in a confined space, probably being watched by a surveillance camera, and having no clue how to either move the damned thing or get out. I tried flashing my lanyard at the screen. Maybe that would fire things up. Still no result. Then, like a complete moron, I held both the card and the lanyard up, wondering if the elevator required a tag team.

It didn't.

I rubbed my chin and thought about it. My security card had opened the door. One would think *that* would've been the most important barrier to overcome, not the act of actually locomoting the accursed machine. Neither the card nor the lanyard brought it to life. There was a small door below the screen, but that only revealed your standard emergency telephone. I slowly turned around, wondering if there might be another card reader tucked somewhere. But why would an elevator manufacturer *hide* the flipping controls?

They wouldn't.

After a few seconds, I laughed at the absurdity of my predicament. I'd heard of people being trapped in elevators, but those were almost always caused by power outages or some other breakdown in the system. I might've been the first person stuck in an elevator simply because they didn't know how to operate it. Still laughing, I put my fingers into the crack of the door, just to see if I could pry it open like a superhero.

No dice.

I looked at the door to the emergency phone and contemplated my options. I could stand here like a buffoon, waiting for someone to stumble across me. Or I could use the phone to call for help. I shuddered to think what kind of questions this would produce—*Who are you? How do you not know how to work the elevator? What the hell do you want on the second floor?*—but I couldn't see another way out.

A decision needed to be made. So I grabbed the phone and, for the first time, something happened. The screen came alive. It showed a standard phone keypad. *Aha*, I thought. With nothing to lose, I hit the two, hoping it would deliver me to the second floor. But that did nothing, either. I hung up the phone, and the screen went dark again.

Wait—Leonard at the security desk had told me his extension. What was it? Two-four-four? No, it was two-two-four. I picked up the phone again and punched in the digits.

Immediately, I heard a ring and, sure enough, the familiar scratchy tones came through loud and clear. "This is Leonard."

"Leonard, this is Raymond Charles. I met you a little while ago."

"Yes, sir, Mr. Charles. What can I help you with?"

"Well, this is rather embarrassing, but every time I rode the elevator with Ambrose, I paid no attention to how he controlled the thing. Now I'm stuck in here and can't figure it out. Is there a YouTube video I could watch on how to operate the thing?"

He gave me the same courtesy laugh he'd shared with Elaine. "Oh, no. I hope you're not claustrophobic, Mr. Charles."

"No, Leonard, but I'm allergic to embarrassing situations and right now I feel like the world's biggest moron."

"Don't you worry about it. Do you want me to open the door now, or take you up one level?"

"Definitely up to the next floor. Then, when I'm ready to come down, I'll just open a window and throw myself out."

Another scratchy laugh. The guy sounded like Rod Stewart had gargled with razor blades. "Okay, hold on just a second."

I heard tapping on a keyboard, and a moment later the elevator began a smooth ascent.

"Bravo, Leonard. I'm airborne. Will the door open on the next level automatically?"

"It will open for you. But I'll stay on the line, just to make sure."

It did.

"Leonard, you're a rock star. I'll call you when I'm ready to come down."

"Okay, Mr. Charles. Let me know if there's anything else I can do."

I hung up and stepped out before the door closed and trapped me again. This level, unlike the frenetic zone below, was quiet. It wasn't exactly dim, but the lights were set to an after-hours feel. All the doors on both sides of the hall were closed. Most, but not all, had full-length windows beside them, providing a glimpse inside. I walked up to one to examine the placard posted at eye level, hoping for some hint regarding the contents of the office. Instead, I was informed that this was #206.

Not helpful.

Again, I'd need to be careful. If video surveillance showed some joker putting his nose to the window and cupping his hands around his eyes, I'd have company in a hurry. The whole reason for making this an overnight visit was to provide me with some relative privacy for snooping.

I tried the door, and it was unlocked, so I slipped inside. The rooms on this side of the hall overlooked the parking lot; through a window and through the branches of a nearby tree, I could see my car. The offices across the hall would provide views onto the assembly line below.

No sense acting sneaky to anyone watching. I flipped on the overhead light, revealing a standard office with one desk, two chairs facing it, and two large, lateral filing cabinets. I nosed around the desk, saw nothing interesting, pulled out a couple of drawers, and still found nothing that caught my eye. Granted, I wasn't exactly clear what I was looking for, but I was pretty sure I'd know if I found it. For the benefit of anyone who might be watching, I pulled a small notepad from my pack and pretended to make the kinds of notes one would expect from a compliance officer.

See what I mean? Nobody knows what they do. But I'm sure they must take copious notes.

The next door down was also unlocked, but it, too, had nothing substantial.

I tried one across the hall, marked #203. It was locked. That instantly intrigued me. I shrugged my bag off my shoulder and extracted a fun little gadget that cat burglars would adore. It did the job of picking a lock without requiring two separate instruments—who had time to kneel down and wrestle with that nonsense? I inserted the piece, gave it a slight twist, and heard the prong do its work. The handle gave easily, and I was in.

This room immediately exuded pay dirt. For one thing, it was larger, with not only a desk and the obligatory two facing chairs but also a sitting room area with two comfy chairs and a love seat. Oh, and against a side wall sat a credenza with an expensive lamp on it. Only people with serious pull at a company put $500 lamps in their office. Look it up.

I closed the door behind me, locked it, and was thankful I didn't have to switch on the lights. The occupant had left the fancy lamp on. It provided a nice, soft glow without alerting people on the factory floor that I'd broken in.

Nothing on the desk seemed helpful, other than to identify the resident as CA Faraji, who carried the title of Senior Vice President of Capture Tech. I had no idea what that meant, but, based on the wall photos of CA at various events with very important people, she carried some clout.

The top drawers of the desk didn't excite me, but the one on the lower right was locked. Desk drawer locks are nowhere near as intricate as door locks; in fact, they're generally worthless, other than to provide a false sense of security. I had it open so quickly that anyone watching on surveillance would assume I simply used a key.

The first thing that caught my eye was the gun—a Canik TP9, made in Turkey. Interesting that Ms. Faraji didn't sport a weapon made by her employer. Even more interesting was an executive vice president packing heat in her office in the first place. It explained one reason for the locked drawer.

Behind the gun, however, were your standard file folders, arranged in a color-coded system with fancy printed labels, rather than the usual hand-scrawled mess. And the very first file I saw was labeled "NGS-3."

NGS. Next Gen Soldier. Had to be.

I pulled it out and set it on the desk, glancing at the door and then out the window into the plant to make sure everything was still humming peacefully along. Flipping open the file, I saw an image similar to the sketch Ty Hedrick had photographed in the vendor's hotel room. This one was sharper and more detailed. More intimidating. Cold. A cross between an angry GI Joe and the Predator. Definitely human. But soulless. That was the only way I could describe it.

I snapped photos, then turned the page. I captured images of what looked like an index, explaining each of the highlighted components from page one. This stretched for nearly 10 pages, a wealth of information.

Placing the folder back in the drawer, I thumbed through the others, wondering if there would be an NGS-1 or NGS-2. There wasn't. But I did find one labeled "NGS-Comp," which turned out to be an inventory list of components. I quickly had photos of every page.

But it was the last folder in the drawer that gave me pause. The stark white label with black type said, "NGS-RGF."

It was thick. Once I had it open on the desk, I froze. RGF wasn't an acronym for a part or a supplier.

It was an acronym for Russian Ground Forces.

I must've sat there for a full minute, scanning the first page. But it was way too much information, and certainly more than I had time to photograph. I thought about just capturing the first few pages, but realized the entire folder was critical.

As I stood over the desk, hands on hips, wondering how to solve the problem, movement out the window caught my attention. A group of five armed men were moving rapidly across the factory floor. At the front, leading the way and pointing toward the elevator, was my buddy, Leonard.

Son of a bitch. His calculated smile and forced laughter concealed the fact that he was nobody's fool. I'm sure my ineptitude in that stupid elevator was enough to trip an alarm in his mind. For that matter, he might've smelled a rat the moment I walked in and name-dropped Ambrose Minor. Either way, I was busted.

Getting out was going to be a problem. Forget the fact that operating the elevator completely stumped me; that irritating contraption was about to be occupied by a small army coming for my head.

I looked back down at the RGF file. "Screw it," I muttered and packed it into my bag. CA Faraji would just have to compile another. Then, for good measure, I also grabbed her gun. Just my luck, if I left it there, some bozo would use it to shoot me. That would be downright embarrassing.

Rushing across the room, I threw on the overhead lights, opened the door, then left it wide open as I exited. A plan percolated in my mind, one that was probably idiotic, but since I'd be lucky to have 30 seconds in which to act, I went with it.

I moved down the hall to the first office I'd entered and slipped inside. Locking the door behind me and leaving the light off, I hurried to the window. It had a crank that opened it. Just as I grasped the handle, I heard movement outside. The assault team had arrived on the floor. I knelt down and peered over the desk at the door-side window. Leaving CA's office door open and the lights on had done the trick. The team slunk past me, weapons raised. As soon as they went by, I silently cranked open the window.

It barely provided enough room to squeeze through, but it would work. I leaned out and dropped my bag to the ground. Then, contorting myself, I worked my way out onto the six-inch concrete ridge circling the building. Holding on to the window frame for support, I stood and looked down. It wasn't a drop that would kill me, but there was every possibility I could jack up an ankle.

A gust of wind rustled the branches of the nearby tree. "Oh, Swan," I said under my breath. "It's not *that* nearby."

But it would have to do. The search team would be back any second. I picked out a branch that seemed within reach and might sustain my weight, and, without hesitating, leapt as far as I could, arms outstretched.

I made contact with the branch and actually had a decent grip, surprising the hell out of myself. But the thrill was short-lived. I heard a snap. The limb gave way. Not entirely, and instead I was lowered a few feet. Perfect. I swung back and forth for just a moment, before letting go and dropping.

It was a textbook landing. I felt terribly proud of myself as I scrambled over to pick up my bag, then walked briskly toward my car, innocent as could be, smiling all the way. Hell, I'd told Leonard I would throw myself out a window, and that's exactly what I'd done.

In the car, I heard a shout from the window I'd just vacated. They couldn't see me, but apparently had figured out my escape route. I waited until they were likely racing back to the elevator, then started my car and pulled out of the lot. In the circular drive in front of the building's entrance, I spotted two cars. Obviously the assault team's rides.

Jamming on the brakes, I pulled a knife from my pack and jumped out of my car. Running to the lead vehicle, I knelt down and punctured the left front tire. Then, moving to the second car, I repeated the vandalism.

When I pulled up quickly to the exit gate, the same guard who'd let me in was standing in the way. He'd probably been instructed to let nobody leave.

Well, leaning on the horn and flooring it will dissuade anyone from holding their ground against a charging two-ton hunk of metal. He dove to the side, I crashed through the gate's bar, and sped toward the highway.

Pulling off the atrocious wig, I let out a long breath and laughed.

CHAPTER THIRTEEN

"Russia? He's selling Next Gen to the Russians?"

I didn't answer the question right away. I was busy chasing a mound of eggs around my plate with a fork. Finally capturing a hunk, I shoveled it in. I was famished, and this was my victory meal: scrambled eggs from a hotel breakfast bar, along with an English muffin and something they swore was bacon. I was on my second mug of coffee.

"I doubt the Russians are his only clients," I finally said to Fife with a mouthful. "But they certainly bring a shitload of cash to the table. Plus, line up a major player like that and it adds an awful lot of social proof to your product."

Fife made a face. "So he won't pitch the product to his own country, but he has no problem peddling it to others."

I slathered extra butter on the English muffin. "It's probably that control thing. He's worried Uncle Sam will move in and try to monopolize it. This way he can push a lot of product internationally and guarantee a massive profit before the US gets a shot at it. But there's another possibility we have to consider. Ambrose might be developing Next Gen, but he may not be the salesman."

Fife reached over and pilfered a piece of the bacon. He chewed it while studying my face. "Beadle?"

I nodded, then stood up. "I'm getting more. Want an English muffin or something?"

"No. I'll just eat half of yours."

"I'll bring you one."

I walked back with more eggs and a paper bowl filled with oatmeal. I tossed an English muffin onto the napkin in front of Fife and picked up the discussion.

"One of the reasons Minor may have partnered with Beadle is to alleviate the issues with the Pentagon. Beadle has a global network of connections, and the bulk of them are potential customers who have no shortage of funds. And since it's all under the table, Minor Arms can put all their time and effort into developing the product while outsourcing the sales. Plus, it offers a layer of plausible deniability. A win-win for Minor; if things blow up, he can claim *he* wasn't pitching the product. And can he help it if some third party misrepresents him? It's the perfect screen. Beadle does the dirty work—for a healthy cut, no doubt—while Minor stays clean."

"Until his product begins killing American citizens," Fife said. "What did Quanta say?"

"Haven't talked with her yet. I forwarded the photos, but I'm going to hand-deliver the Russia folder. She's sending a private plane. I'm leaving in—" I checked the time on my phone. "—in 40 minutes. Just flipping through that file, it looks like we might find out where these soldiers are being built. Or adapted. Or whatever the hell you call it."

I stirred some brown sugar into the oatmeal and sliced up a banana to add. Fife watched this production with mild interest, then said, "I'm going to step up the search for Paige Walters today. She's now been gone long enough to officially qualify as a missing person."

"That's bugging you, isn't it?" I asked.

He finally couldn't resist the English muffin and began spreading peanut butter on it. "It does bug me. Something about her part in this has been gnawing at me ever since she disappeared. Even if she's not an active participant in the murder, I can't help but think she knows something. So while you're jet-setting back to DC, I'll head down to Huntsville."

My phone vibrated with a message from Poole. I read it twice before looking up at Fife.

"Your instincts are good," I said, putting the phone back in my pocket. "Paige must've known something. They just located her. But you won't be able to question her."

He stared at me. "No. Don't tell me—"

"Yeah," I said and pushed away my plate. "We now have two murders. And counting."

I met Quanta on the fourth floor of Q2 headquarters. Poole was there, too, along with a woman named Jenna Macklin. Just as Fife was our plant inside the Bureau, Jenna was our little friend tucked inside the State Department.

She was in her early 40s, shoulder-length brown hair, and smartly dressed. The frames of her glasses were light blue, which matched her eyes. While we'd waited for Quanta to arrive, Jenna and I had chatted, feeling each other out. We'd not met before this, but it took me all of one minute to decide she was my kind of people. Former military, former legal eagle who'd grown weary of defending assholes who deserved to be locked up, and former amateur boxing champ. She could not only go toe-to-toe in a fight, but in a verbal sparring match, too. Jenna was snarky, sarcastic, and clearly unimpressed with the stuffed shirts who paraded around the State Department. I was thrilled she was on our team.

Now, she sat across from me in a conference room, engrossed in the file I'd lifted from the Minor Arms plant. Poole had run copies for each of us.

Quanta, seated at the head of the table, could absorb information faster than anyone I'd ever known. She also was quick to glean which pages could be skimmed and which required extensive study. The room was quiet while we all examined the material.

Jenna tapped a page about midway through the folder. "Their pitch to the RGF includes an offer to do a demonstration. During an actual skirmish."

I turned to the page she'd indicated and read the paragraph. It was within an internal memo from CA Faraji to Ambrose Minor, copied to Antoinette Lazarov.

GS is not content with the virtual presentation from JE, and has requested the use of one NGS during a live operation against an enemy force. As the RGF is currently involved in activities in Eastern Europe and Asia, we should decide whether or not to accede to this wish within the next 30 days. While unable to provide the full experience at this time, I feel confident we could have a 60 percent option available within four months. I recommend agreeing to the live demonstration, under controlled circumstances and with full MA oversight. JE can meet with GS at the 102nd.

"I get the RGF, and MA is obviously Minor Arms," I said. "What about this GS? Any thoughts?"

Quanta said, "The 102nd is a Russian military base in Armenia."

Jenna spoke up. "Agreed. GS is likely General Sokolov. He oversees the 102nd and would be the person most likely to deploy a Next Gen prototype. I've seen some background on him. He's totally the type who'd want a new toy before any other kids on the block had one."

I noted the date of the memo. "This was written three months ago. If Faraji is on point with her prediction, Ambrose could send a working model in about a month. Only 60 percent, she says. But it's possible they've made more progress than that." I looked up at Quanta. "You were right. They're coming into the home stretch with this thing."

Jenna frowned. "Then there's the matter of this JE person. They'd actually handle the meeting with Sokolov. Which makes sense. A layer of protection." She looked around at us. "Anyone have an idea?"

Nobody spoke until Quanta said, "We'll put it on our list."

Poole, who'd been quiet since walking into the room, held up another page from the folder. "They've already put a model through some exercises. In Honduras."

The rest of us turned to that page.

"The Northern Triangle," Quanta said, referencing the part of Central America that had suffered from poverty, corruption, and violence for years. Guatemala, El Salvador, and Honduras had seen more than two million people flee in hopes of finding a better life. It left the area rife with dangerous elements, including a high crime rate—a nearly perfect testing ground for Minor. A chance to wade into conflict without actually participating in a war.

"It's relatively close," Jenna added. "Just a few hours by air. Much easier than traveling around the world to try out his cyborg. I don't see any report on how the test went."

The room fell silent while we all looked. It was Poole who found it.

"Near the back. Um, four pages from the end." She held the page up so we could make a visual connection.

My eyes scanned the block of text. Toward the bottom, there was one quick note:

Honduras test complete. Results mixed. NGS will remain in the field, but will follow up with necessary adjustments as introduced.

. . .

I looked up at Quanta. "'Results mixed.' Does that mean their Robocop killed some people and then went haywire?"

Her only response was a shake of the head. She began rubbing her forehead while reading the rest of the page.

"And those adjustments they mention," Jenna said. "A tune-up, I suppose, based on the data they get during combat. Or however they tested the thing."

Quanta closed the file and laced her fingers together on top of it. "What we have to remember is that these are not machines. They're people. Men and women. We'll be tempted to categorize them as inanimate, but that would be a mistake. It would be much simpler for us if these were simply robots. That would remove the ethical element to the operation. But they're not robots. No matter how much electronic hardware they've had implanted, their minds are still human, and they still have a soul, if you believe in such things. And while they may end up fighting for hostile forces, my guess is that the bulk of them will be American citizens." She made eye contact with me. "We'll need to keep that in mind should a conflict ensue."

There was subtext to her speech. I just didn't know how to translate it. Not yet, anyway. But I'd never heard Quanta express anything about minds and souls before. This was new. And there had to be a reason. I glanced down at the thick folder, wondering if there'd been something she'd seen during her quick scan to generate such a pointed comment. And one aimed directly at me.

She cleared her throat to signal a change of subject.

"There's also the matter of Paige Walters, the woman who was with the Hedricks the night Ty was killed. I was on the phone with the Bureau's special agent in charge of the Birmingham office. He's sent two more agents to Huntsville to investigate. Poole, can you brief Jenna and Swan on what we know so far?"

Poole accessed notes from a tablet.

"Huntsville police discovered Paige Walters' car around 5:30 this morning. They'd had a report called in of a car suspiciously parked in the back of an employee parking lot for more than 24 hours. It was unlocked. When police opened the trunk, they found Ms. Walters. Her hands had been tied behind her back, and she'd been executed. Two shots in the back of her head."

I rubbed my forehead, grimacing, while listening to the report. It was a horrible way for anyone to go, and it disgusted me.

"Any leads yet?" Quanta asked.

Poole shook her head. "They've dusted the car for prints and found those of the victim and of Bryson Hedrick."

"Well, that's to be expected," I said. "They were dating for a while. It would've been strange if his prints *hadn't* been there."

"No discernible footprints around the exterior of the car. Also, no security footage from the parking lot. Plenty around the business itself but not the lot."

"They planned the location well," Quanta said. "This wasn't a last-minute thing."

Poole continued. "Her purse was in the trunk, with her wallet, credit cards, and some cash. Certainly not a robbery. Her cell phone, however, was not on the scene. The agents are trying to find any security footage from businesses nearby, and they're interviewing all of her family and friends."

"And boyfriend," I said. "Although I think I need to talk with him before the FBI. Can we arrange that?"

"Isn't Fife down there now?" Quanta asked.

"He will be later tonight."

"Have him take charge of that element. He can let the other agents know Hedrick is off-limits until further notice. How soon can you get down there?"

"It'll be much sooner if I don't have to fly commercial. I mean, I think the same plane I flew in for this meeting is still just sitting out there at Andrews."

She gave me a blank look while she thought about this. I'd already been treated to some special flight privileges, but Quanta knew time was of the essence.

"All right," she said. "Poole will make the call and set it up." She looked around the table. "Anything else before we adjourn?"

"I have something," Jenna said. "We're at the point where we're going to have to loop in the State Department. Now we have proof we're dealing with an American arms company arranging deals with foreign countries, at least one of which is a major power. The Secretary and the President will need to know. How would you like to handle that?"

"I'd like for you to begin that process," Quanta said to her. "The President's chief of staff was alerted when we first got wind that Minor Arms might bypass the Pentagon and go directly overseas. Please follow up with this new information. If they ask—and they probably will—it was from a covert FBI operation."

The others probably couldn't sense the undercurrent of vexation within Quanta's announcement, but I read it instantly. She'd played the spy game for a long time, not always working for the United States, and she insisted on autonomy. It was likely one of the primary concerns she had when she agreed to sign up with us. Making calls to the Pentagon or the White House were sometimes necessary, but I knew it chapped her. Having to "followup" with politicians and generals was not her thing, so I was sure she appreciated having Jenna on our side.

Which was funny, if you thought about it. For Quanta, calling the President of the United States was a pain in the ass.

The meeting broke up. With a glance, Quanta signaled I should wait behind. When we had the room to ourselves, she looked down at the closed file in front of her and then back at me. "What does your gut tell you?"

"That's easy. We're going to war on our own soil against our own people."

This didn't appear to shake her at all. "I would think a quick battle or two, rather than an all-out war."

I shrugged. "I've known since my dinner with Ambrose Minor that at some point I'd be tangling with his Bulgarian pit bull. Now we know they have working prototypes in the field, so it'll be at least two or three against one. I can live with those odds. Or, if I don't live, I'll give 'em hell the next time." I leaned forward. "I don't mind telling you, just looking at diagrams isn't good enough. I need to see what an NGS is capable of. It's just that I probably won't be schooled on their abilities until I'm fighting for my life."

She was silent for a moment, then said, "There *is* a way to short-circuit any violence."

It took a moment for this to sink in. I said, "Pin the Ty Hedrick and Paige Walters murders on Minor Arms and cut them down in the courts."

She gave a single nod. "Specifically, connect Ambrose Minor himself to the killings."

I let out a long breath, thinking about that possibility. "You and I both know that's an extreme long shot. I think it might be something for you and Fife to concentrate on. But if it doesn't pan out, it's going to get ugly. Well, uglier."

"All right," she said. "Things are beginning to escalate. Stay in touch with me when you're on the ground in Huntsville."

I stood up. "Sure. But it's late, and I've got to crash for a few hours. I'm going home to sleep. I'll leave at dawn."

This didn't sit well with her, but she knew I wouldn't have insisted if I wasn't bone tired. She kept silent, reopened the RGF folder, and started going through it again.

I walked out and headed for home. I wanted a cocktail and at least one hour of couch time with my wife before banking some sleep.

CHAPTER FOURTEEN

The cocktail was perfect. The time with Christina was even better. We rarely slept in the same bed, but tonight we both felt the need for human contact. I put my arm around her, and with her head on my chest, we talked about anything and everything except restaurants and metal soldiers. Every time a work thought tried to force its way into my consciousness, I stuffed it back down and out of the way.

Christina and I both must've reached the conclusion that we didn't have much we wanted to discuss. It was one of those nights where we were happy and content to simply connect physically, without the need to fill the air with words. Some people are uncomfortable with silence; we knew when to embrace it. Both of us toiled in jobs that taxed our reasoning and problem-solving brain cells. Rest was good. Quiet could be an energizing tonic.

At one point, I just lay there, listening to her breathing, looking out through a slit in the window blinds, noticing random lights moving in the distance but not knowing or caring what they were, allowing my mind to wind all the way down. Just when I thought Christina had dozed off, I heard her voice, softly muffled against my chest.

"We've never taken a vacation together."

It took me a few seconds to respond. She'd never broached this subject before.

"Are you anxious to see the Grand Canyon or something?"

She gave me a small pinch on my chest. "I'm serious."

"Okay." I paused, not sure what to say. "I'd love to go on a vacation with you. It's kinda dumb that we haven't, I guess."

Her voice was still muffled, but I felt her smile against my skin. "Hard to schedule a trip with someone who's always off saving the world."

"I could send the world a memo. I'll demand it behave itself for a few weeks while I take my wife to Lake Como or something."

"I'll write the memo and you sign it." She pulled her head away and looked up at me. "I'll have this baby pretty soon. Even though I won't be raising it, I'll still have maternity leave. Would Quanta be okay with letting you go for a while?"

I laughed. "There are times she wishes I was gone permanently. I don't think she'll complain at all."

She put her head back down and nothing more was said about it for now. But it sent my mind whisking away on a whole new tangent, back into the fantasy world I sometimes concocted for myself, where I was the ex-agent. The former spy. The retired assassin.

What troubled me about those thoughts—the few times I allowed them to squat in my conscious mind—was my inability to fathom what a normal life might even look like. It's easy for most people to daydream about the time they retire to the couch or to the beach or golf course. But I'd had a weapon in my hand since my early 20s. I'd either worn a uniform and fought for my country or I'd worn a different body and killed for my government. It was all I knew. I was conditioned.

And now, again staring out the window while my gentle wife dozed on my chest, another thought struck me. I was in the process of hunting down killing machines, manufactured soldiers, products of an assembly line.

How much different were they from me?

It's a parallel thought to the one often coursing through the minds of military personnel and law enforcement officers. We constantly find ourselves tiptoeing up to the line separating us from the so-called "bad guys," and that often will make you question everything. Well, unless you're a psychopath. If you believe you're a normal, decent human being, it's almost painful trying to fit a thin divider between yourself and the other guy. We sometimes scramble to find a justification for our actions, to distinguish between what they do and what we end up doing. We rely on rationalizing, perhaps more than any other occupation in the world. Without it, we might cease to function. Freeze up. Fail to serve. Dissolve into an abyss of self-doubt, even self-hatred.

Then, when a job was finished, I'd instinctively put the assignment away, like stuffing a file into a cabinet, never to be seen again. Without that capability, we'd all be one and done in this job. That's a component that people who've never served would struggle to understand. What we do is not normal.

And that makes *us* not normal.

So, yes, I would love to go on a vacation with my wife. I'm a wretch for never suggesting it myself. But I feared it would be an artificial Eric Swan. A doppelgänger who went through the motions because he knew it was what he was *supposed* to do—but was no more programmed to be a happy tourist than a professional athlete was programmed to be humble. We honestly don't know how to do it.

I slowly stroked Christina's hair, watched her chest and pregnant belly rise and fall with her breathing, and vowed, even if it was only temporary, to find a way to authentically step outside myself—which sounds like an oxymoron, but made sense to me.

· · ·

I grabbed a fast-food breakfast sandwich on my way to catch the plane, ended up buying three of them, and brought the full bag with me, along with a hot coffee. The sandwiches were room temperature by the time I strapped into my seat on the small jet, and I lost interest after the first few bites. I threw the half-eaten one away and gave the other two to the crew while I sipped the java.

During the two-hour flight, I looked over a quick report I'd received from Fife. No leads yet on Paige's killer or killers; family distraught; Bryson Hedrick nearly incapacitated with grief. Fife must've anticipated my skepticism and offered that he didn't think Bryson was putting on an act. I trusted my FBI friend. He'd been handling cases while I was still in college. Years on the job hones your bullshit detector to a fine edge.

There was also a message from Quanta, stating that someone at the Pentagon had gotten wise to the fact that Minor Arms might be hiding a potential game-changing new weapon. Quanta and Jenna Macklin were taking point, determined to quiet the rumblings and keep them from turning into a furor. I'd seen it happen; some generals don't take kindly to being deprived of new toys. They take it personally. And when a general took something personally, that's precisely where shit began its inevitable downhill roll.

Dark clouds greeted us in Huntsville, and a particularly bad storm cell blanketed the base. We circled for a bit before getting clearance to land. The skies continued to unleash a heavy downpour as we climbed out and hustled inside. Fife was waiting comfortably in a leather chair, drinking coffee and reading something on his phone.

"You look like a wet rat," he said. "Let's grab you some of this excellent coffee. By then, the rain may have stopped."

It hadn't. We were both soaked when we climbed into his rental. The coffee helped. Fife was right; it was strangely good for military base brew.

"I know he's devastated," I said, "but I still want to talk with Hedrick today."

"Good luck. He spoke with me for maybe 20 seconds before essentially telling me to piss off. Hasn't answered his phone since then. I spoke with his mother briefly and she's not keen on talking, either. She told me Bryson may never recover from this. The two closest people in his life, killed within weeks of each other."

I sipped the coffee. "Well, he's gonna have to recover enough to help us if he wants to solve both murders. Then he can go back to mourning the losses."

Fife threw me a look. "You're sounding a bit chippy today. Anything in particular eating at you?"

"No." I looked out the passenger window at the wind and rain punishing the trees. "Okay, yes. I like to be able to bull my way through a case without worrying about anyone micromanaging me."

"Quanta isn't the type to—"

"I'm not worried about Quanta. Well, not directly. But suddenly we have the Pentagon and the State Department involved in a case. And you're crazy if you think they're going to sit idly by and just let some rogue agent handle things. They meddle. They always meddle. I can tell from Quanta's body language that she knows it's gonna get messy. When you factor in that hardly anyone at the Pentagon knows we exist? That makes it even worse, because we can't exactly explain who we are and what we do."

Fife nodded. "You can't tell them to back off without telling them who you are."

"And that's gonna be a problem if this case doesn't get wrapped up soon. Quanta wants to connect Ambrose Minor to both murders in order to expedite movement against him. I just don't think that's gonna happen." I turned to him. "No offense to you and your sparkling law enforcement skills."

"Minor is no second-rate punk, knifing people on the street.

He's protected by multiple layers. The best we might be able to do is connect the company."

"And I don't think Quanta will find that good enough." I tapped a finger on my knee. "You know what else kept popping back into my mind during the flight down here?"

"Beadle, maybe?"

I shot him a quick look, then laughed. "Jesus. We're getting to be like an old married couple."

"You're not as hard to read as you think. Besides, I've been wondering about him, too. Mostly I'm puzzled about that mysterious endgame of his. How does one man dedicate his life to creating chaos?"

"Maybe unloved as a child. Maybe he's got a micropenis. Or maybe he's just wired to get high on carnage. There have been lots of criminal assholes wired that way. They're mostly morons. Beadle happens to have that defect while, at the same time, he's brilliant."

When I looked back at him, Fife was staring at me. Then he said, "*Micropenis?*"

"Yeah. It's a thing. I read about it in Cosmo."

He just shook his head and turned back to his driving. "You're the oddest secret agent in the history of secret agents."

I shrugged. "Well, whatever his issue, I don't mind telling you I'm glad he's part of this assignment. It's just another chance to put him down. Hey, pull in here. I didn't have an appetite earlier and now I'm famished."

At one o'clock, we arrived at the luxury building where Bryson Hedrick lived. Fife had left a message that we'd be arriving and that it was important he talk with us. Bryson hadn't responded.

The security guard in the lobby was dutifully impressed seeing one FBI badge and my Homeland Security ID. I could've used my own FBI badge, but two government agencies seemed more imposing. The guy sent us straight up.

When Bryson answered his door, he took one look at us and started to close it in our faces. I did the old movie trick of sticking my foot in. It's cheesy, but it works.

"Hold on, Bryson. Slamming a door in our face will not make any of this go away. We know you're hurting. But shutting us out will not help us catch the people responsible. Now let us in."

He walked back inside his condo, leaving the door open. We followed him.

I stopped in the hallway and inspected some of the photos on a long table. Two of Bryson with his father, one with both of his parents, and one that had to be a group of college buddies on mountain bikes, all mud and smiles. His living room was probably beautiful on a normal day, with its floor-to-ceiling windows and expensive modern furnishings. But this was not a normal day. The room was cluttered with shoes, some clothes, and five empty beer bottles on the coffee table. Another two were tipped on their sides on the floor.

Bryson fell into an oversized chair and picked up the beer in progress. He didn't say anything and he didn't look at us. I toed aside the two empty bottles on the floor and sat down on the couch. Fife stayed on his feet, off to the side.

"First," I said, "we want to say how—"

He threw up an index finger and cocked his head at me. "No. No, you don't get to offer condolences, Swan. You're not sorry. You never knew her. So just save the scripted bullshit. What do you want?"

I took a deep breath. "I want to talk about two murders."

His eyes were slits. Whether that was from the alcohol, excessive tears, or anger, I didn't know. Maybe a combination. Maybe none of the above. The arms company heir was a tough read. Except I knew I didn't care for him and I couldn't exactly pinpoint why. Some people are just unlikable.

I usually got what I was after when questioning someone. But I couldn't deny that Fife had a gentler touch, and it was good to have him along for this interview. Not necessarily a good cop/bad cop routine, but not far off.

"Bryson," Fife said. "Please hear me out. I know you think we're cold, dispassionate investigators. That we're only after the perp and we have no empathy for what you're going through. There's no way it *wouldn't* seem that way to you. Between the death of your father and now the loss of Paige, you won't feel at peace for a long time, I'm sure. But you need to know that the only way we can help you and Paige's family is by finding the animals responsible for this. Your pain will be even worse if we never bring them in. And that means a sacrifice on your part. You have to embolden yourself enough to help us with information. Any information. As much as you're hurting now, we need you to push your way through. Okay?"

Fife was really good at this. But I kept my gaze neutral and locked on Bryson.

After a moment, he shifted in his chair and set the beer bottle on the table. "All right," he said. "I don't know what I can tell you that I haven't already told you. And the police." He turned to me. "Everything I told you on the phone? Well, I don't know any more than that. I never heard from her, and I don't even know many details about—" He broke off and didn't need to finish.

I gave him a moment, turning to watch two birds soar past the window, riding the air currents between this building and its twin high-rise. I wondered if that other building housed its own collection of the disenchanted, another assortment of young, formerly idealistic social climbers who'd run head-on into the cold realities outside the nest. Was that a rite of passage? Or was I simply growing calloused?

After a proper pause, I turned back to Hedrick. "One thing you can help us with: the night of the fire. You and your father went inside the building for a few minutes. You said Paige stayed in the car to call a friend. Do you know who she spoke with?"

He narrowed his eyes. "No. I never asked her that and she didn't offer. Given what happened, Agent Swan, is it really relevant who she was talking with? Calling a friend had nothing to do with what happened inside."

"I would normally agree," I said. "Except Paige never called anyone."

There was silence while he sat, unblinking, processing the statement. "Okay. Then she changed her mind. So what? Maybe she tried calling and they didn't answer. Or maybe she texted them."

I shook my head. "None of the above. No calls placed, no texts sent."

He gave a listless shrug. "Then I don't know."

"Going back to her disappearance," I said. "Did Paige mention anything in the last few weeks about someone bothering her? Maybe following her? I guess what I'm asking is, did she give any indication about something odd going on?"

"Not that I remember. I didn't see her a lot in the last few weeks. We've both been busy."

"What was her mood like the night your father died?"

"She was perfectly—" He stopped and something seemed to flash in his eyes.

Fife saw it too. "Bryson, anything right now might be helpful. What are you thinking?"

It took him a moment to answer. He fidgeted in his chair. "Okay, it wasn't much. But she wasn't talkative. I mean, at all. I said something to her when we were walking back to the car after dinner. Dad had gone ahead. I talked with her just outside the restaurant. I asked her why she hadn't said hardly anything except to answer questions. How it was rude. And it wasn't like her. She was usually very engaged. Very interested in talking to people."

He reached for the beer bottle, then thought better and sat back again. "Funny. I didn't remember that 'til right now."

"What did she tell you?" Fife asked. "When you asked her what was wrong, what did she say?"

"Uh—she said she just didn't feel great. I don't remember if she said it was a headache or something else. Just that she didn't feel her best but didn't want to cancel the date because she thought she'd start feeling better." He looked at Fife. "Maybe that's why I didn't think much of it, because it wasn't that big of a deal. She didn't feel good."

"Yeah," I said, throwing a glance at Fife. "That's probably all it was. I was hoping there might be something more you'd seen or heard."

"No. Nothing else."

"Do you know what had Paige so busy over the past month?" Fife asked. "Her job? Friends? Family?"

He twisted in his seat again. "She made it sound like a little bit of everything. Work was piling up. She had friends in town that she hadn't seen since college. That happened a few times. Then she and her family went on a vacation to Asheville."

"And the boyfriend wasn't invited?" I asked with a slight smile.

His look was icy. "No, I wasn't invited. And that didn't bother me. It's not like we were connected at the hip. She had her life, I had mine, and we enjoyed the time we shared together."

"Do you get along with her family?" I asked, taking a chance.

He shrugged. "I barely know them. Like I said, it's not like we were engaged or anything. Again, Mr. Swan, why is this so critical? Are we talking about my love life here, or are we trying to find the person who killed her?"

"If the first one helps us with the second, it shouldn't be important how we get there. Just relax, Bryson, and let us ask whatever enters our minds."

Fife again tried to smooth things over. "It might help you to understand our questions if you keep in mind all the things intersecting here. We have a competing company you're essentially spying on—" He held up a hand when Bryson opened his mouth to challenge him. "Hold on. We don't personally care what you do to gain an advantage on your competitor, and vice versa. Unless it violates a serious enough law.

"But the point is, we have some pretty alarming technology, the kind that could impact national security. We have the death of your father, and now we're facing the murder of the young woman who was there the night of the fire. We're asking a variety of questions that might shake something loose. Anything that might shine some light. Fair enough?"

Bryson didn't answer but didn't argue, either.

"So," I said. "Her family. Friendly with you?"

"Sure. They're nice people. A little—a little boring, maybe." He looked back at me. "I don't mean that in a bad way."

"I understand. Have you been in touch with her parents since you got the news?"

"No. I mean, I tried to call them just before you got here. I got voice mail and just hung up. I'll try again later."

I nodded and looked at Fife to see if he had anything else at the moment. He gave a barely perceptible shake of his head.

"Okay," I said, standing up. "We'll be around a day or two. Please take our calls. That'll help us immensely."

"Yeah," he said but stayed in his chair and picked up the beer again.

Fife and I left. We didn't exchange a word until we were in the elevator.

"Are you thinking the same thing I am?" Fife asked.

"Pretty sure I am. Let's go talk to the roommate. But what I really want to do is talk with Paige's parents."

The elevator opened to the building lobby, and I added, "Twenty bucks says she didn't go with her family to Asheville."

CHAPTER FIFTEEN

Her name was Rosette. Pretty name, fascinating young woman. Her townhome was decorated with interesting art, paintings you might describe as grim, perhaps even disturbing. But somehow they worked. You had to force your eyes off them. One in particular grabbed me. It showed a man struggling in a violent, stormy sea, his hand grasping the side of his small boat as he fought to climb back inside. Had he been thrown out by a wave? Had he accidentally tumbled out while trying to retrieve something?

Or had he jumped, then had a change of mind?

That question alone moved me. I lingered in front of the painting for a few extra seconds.

Rosette herself was not shy. Multicolored hair framed a bespectacled, thoughtful face with green eyes—either real or lenses, they were dazzling, although currently red-rimmed. She wore a yellow shift dress, accentuating the tone of her arms. She had a way of looking at you that made you think she was reading your mind and unabashedly judging what she found there. Her voice was pleasant to listen to; it reminded me of a cello played by a true artist.

I liked her.

She offered us tea, which we declined. Holding a large mug with both hands, she folded her feet beneath her on a small sofa. Fife and I sat across from her on two wing chairs that looked like they could've been delivered straight out of the 18th century.

We made idle small talk for the first minute in an attempt to put her at ease. But Rosette was the one who steered the conversation to her late roommate.

"It's the worst kind of guilt," she said. "The kind I feel right now. Because my last memory of Paige is anger. And I hate that."

"You couldn't know what would happen," I said. "We all weave in and out of a range of emotions throughout each day. It sounds like you had every right to be angry. Paige left you high and dry with no warning."

Fife leaned forward, his elbows on his knees. "Can you tell us if you noticed anything at all about her behavior in the last few weeks that might've seemed unusual? At least out of the ordinary for her?"

Rosette sipped her tea. "I thought everything about her was different lately. She went from outgoing and friendly to withdrawn. I don't think we had three conversations of more than a paragraph in the last month. And even those were sort of lifeless. It was like—" She thought about it. "—like her spark of life had been extinguished or something. It was sad. I asked her if everything was all right, and she just waved it off."

"Was it stress from work?" Fife asked. "Or do you think it had anything to do with her relationship with her boyfriend?"

She gave a small laugh. "I don't think in her mind Bryson was ever her boyfriend."

"Oh?" I said. "He referred to her as his girlfriend. You're saying she wasn't crazy about him?"

"*Crazy about him*? God no. Paige hung out with him, and I think he was pretty smitten with her. But that was not a two-way street. I could tell when he was over here. She was going through the motions. He's a nice enough guy, but he wasn't exactly doing it for her."

"So why did she keep seeing him?" I asked.

Rosette shrugged. "I honestly couldn't tell you. At first, I'm pretty sure it was just something different for her. She told me she'd always dated boring guys, the safe ones. To me, it meant she was going out with guys her parents would approve of, the ones who would someday be in stable, predictable jobs. So going out with the heir to an arms company seemed somehow edgy. And she said he'd told her some things that made it at least a little more exciting than the accounting majors she'd been seeing. No offense to accounting majors," she added with a smile.

"But that excitement didn't last?"

"I don't think that was it. I think maybe it got a little *too* edgy for her. It's not like Paige was a wild child herself. That wasn't really her personality; she just longed for something different. Like we all do, right?"

"So true," I said. Without looking at my partner, I could sense Fife's amusement at my seemingly innocent observation. Nobody on the planet knew more about changing up your life than a Q2 agent. "Tell me this," I said to Rosetta. "Why didn't she break things off? If the excitement became too much, and she wasn't gaga over this guy, why'd she stick around?"

"Hey, I asked her. Point blank. 'Why don't you just end it?' And she said something like—oh, how did she put it? 'It's not hurting anything.' Which I thought was a strange way to describe a relationship with someone."

"I agree," I said. "Were there other things that happened, besides her becoming more withdrawn?"

She seemed to think about it. "I don't know. Lately, I haven't seen her that much. I know she went out of town a couple of times. Once, she just left me a note, saying she'd be back in four days. That wasn't like her."

"Did she tell you where she was going?"

"No. And she was being so odd and quiet that I didn't ask. If she'd wanted me to know, she would've told me."

Fife said, "How did you two meet?"

"A mutual friend. She worked with an ex-partner of mine. Celine. We still get along, so the three of us went out one night and Paige heard I needed a roommate. Normally I wouldn't invite a stranger like that to move in, but she struck me as very responsible. Had her shit together, you know? Or so I thought. Until she blew out of here in about five minutes."

Fife and I left a bit of silence as a buffer. It allowed Rosette to drink more of her tea and breathe.

Finally, I said, "Let's talk about the afternoon she took off. What happened?"

Rosette puffed out her cheeks and let out a long, slow breath. "I came home and she was loading a suitcase into her car. I figured it was just another trip. Then I went inside and saw she had another bag packed and sitting on her bed. And some other things, like her pillow and a favorite blanket of hers. One box full of things. Totally the look of someone beginning to move out. So when she came back inside, I said, 'Hey, what's going on?'"

"And what did she say?" Fife asked.

"She said, 'I have to go. Sorry to dump it on you. But I can't stay here anymore.' So I asked her if something bad had happened, or if she was in some sort of trouble. And she snapped at me. I mean, a side of her I'd never seen before. She told me we could still be friends if I'd just not pry into her life and accept the fact that something had come up and she had to go.

"Well, I was pissed. No notice at all, and it's not cheap living here. So I asked her if she was going to still cover her half of the costs for the next month or until I could find someone, and she —" Rosette paused and shook her head. "She reached into her purse and pulled out, like, two hundred dollars in cash and threw it on the kitchen table. Picked up the rest of her stuff and said she'd bring more money later when she got the rest of her things.

Then she left. And that was it. No explanation. No real apology. Pretty shitty.

"So, yeah, I was angry. And when Bryson called looking for her, I probably didn't say the nicest things. But I didn't feel like getting into it with a guy who Paige didn't really like, anyway. It was still a sore spot for me. Then I heard the news—"

She broke off again, and I saw her eyes welling up.

"Look, Rosette," I said. "We don't know yet what happened, or what caused Paige to run off so quickly. But we're going to find out. In the meantime, you can stop beating yourself up for feeling angry about the situation. It's not only normal, it's totally under-standable. All right?"

There was no response to this. I didn't really expect one.

Fife said, "Would you be okay with us taking a look in her room? I know it seems invasive, especially at such a difficult time. But even a little scrap of information might help us track down the people responsible."

She waved toward a door. "The police already looked. But go ahead. I haven't been in there. Can't do it."

We nodded in understanding as we stood up. Law enforce-ment may have combed the room, but they weren't necessarily looking through the same lens we were.

The room was bright, not just from the natural sunlight streaming through the window, but from the decorative style. Light colors, happy images posted around the room, in stark contrast to Rosette's taste. There were framed photos with Paige and an older couple, obviously her parents. A collage of images with friends. One of Paige getting the touristy kiss from a dolphin. A pillow in the shape of a sunflower adorned the neatly made bed. The entire room was spotless. Orderly.

Was it artificial happiness? Was the room designed to convince the young woman each day that life could be rainbows and unicorns?

We closed the door behind us to save Rosette the pain of

watching investigators sifting through her dead roommate's things. Fife went to a small desk and began an inspection. I wandered into the bathroom. This was not as tidy—signs of a quick shower and primping—but still cleaner than most. I found nothing out of the ordinary in the drawers.

As I reentered the bedroom, Fife looked at me and shook his head. "Nothing of substance here. Looks like it's been picked pretty clean. Probably in that box of stuff Rosette said she took with her."

"But there was no box of stuff found in her car," I said. "So if there was anything damning, the killer or killers took it with them."

"Or maybe there wasn't anything of interest in the first place. No way of knowing."

"Yeah." I leaned on the desk and took a cursory glance around. "It's always a long shot that we'll find actual evidence. But everything Rosette told us confirms that something was up with Paige. She was definitely involved in this thing. But was she an active participant? Or was she an innocent bystander who just happened to find out something was up?"

Fife raised his eyebrows. "Either way could get her killed. *Did* get her killed."

"Yeah," I said again. "Let's go talk to her parents."

The home of Patrick and Melanie Walters looked exactly as I would've imagined it, based on what I knew of their late daughter. Well-manicured outside, neat and tidy inside, with a faint smell of lemon. Over the fireplace hung the requisite photo of the small family, awkwardly posed on the dunes of a beach, with each of them wearing jeans and a white shirt. And barefoot. Why someone decreed years ago that families should stage photos in this manner made no sense to me. What family went to the beach in jeans in the first place? And we certainly wouldn't all dress alike.

It was a ritual everyone agreed to participate in, regardless of its complete lack of connection with reality. It's as if we all sheepishly gave in to a conspiracy to convince strangers that our intimate, little tribe held a unique bond. Hey, we're all wearing white shirts and going barefoot—what additional proof of a bond do you need?

Never mind that the family probably squabbled about some aspect of the photo right up to the moment they all said "cheese."

Melanie Walters had put on makeup to welcome us, but it was a lost cause. All the eye makeup was smudged. Patrick's face was deeply lined, and I figured a third of those lines had appeared in the last 24 hours. A large wall clock ticked, and for a moment it was the only sound in the house, other than the hum of kitchen appliances. The Walters sat side by side on a couch, his hand covering hers on her knee.

We offered the usual condolences and expressed our fervent desire to quickly find the perpetrators of this awful crime. They greeted these expressions with hollow nods and flickering glances between us and the floor. It dawned on me that they felt embarrassed. Of all the overwhelming emotions that assailed the families of violent murder victims, this one wasn't unusual. Besides disbelief, sadness, and anger, a small thread of shame lay over the top. As if their child had somehow been the sort of person who would attract a crime of this nature—even though it was often the furthest thing from the truth. People didn't know how to feel, and this shade of humiliation often snuck in. It made everything they'd experienced that much worse. I always felt awful for them.

"Mr. and Mrs. Walters—" I said.

"Please," Patrick said. "Pat and Mel."

"All right. Mel, is there anything Paige may have said in the last few weeks to make you think something troubled her?"

She opened her mouth to answer, then paused, thinking about it. "Well. Yes and no. She didn't come out and say anything. But a mother knows."

"Of course. Did you get a sense it was related to anything specific, like work or a relationship?"

"She loved her job. She was so, so good at it, too. The best. And she had a—" She broke off with a sniffle, then tried to rally. "She had a great future ahead of her. So outgoing and smart. They thought the world of her. That's what she always told us."

"And relationships? Could she have been troubled by something in her relationship with Bryson Hedrick?"

Pat spoke up. "I was never fond of that boy."

"No?" Fife said. "Why was that?"

"Because she was too good for him."

"Pat—" his wife said, squeezing his hand.

"No, it's true and you know it. He comes from a lot of money, I know that, and he could spend a lot of it on Paige. But that didn't make him better than her. He didn't deserve someone that nice."

His wife gave us an apologetic look. "I don't think there's anything *wrong* with Bryson. He seems like a nice young man. But I just didn't want Paige to be—" She paused, looking for the right word. "I didn't want her to be an accessory."

I nodded that I understood. And I really did.

"Did they have any arguments or problems you knew of?" Fife asked.

Mel shook her head. "No. I don't think they'd been together long enough for anything like that. I think she only saw him once a week or so. She had her own life."

"And that was okay with me," her husband added.

I studied Mel's face. It was filled with pain, naturally. But there was something else. "Mel? Is there something else you could add to that? Honestly, any little thing that crosses your mind, no matter how minor it may seem to you—it could make a difference."

She glanced at her husband, then said, "I don't even like the way this sounds, but—but I thought, just recently, that maybe Paige was seeing someone else."

Fife and I both shifted in our seats at the same time. "Go ahead," I said. "What made you think that?"

After another quick look at her husband, she gave an embarrassed laugh. "Nothing, really. Again, a mother just sort of knows."

Fife smiled at her. "I'm sure. But any little hint we could work with?"

"Okay. Well, she never spoke that warmly of Bryson. She liked him as a person. I think he treated her well, and that was good. But she kept him at arm's length, you know what I mean? She'd had boyfriends before, and she always connected more with them. Like as a couple. But she never once gave any indication she felt that way about Bryson. It was like she wasn't sure, couldn't make up her mind if he was worth expending more personal energy on."

"Is that the only reason you thought there might be someone else?" Fife asked.

"Um, well, yes. That, and she—" She broke off.

Her husband actually nudged her with his knee. "Go ahead. Tell 'em."

Mel seemed especially pained by having to dish dirt on her murdered daughter. "I'm not saying she was seeing someone else. But Pat and I took a drive over to Asheville. That's in North Carolina, you know?"

"Yes ma'am," I said.

"And we invited Paige to go with us. I wanted to go back to the gardens at the Biltmore. Have you heard of that place?"

"Yes ma'am," I said again.

"We love it in Asheville. We go every couple of years and spend at least four or five days. It's a sweet town, really good food, nice people—"

Pat couldn't take it anymore. He cut in, saying, "Paige decided last minute that she'd go, but she met us there. Took her own car. And on the second day, she said she needed to go somewhere. An overnight stay. Took her bag and left. That was on Tuesday morning, pretty early. Didn't come back until late Wednesday. Mel kept saying she might be going off somewhere to meet another boy. I told her it was none of our business. She's a grown—she was a grown woman." The change of tense hit him hard for a moment, and he faltered.

"Then," he finally said, "she came back and was in a dark mood. Unlike her."

"She wouldn't talk about it," Mel said. "I took her out for coffee, just a mother-daughter thing, but she said everything was fine. It clearly wasn't. But I didn't push. As Pat says, it was really none of our business. I just didn't like to see her so down."

I chewed my lip for a second. "Any clue where she may have gone for that day and a half?"

Mel looked back at her husband, this time longer. It was as if she was urging him to confess something.

"I, uh," he said, haltingly. "I took her key fob while she was asleep and went out to look in her car. I was worried about her. There was a gas receipt from the day before. So I looked at it. It was from Charlotte."

Fife and I didn't look at each other, but I had no doubt he felt the same surge of adrenaline I did. Paige Walters had left her family in Asheville and driven a couple of hours for a clandestine meeting. In Charlotte.

The home of Minor Arms.

Keeping my voice level and calm, I asked, "Did you find anything else?"

"Yes," he said. "In the compartment between the seats she had a phone."

"Her cell phone?"

Patrick shook his head. "No. I know her phone. It wasn't hers. Some other person's phone."

Now Fife and I exchanged a long look.

Paige Walters had come back from Charlotte with a burner phone.

CHAPTER SIXTEEN

Some of the detective novels I read as a young man occasionally compared a criminal investigation to solving a jigsaw puzzle. Putting the pieces together, getting frustrated when a piece didn't seem to fit the design, and total despair when a piece went missing. The metaphor was apt, but it left out an important element: the picture.

Doing a jigsaw puzzle with no idea what the finished image looks like makes it doubly difficult.

I had an assignment on my hands that seemed to hint at one image, but could easily be another. Ambrose Minor was evil enough and his accomplices were not only dangerous, but deadly.

Now, with the possibility that all-American girl Paige Walters may have been complicit in the killing of Ty Hedrick, I was beyond perplexed. The idea of her involvement had danced around the fringes of my mind, but as long as it was only theoretical, it carried no mass. However, if Paige ran off to Charlotte and returned with a burner phone—one that may have been used the night her pseudo-boyfriend's father was burned to death—it bore the weight of a freight train.

Thank heavens for concerned, snoopy parents.

Back in my hotel room, I took out my gear in order to upload. This was intel I couldn't afford to lose, even though Fife had been there, and I'd shared the information with Quanta during the ride back. What I really wanted, though, was to lie on my bed and simply think about everything for a spell. Try to sift through the revelation and make sense of it all. To look at the entire case through the lens of Paige's association with it.

It was this solo brainstorm session I wanted to preserve. We never process information the same way twice.

Here's what I knew for sure: Minor, one of the world's foremost weapons manufacturers, was in the process of developing a new breed of warrior with a hybrid human-machine interface. It would run faster, see farther, shield itself better, and, in general, kill more efficiently. And those were just the advantages we knew about so far.

Ty Hedrick had learned, through his son, about the program. For reasons unknown, he'd been killed because of that knowledge. And his son's love interest—at least on his part—had been at the scene of that murder, perhaps acting as a beacon.

She'd, in turn, been eliminated. Because she knew too much? Had Paige's usefulness died the moment Hedrick did? She'd told her roommate that her association with Bryson was "not hurting anything."

It had killed her.

And what about Bryson? Was he an innocent victim in this game, or was he somehow connected?

The wild card in all of it was Beadle, a man whose entire existence revolved around death and disruption. He was pulling strings somewhere; I wanted to know what those strings were attached to. And how could this entire case play out in a way that provided me a chance of ending him? Now that I knew the asshole was the puppet master behind the Arcetri, it gave me even more motivation—not that I needed another drop of it.

As for next steps, Fife and I agreed we were at the point

where we needed to see one of these damned Next Gen freaks. Enough already with specs and cartoon images. Even if it wasn't face-to-face in battle, I had to see what I—and eventually our military—would be facing. And, as far as we knew, only one active model was in the field.

I closed my eyes. Finishing an upload in a peaceful state was easier once I had a plan in place.

It was time to visit Honduras.

Quanta agreed with my assessment, and when the boss gave a thumbs up, things happened. Fife would stay in Alabama for now and I'd hop a quick military flight to Central America. That meant I had to be back at the army base by 4 for a 4:30 departure. Why so early? It didn't matter. Sometimes my cynical side said military commanders did things like that just to keep troops on their toes. The fact that they were exhausted toes was irrelevant.

It also meant we took off in pitch darkness, but at least I'd be in Honduras before eight, local time. I'd have all day to get myself killed.

It was a bumpy ride, but I'd flown in these beasts plenty of times while in a special ops unit. I knew better than to expect a luxurious experience. A couple of young soldiers, obviously on one of their first deployments, wanted to make happy chat with me, but I had homework.

By the time we coasted over some 8,000-foot peaks and landed at Soto Cano Air Base, I'd studied most of the file Poole had curated for me. That's another element of spy work you never see James Bond or Jason Bourne tackling. When we're waiting around or in transit, we're often reading. And reading some more. Everything we do is built around making split-second decisions based on solid intelligence. Guesswork is a last resort for the ill-prepared and often produces unsatisfactory results. For me, that usually meant a flatline.

Most of us who'd trekked around Central and South America knew which countries struggled more than others. Honduras had remarkable potential but continually battled crime and corruption. Gangs terrorized large segments of the population, while drug and weapons trafficking continued to dominate a not-so-underground criminal economy.

It provided Ambrose Minor with an interesting platform upon which he could test his new toys. There were multiple factions who had no problem assassinating each other, and the government—when not looking the other way—barely kept up. The Next Gen Soldier could be "loaned" to one of the nefarious gangs for work in a hostile environment and it would never make the news. In the rugged hills of Honduras, death and destruction were the featured menu items almost every day.

Further dissection of the file I'd lifted from the Minor Arms plant had revealed one additional clue. The Next Gen Soldier had been involved with a skirmish between two drug cartels; all we knew was that it had eliminated two members of a gang known as the Pájaro Malvado, or PM-44. What we didn't know—yet—was which team the NGS had played for. At any given time, multiple groups could be fighting with each other.

At least it gave me a starting point.

The sun was beginning its daily assault as I climbed off the plane. The airfield, like much of the country, was hot and steamy, ushering back memories of my time as a young grunt, serving in one jungle or another. US forces occupied some of the base, other parts housed the Honduran Air Force Academy. I rode in silence in a Jeep with one other passenger to a building where an American flag drooped in the still air. The commander of the installation, a US Army colonel, was unavailable—my intuition told me he was in but couldn't be bothered with some government agent traveling under intense secrecy. And I didn't blame him. I'd hate that bullshit, too.

Instead, the deputy commander, an Air Force lieutenant

colonel, sized me up after trying to crush my fingers in his hand-shake. His last name was Mondragon, but he insisted I call him Monk.

He hadn't exactly been briefed, but simply instructed to coop-erate with me on a matter of national security. Inwardly, I'd groaned when I found out they'd worded his orders that way. It took all of 30 seconds for Monk to express how unimpressed he was.

"That used to mean something," he said, dropping back into the chair behind his desk. "*National security*. Nowadays, the corpo-racrats in Washington stamp that on every request they make. If you say no to them, you must hate your country. So now I'm supposed to assist you with anything you need on your little mission down here. I'd like to know something before I assign valuable assets to you. Understand?"

"I do, sir."

"Good. So what's the story, Mr. Swan?"

"There's talk of a new weapon being tested here by some of the mountain gangs. I'd like to talk with one of them."

"Which gang are you referring to?"

"PM-44."

He raised an eyebrow and leaned back in his chair. "Uh-huh. You want to have a nice, casual coffee date with the PM-44."

"Coffee. Tequila. I'd settle for an Arnold Palmer if it got me 10 minutes with someone on the inside."

His unblinking stare said I was an imbecile. But he had orders to help me, and that made me his least favorite person of the day. Of course, the day was still young.

"Son, how do you expect me to make this date happen?"

I returned the stare. "Monk, I actually served in places just like this. I know how it works down here. You're not doing your job if you don't have a contact with someone who can reach the bastards. There are damned few gangs in the Triangle that Uncle Sam doesn't at least have a thick file on. And we all know how you compile the data. So I'd be much obliged if you could make a call to your source and find out who I can chat with. I won't take much of their time, and I'd hate to take up any more of yours."

His stony face dissolved into a smile. "You served? That supposed to impress me? The company cook *serves*."

"Hope he's better than the one we had in Pellafong."

Monk's smile disappeared. I'd dropped an arcane reference only a few commanding officers knew about. A code name for an operation that would never go on the books, but had stopped a potentially catastrophic crisis in South America. According to my notes from Poole, Monk Mondragon had been involved on the periphery, but I was sure it was a day in his life he'd never discuss with anyone. Some of his men may have been part of the team of eight who'd perished that night. If not, he at least knew who they were. Their deaths had been reported as part of a tragic training accident. It was no training accident.

Without another word, he sat forward and picked up his phone. He said some names and words that meant little to me but had all the earmarks of action. When he hung up, he stood and offered his hand. "Welcome to Honduras, Mr. Swan. Major Dyess will meet you outside and arrange your meeting. Good luck."

The major was the spitting image of a 1990s version of Meg Ryan. Yes, the rom-com star. I almost said something, but then figured she probably got it from people all the time. Besides, my instincts told me Major Lena Dyess might share physical characteristics with the movie star, but she could probably take down three or four physically fit men at the same time, all without any change to her heart rate. Something about her own hand grip and the hooded glare emanating from somewhere deep behind those eyes. She was cordial, but I knew in two seconds I'd never want to be on her bad side.

"I'm told you'd like to visit with the PM," she said, once we were in her office.

"That's right," I said. "You've spent some time with them?"

"A little bit, here and there. They're not exactly great conversationalists. Of course, they're also sexist assholes who don't think a woman should ever wear a uniform or pack heat."

"You straightened them out on that, I'm sure."

She shrugged. "I have no illusions about changing their caveman tendencies. But even cavemen understood earning respect. So I earned their respect. And they'll never touch me again without an invitation, that's for sure."

"I was always told violence is never the answer."

This earned a half smile from the Air Force officer. "It may not be the answer, but it's often the currency of the land. If you don't trade in it, you might as well stay out of the market." She narrowed her gaze. "Besides, who are you kidding? Something tells me you deal in violence on a daily basis."

"Yes. But in my heart, I'm a lover, not a fighter."

"Uh-huh." She nodded slowly, and I felt like we'd reached an equilibrium of respect. "I can get you into a meeting with the top lieutenant of the PM."

"Not the top dog?"

"Does it have to be the top dog? Or would you prefer to actually get your hands dirty?"

I smiled. "The guy on top stays in his penthouse."

"Oh, he paid his dues. Like his lieutenants are doing today. But he's not even worth talking about right now. We know about him and we know how to find him if we have to. The guy you want to sit down with is named Escobar."

Now I laughed. "How in the hell does he live up to *that* name?"

"Mostly by killing people. I think he sees the coincidence as some sort of marker to live up to." She opened a desk drawer and pulled out a small stack of folders. Flipping through them, she stopped at one that was tattered, with chicken scratch notes covering the outside. Finding a page within, she turned it around on the desk and slid it toward me.

"This is Escobar. Speaks fluent English. Went to college for a while in California. Got deported after some trouble. We get along okay now. He'll talk with you. I think he likes the game."

"The game?"

"Talking with the US military or government. Makes him feel important—which he is, in some ways. Probably the closest he'll ever get to diplomacy. I'm sure he's seen all the movies glamorizing drug cartels. So he works hard helping to build the little empire, then gets to play Hollywood with us."

I studied the photo. Younger than I'd expected for a top lieutenant, but I would never mistake youthful looks with innocence. Escobar had probably packed 10 years of experience into his first year inside the brutal world of drug smuggling and bureaucratic corruption. By now, with multiple years and scores of killings under his belt, you'd find solid ice behind that baby face. A face tarnished by a jagged scar on his cheek, no doubt a relic from his violent past.

"When can we make this happen?" I asked.

"I made the call before I came to get you. Everything goes through channels, but the PM are pretty speedy. Again, I think they like the prestige it gives them. We'll hear something before the hour is up."

Dyess was off by one hour. She found me in the mess hall, eating something akin to the crap we ate in middle school: a bowl of corn chips, chili, and cheese, dotted with mustard and lovingly referred to as Frito Pie. Not exactly the definition of health food. But hey, it was a taste of home and troops always relished shit like that. Well, except Major Dyess. She eyed the glop in front of me and squinted disapproval. Clearly not a Frito Pie girl.

Five minutes later we were in a Jeep, five minutes after that in a helicopter, and in another five minutes we were skimming across the treetops, heading toward a rendezvous point.

The major's voice came through the clunky spaceman headphones. "ETA is 35 minutes. Don't be spooked by the way these particular bandits behave. When we land, you won't hear anyone say a damned word. They'll point and they'll get you where you need to go, but the soldiers don't speak when outsiders show up."

"Odd," I said.

"Yeah. Someone said the PM should stand for 'perpetually mute.' But Escobar will talk plenty when we get alone with him. By the way, he's proud of the scar on his face, but don't say anything about his hands."

"What's wrong with his hands?"

"Pretty disfigured. Some sort of mangling of the left hand, and they've both had extensive burn damage. He's sensitive about that. So don't say anything or stare at them."

I nodded and went back to scanning the jungle below us. With its forests and mountainous terrain, it was easy enough for scoundrels to hide a base, strike without warning, and then scamper back to safety. Their only worry was the usual territorial squabble with other squads of baddies, all lusting to carve out their own piece of the poison pie. It was strange to think such a primitive existence could spawn a multibillion-dollar industry. Well, like many organizations worldwide, the select few at the top enjoyed the fruits of their employees' labor. Only in this case, if a worker spoke up, he wouldn't get a raise; he'd get his throat slit.

We touched down in a small clearing. Dyess and one other armed serviceman walked with me toward a camp, no doubt temporary in nature, used only for meetings of this sort. The primary PM-44 camp would be shrouded somewhere deeper within the jungle.

As Dyess had described, the two dozen or so Hondurans spread out around the camp didn't utter a peep. Half of them kept their eyes on us as we moved in, the other half never took their gaze from the surrounding trees. Every one of them held an assault rifle, and many sported the kind of knife that made Crocodile Dundee famous. I was pretty sure those were just for show, like an extension of their penis.

With the whine of the helicopter's engine dying down, all I heard was the breeze blowing through branches and the somewhat muted daytime sounds of the jungle. From my own experiences on patrol in South America, I knew the jungle's sounds could be almost deafening when night fell, as the animal kingdom went about its daily ballet of life and death. At the moment, I didn't know which was creepier: that nighttime cacophony or this peculiar human silence.

One soldier broke away and fell into step ahead of us, guiding us toward one of the small huts. When he got to the door, he stood at attention outside. It was obvious we were meant to go in. Our own armed escort waited across from the Honduran while Dyess and I ducked inside.

It was well lit. Three more troops were stationed equidistant from each other, two brandishing their own rifles, while the third held what appeared to be an FN Five-seveN, a semiautomatic handgun that had become increasingly popular with the cartels. All three guards stared us down.

Escobar sat expressionless behind a small table. Indicating the two chairs facing him, he said, "Please, have a seat. I have little time." His English, as Dyess had said, was excellent. His hair was longer than I'd seen in the photo and he wore a Los Angeles Dodgers cap, perhaps for show. His clothes were dark and dirty, suiting a man who held onto his soldier heritage while ascending to the top of the cartel food chain.

"Thank you for meeting us so quickly," Dyess said. "This is Agent Swan."

He turned his gaze toward me, now with a half smile on his face. "Agent Swan. And which agency do you work for?"

"You could say I get loaned around to various departments.

I'm what they call a free agent."

"I'm familiar with free agents. I follow all the American sports —although I can't understand your country's resistance to real football. Your *soccer* is pathetic for a population so large. Why do you think your people struggle so hard with the concept?"

I shrugged. "We like using our hands. Bummer about yours, by the way. What happened there?"

It was like throwing a switch. His smile evaporated, replaced with a cold, malevolent look. He threw a glance at Dyess, as if to say, '*Who is this asshole?*' Dyess remained silent, but I felt waves of anger flare my way.

The awkward moment faded. Looking back at me with contempt, Escobar's expression melted back into a faint smile. He gave a slow nod, acknowledging my passive aggressive jab. Then he said, "You're a real *hijo de puta*. Do you know what that means?"

"Well, as I recall, it has a multitude of translations. Some a little more vulgar than the others. Can we just agree on 'son of a bitch'?" I shook my head. "Shit, Escobar, you and I could both have that printed on our business cards. It's practically a prerequisite for the job."

He raised an eyebrow. "Okay, Agent Swan. Anyone else, I might have their tongue cut out and nailed to their forehead."

I did my best to look unimpressed. "As I said to Major Dyess today, violence is never the answer. But that's why I'm here to talk with you. You've experienced some violence lately."

Escobar grunted a laugh. "We experience violence *daily*."

"Sure. But not the kind dished out by something half human, half machine."

Once again, his face betrayed shock. He looked at Dyess, then back to me. Finally, after a long pause, he said, "You know something about the *hombre mecánico*?"

I smiled. "The 'mechanical man'? Yeah. I know a little. But it looks like you know more." I sat back and crossed my arms. "Let's talk about him."

CHAPTER SEVENTEEN

The ride could not have been more uncomfortable. I sat in the back seat of a Chevy pickup truck, wedged between two of Escobar's silent soldiers. The road wasn't exactly a road; it was more of a rutted trail between the trees, washed out in many places and generally worse than the roads in Cleveland, if that was possible. More than once I felt like my head was going to bounce off the top of the truck's cabin. My ass ached after the first 10 minutes.

Just to entertain and distract myself, I made conversation with both of my back seat companions while they sat there like Medusa victims draped in camo. I couldn't tell if they spoke English—although I suspected they knew *some*—but I regaled them anyway with stories of my days as a different kind of football player, embellishing my performances because why not? They'd never know I actually sat the bench for most of my high school sports career, primarily because I couldn't control my mouth. Coaches always get the last laugh.

In the front seat, the driver occasionally threw a tired glance at me in the mirror, probably wishing I'd shut up. In the front passenger seat, an eagle-eyed lookout scanned the road and the trees to each side, watching for trouble. I got the distinct impression that, even if he couldn't show it, *he* was enjoying my show. That made two of us.

Escobar rode in the truck trailing behind, along with Dyess and three more soldiers. Even though I felt like I'd bonded with the Honduran lieutenant, he was content to have me ride in the lead truck, the one that would take the brunt of any surprise attack. It also gave him an opportunity to press Dyess for information about his cocky new American visitor.

We were bound for another encampment, an hour away. All I'd been told was that I'd find soldiers stationed there who could describe the firefight with the *hombre mecánico*. They'd faced it and survived. Five others had not been so lucky. Our sources had said two, which showed you how reliable jungle intel could be.

The last 20 minutes of our ride down the rugged trail was cloaked in complete silence. I'd run out of bullshit, because even I have a limited reservoir. I tried enjoying the scenery but gave up after every mile looked identical. Seeing more than 10 feet into the trees was impossible. While we caught patches of the late afternoon sun on most of the trail, the canopy overhead shielded the depths of the jungle floor, casting it in a perpetual twilight. Branches smacked the windshield every few seconds, and at any moment I expected us to come around a bend and find a jaguar or a crocodile planted in the middle of the trail. I'd once seen a man lose a leg to a crocodile. That's not something you ever cleanse from your memory.

I didn't know we'd reached the camp until we braked to a severe stop and the doors flew open. Climbing out, I attempted to get the blood flowing back into my cramped legs while I glanced around. It took me a minute to spot the first hut, well concealed under a dense canopy. A tall, gaunt man emerged, spied Escobar, and began a hurried walk to welcome the boss.

By instinct, I did a slow 360, taking in the terrain, analyzing my surroundings, noting the personnel stationed in various spots, and also throwing glances into the treetops. I wondered how many snipers might be positioned out of sight. It was easy to imagine someone with a rifle trained on my chest at that very moment, watching me with one eye through a scope, a finger waiting patiently in front of the trigger guard. At least I hoped it would be in front and not resting against the actual trigger. One untimely sting by the aptly named bullet ant could send an accidental round straight into my heart.

Escobar spoke with the tall man, who kept looking over at me, nodding. His right arm was bandaged and in a sling. Then Escobar turned my way and jerked his head to one side, indicating that Dyess and I should join them in the hut.

"This is Hector," Escobar said once we were inside. "He was there and saw the *hombre mecánico*. He can answer your questions." Then he looked at Dyess. "Provided we get the products we discussed."

I looked between the two of them. "Products?" I said. "You want weapons in exchange for telling us what happened? When was that added to the agenda?"

Dyess said, "On the ride over here. Escobar decided that helping us comes with a cost."

The Honduran lieutenant wore a smug look I'd seen a hundred times before, the look of someone who feels they're suddenly in a power position. That look only popped up on the faces of the inexperienced.

I gave a small laugh and shook my head. "That's funny, Escobar. But I want to make sure I'm getting this straight. I've traveled all the way out here, to the middle of BFE, to help defeat the soldier that wiped out five of your people—and will keep *on* killing your people until you're all gone—and you want to *sell* me the information that will save your life? Is that right?"

The smile had been replaced by a venomous look. Escobar puffed himself up, another rookie move designed to intimidate. When he spoke, his voice was a growl. "You could be the next one dead, *Americano*."

"Yeah," I said, looking around. "You've definitely got the advantage there. Major Dyess and I could be dead in about five seconds. And then you'll be able to keep that vital information all to yourself and feel very superior about it. Then the *hombre* will come rolling in and wipe out your operation. Or, since the *Americano* forces will know you killed two of their high-ranking people, you might have to deal with an air strike or two on top of the *hombre*. You won't have any shiny new weapons, but it won't matter, because you won't have any soldiers to shoot them. Oh, and not to mention that *your* boss will also know you cost his organization an awful lot of time and money. Lots of money. Man, what a shitty day that's gonna be for you."

I looked back at him with the most badass look I could summon. "I'd make a really smart decision right now, Escobar. Kill me and get yourself killed later, or give me the goddamned information I want so I can save your ass. You've got 10 seconds to decide. Otherwise, I'm walking back to that piece of shit jeep and driving myself out of this godforsaken jungle and you can shoot me to stop me. Your 10 seconds start now."

To her credit, Dyess remained still and silent, probably wondering what the hell was happening. I'm sure she hadn't planned on this when we'd left the base. I'd died plenty of times, but this would be her first. Well, and her only. Her heart had to be pounding. But she played it perfectly cool.

Escobar used up the full 10 seconds, staring me down. But everyone in the hut knew who had the real power in this situation and it wasn't him. Finally, a smile worked its way back onto his face and he cocked his head to one side. "I was only joking before, when I called you a son of a bitch. But now I am *sure* that you are."

"Wouldn't be standing here otherwise. It's a requirement for the job." I turned to Hector. "*Habla usted Inglés?*"

He glanced at Escobar, then back to me. "A little."

"Great. Tell me about the *hombre mecánico*."

After another look to his boss, Hector launched into a story, using English that was much better than he'd suggested. He told me that he and two other soldiers had been near a disputed area, sort of a neutral zone between the PM-44 and an organization they referred to as the *penes de burros*.

It took me a moment to translate. "They're called donkey 'dicks?'"

Dyess cleared her throat. "The organization is actually called *El Corazón del Caballo*. The Heart of the Horse."

I rubbed my forehead, trying not to laugh at the modification of terms. It was straight out of middle school, but that didn't make it less funny. "Okay. So what happened with the *burros*?"

Apparently what had happened was a good, old-fashioned turf war. Escobar interrupted to say this particular area of the jungle had been fought over for years, between a handful of groups. The land, dense and mountainous, provided great cover and had good water sources. Technically, it didn't belong to anyone but the Honduran government. But the drug cartels knew they'd never be bothered as long as they placated enough people in power. And the government was quite happy having two or three different bands of desperadoes paying to have the authorities look the other way. It basically tripled the graft, which was brilliant. There was no incentive for officials to clean up the mountains; that would only slash their take.

Hector returned to the story. He said it had been late, near midnight. He and his two companions stepped into a clearing and found three men. In the moonlight and from their distinctive attire, two were recognized as being soldiers from their rival gang. At least it would be a fair fight.

But at first, there was no fight. The men they recognized both laughed and one of them said, "If you're smart, you'll leave now and never come back." Hector said the men made no move to raise their weapons. They appeared nonchalant, amused at the situation.

It remained a quiet standoff for a few moments. Neither group wanted to walk away; that would be a sign of weakness, especially with the two sides evenly matched. And yet, nobody was eager to initiate bloodshed, either.

As he told the story, I watched Hector grow increasingly twitchy. He unconsciously flexed the fingers in the hand sticking out of the sling. He clearly was troubled. I already knew the story ended with death; Hector was reliving the details while, at the same time, dealing with the judgment of his superior. I stood still, hands on hips, allowing him the mental space to work through it.

When he spoke again, his voice was softer. He said the two men from *El Corazón del Caballo* did something bizarre. They slowly knelt and set down their guns, then stood and raised their hands to show they were now unarmed. Then, they slowly began to spread out, one walking to the left, the other to the right. They weren't running away; Hector said it was clear they were providing their companion with room to move.

This third soldier, the one who'd not uttered a word, remained perfectly still, sizing up the situation. Hector said in the dim moonlight he tried to get a read on this man. He was tall and fit, but there was more to it than that. His right arm had a sheen to it, glinting like metal. Hector wondered if it was a prosthetic arm of some sort. Glancing down, he discovered the same sort of sheen protruding from the bottom of the man's khaki pants.

But most disconcerting of all was the face. Dark and cold, Hector said. The very face of death. And out of this grim visage, augmented through the darkness of the night, one of the man's eyes appeared to sparkle every few seconds, as if it were an electronic gadget. It all seemed like something out of a movie.

Hector said this man worried him. He was a stranger. He hadn't spoken. He didn't move. Yet he was now the only one of their group who carried a weapon, a pistol held in his right hand at his side.

I understood. Even without the deviant enhancements Hector

had described, this would be the opponent I'd worry about. During my time in the military, in some of the most dangerous places on Earth, I'd learned to pay particular attention to the wild cards who gave away nothing. The ones who talked without thinking were easy enough to manage. A quiet, thoughtful enemy, however, was the most dangerous. When they finally acted, it was often well considered.

The oddity of the situation, with two unarmed men moving aside and a third who seemed unconcerned about anything, became too much. In a move of desperation and fear, one of Hector's men raised his weapon. This one movement spooled everything into action.

The two men who'd moved out on the flank each dropped to a knee. But the one with the flashing eye sprinted off at an angle. No, Hector said after some thought; "sprinted" wasn't the right word. The man streaked away in a totally fluid motion. One moment he was standing there; the next, he was 20 feet away. It had happened in a flash. At the same time, the assailant who would acquire the nickname *hombre mecánico* raised his weapon and fired four shots. Two perfectly placed rounds into the head of each of Hector's soldiers. They collapsed to the ground.

Terrified, Hector scrambled to raise his own rifle. He saw the flash a split second before hearing the report, and a searing pain ripped through his right arm. His weapon clunked onto the jungle floor and he sank to his knees, clutching the hole, now spraying blood from his right bicep. He groaned in agony and a moment later collapsed onto his left side.

Footfalls sounded next to him. Staring up through tear-filled eyes, he made out the images of the two unarmed soldiers, looking down at him. Their expressions weren't sympathetic nor aggressive. It was, Hector said, like they were simply watching a bug struggling in the dirt. Then, between them, the mechanical man appeared. With the moonlight shining on him, and now at much closer range, more of his features could be seen. Hector blinked away the tears from his eyes and choked off the painful cry. If he was going to die, he wanted to know the thing that was responsible.

The dark face seemed ordinary enough, although it, too, displayed no emotion whatsoever. But the glinting eye was clearly artificial. Hector said he could practically see it focusing, taking in the scene, analyzing the condition of its prey. Scanning downward, Hector said the unbuttoned shirt revealed what looked almost like archaic chainmail. It, too, had a shimmer in the faint light.

Then, wondering how the creature had moved so quickly, Hector turned his face to the side and saw, up close, the blades extending from the pant legs.

"Blades," I said. "Like the prosthetic legs that long-distance runners use?"

He nodded.

Escobar spoke up. "He said it almost throbbed with energy, even just standing there."

That made sense. The sketch we'd received from Bryson's hotel espionage revealed a complex form of foot and ankle technology. Incorporating a tension-filled blade could account for drastic speed, especially out of the starting blocks.

I looked back at Hector. "Why didn't they kill you?"

He took a deep breath and again looked at his boss. "They told me I was to come back and warn everyone that *El Corazón del Caballo* now controlled that entire stretch of the mountains. They said the next time, there would be no warning to leave. They would assassinate anyone who trespassed."

"And that's exactly what they've done," Escobar added. "Another patrol, two nights later. All three of our men were gunned down. We found their mutilated bodies. Their weapons had not been taken. I think the bastards wanted us to see that our men had not fired a single round."

I nodded and thought about the description Hector had

shared. It sounded like Minor's prototype had gone far beyond just the one component Antoinette wore. This working model in the jungles of Honduras had the feet, the hands, the body armor, and the enhanced visual abilities that made up the entire package. Well, the entire package so far. It had cut down five soldiers without drawing even a single round from its opponents. It had already produced the kind of terror Minor anticipated—the kind that had Quanta deeply concerned.

And yet the report I'd stolen in North Carolina had described their field test in Honduras by saying "results mixed" and they would "follow up with necessary adjustments." If what Hector had experienced was a mixed result, what the hell would happen once these new adjustments were installed? How much more of a nightmare could Minor Arms insert into a battlefield?

There was one thing left for me to ask the Honduran soldier.

"Hector, this might sound like a strange question, but did you get any kind of feel for the mind of the *hombre mecánico*?"

He looked at Escobar, confusion on his face.

I tried to explain. "What I mean is: At any time, did you feel like you weren't going up against a man—but against a machine?"

He didn't answer right away. I wondered if he thought it was a trick question, something meant to trip him up, to make him look foolish in front of his superior. But a moment later, he took a deep breath and said, "*El hombre no tenía corazón.*"

I thought I understood, but I looked to Escobar for confirmation.

The lieutenant said, "The man had no heart."

CHAPTER EIGHTEEN

The easy play would've been for me to take the information I'd gleaned from the Honduran bandits and head back to the States. I'd file the report and we could base our moves on this second-hand information.

The easy play wouldn't win many battles, however, especially against the beast prowling this jungle. While I listened to Hector's alarming tale of the heartless, Frankenstein-type creature who'd slaughtered three men without so much as breaking a sweat, I knew what came next. I wouldn't be going back to Alabama. Not yet, anyway.

I'd be going on a hunt for the mechanical man.

When I broke this news, both Escobar and Hector looked at me like I'd just slathered ketchup on a peanut butter sandwich. The looks grew even more incredulous when I announced they'd be my travel companions.

Escobar's face gradually dissolved into a leer, but I cut him off before he could tell me I was crazy.

"Don't talk, Escobar. Just listen. I was dead serious when I said I was here to save your ass. And the only way I can do that is to see this mechanical man. I don't need you to put a fighting force together. In fact, that would be a mistake. I want a small team—you, me, Major Dyess, Hector, perhaps one more. That's it. I want the five of us to travel quickly and quietly. In. Out. No one has to die. But I have to see what I'm going up against, and I can't do that unless you take me in. Refuse, and it's only a matter of time before your entire organization is run out of the jungle. Permanently. Because once *El Corazón del Caballo* gets a few more of these monsters, you'll never be able to move them out."

His leer had faded into a blank stare.

"And remember," I added, "the man who pays you will know all of this."

Much of what I'd said to Escobar probably went over Hector's head. But he was smart enough that, even without a strong grasp of the language, he probably picked up the vibe. His eyes darted between me and his boss, and in my peripheral vision I saw him nervously clenching and unclenching the fingers supported by the sling. He knew a decision loomed that could precipitate his death, the kind suffered by his compadres. On one level, I felt sorry for him.

"Okay," Escobar said. "We'll go. But a recon mission only. No foolishness, or I'll kill you myself. Understood?"

He was scrambling to salvage at least a dollop of respect in front of his foot soldier. I decided to grant him this one kindness. "Understood. You and Hector find me this freak in the jungle and I'll make sure we all get home safely."

It was, of course, a promise I had no business making. Even with plenty of experience in jungle warfare—hell, Quanta had recruited me while I toiled with a special ops group in a South American rainforest—the Next Generation Soldier represented a wild card I couldn't prepare for. Teaming with reluctant soldiers presented an additional variable. Who knew how disciplined they'd be if shit went south.

But I'd been honest with the tough-talking drug mobster. I had no intention of battling Robocop. Not yet, anyway. "Look, but don't touch" was the order of the day.

Without knowing exactly where the target might be at any given time, we looked at the points on a map where the two known attacks had taken place and I picked a spot between them. That was the extent of my scientific process.

If we wanted stealth, motorized transport was out of the question. So we began a seven-mile hike, each of us carrying a backpack with some food, water, and first aid supplies. I tucked my Glock into a holster inside my light jacket. Escobar carried the same FN semi-automatic I'd seen another cartel member brandishing. The bug spray Dyess and I applied before setting out had initially brought snickers from Escobar and his men, and the smell was ghastly—but I'd had my share of run-ins with hideous bugs, and that's not something you forget. Let Escobar and his motley crew laugh.

I also carried a special satellite phone along with a homing beacon, so Poole would know precisely where we were at all times. Hector said it would take us about four hours to make the trek.

The path was essentially a tunnel. Heavy jungle growth pressed in from all sides. It was dark, hot, and humid, which you'd expect. But it was more than that. The dense quilt of trees and exotic plants, hemming us in, allowed no sense of direction. The experience would be nerve-shattering for anyone who battled claustrophobia.

We moved in single file, Hector in front, followed by Dyess, then Escobar and me. Our fifth team member, one of the cartel's nameless soldiers, brought up the rear, 50 yards behind us, toting an assault rifle. Other than a few quiet messages and hand signals passed up and down the line, we trudged in silence, camouflaged by the sounds of the living jungle. Those sounds were much louder and more intimidating than you might imagine. Movies could never capture the awe of nature's wildest playpen, where the dance of death played out daily amongst billions of creatures, large and small. In some of the planet's other natural arenas, silence meant survival. Jungles were boisterous.

An hour into the march, I'd fallen into a familiar cadence. I reverted into that special ops soldier, the guerrilla fighter, accessing long-buried files in my brain. It didn't surprise me that they came easily.

You walk differently. You listen differently. You adjust the way you scan your surroundings; instead of simply *looking*, you're *evaluating*. Even your breathing pattern modulates.

But it wasn't just biological changes. My thought patterns had shifted. I, too, was now a creature of the jungle, a participant in that same dance of death. Calculations and problem-solving take on a heightened sense of urgency when a wrong move could be your last. And in the jungle, there's no shortage of things that will kill you.

Including fellow human beings.

Some might jump to the conclusion that this automatically instills fear. It didn't, at least not for me. It elevated my game. I'm compulsively competitive. I have to win, and I compete on the most treacherous playing fields in the world.

As this last thought drifted through my conscious mind, I grimaced. Despite my aggressive attitude toward winning, plenty of losses marred my record. It was to be expected in my line of work, which took the concept of "high risk, high reward" to its ultimate extreme. When you play every game against the equivalent of the 1927 Yankees, the '95-'96 Chicago Bulls, or New Zealand's All Blacks rugby team, you're going to have some shitty days. The difference was that, if he lost a game, Michael Jordan wasn't killed. I wasn't always so lucky.

After some rest stops and a few pauses to confirm our position, we approached the map target. Hector's ETA prediction had been nearly perfect. We were tired from the grueling hike, and spent 10 minutes getting hydrated and eating handfuls of something Escobar called "Honduran trail mix." I didn't want to know the ingredients.

It had been a long shot that the NGS would be strolling this exact spot at this exact moment, but I think we all had a strange sensation that *something* was in the vicinity. The wildlife around us couldn't necessarily be described as subdued, but had definitely dialed back a notch or two. Were they as terrified of the hybrid soldier as Hector? They'd spent millions of years avoiding predators and learning that anything out of the ordinary was, more than likely, deadly.

There was nothing more out of the ordinary in this jungle than the man-made abomination we were tracking.

Escobar made sounds of being in charge of this expedition, but I wasn't interested in his pride. I turned to Hector.

"The *hombre mecánico* is not here. What does your gut tell you?"

He understood the first sentence. When he squinted at the second, I added, "*Tu instinto. Dónde?*"

After again looking to his boss for approval, he glanced around the area. I'd spent enough time in the field to trust the instincts of natives. If Hector pointed north, I'd go north.

He nodded toward the east.

I peered that direction, then leaned in toward the group. "Just so we're all clear: It's not only critical we find this thing, but that we get back to the base to share the information. No one is going to be a hero tonight, no matter how much the odds may seem to be in our favor. No one goes off script. We find the mechanical man, we observe, and we get the hell out. Understood?"

I waited while Escobar translated for his two soldiers, but it was a foregone conclusion they'd enthusiastically agree. They'd already seen five of their men shredded.

We gathered our gear and began working our way through the dense, dark landscape. This was more difficult than the initial

march, with no definable trail. But Hector quietly pushed
through.

Another half hour passed. In an instant, Hector stopped and
dropped to a knee. We all followed his example. His ears, highly
tuned to the normal sounds around us, must've picked up something unusual. I watched him crane his head to one side, then the
other. We held our collective breath, waiting. A few seconds
passed, and then, with his free hand, he motioned toward something at two o'clock. I looked in that direction, but saw nothing.
He slowly spun his head to face me. His eyes radiated fear.

I gave him a silent nod, then placed a hand on Escobar's
shoulder and leaned up to his ear. In a whisper, I said, "Wait here
with your men. Dyess and I are going to move up."

He said something about going with me, and I shook my head.
"You got us here. The fewer people we have pushing ahead, the
less noise we'll make. Besides, I can't have you or Hector killed.
How the hell would I find my way back? Stay here."

He reluctantly agreed and whispered the order to his two
companions. I gave a sign to Dyess, then crept past Hector,
moving in the direction he'd indicated. I heard the major
following.

The jungle floor was damp, which helped deaden the sound.
We stayed crouched, picking our way through the debris, stopping every few seconds to listen. I wondered if Hector had
misjudged whatever he'd heard. Perhaps it had been a bird or
some other creature stirring in the undergrowth.

But the terrified look in his eyes had been triggered by a
memory. He'd heard the *hombre mecánico* before and I was sure it
was an experience he'd never forget—the sight *and* the sound
of it.

Sure enough, after scooting 30 yards, I picked out a sound that
didn't fit in with the background noise. It was high pitched, not
quite a squeal, but definitely electronic or mechanical. Certainly
man-made.

I held up a hand, and Dyess knelt beside me. She, too, had her head cocked toward something ahead. We locked eyes, then she pointed to a spot just to our left. I slipped off my backpack and withdrew two night-vision goggles, handing one to Dyess. Once they were on, I moved toward the area she'd pointed to, one silent step at a time. The adrenaline spike shot up to a 10, putting all my senses on high alert and prepping me for quick action. My military background flooded in, which brought a sense of calm. Specialized training will do that in a time of crisis. Dyess undoubtedly tapped into the same reservoir. She was good. I was glad to have her at my side.

The electronic sound stopped, but was now replaced with a voice. I stooped a little lower and gazed between some oversized leaves. Through the green tint of the goggles, I picked out a human torso. Slowly pushing one of the branches aside, I saw the man. He was about 40 feet ahead, standing in a small clearing. Leaning to one side, I made out another man. As I spotted him, he laughed at something the other had said. They were making no attempt to be silent.

Then, the electronic sound was back, but only for a few seconds. I instinctively dropped even lower, almost prone. Dyess had taken up station 10 feet to my right. She held up two fingers, pointing toward the men. Then she held up one other finger and waved it to the right of the soldiers. She gave a big, slow nod, which I easily translated.

It's him.

My field of vision was blocked by a copse of wide trees. I quietly made my way over to where Dyess knelt and peeked through an opening.

He stood easily six-and-a-half feet tall, perhaps a little more. Muscular yet lithe, a finely sculpted being. My gaze fell to his feet, which glistened in the faint light my goggles picked up. The sheen of metallic blades was evident, but not the thin, functional variety I'd seen on certain prosthetics. These were thicker, fuller, and gave the impression they could crush a human skull without needing much pressure. I wanted to see them in action—but at the same time, I *didn't* want to see that. It might mean the damned thing was running my way.

I scanned upward. The creature's midsection was clothed, preventing any examination of its core. But at the end of each arm, another glint of metal flashed through my goggles. It took me a moment to comprehend that I was seeing both hand *and* weapon, with no clear distinction between the two. It brought to mind the fantastical robot toys of my youth, the kind whose hands were essentially high-powered guns or lasers, bolted onto the ends of the arms.

Here, the gun was definitely a separate entity, but it was designed as a component that melded perfectly into the modified hand. I envisioned an electronic connection as well. Perhaps the gun snapped into place and completed a circuit that helped power the weapon.

I wanted a better look at the face, specifically the eyes. Minor had told me the earliest prototypes had electronic eyes that were noticeable. He'd referred to it as an early defect. That tracked; Hector had described seeing a sparkle and mentioned he could actually see the eyes focusing. Antoinette, on the other hand, featured an updated component. Hell, she may have gone through several iterations, popping out an old one and replacing it with whatever new upgrade came out of the shop.

But at the moment, this mechanical man was staring somewhere off to our right, focused on something hidden from my view. Those enhanced eyes were registering something and undoubtedly recording it at the same time.

Which reminded me.

Moving as slowly and quietly as possible, I brought my own enhanced recording device out of a jacket pocket and spent 20 seconds capturing everything I could. Using the infrared settings,

I zoomed in on the feet, the arms and hands, and waited, hoping to get whatever image I could of the face.

The wait paid off. The NGS swiveled his head from side to side, clearly listening to something. Had we made too much noise? I imagined his super speed and super eyesight also came paired with super hearing.

When he finally moved, the electronic noise returned. I noticed it was a combination of the thing walking and rotating its right hand. The hand twisted, spinning around, a movement I had to think was the NGS equivalent of flexing its fingers. It moved through the clearing, taking large, bouncy steps.

Then, in almost a blur, it streaked to its left and bolted into the jungle. Seconds later, a shot rang out, then two more.

The two soldiers accompanying the NGS sprang into action. One took up a standard defensive posture, the other slipped into the darkness, trailing the beast. A moment later, a human cry sliced through the thick air. A cry of intense pain.

Dyess and I held our breath but exchanged concerned looks. We recognized the sound of the gunshots. They'd come from an FN Five-seveN.

Before we could move to render any assistance—which was surely too late anyway—the Honduran soldier broke back into the clearing, trailed by the NGS, carrying a large bundle. It turned out to be a human form, which the cyborg dropped onto the jungle floor. There was a low moan. The man on the ground slowly tried getting to his feet. The NGS, using one of those heavy blades that acted as feet, shoved the man onto his back.

It was Escobar, his Dodgers cap askew.

His face was contorted in pain, and through the night-vision goggles I made out a discoloration. It was blood. A lot of it. It poured from a slice on his scalp and another gash on his chest. His disfigured hands clutched at the chest wound, trying to staunch the flow.

One of the soldiers from *El Corazón del Caballo* knelt down and stuck a pistol against Escobar's throat. The soldier began asking questions, but his back was to me and I couldn't make out the words.

I silently cursed the PM-44 lieutenant for following us and for putting me and Dyess into this position. We could very well lose our lives if we jumped out to come to his aid. I could come back and try again another time, but for Dyess, this would be the end of the line. On top of that, all of the intel we'd picked up would be lost, which might set us back weeks in our fight against Ambrose Minor.

All because the stupid son of a bitch couldn't just wait in safety. He had to stumble his way into the action, to prove he was tough, to show everyone he was a leader.

I motioned to Dyess that she should take out the two soldiers while I would concentrate on the NGS, but it was too late. The *El Corazón del Caballo* soldier got to his feet and said something to the mechanical man. Without hesitation, it picked up Escobar with one hand and, with its weapon detached and holstered, brought the other hand up quickly. In one movement, it whipped that hand from left to right, severing Escobar's head.

The baseball cap fluttered to the ground, landing beside Escobar's skull.

Dyess started, but held back the gasp. All I could do was shake my head in disgust as the NGS released its grip on the headless corpse, which fell to the ground.

With no outward sign of remorse, the NGS slowly turned his head, staring into the forest, trying to ascertain if the dead enemy soldier at his feet had brought friends.

We were in trouble if we stuck around.

I looked at Dyess, who'd clearly read my mind. She reached inside a flap of her backpack and removed a grenade. With a nod at me, she pulled the pin and launched the grenade as far as she could on the opposite side of the clearing. It landed with a thud, which caused the NGS to swing its head that way. A moment later, the weapon detonated, causing the Hondurans to throw themselves onto the ground.

Then, as the sound died away, they jumped to their feet and, with the NGS breaking out to their right, plunged into the overgrowth.

It was the distraction we needed. Dyess and I quietly back-tracked, putting as much distance between us and the Hondurans as we could while remaining silent. A minute later, we heard a shout from the soldiers, and I judged we now had a good 70 or 80 yards between us. We picked up the pace, scrambling across the jungle floor, leaving behind the body of Escobar, lying alone in a pool of blood.

And leaving behind a nightmare, unlike anything I'd ever seen before.

CHAPTER NINETEEN

The drive back to our original meeting spot was probably just as bumpy as it had been on the way out, but I hardly noticed. My mind was busy reliving the bloody scene we'd managed to escape. I replayed it in my mind several times, watching in a type of slow motion as the NGS sliced off the head of our guide. In normal circumstances, we would've taken out the enemy, cutting them down in retaliation for the murder.

But these were not normal circumstances, and the *El Corazón del Caballo* soldiers were not *our* enemy. Dyess and I weren't even supposed to be there. If we'd killed Honduran citizens, there was no telling what kind of diplomatic nightmare that could've caused. All we could do was watch and try to escape. I didn't like it, but I knew enough about procedures to recognize when my hands were tied. I'd had those hands slapped many times.

The helicopter journey passed in a haze, too, as I stared below at the treetops whizzing by. Major Dyess attempted to ask questions, but she soon realized my mind was elsewhere.

In truth, my thoughts were fragmented and strewn all over the place.

There was no real evidence Ambrose Minor was involved in

anything that would directly harm the United States or any of its citizens. And yet he was clearly behind the explosion that nearly killed Fife and me. He was the leading suspect in the killing of his rival, Ty Hedrick. He'd supplied a Next Gen Soldier to one of the competing drug cartels in Honduras, taking advantage of the precarious situation in that Central American country to foster his own testing ground. That mechanical soldier had already killed five cartel members and now had decapitated a rival lieutenant.

But there was more.

We had every reason to believe Minor had communicated with a Russian general, and there was a possibility he was open to selling his NGS—or an entire squadron of them—to organizations with a vested interest in bringing chaos to the US or its allies.

But he'd remained one step ahead of the law. He was the Teflon Man, making it damned hard for us to find anything that would stick.

And yet I knew the proof was there. Somewhere. Without that proof, Quanta was right: We couldn't legally move against Minor Arms. He was free to build and peddle his weapons to anyone he liked. What made it worse was that I knew the bastard was aware of our dilemma. He was likely somewhere at this very moment, smiling.

I needed the bastard to make just one mistake. Something that would allow us to pounce.

My mind also danced around the situation with Bryson Hedrick. From the moment we'd met, I'd had a bad feeling about the guy. And again, I had nothing I could pin that feeling to. But it was asking too much to believe he was unblemished when it came to either the death of his father or the death of his pseudo-girlfriend. Or both.

All of this put me in a tough situation. Q2 might be a stealth agency and we might technically be invisible to the public and most politicians, but we still had to follow basic rules. That meant I couldn't storm in and blow up Minor's operation without justification. Unfortunately, I'd been stonewalled at every attempt to produce that justification. I was beginning to feel as powerless as the startled PM-44 soldiers who'd fallen prey to the NGS prototype.

As we approached the air base, I mentally circled back to Bryson Hedrick. As inept as he seemed to be, the young heir was still somehow the linchpin to this whole mess. If I could crack the code of his involvement, I might weaken the foundation enough to bring it all down. Sometimes it took only a single domino to fall.

Once inside an empty office at Soto Cano, I closed the door and used a satellite connection to make a secure call to Quanta.

She listened to my description of the jungle nightmare. "We could have you stay in Honduras and lead a larger, better-equipped group to try to capture the NGS. But that could take more time than we have. Besides, it makes no sense getting you killed before we have more information."

"Your faith in my abilities is touching."

She ignored that. "Not to mention we don't want to end up having to explain why an American agent was in a Honduran jungle, fighting for a known drug cartel and potentially killing another American citizen. You have the information we wanted—we now know the Next Gen is operational. We've got the video you took and the second floor is already working on it. It's time to bring you back home."

"All right," I said. "Any update on Minor's relationship with the Russians?"

"Poole is working to zero in on that connection. What we need is the actual link between them. We have an illegally seized memo, but there's a conduit in all this that we don't have yet. We need the actual chain itself. It may not be enough to prompt action on our part but it would be an important piece of the puzzle."

"I've thought about that," I said. "My gut continues to tell me that Bryson Hedrick is the key. I've felt that way from the beginning, but the murder of Paige Walters underlined it. All I need is one scrap of information tying him directly to Minor, or at least to the operation of Minor Arms. I'm telling you, the guy is dirty."

"I don't disagree with your instincts," Quanta said. "Unfortunately, we don't have that scrap. Not yet. And it's possible the only way to dig it up would be through techniques that would make everything against Hedrick inadmissible in court."

I chewed on that for a moment. "Well, you know what? I don't care. I'm not looking to try the bastard on anything right now. I just want something I can use to turn the screws on him. To hell with anything that would stand up in court. I say we let loose the hounds."

It was Quanta's turn to sit quietly. Finally, she said, "That's treading on dangerous ground, Swan. It's the epitome of the slippery slope."

"Well, shit, boss. Seems like everything we do is slippery and dangerous. I won't tell if you won't."

Even from this distance and routed through a satellite 22,000 miles above the equator, I heard the wheels turning in her head. Quanta did her best to remain on the right side of the law, mostly because it was her ass if things went to hell. But in our business, staying perfectly clean was damned near impossible. We fought people who scoffed at the notion of following laws and rules, and some well-meaning souls felt we had to stay above it all. I've read more than one op-ed piece suggesting that national security teams should never sink to the level of the scum they battled.

But the people who wrote those essays did so from the comfort of a warm, safe room in a city protected by people like me. To think we could safeguard our citizens and remain pure as the driven snow was noble, but naïve. You had to pick: Did you want to be as safe as possible and have your agents occasionally step over the line, or would you insist on agents always following the law and risk a smoldering hole in the ground where a city once lay?

My years of service, both in the military and for Q2, had convinced me that the average citizen wanted Option A—as long as they didn't have to see it happen. *Protect me*, they seemed to say, *but in a way that won't make me lie awake at night, feeling guilty about it*.

Quanta knew I was right. We needed the dirt and we needed it now. To hell with legalities. We could deal with the repercussions after we'd stopped a power-hungry madman from selling out his country to people who'd love to see it in flames.

"Fly back to Huntsville," she finally said. "By the time you get there, I'll see if the second floor can sniff out something that gives you a toehold. After that, it'll be up to you. Handle this as carefully as possible, Swan."

"You know me, boss: Mr. Delicate."

I thought I heard her scoff as she hung up, but it could've just been the satellite connection.

It was an overnight flight to Alabama, and I arrived exhausted. Back in my hotel room, I debated getting some sleep first and then uploading, but I knew I'd be better off getting the work out of the way. Otherwise, I'd wake up grumpy. I preferred to roll out of bed and be ready to challenge the day.

It took 45 minutes. The process was definitely getting quicker. I used those minutes to lay out a rough plan for confronting Hedrick. I put a lot of faith in the weasels on the second floor uncovering some dirt. When they set their sights on someone, it was hard to hide anything. And I mean *anything*. If divorce lawyers had access to this help, they'd be undefeated in court. Phone calls. Emails. Social media messages. It was all vulnerable. I didn't know how in the hell they did it and I probably didn't *want* to know. We live in a fantasy world where we're convinced our cute little passwords keep our secrets safe. It's a joke. In the hands of the real experts, there's almost nothing you can hide.

When the upload was finished, I crashed for five hours. It was a hard, dreamless sleep, an angry sleep. I awoke to the sound of my phone buzzing on the nightstand. It was Poole.

"Don't tell me the brains on the second floor have already come through."

"Yes, they have," she said. "I'm sending you a folder as we speak."

"Excellent. I don't mind spoilers—what's the headline?"

"Someone at Hedrick Sky made a phone call from their offices to someone at Minor Arms four weeks before Ty Hedrick's death."

"Well, that's interesting," I said. "But it could've been straight business, too. I mean, they *are* in the same industry."

"Yes, that's true. But the file will also show you Bryson Hedrick's personal phone records. I've highlighted what I think you'll find important."

I smiled. "Okay. That's enough of a tease. I'll read all of it over breakfast."

Thirty minutes later, devouring an omelet and hash browns, I skimmed the folder. Sure enough, a business line call from Hedrick Sky to Minor Arms had taken place 25 days before the fatal fire. There would be no way to tell who had specifically placed the call and to whom it had been directed. The call had lasted nearly 40 minutes.

But Bryson's phone history was tantalizing. The usual tsunami of text messages, several to his father, a slew directed to other employees and clients, and the usual amount you'd expect between a guy and his love infatuation. Not surprisingly, he'd initiated the vast majority in the latter category.

A smattering of phone calls showed up that were clearly business, along with a couple that Bryson certainly wouldn't want anyone knowing about. Hey, adult entertainment stores made a lot of money off young executives like young Master Hedrick. I had a fleeting image of Poole blushing as she identified the number, which momentarily sent me off on a tangent, wondering who Poole's new love interest might be. Part of me hoped I'd never find out. I liked the idea of a mysterious side to Poole.

Looking back at her highlighted notes, I saw what she'd hinted at during our brief conversation. Either Bryson had not considered law enforcement's ability to scan phone records, or he was just plain stupid.

Two phone calls pinged a tower in Charlotte. The first number belonged to an unknown cell number—a burner phone, no doubt. The other, a four-minute connection, was traced to a number attached to Antoinette Lazarov.

I set down my tablet and stared out the dining room window. Could we label this a smoking gun? Probably not. But we were getting closer and closer to throwing a lasso around the little shit. These were legitimate pieces of evidence that Bryson Hedrick was somehow connected with the people who'd spent decades trying to put Ty Hedrick out of business. And who'd probably killed the man.

With help from Ty's own flesh and blood? For the first time, I entertained the idea that Bryson was dirtier than I'd imagined.

There was now no question what I had to do. It was time for another face-to-face. With a well-placed shove, I was sure the guy would collapse. "In over his head" didn't begin to describe it; he was dog-paddling over the goddamned Mariana Trench and the swells were building. I wanted to personally hold his head beneath the waves until he sputtered the truth and revealed exactly what the hell was going on.

I felt a presence looming over me and looked up, a forkful of omelet halfway to my mouth. It was Fife.

"Well," he said, "at least you didn't get yourself killed in the jungle. Did it bring back fond memories?"

"I never romanticize those days. Hot. Wet. Sweaty. Bugs. Bats. Bad guys with guns. Bad food, which led to what my grandma called 'gastrointestinal distress.' I miss the camaraderie, but nothing else."

"Which part was the worst?"

"For me? The bugs. For our Honduran contact? Losing his head. I guess I win." I nodded to the seat across from me. "Have a seat. Grab some chow."

He sat down. "Really? The bugs? Assholes are shooting at you from the trees and you're worried about ants?"

I finished shoveling in the large bite of eggs. "Yeah. Spoken like someone who's never seen ants the size of a Honda. What would you know? You FBI weenies sleep in a warm, comfy bed every night."

"Because we're smart."

A server stopped by and Fife ordered coffee and toast with jam.

I chuckled. "With an order like that, you can never again give me shit about anything. But if you're here, you either missed me or you have something to share."

"Both, actually. We may not have the superhuman powers of the second floor, but all of us dweebs at the Bureau can still pull a few rabbits out of the hat occasionally."

"Quit teasing. What's so spectacular that you had to tell me in person?"

He made a production of it, placing a tablet on the table and giving it a dramatic spin to face me.

I stared at a hodgepodge of reports, two columns packed with data. "What am I looking at?"

"That, my secret agent friend, is a comparison between the customers of Minor Arms and Hedrick Sky. Two competitors, two separate lists of clients and contacts, the very lifeblood of both organizations. These are the sources of funds. It's where the money comes from to pay for private schools, luxury cars, and beachfront property. And it's very proprietary."

"I'm sure. And since you're practically giddy—even *before* getting your toast and jam—I must assume you've stumbled across something out of place."

"You could say that." He placed a stubby fingertip against one entry in the column on the left. "This is one of Hedrick Sky's most important contacts. A guy named Epperson. He's sort of like a middleman between the manufacturers and the militaries of some other countries and militias. One of those jobs nobody talks about. But it's lucrative for Hedrick *and* for this guy, who marks up the goods before peddling them to others."

"Okay," I said. "And I'm guessing Hedrick works with him because they can't sell directly to certain groups."

"Exactly right. Either because the US frowns upon it or because it would create a PR problem for a righteous American company. Sell the stuff to Epperson and let him use his own Rolodex of ruffians to make the sale."

I grinned. "You've waited all morning to use 'Rolodex of ruffians' on me, haven't you?"

"Didn't sound as corny when I first thought of it. Anyway, here's where things get interesting." He moved his finger to my right, landing at a spot on the other column. "This is from Minor Arms. Some of *their* contacts."

"And where did you get this?"

He laughed. "From a super sleuth named Swan."

"Oh. This is from the file I snatched from their offices?"

"Correct. And it wouldn't necessarily stand out, except you recall exactly what that file represented, right?"

I paused. "The Russians. The RGF." When Fife just sat there, smiling, I glanced back and forth between the two entries. "Small print at the bottom of each. Ten digits. The same in both columns."

"Uh-huh," Fife said. "What normally comes in the form of 10 digits?"

"Uh, phone numbers." I looked up at him.

He gave a low whistle. "Look who gets a gold star. Should I let you figure the rest out for yourself, or do you want me to fill in the blanks?"

I pushed the tablet back toward him. "I'll be go to hell. That little scumbag, Bryson Hedrick. His phone number. In both files. Both attached to Epperson."

"Gold star number two."

After a pause, I said, "Wait a minute—what's Epperson's first name?"

"Jacob. Why?"

I gave a slow nod. We now had the mysterious "JE" from the Minor Arms memo. That answered one question, but the whole thing presented another. I squinted at Fife. "I don't get it. This suggests that Minor Arms used their connection with Hedrick to arrange a sale of the Next Gen Soldier through Epperson, who could funnel the product to the Russians—and to others, for all we know. Which means the young asshole sold out his father and his father's company. But why the hell would Minor put Hedrick's phone number in an official file where anyone could see it?"

Fife grunted a laugh. "Because this is far from an official file. They're not showing this to anyone, my friend. This is just the file you stole from a locked drawer." He leaned back while the server placed his order of toast in front of him. When she'd moved off, he said, "And I'll bet Ambrose Minor is very unhappy with you about that, Mr. Swan."

He slathered some strawberry jam on a piece of toast and pointed at me with it. "Unhappy enough to try blowing you up again." After taking a large bite, he added, "I probably shouldn't even be sitting here."

CHAPTER TWENTY

The only question I had was whether or not to take Fife with me to confront Bryson Hedrick. In the end, I chose for him to go. Things could take an ugly turn.

We arrived at Hedrick's building just after 6 p.m. It took nearly a minute of knocking before he opened the door to his condo. The look on his face was a combination of surprise and fury.

"You're not coming in," he said, pushing the door closed, an exact replay of our first visit. This time, I placed my hand on the door and shoved it back open. It banged into his shoulder.

Sticking my head through the opening, I gave him my best throaty voice. "You've always been a dick, Bryson. But trust me, you don't want to be a trust fund baby in the county lockup. There's almost no bigger bull's-eye you could paint on your forehead. Now move out of the way."

"Lockup?" He stood his ground, a smirk on his face. "You obviously don't know my legal team, Swan."

"You're right. I've never met them. I'm sure they're delightful people and snappy dressers. And you know what? I've also never met Jacob Epperson. He's probably not as charming as your attorney, but I'll bet he'd have a lot more interesting things to tell me."

The effect was almost comical. The second he heard the name, Hedrick's eyes flared wide and his mouth fell open. The pressure he'd been applying to the door went slack. I pushed it open the rest of the way and marched past him, followed by Fife, who, with a smile on his face, gave a perfunctory nod and said in polite greeting, "Mr. Hedrick."

Soft light spilled through the magnificent windows encasing the living area. In the building across the street, small stick figures shuffled around, unaware or uncaring that their lives were on display.

Hedrick's living room had been straightened. The beer bottles were gone. In their place, a single martini glass sat half empty on the coffee table next to an open briefcase. A handful of report binders were stacked on the table and two more on the couch.

"A nice, quiet evening at home," I said, glancing around. "Anyone else here?"

Hedrick had glumly followed us into the room. He stood behind the couch, seeming to process what had just happened. It took a moment for my question to work its way into his consciousness. He shook his head once.

"Good," I said. "Take a seat. We can have a nice chat while you finish your drink. Maybe make another. You might need it."

It took him a few seconds, but he finally got his feet to move. Circling the couch, he sat down, ignoring the glass. Fife and I remained standing.

"You've made us take the long way around, Bryson," I said. "A lot of wasted time, all to wind up right where we were always going to finish. Sitting here with you, talking about your secret association with Ambrose Minor."

He didn't answer. I kept going.

"It should've dawned on me from the beginning. Your bullshit story about just casually meeting up with a vendor who'd gone to a Next Gen presentation at Minor Arms. And then that fairy tale about breaking into the guy's hotel room and just happening to find a convenient brochure. I probably wanted all that to be true. But it wasn't."

Bryson looked deflated. He shook his head.

"Right," I said. "So now, tell us exactly what happened. And Bryson—" He looked up. "No more bullshit. Waste my time again and I *will* march you downtown. You'll find yourself in a cell with people who will happily introduce you to the incarcerated life in ways you'll find distasteful."

As I expected, he reached for the martini and finished it in one gulp. Then he sat back and ran a shaking hand across his mouth. I'd normally feel sorry for someone facing their first real interrogation, but this guy deserved no sympathy.

"None of this was supposed to happen this way," he began. "Everything went wrong. I mean *everything*. And the more I tried to navigate my way through, the worse it got. Like trying to run across a sand dune. Just—just horrible."

"All right," Fife said. "Start by telling us how you connected with Minor. When did he approach you?"

Bryson gave a quick snort of laughter. "Well, that's the thing. It might be easier to forgive myself if he'd approached *me*."

I cast a glance at my partner then back at the miserable figure on the couch. "Oh. So *you* initiated things."

"Yeah." He looked up at us. "But I'll say it again: Nothing like this was supposed to happen. Everything I did, I did it for my dad's company."

"Sure," I said.

His eyes widened, and he barked, "Screw you, Swan. You don't know shit about this."

"I know plenty, Bryson. But it's going to be interesting listening to you explain how all this was a good thing for your father. Especially considering that you just buried him."

He glowered at me for a long time, then looked back down and lowered his voice. "It *should've* been good."

"So tell us," Fife said.

After a deep breath, Bryson said, "I've wanted to fast-track my career from the day I left college. Dad's plan was for me to learn a little bit in all the departments, which was fine. I understood that to a certain extent. But I didn't want to spend too much time getting experience in departments I'd never specialize in. I knew I could make a difference if he'd let me take on the *big* projects. Develop new systems. Bring a fresh outlook to things, you know? Help guide Hedrick Sky out of the old ways and into a modern way of doing business. Otherwise, why make me spend all those years in school?"

"Makes sense," Fife said. I wanted to punch him for his kid-glove treatment.

"And I tried telling Dad. Several times."

"He wasn't interested in scrapping his tried-and-true ways," I said. "You wanted to move faster than he was comfortable with."

"Something like that. And it all came to a boil when we heard about the Next Gen Soldier."

Now I sat down on the chair across from him. This was the good stuff.

He took another long breath. "Dad discovered Minor was exploring some new weapons prototype—"

Fife interrupted. "How did he find out, exactly?"

Bryson shrugged. "The arms industry may be huge, but it's still a community of sorts. It's really hard to keep something under wraps when you're dealing with a variety of vendors, part-ners, and especially potential buyers. You don't want to invest too much money into a new project unless you know you'll have the buyers. So people find out, and they talk."

"All right," Fife said. "Keep going."

"Well, to me, it was exactly the kind of thing I'd tried to convince Dad to look into. Maybe not this exact thing, but at least something different. I told him we were set up with vendors who could expedite things. All we'd have to do is look into a partnership with Minor. Nothing critical, and certainly not anything that would jeopardize our autonomy. Just a one-time contract to help develop this new system."

"Your father wasn't interested," Fife said.

He grunted again. "That's an understatement. He came unglued. Accused me of being shortsighted. Of being greedy. And then he said I was disrespecting everything he'd worked hard to build for decades, mostly because I was talking about getting buddy-buddy with a man who'd tried for years to ruin us."

"And you could've left it right there and gone back to your apprenticeship," I said. "But you wouldn't take no for an answer."

"Look, it's not like I was trying to openly defy my father. I wasn't *angry* with him; I loved him. I was just anxious, and I didn't think it was a good idea for us to play conservatively. Not only is the arms world changing, *everything* is changing. If you don't evolve, you die."

He leaned forward and held out his hands to make a point. "But if there was a way I could come to him with an actual plan, so he could see that it was a good thing? Maybe all Dad needed was a road map. That's what I was hoping to do. I wanted it to be a pleasant surprise for Dad, something that would make him sit back and think, 'Yeah, Bryson can do this job. Look at the initiative he took on this deal.' So, I gave it a lot of thought and then got in touch with Ambrose Minor. Just to talk. Nothing else. Testing the waters."

"Probably made his entire year," I said. "The heir to the throne of his chief competitor, sniffing around to see about a partnership."

"Yeah. Probably." He gave a mirthless chuckle. "I was terrified. First of all, I knew my dad would probably kick me out of the company and disown me if I botched it. So I was very careful, very noncommittal. Just a call to say, 'Hey, what if we just talked, the two of us?' And he immediately said yes. Thought it was a brilliant idea."

"Uh-huh," I said, trying—and failing—to keep the sarcasm from my voice. For such an educated young man, and for someone who'd spent his entire life around the industry, it was incredible how clueless Bryson Hedrick was. Some might call it optimism on his part; well, that optimism had gotten his father and girlfriend killed. He'd had no idea what kind of viper he was getting into bed with.

"Anyway," he continued. "I flew to Charlotte, like I told you. But the business wasn't with any of our vendors; it was to meet with Ambrose over dinner. We hit it off, and he wasn't high pressure at all. The next morning, we had another meeting at his place, and he told me he looked forward to the day I was running Hedrick Sky. Said he knew I'd bring the kind of change necessary for real, scalable growth. I told him it would be a while before Dad retired. At least another 10 years.

"And that's when he said the thing that hooked me. He said, 'Everyone is capable of having a vision, Bryson. What we've lost are the people who convert their vision into reality.' He said visions are for dreamers and fools. The heroes are the ones who get off their asses and do something. Then he said, 'Are you a dreamer? Or are you a hero?'"

It was my turn to grunt a laugh. "Quite a speech. Very rah-rah. And of course you jumped up and said, 'I'm a hero, sir!'"

Bryson looked at me with disdain. "Piss off, Swan. You're all gung ho, barreling your way through life, probably destroying everything you touch. What the hell have you ever created, other than bloodshed and misery?"

I couldn't let him see the impact of his words. I kept my face of steel.

But the son of a bitch was dead right. He wasn't the first to point it out, either. I could blame it on my job, which in some ways acted as a salve. But I wasn't a creator, a dreamer, a visionary

—none of those. I was a destroyer. I did it in the name of good-ness, or at least that was the story I'd been sold. And I mostly believed it. That still didn't prevent my soul from shredding a little more every time I thought about it.

I camouflaged my doubts with bravado and by reminding myself that I *was* on a journey of discovery. The bodies I left in my wake—both villains and my own—I chalked up to the price I had to pay to find my answers. I suppose I could twist that journey into a semblance of something noble and creative. But only if I *did* eventually find those answers. Otherwise it was a trail of blood with no real meaning other than duty, whatever that was.

It was a heavy burden carried by plenty of people who'd come before me, in combat, in pursuit of national defense, in hopes of ultimately bettering the world.

But at what cost to our own private world?

I let the thoughts rush through me, then locked them away, prepared to take them out again at some future date and ratio-nalize my way through. Like I always did.

For now, I couldn't get distracted from the case at hand. Bryson may have hit a nerve, but I'd have to limp my way through.

"Yes," I said. "*I'm* the horrible person. Coming from a guy with the blood of two loved ones on his hands and the day ain't over."

Bryson began to jump up. Fife, standing nearby, put a hand on his shoulder and gently pushed him back onto the couch. "Let's take it easy," Fife said in a soothing tone. "Keep going with your story, Bryson. What happened next?"

He reached for the martini glass, noticed it was empty, and put his hands back in his lap. "Nothing happened for a while. You don't grow up under the thumb of Ty Hedrick and immediately start freelancing. Especially when he's ordered you to *not* do something. So I had to figure out a way to make incremental progress. To tiptoe into a vague relationship with Ambrose without causing all hell to break loose.

"Then it dawned on me: I didn't have to get too deeply involved. At least not yet. I could connect Ambrose with one or two of our vendors, ones I knew would remain loyal to Hedrick Sky. Dad had built up a lot of personal capital with people through the years, which was good and bad."

"How so?" Fife asked.

Bryson looked up at him. "If I could convince them that their participation would not only be beneficial to their business but also to Ty Hedrick, they'd be all in. They'd be happy to help. The downside was that the personal relationships were just so strong after all those years. These people were not only Dad's customers, they were his friends."

I got it. "Someone would blab."

"Yeah. I had to get them on board in a way that they wouldn't say anything to anyone, and that included Dad. Not an easy ask."

"No, I wouldn't think so," I said. "How did you convince Jacob Epperson?"

He grimaced. "I took him out for cocktails and bared my soul. I knew he was the right person to act as a conduit between us and Minor Arms. He's brilliant, and he's got connections all over the world. So I began by telling him I wasn't going behind Dad's back; I was just wanting to stack a few wins to surprise him. Told him what a gigantic score this could be for him and for Dad. But I needed absolute confidentiality."

Bryson paused and rubbed his forehead. "The guy lectured me for a solid 10 minutes. Told me how he'd been through the fire with my father and how he was disgusted that I'd try something like this."

A slow smile crept across my face. "He lectured you like a school principal and then said 'I'm in.'"

"Pretty much."

I looked at Fife, who gave me a grim look.

"All right," I said. "So you found a connection to use with Minor. Then what happened?"

"Uh, the Next Gen project picked up steam. Ambrose was a lot further along than I'd thought. He had some connections to potential buyers, but he seemed reluctant to use them. He glommed on to Epperson as soon as I suggested it."

"Of course he did, Bryson. It's another layer of protection. If things go to shit, it was your guy who made the deal with the bad guys."

Fife spoke up. "Plausible deniability. Ambrose will say he designed and built the things, sold them to a reputable dealer that *you* arranged for him. How did he know the guy would sell the death machines to the Russians?"

"Or sell them to other sketchy groups who should never have a Next Gen Soldier?" I added. "All right, keep going."

Bryson stood up and began pacing. "After a while—after he saw exactly how nasty these things could be—Epperson had an attack of conscience."

I grunted. "Right. An arms dealer with a conscience."

"Oh, not about the sales. He was totally cool with that. He just began to feel like he'd perhaps ruined his relationship with Dad. So he took Dad out and spilled his guts."

"I'm sure that went over well," I said.

Bryson continued to pace, but his hand went to his head again. "I thought he was going to have a stroke. It's the angriest I'd ever seen him. Took me two days before I could get him to have a normal conversation with me. Then I showed him everything. Told him my plan, how it would bring Hedrick Sky into the modern world of military technology. How it could actually help us leapfrog some of the more traditional arms companies."

"Did he buy it?"

"No. I mean, he wasn't a stupid man; he saw the financial benefit of it all, and after he calmed down, he actually commended me for having the guts to put the whole thing together. I think he might've even been a little proud of me on one level. I'd broken his heart—but a part of him was happy I'd at least showed some balls."

Bryson stopped pacing and turned to look at me. "Then he fired me. And that—well, that turned out to be what got him killed."

CHAPTER TWENTY-ONE

I blinked, trying to absorb the blunt force of the comment and the matter-of-fact manner in which Bryson had said it. At first, all I could say was "Oh." I looked at Fife, then back to Bryson. "Well, if he fired you, then, uh—"

Fife finished the question. "How were you still working for him?"

"Just throwing me out wasn't an option. I was working on several projects and those couldn't be abandoned. He said I'd be phased out and then be free to go out into the world and find my own way. Like *he* did. 'Take those big ideas you have,' he told me, 'and see what you can do with them. Just never compromise your integrity again, like you did here.'

"So we were going to transition. I'd finish up the work on my desk and then turn things over to one of the other executives. I called Ambrose and told him I'd be working with him on my own moving forward. And—"

I cut in. "Ambrose broke the news to you. That you weren't worth a damn on your own."

Bryson let out a long breath. "Yeah. He said the only way we could work together was if I took charge of Hedrick Sky. And the only way to do *that* was to encourage my dad to step down."

The room fell silent while he mentally hefted the weight of the situation, probably for the hundredth time. I couldn't let it drag on too long, though. I pushed the conversation forward. "What was his plan for that?"

He took one glance at me, one at Fife, then looked back at the floor. "He said the pressure of the situation might be enough, given time. But Ambrose isn't a patient man, and he was heavily invested in the Next Gen project. I mean, from what I gather, he's put *everything* into it. Like a poker player going all in. There was no way to put Next Gen on hold. He suggested we add additional pressure. Basically damage some of Hedrick Sky's business, enough to make it easier for Dad to step down. He said Dad was too old to roll his sleeves up and start over, and that he would see it as a reason to retire and make way for the next generation. And that we should do it while I was still an employee. He convinced me that Dad ultimately wouldn't want the company in someone else's hands—that Dad was only acting impulsively out of pain."

I squinted, trying to see the logic in any of this, and found it lacking. "Wait a minute. Your dad essentially fired you, and you believed that if you sabotaged the company, he'd suddenly change his mind, retire, and hand it over to you?" I looked at Fife for confirmation that this was an insane line of thinking. He merely gave one sad shake of his head.

"Look," Bryson said. "You've got to understand something. Everything was moving at light speed, okay? I was in shock, my dad was a wreck, the Next Gen project was moving forward whether I was part of it or not. I was watching everything go straight to hell, and I was desperate to try anything." He closed his eyes for a long moment. "Let's just say I wasn't exactly thinking clearly."

"All right," I said. "So then what happened?"

He began pacing again, trying to put all the pieces together. "A couple days before the fire, I had a meeting with Ambrose in Atlanta. He said his team had identified some things that would hurt Hedrick Sky, but not cripple it."

"Why Atlanta?"

Bryson shrugged. "I don't know. Other business, I guess. He's apparently there all the time."

"Did he tell you how he was planning to damage Hedrick Sky?"

"No, he said it was better if I didn't know. That way I wouldn't accidentally say or do something to compromise the operation. I should just go about my business and act surprised."

"And the fire was the surprise?" Fife asked.

"Yeah. I didn't know they'd be doing anything that night. I didn't even understand how they knew we were there. Until later."

I exchanged a look with Fife, then said, "Paige."

Bryson didn't respond at first, then gave a slow nod.

"Ambrose recruited her," I said.

"Yeah." He looked up at me. "I swear I didn't know until she told me."

"When was that?"

"The day she disappeared."

It was my turn to rub my forehead. It was such a mess, with so many twists. "You better tell us everything she said to you."

He walked back to the couch and fell onto it. I watched him wipe his eyes, then sniff a couple of times.

"Something wasn't right with her," he said. "She'd been acting weird for weeks, and the fire just put her over the edge. She'd stopped taking my calls, wouldn't answer text messages. It had been a traumatic night for all of us, but I didn't understand why she was hiding.

"Then she suddenly showed up here. Said she had a lot to share with me. Started by telling me she needed to go away for a while. When I asked why, she said she'd played a part in my dad's death. Unintentionally, of course. She'd been as shocked as everyone when the building caught fire. But she said she was partly to blame."

I didn't want to hurry him, so I sat still.

"Ambrose had contacted her and said he was quietly working with me. He asked if she would join the team. There would be a lot of money in it for her, and said all she had to do was keep him apprised of some things. It was basically corporate espionage, but he never used those words. She said it just seemed, uh, exciting."

Everything we'd surmised about Paige had been spot on. She'd had an opportunity to inject some spice into her life and was probably flattered that a major player like Ambrose Minor was recruiting her. It also explained why she stuck it out with Bryson, even though, by all accounts, she had no long-term interest in him. He was simply a ticket to an adventure, something edgy, allowing her to cross a line she'd never even come close to in her previous life.

She couldn't have predicted that tragedy would strike, so it must've seemed like a dream for her. Make some cash, live a spy's life for a week or two. Get off the "proper Southern girl" tread-mill, even briefly. As ridiculous as it sounded on the surface, it made sense. I knew how persuasive Ambrose could be, especially to someone longing for even a glimmer of intrigue.

And what a brilliant chess move by the arms maker. Luring not only the son of his chief rival, a young man who was confused and had completely lost his compass, but also roping in the son's girlfriend. She would be a useful pawn, a piece to be deployed and then discarded.

"Paige called Ambrose," I said, "and reported that you and your father were going to the remote office. Then waited in the car to signal that you were inside."

Bryson gave a short nod and his eyes welled up again. "She swore to me she had no idea anything bad would happen. She thought someone would simply sneak in and steal papers or some-thing. When the fire broke out, she was terrified. And when—"

His voice cracked. "And when Dad didn't make it out, she felt like she'd been an accessory to a murder. She fell apart."

"And instead of telling anyone about it, she ran," I said.

"*Tried* to," Bryson said. "Ambrose had her killed. And that was a message to me. A warning that if I tried to back out of our deal, the same thing would happen to me."

Now a sob escaped his lips. He wiped away more tears, and I saw him shaking.

"God," he said. "It's all such—such a nightmare."

"Yeah," I said. "And I'm afraid it's far from over."

He looked at me through watery eyes. "You think he'll try to kill me?"

I opened my mouth to answer, but never got the words out. One of the massive windows exploded in a shower of glass and Bryson's head snapped back in a shower of blood.

Fife and I reacted instinctively. We dove to the floor. But that provided no cover from the gunman who obviously was in the building across the street, looking straight into Bryson's condo.

"Move," I yelled, and we both scrambled to our feet and lurched for the hallway, out of the line of sight of the shooter. As we did, we heard five rounds punch into the couch, as if counting off a rhythm.

Once in the hallway, Fife looked at me. "You hit?"

I shook my head. "No. And I could've been. Easily. You too." I glanced around the corner at the living room, where Bryson still sat, his face pointing up at the ceiling. The back of his head was gone and a smear of gore coated the floor behind the couch. "Whoever did this, they let us go. Look at the holes in the couch."

He leaned out for a moment, then pulled back. "Jesus. Five across, perfectly spaced."

"Yeah. This guy corked Bryson, then just played around with us. Those shots were to let us know he could've killed us at any time. Probably laughing the whole time."

Fife grunted. "I'll say it again: I need new friends. Hanging out with you will be the death of me."

"Probably. Sure you don't want to upload and join the party?"

"No, thanks. Retirement actually sounds much better right about now."

I pulled out my Glock. "Ready to go catch this guy?"

"You know he's already long gone, right?"

"Yeah. But I'm sure there's security footage. Ready?"

We'd have to step into the line of fire, but we clearly weren't the targets. And I was sure Fife was right; the shooter would've made an exit by now. Regardless, we still hightailed it to the front door and the safety of the building's corridor, leaving behind the bloody remains of Bryson Hedrick.

An hour later, I was on a video call with Quanta. She was not happy.

"What have you found?"

"Security cameras show someone clearly in disguise, wearing thin gloves, and carrying a case that must've contained the rifle. They entered the building, took an elevator to the 19th floor, then walked directly to one of the units. They knew exactly which one faced Bryson across the street. We checked out that condo. Found the owner, a man, 40 years old, dead. Two rounds to the back of the head. The sliding glass door was open, and it provided a perfect angle. The shooter was in and out within two minutes. So they came in, shot the owner with a silenced 9 millimeter, pulled out and assembled their rifle, took aim, and blew Bryson away. Then they toyed with me and Fife, lobbing a few shots into the room. Disassembled the rifle, stowed it, and walked out. Outdoor security shows them casually walking up the street and disappearing."

"You said 'clearly in disguise.' What was the disguise?"

"I just sent you a still shot lifted from the footage."

I waited while she accessed the photo. It wasn't great quality, which figured. We were able to get perfectly clear images from galaxies halfway across the universe, but simple security video from 20 feet away generally sucked. In this case, it was good enough to tell that the killer had worn facial distortion items, like a phony nose, along with a long-haired wig, a hat, and tinted glasses. Even the clothing was baggy, obscuring their build. They knew they'd be on camera and made sure we'd get practically nothing from it.

"Fife has the lab folks at the Bureau working on it anyway," I said. "Seeing if they can get some sort of match on facial recognition. I'm not optimistic."

"And now both of our witnesses to the murder of Ty Hedrick are also dead."

I sighed. "Yes. It's pretty much a disaster all the way around."

It chapped my ass. We knew Minor was behind all of this, but we didn't have a single piece of evidence to tie him to it. We had phone records showing he may have spoken to Bryson and Paige, but we couldn't even prove that. There were no fingerprints at any of the crime scenes, and security footage that was either entirely unhelpful or nonexistent.

And while we ran around in circles, trying to piece it all together while simultaneously dodging bullets, Minor Arms kept making strides toward developing and selling a hybrid soldier already proven in the field to be deadly efficient.

Quanta was silent while these thoughts went through my mind. She was likely coming to the same conclusions and chafing just as much as I was. We were both sore losers.

Finally, she said, "It's going to be complete chaos now for Hedrick Sky. I don't know who inherits it, but I imagine the company will be lucky to survive this. The owner and his son, both murdered? That's enough to scare away even their most loyal customers, especially with the company's future in question."

"Which is exactly what Ambrose wanted from the beginning.

He must be giddy. He not only siphoned away a contact from Hedrick that he can use to peddle his goods under the radar, but he pretty much put a dagger into the heart of a competitor. He's probably wondering why he didn't do this long ago."

"So," Quanta said. "Next steps?"

I knew she was going to ask this, and I was ready. "One thing we've wanted to discover was the site where Minor Arms either finishes production on the Next Gen, or the testing grounds where they're run through their paces. There's a good chance it's both, in one location."

She perked up. "And you think you may have a lead on that?"

"Maybe. Or it could be nothing at all. But just before someone shut his mouth for good, Bryson mentioned that Ambrose spent much of his time around Atlanta. It could be unrelated to Next Gen; I mean, he's got an awful lot of contracts in other areas. But after all these years, it wouldn't seem like the boss would make multiple trips to see a vendor or customer. Most of that stuff would seem to run on autopilot most of the time. On top of that, Bryson suggested Ambrose has put all his chips on this one bet. Sounds like a man who wants to oversee everything."

Quanta stared back at me, then said, "There's a lot of mountainous terrain in northern Georgia. Lots of tree cover. And it's relatively close to Charlotte."

"About 250 miles. I think Minor would find it almost poetic to use one of his new toys to take out Bryson. Maybe one of the models with the same precision eyeball that Antoinette Lazarov has. That might explain their pinpoint shooting, too. So if that soldier has retreated to Georgia, we might potentially be able to recover the weapon. That would provide a direct connection to Ambrose."

"I'll put the second floor on it," Quanta said. "We'll try to narrow down where he goes once he arrives in Atlanta."

"Sure, we could go that route. But it would probably take time. So here's another angle: Jacob Epperson. If he's brokering deals for Ambrose, it's possible he knows where this training ground is. He may have been there to see the goods before agreeing to sell anything."

"Yes. I concur."

"Good. See if Poole can find where he is, and I'll leave first thing in the morning. Let's hope he's in the country."

She gave me a hard look. "Be careful how you handle this one, Swan."

I understood what she was saying without her having to verbalize it. Get the information out of Epperson without revealing just how much the government knew. In other words, play dumb.

We ended the video call, and I knew the first thing I had to do was upload. There'd been an information tsunami in the last few hours, none of which I could afford to lose.

The second thing I had to do was track down the salesman who would lead me to a bionic assassin.

CHAPTER TWENTY-TWO

As usual, Poole was a magician. She'd located Epperson and had the map coordinates to me before my head hit the pillow. By seven the next morning, I was on a commercial flight to Jacksonville. Epperson's credit card information showed him staying at a luxury hotel in that Florida city, along with a smattering of restaurant and bar charges, too. He clearly was entertaining people, which is exactly what a good salesperson specialized in—especially those who deal in multimillion dollar contracts. Never underestimate the power of the schmooze, an art that impressed me and, at the same time, repulsed me.

When I touched down, an update from Poole provided me with some ammunition—sorry—for me to use against the arms broker. Her snooping also suggested it had been a late night for Epperson. His final charge had come just after 1 a.m. There was a good chance I'd be waking him up. I hoped so. I also hoped his head would be pounding. It's easier to intimidate someone with a hangover. They'll cave to almost anything just to nurse their self-inflicted wounds.

The assistant manager at the hotel's front desk was reluctant to reveal Epperson's room number until I flashed the FBI credentials. That usually worked like a charm. I went to the ninth floor and noted the "do not disturb" placard hanging on the doorknob. I pounded a few times, waited, then repeated, adding a little mustard to it. The light dimmed on the other side of the peephole, which meant Epperson was peering at me. Probably with a bloodshot eye.

I held up my badge and spoke in a voice loud enough to penetrate the door. "Open up, Jacob."

He waited the length of time I'd expect for him to wonder 'What the hell is this?' before giving in and pulling the door open a few inches. I almost laughed when he actually said, "What the hell is this?"

I placed the badge into the crack of the door to make sure he felt the power. "We got a report from a hotel employee that you have a goat in your room, Jacob. I'm here to make sure you're not doing something that will traumatize the goat and that you'll regret later. Unless you're really into that stuff, in which case I'm here to simply rescue the animal."

"Goat? What the—"

I shoved the door open, causing him to stumble backward, right onto his ass. Once inside, I kicked the door closed, put my badge away, and grabbed him by a bicep, pulling him to his feet. He was tall but not muscular, sporting a shaved head, a goatee, green boxer briefs, and multicolored socks. Not the most glamorous look. I guided him, stumbling, back into the room and plopped him down on the edge of his bed.

He adopted the look, the one that said he was offended, outraged, and ready to sue as many people as his lawyer could fit on a court document. He opened his mouth to spout all this, but I cut him off by pulling out my Glock and placing it right up against his nose. That, too, works wonders.

"Before we get down to business, Jake—do you mind if I call you Jake?—I need to let you know that normally I'd give you endless shit about sleeping in socks. But these are actually quite stylish and I think if I owned a pair, I'd never want to take them off, either. So you get a hall pass for being a dork. What you don't get a pass for, however, is being an accessory to multiple murders. Three so far, and probably more to come."

His eyes, which were, indeed, quite red, flared wide. When he finally spoke, he stammered, to the point I had to hold a finger up to my lips and shush him.

"I can't understand you when you're about to piss your shorts, Jake. Take a deep breath and try again."

He swallowed hard. "I don't know what you're talking about."

"No? Need a hint? Ty Hedrick."

"Ty Hedrick? He died in a fire. What the hell do I have to do with that?"

I clucked my tongue. "Oh, no, Jake. The fire was an amateurish attempt to disguise a murder. I say *amateurish* because professional assassins know that kinda shit never works. Better to take the body out somewhere and either bury it or send it to the bottom of the ocean. Arson to cover up murder? That's right outta *Murder, She Wrote*. Ask your mother; she probably watched that. My mom never missed it."

It was my favorite tactic. Overwhelm them with a torrent of crap so they can't figure out what to focus on. It's the ultimate move to keep assholes off balance. And it was working.

"I don't—I don't know anything about that," he said. "Look, can you put that away? Guns make me nervous."

Now I really did laugh. "You sell the goddamned things all over the world."

"That doesn't mean I enjoy people waving them in my face."

"Well, I'm not sure I want to put anything away yet, Jake. Not until I know I have your complete and undivided attention, and that you won't feel tempted to dish up any bullshit to my questions. I feel the same way about bullshit answers that you do about guns in your nose."

He shook his head, perplexed. "I—I still don't even know

what you're talking about. You barge in, stick a gun in my face, and accuse me of murder—"

"*Accessory* to murder. Probably doesn't get you life in prison but doesn't prevent you from becoming the cell block's hot date on Friday nights, either. Actually, now that I think about it, probably every other night, too. There are no weekends in prison. Just one long, cold, painful day after another."

Another shake of the head. "Mister, whoever the hell you are, I don't know what you're—"

"My name is Swan. I'm here to gather some information from you. I expect your total cooperation. Otherwise, I tell Ambrose Minor that you *did* cooperate and helped finger him for the murders. Then Ambrose will dole out whatever he thinks is the appropriate punishment for a rat. And since he's shown no remorse yet for any of the killings already on his ledger, I'm guessing you'll be the next person to get the extra-crispy treatment."

Now he squirmed and held up a hand. "Whoa, whoa, whoa. Hold on just a moment."

I pulled the gun back. "Oh. You're ready to talk with me? Did I say the magic words?"

He licked his lips. "I'd like to know exactly what's going on." He glanced down. "Is it okay if I put on some clothes?"

"No," I said. "We're gonna keep you in your undies and socks. The sooner you give me the information I want, the sooner you can either get dressed or go back to sleep."

A glare crossed his face but dissipated the moment I pushed the gun back against his nose.

"Okay, okay," he said. "Put the gun away and I'll tell you what you want to know."

I took one step back, pulled a chair over with a foot, and sat down, leveling the gun at his chest. "I appreciate reasonable people, Jake."

"Please stop calling me that. I detest it when people call me *Jake*."

I shrugged. "Suit yourself. But remember—this is a no bullshit zone."

He let out a long breath. "What do you want?"

"You're in the process of making some arms deals for Ambrose Minor."

"So? It's what I do. It's not illegal."

"Well, some of the deals *could* be construed as illegal. I'm not a lawyer and, honestly, I really don't give a shit about legality, as evidenced by my casual use of this firearm. What I do care about, *Jacob*, is the Next Gen Soldier and who might get their grubby hands on it."

He sat back. "Uh—"

"Ah, ah," I said, waggling the gun. "I see you're already teetering on the edge of the bullshit zone. I thought we covered that."

He again held up a hand. "No. I mean, yes, I helped broker a deal for Ambrose and his new toy."

I grunted. "That *is* bullshit. For one, the Next Gen is not a toy; it's a goddamned killing machine. In fact, it's already killed several people, with more to come. A *lot* more. Many of those will be innocent Americans. And two, you aren't brokering just one deal. You started with General Sokolov and the Russians but certainly didn't stop there. Got some nasty little side groups interested. I'm gonna wanna know who, exactly." I waved the gun again. "Don't forget our little pinky swear regarding the truth."

His mouth fell open. He looked like a high school football player who'd been asked to name three state capitals. I'd obviously staggered Epperson by dropping Sokolov's name. That would go a long way toward prodding him to shoot straight with me.

He lowered his head and seemed to weigh his options, which were limited. He could give me what I wanted or face getting whacked by Minor's hit squad. I decided to give him a glimmer of hope, a lifeline he could cling to.

"Jacob, you might think I'm gonna extract what you know and then throw you in a cell. When, in reality, I don't give two shits about you or what you do, with just a few caveats. If you provide weapons to small-time hoods in foreign countries, it's unfortunate, but it doesn't make me lose sleep. When you sell to people who might kill my neighbors? Well, that makes my trigger finger get all twitchy. So, if you tell me everything I want to know and stop selling to terrorist groups and the RGF, I will let you and your groovy socks walk right out of this swanky hotel. I got bigger concerns than your skinny ass.

"But," I added, leaning forward, my elbows on my knees, keeping the Glock trained on his heart. "All my threats were *not* bullshit, my friend. I'll not only throw you under Ambrose Minor's bus, but I have connections with the CIA. They'll be happy to let Sokolov know you're telling his superiors in Moscow that he's planning to use the Next Gen to overthrow the Russian government."

He looked shocked, then grunted a laugh. "What a crock."

"To you, sure. To Sokolov? Man, I read a few reports of what he did to people who pissed him off." I gave a cartoon shudder. "So, to sum up: Tell me everything, walk out of here, and keep running up ridiculous bar tabs with sleaze bags. Screw with me, and you're dead without me having to do anything. Well, dead after they mutilate you a bit first. Minor and the Red General might race to see who can get to you first."

He sighed. "All right. But look, I really gotta pee. Can you let me do that? Then I'll talk to you."

I chuckled and stood up. "Sure. Let's go."

He looked up at me in horror. "You're not going in there with me."

"No. I'm going to check out the bathroom first, then let you stand there with the door open and do your business. Come on."

That's exactly what we did. I scanned the bathroom and poked around beneath the stack of towels to make sure he was serious about his timidity concerning weapons. Then, I waited just outside while he let loose an enviably powerful stream. When he finished, we went back into the bedroom.

"You've been a good boy so far," I said, "so I'll be magnanimous. Go ahead and put on a T-shirt. Then start talking. I got things to do."

When he was halfway dressed and situated on the edge of the bed again, he gave me a quizzical look. "Give me some direction here. What exactly are you looking for?"

I pulled out my phone and began recording our conversation. "I want to know everyone—*everyone*, Jacob—you've pitched the Next Gen to."

"Well, you know about Sokolov. I also mentioned it to someone with the ZRG."

I squinted. "ZRG. The cell in Africa?"

"Yeah."

In the grand scheme of things, they were small potatoes, a group involved in some of the nastier skirmishes on the continent. But definitely not big enough to afford what Ambrose would want for his technology. I felt like Epperson was stalling. He named another group or two, slightly more interesting.

Then he said, "And, uh, I've had one conversation with Viktor Ure."

I gave him a cold stare. "You what?"

He swallowed hard. "Hey, you wanted everything, so I'm telling you everything. I talked with Ure."

Viktor Ure was one of the more heinous up-and-coming terrorist leaders, responsible for a half dozen ugly attacks in Europe, Japan, and Australia. He was rumored to be gaining strength, attracting the usual sycophants who wanted to associate with anyone who held power and threatened violence against the status quo. He was like a freelance version of the world's name-brand terror groups. But Ure's attacks were savage and without the common religious motivation. More than once he'd hinted at an attack on US citizens overseas.

"How the hell did you find him?" I asked.

"I didn't. Some third party—someone working with Minor, I think—arranged for me to talk with him."

I knew damned well who that third party was.

I shook my head. "You know, I should just shoot you right now. You're going to put the Next Gen technology into the hands of someone you know will use it to wipe out thousands of innocent people? For a freakin' paycheck?"

He didn't answer. Just sat there with a glum look on his face. I mean, what *could* he say? The guy knew he was a scumbag. He just wanted our little interview to be over as soon as possible.

I sighed. "All right. I'll need you to write down the way you contact Ure." I saw him open his mouth to object; it was my turn to raise a hand. "No, that's not open for discussion. I know you probably don't talk to him directly, but you'll write down your contact information for his peons. Don't give me grief, Jake. You went from jerk to primo asshole really, really quickly, so you're in no position to bitch."

Epperson's voice came out as a whine. "What I'm trying to tell you is that whatever contact information I had is useless now. It never stays the same for more than a few days. They reach out to me." He leaned toward me. "Listen, whether I broker the deal or not, it's going to happen. Ure knows about Next Gen; he'll get it one way or another. Directly from Minor, if he has to."

"I doubt that."

"Why?"

"Two reasons. One, because Ambrose is too smart to show a direct link with anyone like Ure. He'll always use a dirtbag like you. And two, because Ambrose will either be in prison or dead. That's why. All right, let's move on to something else. I want to know where Ambrose is testing his handiwork."

He hesitated before answering, causing me to raise an eyebrow. That did the trick.

"Yeah, okay. It's in Georgia."

"I already knew that much. But I don't want to go door-to-door in the whole state. Narrow it down for me."

"I don't know." When I groaned in disgust, he quickly added, "They kept me in the back of a box truck for a couple of hours. It was better than being blindfolded or having a hood over my head."

I pursed my lips, thinking. What he was saying was believable. If I was Minor, I wouldn't want Epperson knowing where my testing grounds were, either. Or anyone else, for that matter. But I couldn't leave this hotel room without *something* to go on. It was actually Epperson who provided the answer.

"Look," he said. "I'm not a bad guy. I can help with this."

"I'm listening."

He fidgeted for a moment. "I'm supposed to have one more meeting at the training facility. I'm, uh, bringing someone to see for themselves."

I studied his face, which looked like the face of a six-year-old admitting that he'd just shoplifted a candy bar. And then it hit me.

"You've got to be shitting me. You're not seriously escorting Viktor Ure to a presentation."

He chewed his lip, then turned and looked out the room's window. "He says he won't use them against us. He says he just wants them for—"

"Oh, shut up, Jake."

I stood up again and paced the room, considering everything. My brain was reeling. One of the world's most wanted terrorists was either in the country or would be, attending a private showing of a tool he could later use to kill people. Lots of people. And the little shithead sitting in front of me could not have cared less about it, as long as it afforded him a glamorous lifestyle.

But he was right about one thing: It could definitely help me.

I sat back down and pointed the gun at his chest, just to let him know how deadly serious this conversation really was. "All right, Jacob. Here's what's going to happen. And, just so you know, this is not a negotiation. You're going to do everything I say, to the letter, or I won't wait for Ambrose or the Russians to kill your ass. I'll do it myself. And, if you couldn't guess, I'm really good at it. Are you following me?"

He gave a nervous nod of his head, still chewing on his lower lip.

"All right. You're going to that next appointment in Georgia, and you're going to be taking a little electronic toy along for the ride."

He shook his head. "No, man, that won't work. They scan everyone for a wire, a bug, anything like that. No phones allowed, obviously. It's serious security."

"Yeah, I'm sure it is. But we've been doing this spy game a lot longer than Ambrose Minor. They can scan you all day long and check all your body cavities, but they won't find what we're going to equip you with. And don't worry, it won't hurt much."

His eyes got wide. "Hey—"

"Remember, we're not negotiating. Now, tell me—when is this little field trip taking place?"

The answer surprised me but shouldn't have. I'd grown accustomed to government entities that would have a hard time keeping pace with a sloth. Private industries, especially boutique outfits like Minor Arms and Hedrick Sky, were nimble. They made things happen with a phone call, and sometimes not even *that* much prep. Factor in a wild card like Viktor Ure and you could toss out any semblance to routine. Fifty million dollars might turn on a split-second request and the subsequent reaction. A one hundred million dollar decision might take a *little* longer, pondered, perhaps, during the time it took to sip a cocktail.

And with groups skirting the boundaries of the law—or making no bones about dancing over those boundaries—payment was generally bloated and prompt, an added jackpot for people like Ambrose Minor.

So when Epperson told me he was due to visit Minor's facility in Georgia "sometime in the next three days," I blinked twice, then realized our entire operation could be decided—one way or another—within 72 hours. If I couldn't find a way to connect the dots between Minor and the trio of violent deaths we'd encountered, the crafty weapons dealer might actually get away with murder. Make that *murders*. Not to mention the countless bodies that surely would pile up in the near future.

I left the scuzzy middleman and his fancy socks with clear instructions: When he heard from Minor, he was to immediately contact us at the number I left for him. It would forward directly to me. He'd thrown a nervous glance at the Glock, but I was sure the most potent threat was the possible retaliation by Sokolov. I'd seen it in Epperson's eyes, the immediate fear. Hey, that kind of threat would've scared me straight, too.

On my way back to the airport, I spoke with Quanta and filled her in. As expected, she reacted to the same name that had shaken me.

"Ure," she said. "He's in the country now?"

"Or will be. Which puts us in an interesting spot. Can we capture him without jeopardizing the assignment at hand?"

The boss didn't hesitate. "I wouldn't look at it that way. I'd say there are now two assignments. If Mr. Ure decides to enter this country, it's your job to make sure he becomes a permanent guest. Understood?"

"Understood. I'm about to send Ure's contact information to Poole. A couple of names Epperson gave me. Might not do us much good right now, but if they're a conduit for Ure, they may do the same for other sleazy types. I'm leaving for Atlanta now. I'll wait there to hear from Epperson."

"All right," she said. "Anything else?"

"No. Nothing else at the moment. It looks like we'll be putting all our eggs in the Epperson basket. But, at least—" I stopped and looked at another incoming call. "Well, I'll be damned."

"What is it?" Quanta asked.

I chuckled. "Gotta hang up on you, boss. It's a call from Antoinette."

CHAPTER TWENTY-THREE

I answered the call and immediately asked the Bulgarian soldier if I could place her on a brief hold. I sounded like a customer service operator. But it wasn't often I was caught so totally off guard, and I wanted a moment to think through this unexpected development.

Minor knew I was bearing down. No matter how legit he positioned his business, he was smart enough to know things were precarious with the NGS project. In his mind, it made sense to stay in touch with me. Probably hoping I'd reveal what the government knew.

Or he just wanted to kill me. Which was more likely.

Putting Antoinette on hold was also a bit of a pissing game. After letting her sit for nearly a minute, I punched in the call. "What can I do for you, Ms. Lazarov?"

"I'm glad I was able to reach you, Mr. Swan. I'm calling at the request of Mr. Minor, who was interested in another social meeting."

"Another *social* meeting? Wow, we're really becoming pals, aren't we?"

She paused. "By social, I meant only that he'd like to meet for dinner someplace, rather than at the office."

I let her wait again, the seconds of silence dragging on. Finally, I said, "All right. When did Ambrose have in mind?"

"He's relatively free. What would work for your schedule?"

"How about tomorrow night?"

"Oh," she said. "Excellent. I will confirm that with Mr. Minor, but I'm sure he can accommodate it. As for location—"

"Yeah, about the location," I said, cutting her off. "I have another matter I'm investigating in Georgia. How would Atlanta work for him?"

I smiled as I pictured her on the other end of the call. A scowl on her face, her eyes—including the bionic one—narrowed. Pondering the significance of my request, calculating the odds of a coincidence, and realizing she had no choice but to say yes. I savored the moment while she silently worked through it.

"Yes, we can make that work," she said, just a touch of caution in her voice. "I'll send you details of the meeting location."

"Actually, I'll pick the spot this time. I'll text the time and location to you tomorrow afternoon."

I hung up before she could reply. Let her and her boss stew on that for the next 30 hours.

Poole arranged a car for me to make the commute from Jacksonville to Atlanta. I could've flown, but we had plenty of time before my meeting with Minor. And, honestly, I wanted the five hours to think. I'd always found long stretches of highway to be an incubator for puzzling out problems.

Now, with my playlist on shuffle, I steered the Audi west on I-10, letting my mind sift through everything. This case had already taken turns I'd never expected, and now, with the addition of an international terrorist thrown into the mix, it had achieved critical mass. Selling arms to a Russian general was concerning;

funneling those arms to Viktor Ure was something else. It shifted everything from a hypothetical scenario to the probable. Terrorists had no fear of the mutually assured destruction that helped to keep superpowers from doing something stupid.

By the time I reached the exit to I-75 North, I'd plunged deeper into the guts of the case. Down a different highway of the mind, a path I inevitably had to travel.

For Quanta, the assignments—now plural—involved Ambrose Minor, Antoinette Lazarov, Jacob Epperson, and the latest wild card, Viktor Ure. But for me, a fifth name bubbled beneath them all. The person who'd remained in the shadows from the beginning. The ultimate mastermind of this entire, sordid drama.

Somewhere out there, Beadle played the enigmatic role he'd perfected years ago. While we focused on Minor, Beadle worked as puppet master, pulling every string, all from the safety of a lair. He clearly orchestrated the connection with Ure. The darkest side of networking? That was his specialty.

All I wanted to do was drive this rat from his nest, out into the open, and eradicate him.

I no longer lied to myself about the obsession, which in some respects made it easier to pursue. It's more corrosive to our souls when we deny a fixation exists. I may never find absolute peace, even after dispatching the monster, but acceptance of my own personal vow of vengeance made the journey itself less damning.

My protective shell could be said to parallel the quest of Sir Galahad. Legend had it he was born to find the Holy Grail, that it represented his very reason for being. Late at night, before dropping off to sleep, I'd often wondered if that romantic notion of a sole purpose might apply to me. That everything I'd ever done, every choice I'd made, every *death*, had been put into play in order to deliver me, eventually, to Beadle's doorstep. My own quest.

And yet, if that were true, it would mean *everyone* was born with a singular purpose. I wasn't sure I subscribed to that concept. A world of people, each preloaded with a unique life mission, reduced our species to the level of ants, carrying out a task for no other reason than because it was in our genetic material, out of our control. The idea was far from romantic to me. It was depressing.

Easier to believe I was simply different. As long as I was an oddity, it didn't reflect on humanity as a whole. And, lord knows, I certainly qualified as an oddity.

I turned up the tunes and sped onward, toward Atlanta. And toward a showdown.

Traffic on Atlanta's highways, notorious for their gridlock, was unusually light. I made my way north to an area known as Buckhead, which, for purely juvenile reasons, always made me snicker. It's doubly funny because it's one of the snootier parts of town. But it's also one of my favorite spots in one of my favorite states. Although Georgia is dinged a few points for being overly infatuated with using the word "peach" in street and business names, to the point that directions can be confusing. Besides, if you ask anyone, the state's peaches don't drum up nearly as much loyalty as their biscuits. I mean —damn. But, even so, you're not likely to find any Biscuit Boulevards.

The Audi purred to a stop at the valet station in front of the St. Regis hotel. Poole had reserved a suite for me under one of my fake identities. No need to telegraph my location to Minor and his minions. After checking in, I left to catch dinner at one of the ritzy neighboring restaurants. I strolled several blocks, thankful to work out the stiffness of the long drive. I also used the time to phone Christina and was lucky enough to catch her.

"The last time you were in Georgia," she said, "you promised to bring me some peach jam."

She was right. But during that case I'd also been gunned down, a nasty shoot-out in a little place called Locust Grove. It was a valid excuse for neglecting the jam but not something I enjoyed talking about with my wife. She didn't need to know details about my various demises.

Instead, I chuckled and said, "I'll bring you a case this time. How are you feeling?"

"Oh, mostly the same."

"Mostly?"

"Things just feel like they shifted around in the last day. It's probably the baby dropping."

I stayed silent, mostly because I didn't know what that meant. In all of my multiple lives and in all the stressful situations I'd been in, I'd never dealt with a pregnancy. I was about as ignorant as you could get.

Christina picked up on my hesitation and laughed. "Don't worry, that's normal. It just means she's getting into position to be born."

"Oh. All right. In other words, she's the quarterback and she's now gone under center, ready to take the snap."

"Yes. Crudely put, but yes. How's my super spy? Nailed any bad guys today?"

"No, but they're in my sights. I'm having dinner with one of them tomorrow."

She let out a snort. "Babe, you have the oddest job. Dinner with the enemy."

"And since he's buying, I'm getting steak and an extremely expensive Pinot. I intend to enjoy every minute of his last meal, if that's the way it turns out."

"Oh, yum. That's one thing I've really missed these last few months: a bottle of wine. Tell me this: Does the bad guy know it could be one of his last meals?"

"This guy is pretty slippery. But I honestly hope to wrap everything up in the next few days. I need to put a bow on it in time to be there for your delivery."

"You're sweet, but we've talked about this. Antonio and

Marissa will be there, and I won't exactly be able to explain why some strange man is in the delivery room with us."

"Tell them I'm your cousin, in town for a few days. Or tell them I'm your life coach."

"You just wait at home and then I don't have to tell them anything. I really appreciate your kindness, Swan, and just knowing you want to be there is sweet. Believe me, I'll have enough of a cheering section on hand."

"All right. Well, I'll check back in tomorrow if I can. Tell me how much you miss me."

"Almost as much as I miss the wine."

"Hey, as long as I'm in the top three."

We said good night and ended the call. I let her think she'd allayed my concerns about not being there to support her. But the truth was, I felt like shit about it. While she was right about the awkwardness of having to explain my presence, it still felt like I was letting her down. Again.

Christina had known what she was getting into when we exchanged vows. I was gone way more than I was home, and even "home" wasn't normal, with each of us having our own place. But she insisted the arrangement worked for her and her sensibilities when it came to a relationship. And I went along because—well, because what choice did I have? Other than to retire from my life as a Q2 agent and maybe start selling real estate, like everyone else who left a career with no real plan in place.

I tucked my phone back into my pocket and hoped some fried Southern food and an old-fashioned made with good bourbon would numb the thoughts. Instead, I found myself standing outside one of those urban dog parks, a place where guilt-ravaged people who lived in a city condo brought their canines to give them at least a taste of what a dog's life should be. Every breed imaginable ran around within the fence, chasing each other, chasing a tennis ball, some just chasing the wind, running because they hadn't been able to since the last time they'd been inside their version of Oz. There was a palpable joy on each furry face, which, in turn, lifted my spirits. Sure, it was artificial turf instead of grass, but the dogs seemed okay with overlooking that minor detail in exchange for this splash of freedom.

We all—creatures of every type—find ways to adapt and make the best of it.

Even a freak of nature like me.

After walking around for another hour, I popped into an Irish pub, grabbed some shepherd's pie and a pint—the bourbon would have to wait—then went back to the hotel, uploaded, and crashed. In 24 hours, I'd be face-to-face with the man who'd already tried to kill me once, and who'd made his mark in this world by stopping at nothing until he succeeded.

CHAPTER TWENTY-FOUR

My text to Antoinette the next day at five o'clock was short and sweet:

7:15, Atlas, inside the St. Regis.

That gave me a couple of hours to kill. I picked up my car from the valet and disappeared for a while, so when I showed up at the appointed time, it didn't look like I was staying at the hotel. Minor would definitely have people watching and reporting.

In other circumstances, it might've been prudent to have my own backup present. But I was confident I'd taken enough precautions. I didn't expect Minor to have his people shoot me in the head. Not yet, anyway, and not in a public place.

I made sure to be properly tardy. At 7:25, I walked into the hotel and took the winding staircase to the restaurant on the second floor. Atlas is one of those dark but lively places where money is spent without a care. The bartenders maintain that perfect balance between fun and professional, and the food is first rate, even better when it's on someone else's tab.

The artwork on display was remarkable. The restaurant was owned by one of the world's largest collectors of fine art, and he shared his delights with the patrons.

This time, instead of sitting at a table in the back, Minor had reserved one of the private rooms. My favorite, actually. The restaurant called it the Papillon Room, and it sat right off the entrance. Floor-to-ceiling glass along one side allowed passersby in the hotel to gawk and wonder who the big shots might be who dined in this very expensive fishbowl.

The opposite wall was a bookshelf filled with impressive volumes, but also proudly displaying exotic stemware and a set of small teacups you'd never break out, not even for special occasions.

The walls and ceiling were adorned with small blue butterflies. Three thousand of them, to be exact. Papillon was, after all, the French word for butterfly. All I could think of when I heard the word, however, was the Steve McQueen movie.

Minor sat at the far end of the table, with Antoinette on his right, her back to the bookcase. Minor had his customary vodka martini in front of him, half empty, while the Bulgarian soldier sported a glass of water. With his thundering voice, Minor greeted me, getting to his feet but not offering a hand. We'd apparently left that stage of our relationship behind. Not a lot of handshakes when one person tries to kill another.

Once seated, I nodded hello across the table to Antoinette, then requested that overdue old-fashioned from the server.

"This was an excellent choice," Minor said, looking around the room. "It's been quite some time since I was here. I appreciate your taste."

"And I appreciate you securing this room," I said. "If we get crazy enough tonight, maybe we can break into one of the displays." I looked to my right, where a bottle of 1940 Macallan

Scotch—the only one of its kind left in the world—glistened from within a glass case. Across from it, in its own display, a bottle of Louis XIII Cognac beckoned. "Or we could just have wine."

He replied with a polite, quiet laugh. Quiet for him, at least.

"Glad you could make your way down to Atlanta," I said. "Hope it wasn't too much of an inconvenience."

He shook his head. "No, no. I love this town. Until I fell in love with the NGS project, I might've considered retiring here."

"Hard to imagine you retiring, Ambrose."

He chuckled. "I've spent the last 10 years staking out comfortable spots around the world. Even so, I originally thought about buying a second home here. Well, third, actually. I have a small place in Aspen."

"I didn't know Aspen had small places."

He answered with a half smile. "Thank you for agreeing to meet at such short notice. I was hoping we could—well, come to some sort of understanding."

I cocked my head to one side. "An understanding? Ambrose, I'm just trying to understand how you've managed to pull off everything you've done."

"You mean building a successful business?"

"Uh, no. That's not exactly what I had in mind. Given your personality type and ruthless business sense, it's no surprise you've kicked ass."

He pursed his lips while reaching for his cocktail. "I'm not sure I'd describe my business sense as 'ruthless.' Can we just say I'm very determined? And what's wrong with that? You strike me as a very determined man, as well."

I wanted to fire back, "I'm determined, but I don't kill people." The only problem was, I *did* kill people. And Minor knew it. Instead, I said, "I'm mostly curious about your relationship with Bryson Hedrick. You played along with his bullshit story about breaking into that hotel room, about stealing plans for your toy soldier. You conveniently ignored the part where you brought him aboard—temporarily—as a partner."

After leisurely glancing out the glass wall, an obvious move to stall for time, he shrugged. "I left out parts of my relationship with young Mr. Hedrick at his request. He couldn't let it be known he was operating without his father's blessing."

"But now that he's been murdered, there's no need for secrets."

"I was very sorry to hear of Bryson's death. He was an impassioned young man."

It was an odd way to describe someone you'd had killed, but I let it pass. "You terminated him."

I was well aware of the double meaning, and I watched his face as he absorbed the words. A flash of hatred passed through his eyes, and I swore I saw a small twitch beside one of them. Before he could answer, I clarified. "You ended the partnership."

This calmed him a touch, but not much. "By now you've done enough investigating to know this was a delicate relationship to begin with. Bryson Hedrick was enthusiastic about the future of the industry, but his father was—well, set in his ways. As much as I would've liked to nurture the alliance between our companies, I got the sense it could never work out."

"Even with the old man conveniently out of the way?"

I was pushing hard, which often delivered results. But I delighted in it, too.

Ambrose Minor, on the other hand, was not enjoying it one bit. Splotches of red had popped up around his neck, and the twitch intensified. He set down his empty glass and leaned back in his chair, trying to physically and symbolically distance himself from me. "I find your choice of language tonight quite distasteful, Mr. Swan. I'm not sure why you insist on trying to provoke me with these crude remarks. Would you like to clue me in?"

Taking a page from his book, I savored a long, slow sip from my cocktail while scanning the books staring back at me from the shelves. There were so many things I wanted to hurl at this smug killer, but there were far too many cards in play. The joker in the deck was Viktor Ure, and I couldn't say anything to spook Minor into canceling his appointment with the terrorist.

I threw a quick glance at Antoinette. She sat placidly, her fingers laced together on the table, her eyes, unblinking, focused on me. For a moment, I tried to peer inside the bionic eye. What exactly could she see with it? Did it read my body temperature? Could she detect the throbbing of the veins in my neck, instantly calculating a pulse rate, acting as a sort of lie detector? I had so many questions.

But there would be time to deal with Antoinette Lazarov later.

"All right," I finally said to Minor. "I'll tell you what's putting me in a foul mood. I think your Next Gen Soldier is going to wind up killing innocent people. You've put a lot of time and undoubtedly a lot of money into this creation of yours, a creation whose only purpose is to kill. Sooner or later, it's going to fall into the hands of someone—or a collection of someones—who will turn it against American citizens."

Minor caught the attention of the server and signaled for another round of drinks. Then he gave a low chuckle. "A very passionate argument, Eric. Spoken like a true patriot. But there are two flaws in your logic. For starters, there has never been a weapon of any kind that hasn't been used against all the peoples of the world. The first sticks and stones were used to batter neighboring people. Then knives and spears. Swords. Lancets. Crossbows. It took no time at all before they employed gunpowder to slaughter millions. There is no invention of war that has been exclusive to one group. Even the atomic bomb, the most deadly killing machine we've ever known, went from a secret American weapon to the point where nine countries now possess the capability. And those are only the ones we know about."

I grunted. "The fact that warfare escalates is not the issue here, Ambrose."

"It most certainly is. Your position is that the Next Gen Soldier will be employed to take innocent lives. I counter by saying that *all* weapons take innocent lives. They also are maintained to *protect* those same lives."

I opened my mouth to answer, but he raised a hand to cut me off. "Before you discount that argument, let me address the second flaw in your position. What you're neglecting is the peaceful application of the work we're doing."

"Oh, by all means, tell me how your killing machine will be our friend. Will we find them working as school crossing guards or something?"

He smiled at me and nodded thanks to the server who deposited our fresh drinks on the table. He held his vodka up to me in a toast, then took a sip.

"I've come to expect your snarky repartee," he said. "I suppose, to your way of thinking, it has a certain charm. But I must tell you, it often paints you as obtuse."

I laughed. "Guilty as charged, Ambrose. So educate me. How will your deadly machine make the world a better place? I'm all ears."

Now he leaned toward me, his forearms on the table. "Not the 'deadly machine' itself. But much of the basic technology. Specifically, the brain interface."

A cold dagger swept through me. There it was: confirmation of what Bryson Hedrick had casually mentioned. I slowly set down my drink and stared at him. "So, you've built a BCI to go with your cyborg?"

He answered by simply smiling.

"Those aren't new," I said. "But I'm guessing, just by the shit-eating grin on your face, that *your* interface is more developed. Otherwise, why mention it at all?"

"Oh, we've made good progress, yes."

My thoughts raced out of control. From the beginning of this assignment, we'd assumed the weapons maker was invested purely in the hardware side. His bionic soldiers could run and shoot, and their senses were electronically adapted beyond anything a normal human could manage. This already put them at a huge advantage on a battlefield or in an urban assault scenario.

But if his team had truly cracked the code on a brain-computer interface, or BCI, it added a layer of complexity far beyond a killer robot. It combined the physical tools with the marriage of a human brain and a supercomputer. The complete package.

Inhuman. Far *beyond* human, actually.

And even more deadly than we'd ever imagined.

He still said nothing, just enjoyed a slow sip of his drink while staring me down.

I inclined my head toward his assistant. "And your hired help —have you planted one of these chips in *her* head?"

"I'm not willing to share *too* much information. I've already given you far more than you expected. But—" He cast a quick glance at the soldier. "Antoinette is very gracious when it comes to keeping an open mind about any and all technological advances."

"Uh-huh. So she's willing to be your guinea pig. For a price."

Minor gave another grunt of laughter. "You keep talking about her as if she's not in the room. That's very rude. If you have a question, why not ask her directly?"

"All right." I turned toward her. "Do you have a BCI chip in your noggin, Ms. Lazarov?"

Her blank expression never changed. "That's none of your business."

Minor let out a laugh, and, with the magnitude of his voice, it caused the hostesses at the front of the restaurant to turn and look. I kept my eyes locked on hers.

Just for fun, I leaned close and pretended to peer deeply into her artificial eye. "Would I be able to tell by looking?" I paused, then added, "Open the pod bay doors, Hal."

She didn't hesitate with her answer. "I'm sorry, Dave, I'm afraid I can't do that."

Now it was my turn to laugh. Hearing the movie quote in her Bulgarian accent was the jolt I needed to get out of shock. I leaned back and held my drink up to her. "Touché."

Something wasn't right with this big reveal, and it was obvious. "Why are you suddenly telling me this?" I asked Minor.

He started to answer, but at that moment, the server returned to take our orders. I didn't need to look at a menu. I ordered the filet, medium well. I didn't hear what my companions ordered; my mind was whirling.

When we were again alone, Minor said, "To answer your question, Eric: I'm telling you this now because I think you and the people you answer to need to understand this project a little better than you do. From the beginning, I know you've approached the Next Gen program with fear and distrust—and I can't say I blame you for that.

"But what I've held back is the most critical component of our work. And I've held back that information for obvious security reasons. My company's security, not yours."

He paused, but I didn't interrupt.

"You see, my initial interest in the research was purely for military production purposes. That is, after all, where the bulk of our business is generated. It has been a lucrative and personally satisfying pursuit, and I could've easily retired by now. Many times in the last 10 years, I've considered turning the company over to a successor. And then I heard about the possibilities of an advanced fighting machine."

He tapped a stubby finger against the table. "I tell you, Eric, it's been a long time since I've been as energized at the potential of a new system. Building a new, large gun for a warship, or designing a ground-to-air defense system is strategic to our goals, naturally. But they're—let's just say they don't inspire me anymore."

He took a sip of vodka, glanced at Antoinette, who, of course, sat passively, then continued.

"The very concept ignited my passions. A soldier with such advanced physical tools—the eyes, the ears, the hands, the feet, the synergistic connection with its own weapons—well, I knew this was a futuristic soldier that was entirely achievable today. We've had the technology, for the most part, but no one has ever been able to make it work as one complete package. I knew I could do that, by building the right team around me, and by focusing all of my energy into every aspect. I oversaw the best researchers in the world, hired the greatest engineers, and spared no expense with materials."

I finally spoke up. "And poached the son of your biggest competitor."

His face clouded for a moment, but he let this latest jab pass without comment. He straightened his silverware before continuing.

"But what really made the entire enterprise complete, as you've now heard, is the brain component. Ms. Lazarov's eye was a great step forward. The advances in locomotion and dexterous abilities are nothing short of remarkable. All of that is true. But when our new scientific team showed me what could be possible with the neurological component? Well, it's made me eliminate the idea of retirement altogether."

I gave a slow nod. "I understand all that. But it doesn't answer my question."

Minor let out a long breath. "If it were up to me, I would never have told you any of this. But it's clear you report to people who would undoubtedly be interested in what we're accomplishing at Minor Arms."

"Of course we are," I said, growing irritated. "But—"

"Just a moment," he interrupted. "What I mean to say is: You've always been interested in the Next Gen program for its military applications, of course. But with the neuro-connection component, I believe it makes us indispensable to your government."

I stared hard at him, letting the words sink in. What Minor was basically saying to me was that his work before had been desirable to us. Now, it was critical. And that we needed to back off to assure he'd eventually play ball with us.

A subtle form of blackmail: Leave me alone, because toys you *thought* I had are nothing compared with the ones I *really* have. It was like worrying over an atomic bomb, and then discovering your enemy had a hydrogen bomb, which is 1,000 times more powerful. We had finally tiptoed up to the crux of the issue. This was Minor's hole card. And it was truly an ace.

And yet something was *still* wrong. There was a lot Minor didn't know about my progress in this case. He didn't know about my scouting trip to Honduras. He didn't know I'd tracked down Jacob Epperson—unless Jacob had been foolish enough to tip him off. And he didn't know I knew about Ure. For the time being, Minor was simply trying to swat away a pesky mosquito.

So why would he reveal his ace? What would have worried him enough to spill his guts, especially when he was within hours, practically, of making one deal with a Russian general and another with a terrorist? It didn't make sense. And things that didn't make sense worried me.

Could it possibly be nothing more than a stalling tactic? Something to get me to back off so he could make his dirty deals without me mucking up the works?

Possibly.

But Ambrose Minor hadn't come this far in a cutthroat industry by being careful. I looked at him, then at Antoinette—who'd spoken fewer than 20 words the entire time—and back to Minor. His smile seemed to say: *I've got you right where I want you: tied in knots, unsure how to maneuver.*

And he was exactly right.

CHAPTER TWENTY-FIVE

It was Quanta's idea for me to meet with our State Department friend, Jenna Macklin. It was late, and I'd just finished uploading after my unsettling dinner with Minor. I was tired, my brain was frazzled, and I wanted to sleep to satisfy both issues. But I agreed it would be wise to get Macklin updated on the most recent developments.

She answered on one ring and said Quanta had told her to expect my call. We kept it brief. She would fly to Atlanta in the morning for a late breakfast.

Before dropping off, I went back over everything Minor had told me. In the short time I'd investigated this case, he'd flip-flopped between extreme caution and gutsy risks. He'd kept his nose clean by using the services of people like Antoinette Lazarov, Bryson Hedrick, and Jacob Epperson. He let them do his dirty work while remaining behind a shield. But it was obvious he'd ordered a hit on me and would no doubt try something again when he got the chance.

What kept me awake for an extra hour, though, was the notion of his Next Gen Soldiers equipped with a BCI. As a science nerd, I'd read several pieces on the advances being made with artificial intelligence and robotics. The concept of a direct link from a computer to a human brain—itself naturally a super computer—was fascinating. Once the playground only for science-fiction authors, it had catapulted quickly from theory to design. The only problem had been perfecting it. On paper, it could work. In reality, it was a decade or two away.

At least, that's what we'd been told.

Intelligent cars had leaped ahead, to the point where they were cataloging millions of miles per year, improving each day. The technology used in aircraft basically allowed them to fly themselves. In financial services, computers could manage thousands of instant transactions that would take a human months to accomplish. And not just acting on instructions, but thinking through the various scenarios themselves and making decisions.

Now imagine those capabilities planted in your own brain. Imagine the quantum leap in learning, calculating, and implementing those decisions. Think what a weapon of war would look like if it could think like Japan's Fugaku supercomputer and fight like the Terminator. Now picture this away from the battlefield and walking beside you on the street.

At what point would so-called *normal* humans be able to compete in any endeavor? In many respects, a human-digital interface could be positive. Perhaps it was inevitable. As some say, "We're living in the future."

It's just that visions of the future alternate between phenomenal and frightening. Often within the same application.

Adding to my sense of uneasiness was how I personally fit into this discussion. One could argue I was already an absolute freak of nature; what would happen if we combined Q2's investment technology with a workable BCI implant? You'd essentially have a being who could stack life upon life, gathering not only physical experience through reanimation in new bodies, but with an exponential expansion of data.

I'd always suspected I was becoming a monster. With Minor's

BCI work married to God Maker's investment program, the debate would be over. It could—perhaps—make for a vastly superior being. But would that being still be human?

My soul—or what remained of it—screamed "No."

My last thought before falling asleep was how a tech advance of this nature would affect the last vestige of any personal life I held onto. Would it still be possible to have a relationship with Christina if both my body and my mind were artificial? Would my feelings be artificial, as well? How would I *know* what was real and what was programmed?

It was not a good night of sleep.

Jenna carried a to-go cup of coffee into the restaurant, something I always felt guilty about doing. She didn't care, even waving to the hostess with the hand holding the java. She sat down across from me and pulled a tablet from her bag.

"I understand you had an interesting dinner last night," she said. "How's our little arms dealer doing?"

"He's the kind of person you'd want coaching your football team. Always pressing, putting the other team on their heels, and never once going into a prevent defense. Attack, attack, attack. Smiling, of course."

She tapped her tablet to life with an electronic pen and smiled. "Do I detect a hint of admiration, Agent Swan?"

"Sure. Other than being a cold-blooded killer with perfectly clean hands, I wouldn't mind him calling the shots. It would never be a dull day, and you'd never find yourself playing catch-up. I admire the hell out of him." I paused, then added: "Which, to be honest, isn't new. There have been lots of creeps I've eliminated who I actually admired. It won't earn Minor any mercy points when the time comes."

She raised an eyebrow. "*Now* who sounds like a cold-blooded killer?"

I grunted a laugh. "Christ, Jenna—I've never denied that. Although I like to fool myself into thinking I'm more of a luke-warm-blooded killer."

"The killer with a heart?"

"More like the empathetic killer. I've learned to appreciate my foes, even if I have to wax them."

She gave me a look I recognized from countless discussions before with people who lived on the periphery of my work. They wanted to support what I did, while at the same time wondered how I could live with myself.

I didn't quite know the answer to that one.

"The reason I'm here," she said, "is because Quanta mentioned Viktor Ure. How reliable is the intel that he's coming to Atlanta?"

"I'd say pretty solid. You tell me, though, what you know about him. I only have a snapshot."

She tapped a file on her laptop. "I just sent you everything we have on him. It's more substantial than you might assume. Unlike many of the world's baddest bad guys, he doesn't remain holed up. He shows his face fairly often—not for long, naturally, but enough for us to have a healthy file on him. I think he likes it that way."

"That's your modern terrorist," I said. "Can't live without the notoriety. In most cases, it's more important than their 'cause.'"

"As you said, you already know about some of the items I sent you, but let me share something about his last known action. A tidbit you *wouldn't* have heard about." She paused. "And it's one reason I've come down here."

Over the next 15 minutes—and over some of the best biscuits and gravy I've had throughout my various lives—she told me about an operation Q2 wasn't privy to. Which was fair. We certainly didn't share the details of *our* adventures with the other alphabet agencies in the government. Sure, it might be more helpful in some cases if every agency disclosed all of their activities with the other guys. Might even reduce some redundant work.

But it also would create a headache of nonstop bureaucratic bullshit. It was bad enough having to write reports for your own supervisors; making sure all the other supervisors were up to snuff? Who needs that hassle? And let's face it, one group or another would ultimately complain they were being more forthcoming than their brethren. Finger-pointing would ensue. The CIA would cry that Homeland Security hadn't revealed everything, while the folks at NSA would bark at the special ops forces for not fully briefing them. Charges of favoritism would be lobbed at government officials who already were in over their heads, and everyone would end up distrusting the other teams even more than they did now.

Better to just let us each have our assignments, do our thing, and report back when it helped. We won't tell you how to kill your bad guys, and you stay off our backs, too.

According to Jenna, Viktor Ure's last confirmed attack had been the French train accident that had claimed nearly 80 lives and injured 130 others.

I frowned. "That was claimed by—shit, what are they called?"

"Well, they're known as Blood PMG. But *claimed* is the operative word. They took credit; but the point man on the operation was Ure. The CIA discovered he *loaned* his services. At least that was the word they used."

"So what is he now? A mercenary? Hiring himself out?"

"Yes. French intelligence told the CIA he's doing a few select jobs for various extremist groups, not only for some money, but as a way of building up a sort of terror capital. He wants these groups to owe him."

I shook my head and muttered, "What the hell?"

"There's more. My source at Langley tells me they've had someone inside Blood PMG for nearly a year. And the word there is that Ure is claiming he'll hit an American or British target within the next four months. He says it will get everyone's attention."

I pushed aside my plate. "And now he's coming to check out the Next Gen. If he's really hiring himself out these days, no doubt he's banking enough money to make some sort of deal. And yeah, any attack with an NGS would get everyone's attention."

Jenna let out a sigh. "Bombs, it would seem, are becoming passe, Eric. Today's terrorists are inspired by comic book movies. They don't want bombs, they want bombastic. Look at the train attack; it wasn't an explosion. It was an intricate act of sabotage on the rail line. Same effect, same carnage."

Jenna paid the tab—thank you, State Department—and we walked outside to a brisk, late morning. We still had plenty to talk about, so we turned right, crossed Peachtree Road (again with the peaches), and made our way toward a park. I needed the walk and the fresh air.

We strolled along a path that could use some maintenance work, then cut across the grass. It was a weekday, and the park was mostly empty. We passed a knot of college-aged kids congregated beneath a large, shady tree, and a certain aroma reached us a moment later. Jenna and I smiled, but said nothing. Hopefully they were done with classes for the day.

"Shouldn't you have heard from Epperson by now?" Jenna asked when we were again alone. "You don't think he's skipped out, do you?"

"I doubt it. He's pretty well invested with this now. Besides, he's legitimately worried about me turning General Sokolov against him. He'll call me. And with Minor in town, it should be any day now. What's really interesting is that—"

I broke off and Jenna looked up at me. "What is it?"

"Just keep walking for a minute," I said in a low voice.

She was former military, and it showed. She asked no more questions, and she didn't look around. She kept walking as if nothing was wrong.

And maybe nothing was. But after we'd gone another 100 feet, I said, "There's a man I'm pretty sure is tracking us. He was on the street across from the restaurant, supposedly talking on his phone. But three blocks later, I saw him on the other side of the street from us, paralleling us. Now he's here. In the park."

Jenna's voice level matched mine. "Could be a coincidence. It's a nice day."

But she didn't believe it. I certainly didn't. Especially since he'd disappeared when we were about a block away from the park, then showed up again a minute ago, coming toward us. He would've had to have run pretty fast to get ahead of us on a side street and then circle back our direction.

The man was in his 20s, tall and athletic, dressed in your basic tracksuit. As soon as I looked up and saw him heading our way, he pretended to look at a running watch and veered off in a jog, toward a stand of trees.

Something about the way he ran did not seem normal. I felt a tingle of alert ripple through me, and an alarm of sorts sounded in my brain, saying *You've seen this before*.

It was broad daylight in a park in Atlanta. What better time and location to catch someone off guard?

"Do you still see him?" Jenna asked, her pace picking up.

"No. He started running. About two o'clock." She understood I meant a direction. That's where the copse of trees stood. Our path was gradually circling that stretch of woods.

"Listen," I said. "We're going to stop in a few moments and act like we're going our separate ways. Maybe even a handshake. Then I want you to head back the other way. When you get about 50 yards back, swing around to the far side of those trees and circle around toward me."

"Will do," she said.

And that's what we did. We stopped, faced each other and carried on a bullshit conversation for a moment. Then she stuck out a hand, I shook it, and she walked away.

I leaned my head back, as if soaking in the sun's rays, then continued my walk. Two women passed going the opposite direction, but after that, the trail seemed empty. I could hear the busy sounds of Buckhead going on around me, but there was no one nearby. It was a perfect scenario for my mystery runner.

When he struck, I was lucky. I just happened to glance to my right, otherwise I would've missed the blur of a tall shape, speeding up on my right flank. At the last moment, I fell to a crouch as something whizzed over my head. Whatever it was, it missed me by no more than an inch or two.

I quickly discovered what it was. The blur came to a sudden stop, then swung the same object. I lunged to my left and heard it cut the air just beyond my face, again much too close for comfort. I put some space between me and my attacker, and the first thing I did was size up the weapon in his hand.

To call it a knife wouldn't do it justice. This had to be the most wicked-looking knife I'd ever seen, and I'd been in my share of nasty confrontations in some of the most frightening locations you can imagine, like jungles, terrorist camps, and St. Louis. The blade was a good 10 inches long and appeared razor-sharp on both edges. Sunlight actually glistened off one side, producing a brief, blinding flash. The handle was form-fitted to the hand—and that hand moved closer to me.

This is where my training kicked in, and, for one of the few times, I was grateful for the ass-kickings Quanta doled out on a semi-regular basis. I'd screwed up by leaving my gun back in the hotel room's safe. But while this guy had the weapon, I had the experience.

At least I hoped so.

I felt the initial blast of adrenaline ebb, and I centered myself, taking in everything. As he took one more step, I feinted back, which anyone with a brain would do when confronted with a killing machine. He probably expected me to back off, but he certainly didn't expect me to follow that with a leap-kick to his chest.

It was like kicking a brick wall. I staggered backward, and, for the first time, looked up into my opponent's face. He had a sharp jaw, a small nose, and close-cropped blond hair. Two large blue eyes sized up his surroundings.

And he was smiling.

He probably loved my reaction at bouncing off his chest. So much, in fact, that he paused to soak it in while I stood there, looking stunned and a little deflated. The bastard.

Well, I wasn't in the mood to start over fresh with a new body. That would set me back at least a couple of days and, by then, Minor could very well have finished up his business with Ure. I knew I was getting close to a showdown, and the last thing I needed was for this brute to jack up my plans.

My next move was something I often fell back on: Talk to the asshole.

"Where you from, cowboy?"

His eyes flickered, no doubt surprised at any conversation, given the setting. It usually scrambled the mind of an attacker, which gave me a slight advantage. But a moment later, he leapt toward me again, with a speed I could barely process. Again, I slipped to the side. Only this time, the blade made contact. I felt an intense, burning pain in my left shoulder and let out a small cry.

This emboldened my vicious friend, who planted his feet and took another swipe. It didn't kill me, but it clipped the little finger of my left hand.

Well, now I was pissed.

"How many gadgets do you have installed?" I asked. "Obviously the feet and the chest. Do you have Antoinette's eye? That's what I'd request."

He squinted at me, either out of confusion or as a way to use that eye to see something I couldn't.

I shuffled backward again, toward the stand of trees, and felt a small branch under my foot. I bent down and picked it up. It wasn't big enough to do damage, but it might act as a tool to deflect the next lunge by Edward Scissorhands. Although, to be honest, I felt a bit like a fool, brandishing a twig against his razor of death. But hey, you make do, right?

He must've found it amusing, too. His smile returned. And now he just toyed with me, feinting one direction, then stopping when I reacted, then feinting the other way. It had to be the most fun he'd had in ages, stalking a top-level government agent, like a cat tormenting a cornered mouse. The warning bells in my head told me I had less than a minute before the lights went out. I looked behind him to see if there was anyone who might call for help, but we had this little spot to ourselves. He'd picked the perfect place for his ambush.

All I could do was try for a lucky shot. Perhaps a kick to the head. Maybe, if the stars were aligned, I could dislodge the knife and shove it between those blue eyes.

At last, he spoke. "Drop the stick." The voice, higher than I expected, sounded European, although I couldn't place the origin.

"I can't," I said. "This is a magic stick. It's going to help me kill you."

He laughed again and, moving faster than I expected, rushed in, attempting to snatch the tree branch from my hand. I slipped to my right and, as hard as I could, brought my left knee up into his groin.

Listen, I don't care how many bionic components you've got, if one of them is not a ceramic willie, this will slow you down. He grunted and bent over. I slammed the side of his head with my magic branch, then got in another kick, this one to his chin. His head snapped back and he let out a roar. As he raised his knife, I lunged and punched him as hard as I could in his throat. This staggered him, but not as much as I needed. With his free hand, he shoved me backward with a force unlike any I'd experienced in hand-to-hand combat. I flew back, my feet unable to get traction, and I spilled onto my back.

With another growl, he took a step, raising the knife over his head. I started to roll to one side, but knew this was the end. Dammit.

But then it wasn't.

There was a small explosion of sound and the bionic beast, halfway down to me, suddenly flew sideways. I felt a warm spray cover my face, with a scent I'd smelled a thousand times in battle.

I scrambled to my feet and looked down at the man who now lay on his side, breathing hard, his hand clamped against a large wound in his left hip. I picked up the impressive knife glimmering in the grass and stared at the writhing monster who'd come that close to finishing me off.

I was aware of someone standing beside me, also breathing hard.

"I guess I should've mentioned that I wanted you to actually hustle around the trees, not saunter," I said.

Jenna chuckled. "Then there would've been no drama whatsoever."

I was conscious for the first time of a screaming pain in my left hand. I held it up, which brought another laugh from Jenna.

"Oh, no," she said. "How are you ever gonna count to 10?"

The little finger was missing the tip, sliced off cleanly, right at the last knuckle. The ring finger was mangled, too, but at least holding on.

"Well, that's just great," I said. Then I turned to look down at the weapon she held at her side. "I'm damned glad one of us brought a gun."

She gave a shrug. "Agent Fife told me I'd be foolish not to, especially if I was going to be hanging out with you."

CHAPTER TWENTY-SIX

The crew from Sanitation arrived minutes after the police and did their usual spit and polish act on an ugly situation. Jenna's badge helped, too. While one paramedic treated the NGS, I had the other bandage my hand.

I motioned to one of the Sanitation workers, the woman who'd smoothed things over with the cops, and she walked a few feet away with me. Two police officers kept watch over the bleeding man on the ground in case he tried to do his Road Runner trick.

I nodded toward the assassin. "As soon as they make sure he doesn't bleed to death, I want him shipped to DC," I said. "He's our lab rat. And the sooner, the better. I'd rather Atlanta police didn't spend too much time with him."

She didn't answer, but walked away to start working on whatever procedures would be necessary. God, I loved those guys.

Jenna came over, holding the knife. "I figured you'd want this as a souvenir."

I took it from her. It was a thing of beauty, if you overlooked my blood on the edge of the blade. I wiped it on my pants and examined it in the sun. "Nice heft," I said. "But I think it's designed for his style of hands, not mine. We'll give it to the lab people and see if they can figure out the connection."

She looked back at the NGS, now being attended by medical personnel. A third police officer, service weapon drawn, stood watch now. But I didn't think our mechanical man was in any condition to run for a while.

"Listen," I said to Jenna. "I haven't officially thanked you yet. You saved me from getting killed, and that would've been a terrible inconvenience right now. So thank you."

"Glad to be of service. And good to know military training doesn't wear off." She turned serious. "I assume you're taking him away for questioning."

I shook my head. "Honestly, I don't think there's anything he could tell us. Well, maybe under drugs. But I don't want him for his intel."

"No?"

"No. I want our people to go over every inch of him so I know what I'll be dealing with when Epperson and Ure get here."

She raised an eyebrow. "What are you saying? You want them to dissect this guy? Swan, I don't think they'll do that."

"Well, not that he doesn't have it coming, but we won't need to go that far. Just a solid inventory of his skill set would help. It's like when Alec Baldwin helped steal the submarine."

"What?"

I laughed. "*Hunt for Red October*. The movie. The US got their hands on a supersecret Russian sub so they could uncover all its surprises. With the help of Sean Connery, of course, playing a Russian captain with a Scottish accent." I looked over at the NGS. "This guy is our Red October."

We could've pulled off the debriefing over a video conference, but it was only 90 minutes to DC, and we had cargo that needed to be delivered there, anyway. I could be back in a flash when I heard from Epperson. This chat was too important to not be in person.

Quanta arranged for a private jet—she seemed to have them stashed all over the place. Within an hour, Jenna, two Sanitation workers, and a very sedated bionic soldier joined me for the ride. Besides being fast asleep, our mechanical man was under heavy restraints.

When we landed, a fake ambulance took charge of Sleeping Beauty, accompanied by the Sanitation duo. Jenna said her good-byes and headed back to her office at State. My ride patiently waited behind the wheel of a dark SUV, a smirk on his face.

"Cheating death again, I see," Fife said.

"Kinda the story of my life," I said as we sped toward Q2 headquarters. "But please, no questions. You'll just have to wait 'til we get there. I don't want to tell every story twice. When did you get back from Alabama?"

"Six hours ago. Been pulling data on private land in north Georgia, and looking for any possible thread to Ambrose Minor, his company, or even known associates. But this guy—I'm telling you, if someone really knows what they're doing, they can camouflage their activities pretty well."

"And if they can pay for it."

He laughed. "That helps. But it's crazy. We know he's got a base there but we can't find it. Not yet, anyway."

I looked out the window at the scenery racing by. "It almost doesn't matter. We'll track Epperson to the meeting."

"Right. I just wanted to get a jump-start so we could have some help scattered around. You won't always have a State Department employee hanging around to save your ass, ya know."

"Shut up and drive."

Quanta arrived at the drab Q2 building minutes after Fife and I walked in. Her gray expression conveyed weariness from making multiple trips to HQ. But it was more than that. We also had an NGS in custody and one of the world's most dangerous terrorists preparing to breach US soil. That was a lot of weight piled onto her small frame.

Poole had coffee, water, soda, and a nice selection of snacks set up. I helped myself to one of everything that contained sugar.

The boss wasted no time.

"You barely survived this ambush, Swan. And you wouldn't have done so if Jenna Macklin hadn't shown up."

"Well, I've often found the trick is simply to stay alive until help arrives. I might even have that put on a T-shirt. Where's our toy soldier?"

"One of the basement labs. I know you're hoping for a full analysis as quickly as possible, but I'd be surprised if you had much information before you fly back to Atlanta. Tell me your observations from your one-on-one."

I took a bite of a chocolate chip cookie—Poole was a goddess —and sat back. "If the NGS we saw in Honduras was an early prototype, I'd say this guy is version 2.0. Or maybe even 3.0. Both are remarkably quick, but the new model has lightning-fast hand reflexes to go along with ground speed. We wondered what combat with an NGS would look like; well, it's uncanny. That's the only way I can describe it. You could see him sizing up the situation and reacting within milliseconds. At least it seemed that fast."

Fife spoke up. "Is it possible Minor installed his bionic devices into a man who already had quick reflexes?"

"I've been in more *mano a mano* dustups than I can count, and there is *no one* who moves like this. He's human with inhuman characteristics. I'll be especially curious to see how the lab geeks break down the relationship between hands and weapons. He controlled that knife not like it was a tool, but more like it was an extension of his arm. Moving forward, I'm sure we can extrapolate what that might mean with a firearm."

Quanta said, "A direct link from the cerebellum in the brain."

I nodded. "Which would jibe with what Ambrose Minor talked about last night: the neuro-connection."

"Now, wait a minute," Fife said. "That's quite a technological jump, isn't it? How could something so new and so complex be kept quiet?"

"It's not new," Quanta said. "There have been major developments over the last few years. Much of it is being studied for helping people with spinal injuries, as well as prosthetics. No, it's not the technology that's surprising today; it's the leap into weaponization that has me concerned." She turned to Poole. "Do a deep dive into Minor's scientific team. I'd like to see if he's poached an expert or two from companies doing biometric and medical device engineering."

"Makes sense," I said. "But what we need right now is a way to defeat them. Other than relying on someone sneaking up on them and shooting them. We need a strategy to compete with them face-to-face. If Viktor Ure or some foreign agents or, hell, even a drug cartel, deploys a squadron of the things, we're hosed. We need a plan. And frankly, I think that's going to be a tough nut."

The room was silent for a moment. Then Quanta said, "We're on shaky legal ground here. This is not a robot we have in the basement; it's a human being. A sophisticated, highly modified human, but still a sentient being. We can't detain him indefinitely without charging him with a crime. And that supplies its own difficulties. Do we want to put a Next Gen Soldier on trial and expose the technology to the world? I'm sure we all agree that would not be ideal."

More silence greeted this. I imagined everyone was probably thinking what I was thinking, but no one wanted to say. So I finally did.

"We're not going to put this man on trial, and I think we all know that. It would be disastrous. And while I'm all in favor of due process, this man attempted to assassinate a government agent in order to aid and abet a transaction with a known terrorist. He's a casualty of war."

I watched Poole knit her brows over this. Even Fife seemed uncomfortable. But neither of them spoke up. As much as it might have made them squirm, they were content to let me be the bad guy.

It wasn't the first time. In my first few years with Q2, I'd suffered through these moral dilemmas, thinking and rethinking every position, questioning why I would do something a normal citizen might find reprehensible. But I finally reached a point where I realized it was a guilt I would just have to live with. I rationalized it by remembering what crimes we were talking about. The guy currently in the Q2 basement wasn't accused of embezzling or parking in a red zone. He was a party to not just murder, but mass murder. I was willing to shoulder the guilt on this call.

That still left us unclear on just what exactly we'd do with him. That decision would have to wait until after we'd examined him.

Something else occurred to me. "I know this might sound crazy, but when our medical and research guys are finished studying the NGS, could we—I don't know—reverse the process? You know, turn him back into a regular human?"

Fife leaned forward. "But he'd have to surrender some of his parts. Are you suggesting he go without a right hand? No feet? One eye? That's pretty ghoulish, isn't it?"

"Yes, it is, but that's not what I'm suggesting. We can fit him with traditional prosthetics. Do that, and rip out the neuro-connection from his brain, and he wouldn't be the same killing machine. I mean, he might have violence in his genes, but we could remove the unfair advantages he's been given so that he's just your regular, everyday, run-of-the-mill asshole."

Fife looked at Quanta. "He's got a good point. We could treat the bionic parts as loaners."

"And," I threw in, "maybe use those parts ourselves."

Quanta stared at me. For a moment, I thought she was going to scoff at my casual suggestion. But as the seconds ticked by, she may actually have been considering it. I had to admit, for an idea that had just popped into my head and out of my mouth with no gestation time whatsoever, I kinda liked it.

It was a shame we didn't have more time before the meeting between Minor and Ure. Why couldn't the NGS have tried to kill me a couple of days earlier and sped up this process?

"I'm going to table this discussion for the time being," Quanta said. "We'll learn as much as we can, as quickly as we can. Assuming we won't be able to ascertain enough before the confrontation in Georgia, you'll have to go in without any additional intel on the NGS."

When nobody spoke, she continued. "We've actually been given quite an opportunity, thanks to Ambrose Minor. By arranging a meeting on his property with a known international terrorist, he has unwittingly given us a legitimate excuse for an incursion. All we need is proof that Ure is on site, and that will eliminate any legal conflicts. It will instantly become a national security issue."

I tapped a finger on the table. "All I've wanted is for Minor to make one mistake. He's kept himself clean the whole time. This —" I glanced at Quanta. "This is the gaffe. Viktor Ure. Don't worry. I'll get the proof."

"Unless I beat you to it," Fife said. "I'm going in on this operation."

"You're not," I said.

"He is," Quanta said. "But not front line. He'll be running the operation from the perimeter. We are, however, allotting a tactical team to help with the incursion." She let out a long breath and rubbed her forehead. "I shouldn't have to remind anyone that this, too, is a massive legal nightmare. Get me Ure, and that will go a long way to validating the entire exercise."

She turned to Poole. "What's the status on Jacob Epperson and the tracking bots?"

Poole glanced at a note on her tablet and said, "Should be taking place right now."

While they talked, Fife leaned over to me and spoke in a low voice. "Tracking bots? Is this new?"

I put another cookie in my mouth. "Like little GPS trackers injected into the bloodstream. Only they're mostly alive, so they aren't detected by any electronic scanning device. Just the kind of nastiness they dream up around here."

"Why don't you have them in you?"

I shook my head. "You know I hate needles." When he opened his mouth to call bullshit, I smiled. "Kidding. No, the problem is, they only last about 72 hours." I popped in another small cookie. "I'm sure Jake is the most unhappy person in Jacksonville right about now."

The plan was for me to hurry back to Atlanta. A plane waited at Andrews Air Force Base.

But I told Quanta I'd need an hour for a quick errand. I'm sure she knew exactly what I was going to do.

The small bakery and coffee shop across from Christina's restaurant was mostly empty. I was at a table in the back when she walked in.

"Doesn't this place smell fantastic?" I asked as she lowered her very pregnant self into a chair.

She nodded and looked toward the display of baked goods. "I've been known to pop in for either their banana nut bread or the red velvet cake."

I grinned and moved a menu out of the way, revealing a small plate with a slice of banana nut bread. I pushed it over to her.

"God, if it wasn't so hard to maneuver right now, I'd climb

across this table and kiss you." She picked it up, then held it out toward me with raised eyebrows.

"No, thanks," I said. "I just put away so many cookies, the Keebler elves are threatening to go on strike. How's the restaurant been this afternoon?"

"Hectic. I wanted to work up to as close to delivery as I could. But it's getting to be too much. I'll give it at most another few days and then start my maternity leave."

The words rocked me. I mean, I'd obviously known she was pregnant for months, but the term "maternity leave" somehow made it all more real. And more frightening. I could only imagine the emotions ping-ponging through her mind and soul. My heart swelled more than usual—and I was already crazy about this woman, even after so many years. For a few seconds, I just stared across the table as she savored the bread.

I reached out and took her free hand. "I'm sorry I have to leave again. It's critical; otherwise, you know I'd be here."

She squeezed my hand. "I know. It's what I signed up for when I married a spy and when I agreed to be a surrogate." She laughed. "Don't worry. I'll be quite happy at home, watching my favorite shows, lying on my side on the couch. Oh, and I've rediscovered our building's pool. I love the feeling of weightlessness, even if it's just for a half hour."

Again, I felt a heavy sense of guilt. She was entering the home stretch, and I was getting back on a plane.

"Listen," I said. "I'll put this spy stuff to bed as quickly as I can. Quanta knows I'm taking a break after that to spend some time with you. So don't evict the little bugger until I get home, okay?"

She grinned. "Sometimes the tenant leaves on their own, you know?"

"So I've heard. Well, if you're confident you've got another week or two, I'm confident I'll conclude my business before then. But overall, you're feeling okay?"

"I feel sluggish, but nothing terrible. I've had it easy compared to a lot of women. But—" She paused. "You know what's funny about this? I'm sailing through a pregnancy with a child that's not even mine. The other night, just lying there, thinking about everything, I wondered if that had something to do with it."

I reached over and broke off a small piece of her banana nut bread. Some things are impossible to resist. "What do you mean?" I asked.

"Oh—" She paused again. "I agreed to help Antonio and Marissa because they're not able to do it, and I love them both, dearly. And a part of me wonders if I've had it easy because it's— oh, how do I put this? Because it's a gift for someone else, not for me." She flushed. "I know that sounds silly."

It was my turn to squeeze her hand. "No, it doesn't. And it makes sense to me."

"Really? Because I'll tell you something else I thought about, but I don't want you to brood over it or take it the wrong way."

"Uh-oh."

"No," she said, laughing. "It's not bad. But I've had a lot of time to think about what I'm going through. How I'm doing a job, really, to help someone else. I'm going through a sacrifice of sorts to bring life to their family. And last night—"

Her voice faded away. I forced her to make eye contact with me. "Go ahead. Last night what?"

She took a deep breath. "Last night, I thought about *your* job. How you sacrifice so much. Hell, you sacrifice *everything*, including your life. And you do it to help people you'll never meet. I know Marissa. I know Antonio. I care about them. But you'll go off today on some assignment and risk your life—and you'll do it for total strangers. I just find that . . . beautiful."

I was the one who broke eye contact. My chin sagged. Never —*never*—had I looked upon my job as something beautiful. My job was dirty. It was ugly. I felt like shit that my wife, doing such a selfless, altruistic act, was somehow trying to equate her generous and good-hearted deed with the bleak, horrific duties I performed.

Her soft fingers took hold of my chin and raised it back up until she was looking into my eyes.

"Listen to me, Swan. Don't think I'm unaware of the darkness you sometimes live inside. I know what torments you. I know you're searching for answers. And I know you often put on a mask for me. You pretend everything is rosy when I know it's not. You use gallows humor to compensate, probably to survive without losing your mind. Losing your sense of self. I *know* this."

The smile returned. "But I also know your heart. And I know you're doing a job very few people could ever do. It's difficult and it's messy. So when I say what you're doing is beautiful, I don't want you to discount that. You're sacrificing something I would never have the courage to do. You're sacrificing a piece of your soul. And I want you to know I appreciate it. If people could only know what you do, they'd appreciate it, too."

I waited a moment, then got up from my chair, went around the table and sat down beside her. I put an arm around her and rested my head against her shoulder. She leaned against me and we stayed like that for a long while.

I whispered into her ear. "I love you, Ms. Valdez."

She kissed my forehead. "I'm only Ms. Valdez on paper. In my heart, I'm Mrs. Swan."

CHAPTER TWENTY-SEVEN

It was 6 p.m. when our plane touched down in Atlanta. While Fife drove us to the hotel, I picked up a message from Poole. We had confirmation that Epperson had received his dose of tracking bots and—as expected—had pitched a fit. The little shit. I wished I'd been there to actually plunge the needle in myself. I would've given it an extra twist at the end.

Our timetable was almost perfect. As the hotel came into sight, my phone rang. It was Epperson.

"What's the word, Jake?" I said.

"I told you—I don't like being called that."

"Which makes no sense. *Jake* sounds like someone who'd be fun to hang out with, have some beers, catch a ballgame. *Jacob*, on the other hand, sounds like a skinny weasel who'd sell out his country to a foreign terrorist. So, again: What's the word? Did our friend call you?"

"I heard from his assistant. It's a woman—"

"Yeah. We've met. She gave me the eye." Next to me, Fife grunted a laugh. "So when do you arrive?"

"Tonight."

"*Tonight?*" I said.

"Yeah. I'm at the airport. I fly into Hartsfield-Jackson at nine o'clock. Then, I make my way to Sandy Springs. There's supposedly a room reserved for me there. They'll pick me up early tomorrow."

"How early?"

"Five-thirty. I'm only told it's a dark van. It's *always* a dark van. I don't know the license plate or anything like that."

"Doesn't matter. We'll be able to follow you."

His voice turned dark. "Yeah, and that's another thing. I don't appreciate you guys shooting poison or whatever into me."

"It's not poison, Jake. Although you might deserve a dose before this is all done."

"If I get cancer—"

"Christ, you bitch more than any traitor I've ever dealt with. You won't get cancer. At least not from this. You'll eventually sweat it out. Or piss it out. I can't remember the exact science. The point is, it's temporary, so relax. Now, what about the terrorist?"

"He's in the country. Somewhere on the East Coast."

I felt a shudder go through me. The fact that one of the world's most vicious killers could sneak within the borders made me sick. Well, as Quanta had pointed out, it was my job to make sure he never left. And it gave us an excuse to crash the party in Georgia. "Okay," I said. "How will you connect with him?"

"I don't know. I don't know when he arrives or where he's staying. He might already be with Minor."

I thought about this. It made sense that Minor would keep them separated.

"Any word on the demonstration?" I asked.

"Nothing. Just the flight, the hotel, and the pickup tomorrow morning. And if something changes, I can't exactly call or text to tell you about it once I leave the hotel. I'm not taking any chances for you."

"All right. Well, if things change, the little cancer bots will alert us."

"Screw you, Swan."

"While you're in such an agreeable mood, I'm going to tell you one more time: The most important thing for you to remember—and this is *very* important, Jacob—is to keep your mouth shut. One little slip, to anyone, and your world will become a nightmare of proportions you can't even fathom. Not a word. Especially once you get into that van tomorrow. Don't be fooled into thinking you're in a safe spot, because Ambrose Minor has killed people who meant a helluva lot more to him than you do. Are we clear?"

"Yes," he said in his sulking voice.

"Good. Text me the hotel information. Night night." I hung up.

Fife brought the car to a smooth stop at the valet stand. Before opening the door, he turned to look at me. "I take it we're set for launch."

I gave him a grin as my phone pinged with Epperson's text. "All systems go, Houston."

He laughed. "Godspeed, Eric Swan."

I went straight to my room, ordered room service, uploaded, changed the bandage on my hand, and made sure I was asleep before 10.

Fife met me in the lobby at three o'clock in the morning. The usual butterflies had set in. For some people, that might mean crippling nerves; for me, it was a high octane burst of adrenaline. On days when I knew the action would be cranked up to 11, I was like a racehorse in the gate, bristling for the start. That energy served me well.

My FBI friend and I didn't talk much on the drive, other than to go over the loose plan we'd already put together. There had been some discussion about when to make our move. Should we wait for the demonstration to begin? Or just confirm all the players were there and rush in? As I'd pointed out to Quanta, there were far too many jokers in this deck and I didn't want to take a chance of anyone leaving. Better to round them up as soon as possible.

Fife would drop me at the airport, then make his way north to Sandy Springs. From there, he'd track the van but would stay a healthy distance back. We didn't want to give Minor any idea we were on the prowl. With Epperson's tracking bots, it wasn't necessary to stay right on his tail.

Meanwhile, I would be airborne. An FBI helicopter awaited me at the airport. No matter where the dirtbags were headed, they wouldn't be able to give us the slip.

Fife took us through a security gate and cruised up to a private terminal. Before getting out, I shook his hand.

"Good luck," he said. "When you run into trouble—and we both know you will—be sure to holler, so I can rush in and save your ass."

"No one gives a pep talk quite like you, Fife." I winked and got out of the car.

Ten minutes later, I stood outside a converted Black Hawk helicopter. The pilot, a woman who went only by MJ, gave a thumbs-up in greeting. Her copilot looked young but capable. They both held large coffees. Three armed tactical agents were there, too, and each gave me the all-business nod while sizing me up, no doubt wondering what kind of hot dog they were risking their lives with. I didn't try to win them over. I'd been in their shoes many times during my military service, often assigned the task of supporting some hotshot I didn't know. You work shoulder to shoulder with your team and you trust them with your life. But a newcomer is a wild card—and those can be dangerous. Deadly, even. For these highly trained agents, *I* was the joker in the deck.

We made introductions, and I spent a few minutes finding out how much they knew about the assignment. They knew about the NGS, but not the fine details. I filled in the gaps and watched the information sink in. There were some exchanged glances, the kind that said, "*Is this shit for real?*" So I told them it most definitely was.

"You've never seen anything move like this," I said. "Don't assume I'm exaggerating, and don't be startled when it happens. Know that your enemy is lightning fast and react quickly yourself." I made eye contact with each of them. "Most importantly, remember that while it might seem like a machine, it's still a human soldier. Its enhanced abilities can be defeated with steady nerves and quick thinking. Fair enough?"

I got more nods in response.

They had no idea what they were in for, and there was really no way to prepare them. I hadn't been prepared in the Honduran jungle, even though I'd been told what to expect.

A minute later, another young man walked up, pulling a case on wheels behind him with one hand, holding a Mountain Dew with the other. He went straight to the chopper, stowed his gear, then came back and stretched out his hand to me. I shook it. It was sticky from his soda.

"I'm Sanchez. They usually call me Chez."

"Swan. What's your role here, Chez?"

He nodded back toward the helicopter. "Drone pilot." Then he took a swig and walked away.

He was an odd duck, which meant I immediately liked him. Even with his gross handshake.

We lifted off at 4:45.

Fife, who'd now been joined by two other agents, came across my earpiece at five. He was parked within sight of Epperson's hotel. Another team of eight agents were deployed nearby, some FBI, some Homeland Security. Not counting the two helicopter pilots, we numbered 15. Seemed like a good number to me. Enough to get the job done—I hoped—but not a damned platoon that would give everything away.

I was anxious that we didn't know where Viktor Ure might be, nor what kind of disguise he might employ. I doubted he'd be staying at Epperson's hotel, especially if, as I suspected, Beadle was behind the connection. Our only chance at nailing the terrorist would probably come at Minor's camp. If he was really there.

At 5:27, Fife's voice came through again. "Dark van just pulled up." After a pause, he said, "Yeah. Epperson just got in the back."

I checked the screen on my tablet. The little pale blue dot representing Jake—or, rather, representing the microscopic particles currently hitching a ride inside him—sat still. The goons sent by Minor were likely checking Epperson for a wire or other electronic devices. I could only imagine how freaked out he was by everything, perhaps on the verge of wetting himself, which brought me a measure of joy.

Two minutes later, the dot moved, coasting along gently on the map. I watched it make a few turns before settling in on Northbound 400, the highway snaking up into northern Georgia. I relayed this information to everyone.

"He'll be going right past us," Fife said. He was watching the same video game I was. "We'll wait till he zips by, then swing in behind him and stay about a half mile back."

I looked over at the three armed agents sitting in the rear of the helicopter with me. One was chewing gum, just staring straight ahead, while the other two looked like they were either asleep or meditating. Trained combat and SWAT personnel can always stay in a low gear until it's go time. They'd obviously paired me with experienced personnel. Quanta wouldn't have it any other way.

I had MJ take the helicopter onto a parallel course with the highway, but a few miles to the east and behind the moving dot. We'd be content to wait and watch. This might take a while.

The gum-chewer and I made eye contact, and I gave him a faint smile. He gave me a traditional bro-nod in return. For the first time, I noticed a scar along one side of his throat. Looked like an old knife wound he'd survived. Through our headset intercom system, he said, "You serve?"

"Did some time. You?"

"Four years."

I put a finger up to my own throat. "That where you got this?"

He shook his head. "That was a little misunderstanding back in the 'hood."

I raised an eyebrow. "Let me guess. That's how you ended up in the military."

"It was that or jail. But I did my time, got my degree, then went to Quantico."

"Gangs to GI to G-man," I said. "Impressive path. I'm a dropout, myself."

He gave me a quizzical look. Special agents needed at least a bachelor's degree.

I smiled at him again. "I'm what they call a special case."

He didn't look appeased at all, and I noticed his two sidekicks were now paying close attention, as well. Gum-chewer looked down at the shitty job I'd done on my new bandage, then back at my face. To his right, Chez fiddled with a tablet, totally disinterested.

"Don't worry, guys," I said to the attack team. "I'm smarter than I look."

They exchanged quick glances, but the conversation was over.

Near Lake Lanier, the vehicle carrying Epperson left the highway at a town called Cumming. This couldn't be the site of Minor's camp; it was too close to civilization. Something else was going on. Fife and his small team closed the gap. The two trucks with the other eight agents followed suit.

"Going into a parking garage," he announced over the radio. "Stand by."

We stood by, circling safely out of the way. Fife would linger outside the parking garage. It would only cause suspicion if he drove in and then followed them back out.

I noticed Chez crawl over to his fortified case and pop it open. Inside, a dull gray object sat secured in foam. It was the top of the drone. I watched the specialist tinker with it for a moment, checking something on the tablet. Then Fife was back.

"They weren't in there even two minutes. Exiting now."

I thought about this. "It's a transfer. My guess is they had Epperson in the van and Ure in another vehicle. This was consolidation."

"Same dark van," Fife said. "Mercedes Sprinter, the cargo variety. No windows in the back."

"Of course. All right, next stop should be the target zone."

The dot began moving again, returning to the highway and continuing north. Out of habit, I pulled out my Glock, did a quick check, then confirmed four spare magazines in my small pack.

The trek continued, and before long the van was cruising up Route 9. It passed through the small town of Dawsonville as the sun broke above the horizon. Dawsonville, according to a quick search on my phone, was the home of the Georgia Racing Hall of Fame. Must be heaven, I figured, for good ol' boys.

More time passed, and the dot migrated from one state route to another, until it was on 52. I heard a squawk from Fife. "He's turning."

The dot left 52 not far from a state park. I did a quick online check. It was called Amicalola Falls, and the photos were impressive. And, although it might not be relevant, the park had a feeder trail connecting to the Appalachian Trail. There was plenty of wide-open space in the area. Plenty of room for Minor to hide a small base.

"He's on a dirt road," Fife said. "I'm not comfortable following right behind him."

"We've got him," I said. "You can find a place to park."

MJ needed no prompting from me. She knew exactly how to pilot the ship in order to remain fairly invisible, keeping us high and wide, unlikely to be picked up by anyone in the van. Within 10 minutes, the dot pulled to a stop.

"This must be the place," I muttered into the radio. "Let's get some research on that property, okay? While you're doing that, we'll find a good spot where we can park this bird."

Another 10 minutes passed while Fife did some digging. Meanwhile, the eight trailing FBI agents had joined up with him in a parking lot. Everyone was coiled and ready.

"Sending you an info packet now," Fife reported. "And some people on our side are clearing things so you're not disturbed."

I smiled. My friend was speaking in a loose code, but I understood. Quanta had made calls to someone who made calls. Local law enforcement would leave us alone. There was no telling what was said, and it wasn't important. All that mattered was we'd be free to move around without having to answer to a curious deputy who might wander by.

I wondered if it would be enough. With a state park right next door, we had to provide for the possibility that things could spill over and get innocent civilians hurt. If that happened, it might be too much for even our brilliant Sanitation department to hush up.

The file sent by Fife pinged my phone. As expected, it didn't come right out and tell us much. Some of the land around the park had been in a private trust for years, predating the formation of Minor Arms. Another swath belonged to a family and, again, they'd held possession for many years.

Then I saw it. About 6,000 acres—roughly nine square miles —abutting the park, and held by another private trust. But this large, rectangular parcel of land had changed hands six years ago. This had to be Minor's playground.

I scanned the map and associated satellite photos for a minute, then radioed back to Fife, sharing my hunch. "The property just to the north of Minor's," I added, "is owned by a private family trust. How long will it take for you to get official clearance for us to muster our team there?"

"Officially? A while. Maybe even a day or two."

I chewed on that. "All right. Get someone to start the paperwork now, so it's on record, and we'll offer sincere apologies later."

Let Quanta worry about soothing hurt feelings among any outraged land owners. She had the political contacts to do that. We had business to attend to, and I wanted out of this helicopter. My butt was sore.

I worked my way up beside MJ. First, I showed her the map, then relayed the coordinates. I asked her to circle wide, come in low from the north to avoid flying over Minor's camp, and to find a good place to touch down. She gave her standard thumbs-up and went to work.

The landing zone was perfect. According to the satellite link, we were just under two miles from the edge of Minor's property, behind a large knoll and a shitload of trees. Of course, this was north Georgia; the whole place was a shitload of trees. The only building in sight was a long, low structure I recognized as a poultry house. Now deserted, it must've once held thousands of chickens. There was no sign of people.

It was 6:40, and daylight was in full effect. We climbed out of the chopper, dragging a couple of boxes of gear with us. Chez immediately went to work prepping the drone.

"Tell me about the camera on this thing," I said as he assembled some parts. He had another Mountain Dew sitting on the ground beside him. He must've carried a supply of them wherever he went.

He didn't look up from his task. "I can tell if someone's shoe is untied from 2,000 feet. In any kind of light. Or no light, for that matter. It's pretty cool shit."

"Quiet?"

He chuckled. "We'll be high enough they won't hear anything. But even if the thing was 20 feet overhead, they wouldn't be able to distinguish it from the wind." He finally looked at me with a half smile. "You must be an important dude. They've given you the best."

"The drone or you?"

"Oh, man, you have to ask?"

I'm telling you, I liked Chez. If his results panned out, I'd have to remember his name for future missions.

After studying the maps and data a little longer, I'd formulated a plan. We'd filter down from the north. The eight FBI agents currently gathered with Fife would split into two details, one approaching from the east, one from the south. That would give us coverage on three sides, with teams small and nimble enough to provide the stealth we'd need to get close.

All we needed now were the right players to show their faces.

CHAPTER TWENTY-EIGHT

A drone under the control of an amateur is basically useless, except as a toy.

A drone guided by a master technician is a remarkable weapon of war.

The sky had gradually slipped into an overcast gray, and Chez sat on a tree stump, a gamer's headset over one ear, his fingers deftly manipulating a pair of joysticks. His latest trusty can of soda, as yet unopened, perched beside him. There was a look of bliss on the young man's face, the expression you see when someone is dialed in, fully engrossed in a labor of love. Chez was born to do this work.

We'd trekked to within 200 yards of the border to Minor's property. I'd scouted ahead and found what appeared to be an innocent wire fence marking the boundary. I knew there wasn't an innocent bone in Minor's body. Opening my pack, I'd attached a couple of alligator clips to one of the wires and fed their signal into an app on my phone. As expected, the innocuous fence was part of an elaborate security system. One snip would sound an alert and we'd soon have a welcoming party bearing down on us. But I could disable the fence alarm easily enough.

I wasn't worried about motion sensors up ahead; there was way too much wildlife bounding around these parts of Georgia. And cameras, although possible, seemed impractical. Covering this much rural property would take a ridiculous number of units, not to mention an unwieldy number of people needed for monitoring. It was more likely we'd encounter a random patrol until we got close to the actual buildings. Until recently, Minor had probably never worried about his secret training ground being revealed.

Just to be safe, however, I did an electronic sweep with another gadget invented by the geeks on the second floor. It gave a negative response. Reassuring, to a certain extent, but nothing you'd want to gamble your life on.

I looked over Chez's shoulder. "Good to go?"

"All good," he said. "The little man is hovering at about 500 feet."

The gum-chewer stood to one side. "You sure that's high enough they won't see it?" he asked.

Chez grunted a laugh. "Got this thing in octopus mode."

"What does that mean? It has eight arms?"

"No, man. Octopus mode. The way an octopus will blend in with her surroundings. Practically invisible." He pointed up toward the sky. "My little man's main shell is coated with a sort of crystal ink. It looks at the sky above it and adjusts its belly to match that background. Not perfect, but I guarantee you'd never notice it unless you were looking for it."

He turned and looked at me. "You wanted the best? You got it. The camera is tuned, winds are light, and the digital gods are happy."

"Digital gods?" I said.

"Well, yeah. You're not wise to the ways of the digital gods?"

I just stared back at him, a smile on my face.

Chez shook his head, as if he were dealing with a moron. "Early humans had gods for the sun, for the rain. Gods provided the food. It was a god who guided you to the afterlife. Well, it's a new world. A digital world. You think the gods just retired or something? Hell no. The gods went back to school and learned how to code, man."

Now my smile turned into a laugh. "You're one weird dude, Chez. But if you work wonders for me tonight, I'll bow down and worship any digital god you put in front of me."

"Well, shit, Mr. Swan. They're *all* right in front of you. You deal with them every day." He turned back to his work. "But I'm tight with them. We'll give you a good show today."

I patted him on the shoulder and walked away, then radioed Fife. "Everyone in position?"

"In position and holding. I'm in the lower lot of the state park. Normally it opens at seven o'clock, but we've just closed the main gates and had the rangers rounding up the few people who already got in. They're telling them there's emergency maintenance going on. From what I understand, there are only a few stragglers right now, and we expect them out of here in the next half hour."

"Good. Stand by." I adjusted the radio for all of the team members. "All right, listen up. We're sending in the eye in the sky. Stay alert, we might have to move fast."

Each group checked in, and I turned back to Chez. "Any time you're ready."

Without saying a word, he flexed his fingers in the air in front of him, then sent the drone on its way. Even though I had access on my phone to the same digital picture Chez was getting, I hunkered down and watched his screen. The airborne robot gained altitude as it approached some buildings on Minor's property, reaching 900 feet. As promised, the image was crystal clear.

And disturbing. Every time I saw a new iteration of our surveillance capabilities, I wondered again what kind of existence we'd condemned ourselves to: a world where we were no longer safe from prying eyes in our daily life, and where there were fewer places you could hide. Hell, we were practically in the middle of nowhere, and Chez's "little man" was primed to reveal anything and everything about the people strolling through the woods three football fields below its sharp eyes. Sure, it was about to help me against some really bad people—but you had to wonder how many good people had their privacy invaded on a regular basis.

We want the security. I'm just not sure we truly comprehend the price.

I watched the detail as it filled the screen, and that made me think of something else. How close to this resolution did Minor's bionic eye reach? What did Antoinette see with that optical marvel when she cooly appraised me at dinner? It wasn't hard to imagine she had X-ray vision with that thing and she knew exactly what kind of gun I was packing under the jacket. Or what I was packing elsewhere. Oh, my.

"Got a citizen," Chez said.

Sure enough, a man showed up on the high-def screen. He wasn't from the primary cast of characters; based on the weapon slung across his shoulder, he was hired help, part of the patrol I'd imagined. We marked his position on our maps and the drone continued on course.

"The cool thing about my little man," Chez said, "is he'll find people without even looking for them."

"Heat signature?" I asked.

"Yeah. It's not perfect yet, but it's getting there. The really cool shit, though, is coming in a few months."

"Describe the cool shit."

"Listening for human sounds."

"Shut up."

Chez laughed. "I shit you not, man. He'll be able to detect sounds up to 3,000 feet. Heartbeats. Respiration. Coughing. Farts. He'll collect it all."

"How the hell will he distinguish it from animal life?"

This earned another glance over the shoulder. "Oh, man, come on. Artificial intelligence. It sees all; it knows all."

"And hears all."

"True that."

"All right. For now, try to find anyone who might be along our path. Even if they're hidden."

Chez gave a snort. "Before long, assholes won't be able to hide from the little man unless they're dead."

All I could do was shake my head. A few seconds later, to prove Chez's point, the camera spun its field of vision to one side and zoomed. This time there were two men, both sitting on large rocks, deep in conversation, oblivious to the probe overhead. They, too, became red marks on our map.

"Coming up on the main complex," Chez said. "Pulling up another hundred feet."

The boost in altitude didn't matter. My funky drone master simply adjusted the resolution on the camera. Soon, we had a wide view of Minor's primary operating area. I leaned forward and studied it.

"Confirming that you're getting all this," I radioed to Fife.

"Just like a movie," he said. "All I need is the popcorn and some Junior Mints."

"There are quite a few people down there," I said. "We know who our key players are. But everyone keep their eyes peeled for Ure. I want confirmation he's got a ticket to today's show. Sing out if you think you spot him."

Another five minutes passed. For a moment, my mind wandered back to my military experiences, to some of the sorties I'd undertaken in tough spots around the world. How much I would've given to have access to this remarkable technology. Some people would've come home with us in the passenger section of the plane instead of the cargo hold.

I spotted something. "Wait," I said. "Pan back. Yeah, there. Give me just a touch more zoom, please."

Chez fiddled with something and the screen shifted. A familiar face came into focus.

"There's our host," I said. Ambrose Minor stood outside the door of a small building. It looked like he was—

Yes, he was. He was smoking a cigar. What a tool. "Okay, if Minor's right here, I don't think Epperson or Ure will be too far behind." To Chez, I said, "Pull back just a touch. Show me the area around Minor."

A moment later, someone else came into the picture.

Antoinette Lazarov. Minor's test subject and Bulgarian guard dog stood at his side, listening to instructions.

Since the day we'd met, I'd suspected we'd eventually come face-to-face in some sort of conflict. So there was no real surprise here. Just acceptance.

I chewed on my lower lip. "Total distance from here to that main camp?"

"Two and a half kilometers."

I was about to radio Fife when, on the video screen, Minor and Antoinette both turned. Two other people had joined them.

"Oh, that's definitely our target," I heard Fife say.

He was right. As clear as if he were standing 10 feet from me, I looked at the face of Viktor Ure. "Gotcha, you son of a bitch," I muttered.

Then, louder, I added for the group: "That's Ure. Next to him is Jacob Epperson. I want to be clear: Taking Ure alive is a priority. Unless your own life is in jeopardy, it would be best if we could question this sleaze. And one last reminder: Do not take the Next Gen Soldiers lightly. We don't know how many are here, but do not be startled if you encounter one or more. React with your training. Copy that?"

Each group responded, and all I could do was hope they took me seriously.

"Chez, keep watching for a minute or two, then send your little friend to check out the routes for the other two assault teams. Feed the results to them so they know what's between them and the main camp. Meanwhile, my team will start. We'll make our way to the three lookouts and incapacitate them. Then, once we're within 100 yards, we'll hold until each team is in a similar position. Everyone clear?"

They were. I tapped Chez on the shoulder and said, "Keep in touch. You're the eyes and ears until we jump into the fire." He just nodded, then finally opened the Mountain Dew that had been sitting beside him.

I turned to my three armed companions. "Okay. Let's go hunting."

They picked up their gear and started toward the fence. I was about to join them when I happened to take one more glance at the video screen. Another person had joined Minor, Antoinette, Epperson, and Ure. A man of about medium height and build.

I didn't think much at first, figuring it was just another one of Minor's flunkies.

Then I froze. My eyes zeroed in on the man who now spoke to Ambrose Minor. I felt a cold chill run through me, and my fingers involuntarily clenched into a fist. It had been a while since I'd seen that face, but it was certainly a face I'd never, ever forget.

Beadle.

CHAPTER TWENTY-NINE

Of course. It had to be him. Who else could've arranged everything to get Viktor Ure safely into and—ideally for them— back out of the country? He was the monster behind multiple tragedies that had taken thousands of lives, both in the US and around the globe. He was more than just a heartless mercenary; he was evil personified. I'd hunted him for too many years, and failed again and again to bring him down.

The last time I'd seen him in person, I'd managed to wound him. But, like every other time, he'd wriggled away.

Now I stood less than two miles from him, staring at his image.

After a few seconds, I tore myself away from the screen. I didn't want to waste any more time. Now, on top of my assignment with Minor and Ure, I had a separate agenda. It could easily be categorized as a critical job for Q2, as vital as the need to capture Viktor Ure. But this was also personal.

My heart rate had picked up, and I took a series of deep breaths to flush out the wave of emotions suddenly vying for attention. I had to stay focused on the primary mission.

"Let's go," I said to my team. We set off to the south, with the gum-chewer—okay, so his name was Oberg—taking the point. He insisted on it. Gung ho, that one. Bolton, tall and muscular, was next. Then me. The quietest one of the bunch, Kemp, brought up the rear. I got the sense he might be the most reliable of the three, and I was good with him protecting the flank.

Memories of my special ops days swept back to me, and I felt the familiar surge of healthy adrenaline beginning to work its magic. I didn't have Antoinette's bionic vision, but I always swore my eyesight grew just a bit sharper whenever I was on a patrol. Maybe it was survival instinct. Or maybe I was somehow wired that way. If so, it wasn't a purely physical trait because it migrated with me from body to body. I'd decided it was part of my mental makeup, as if my brain performed a manual override of the body's visual acuity center.

We'd paired our phones with the data from the drone, which would lead us to the three guards standing between us and the main camp. First, we had to deal with the fence.

Oberg reached it and looked back at me. As much as he seemed to distrust me, he knew I'd have some gadget to get us in.

Naturally, I did. I knelt at a likely spot along the wires and studied them for a moment before opening my pack. I removed a series of small clips and a tiny black box. Taking my time, I attached one of the clips along the top wire, then flipped a switch on the box. Opening an app on my phone, I studied the signal from the clip. It registered a flat line. Removing the clip, I repeated the procedure on the other four wires.

Two of them—second from the top and second from the bottom—pegged the meter on the black box. Fair enough. Two of the wires were charged, not with voltage for defense purposes, but as an alert system. I spent three minutes attaching more of the clips on those two live wires, then performed some tasks on both the box and my app.

"Not to mess with your mojo," I heard Oberg say beside me. "But I'd love to know what you're doing."

"I'm fooling the system monitoring the perimeter," I said. "Once I get this set up, we can cut the wires between these clips and the system will continue to read that they're intact. Sort of like a digital patch." I tapped two more buttons on my phone. "In fact, it's done."

I stood up. "If you'd be so kind as to snip these, we can waltz in."

He hesitated, then, without a word, took a pair of wire cutters from a jacket pocket. In seconds, he'd finished the job.

"You're sure this didn't set off an alarm up ahead?" he asked.

I shrugged. "Well, if it did, we'll know pretty damned quick. Or, at least, you will, since you're on point." I gestured ahead. "Lead the way."

He shook his head but slipped through the opening in the fence. The rest of us followed. In a low voice, I contacted the other teams. One of them was in on the north side, using the same toy I had, and the other was in the process of setting it up. Fife chimed in, saying the park was officially empty of civilians.

"One empty vehicle, an SUV, in the lot at the top of the falls," he said. "Otherwise, no one around. There are rangers stationed at the hotel to keep people from wandering into the park. Same with the hiking trails that empty into the park. They'll keep people out.

"But just a heads-up," Fife added. "Some big shot with the parks service is insisting on staying on site with a team of people. Kinda being territorial, if you know what I mean."

It wasn't that unusual. Local police and, yes, even park rangers usually resented being elbowed out of the way by the feds. Guess I couldn't blame them. It was their turf, after all.

We went silent and continued our trek through the woods. According to the drone's map, we were 50 yards from the first guard. I signaled Oberg, who nodded. We crept forward, keeping low and being mindful of every step, wary of making any sounds.

A few seconds later, I saw Oberg stop and drop to a knee. The rest of us did the same.

My point man looked back and waved me up. Kneeling beside him, I peered in the direction he was pointing and easily saw the guard, standing in the shadows. He was looking at something on his phone, the glare illuminating his bearded face. I retrieved a tranquilizer pistol from my pack and checked to make sure it was ready. Motioning for Oberg and the others to stay put, I moved a little closer to the man studying his phone. He was in profile, so he'd need good peripheral vision to pick up any movement. I relied on him being completely absorbed by whatever was on his screen.

At 20 feet, I knelt again, and waited for him to pocket the phone. I couldn't take a chance that he was communicating with someone. After a minute, he chuckled about something, and slid the phone into his jacket. I immediately raised the pistol, took aim, and placed a dart perfectly into his neck. His right hand shot up, like he'd been stung by a wasp, but two seconds later, he collapsed in a heap. He'd be sound asleep for the next five hours.

I waved the team up. While I reported the news to Fife, Bolton and Kemp secured the guard with zip ties and collected his weapon. After marking the exact spot on our map so Sleeping Beauty could be retrieved later, we moved on.

The next two sentries went down just as easily, leaving us a clear path to Minor's base. Chez confirmed we were 100 yards due north of the first building. We waited five minutes, until getting word that the other two teams were in place, also a hundred yards out. We essentially had Minor's camp bracketed.

"All right," I said to my unit. "I'll move to point. Oberg and Bolton, to my right. Kemp, hang back for a few minutes, then track to my left." They each nodded, and we moved off.

Soon, we made out some buildings of the camp. Not long after that, we heard the sounds. I stopped and checked in with Chez, speaking in a low voice. "Any changes?"

"Everything is peaceful. The gods say you're good to go."

"Amen," I said.

Fife's voice came in. "You might want to hold up a second, Eric."

"What's up?"

"A message from the boss."

I scowled. "*Now?* We're a little busy."

"Well, hunker down for a second. It's labeled a priority. You need to check it out before moving forward."

With a sigh, I motioned for the others in my group to hold. "All right, send it through."

I pulled out my tablet just as the file arrived. It included one long text document along with what looked like diagrams.

"Shit, I don't have time for this right now," I repeated. "Fife, have you skimmed this already?"

"I did."

"Give me the highlights."

"There's been a breakthrough in regard to that NGS you brought back from Atlanta. They still have a long way to go, but they feel that one bit of information could be helpful with our assault. So they're passing it along."

I looked ahead toward Minor's camp. It was true; any piece of news about the cyborg soldiers in that camp might save lives. Maybe my own.

"Okay," I said. "Share it with all of us."

"The research team put the bionic elements on the back burner once they heard about the neuro-link component. We can always figure out the enhanced eyes and limbs. They felt the brain connection was the most likely shortcut to overcoming these things."

"Makes sense," I said. "What'd they find?"

"They found the small pack these things have attached to the back of their neck includes a thin probe that enters the base of the skull and creates some vague interface. They think it's crude for now but will likely expand quickly. They just need more and more data, which is what these current NGS models are delivering."

"Fife," I said. "Do they have something to help us or not?"

"Sorta." Before I could cut him off with an expletive, he pushed on. "What they *do* know is that the connection is electrically based. So it can—"

"It can be jammed!"

The exclamation wasn't from me. It was Chez, his voice animated over the comm connection.

"Yeah," he continued. "It would all have to be electricity. And anything electrical can be interfered with."

"Chez, are you saying you could do this?" I asked.

"I could try. The little man can broadcast as well as he receives. How much information do they have on this electrical connection?"

Fife said, "It's all in the documents they sent. But they warned us it's not much. In a nutshell, each soldier will not only be wired differently, but will interface with the control unit through their own biomedical frequency. And that can be as unique as a fingerprint."

I thought about this, still looking ahead at the camp. "So it would have to be a series of random signals. Trial and error." I grunted. "That doesn't help us much. Chez would need to pick a frequency, send a jamming signal, and we'd have to report on whether or not it worked before he could try again. There must be thousands of possible frequencies."

"No," Fife said. "They all fall within a range. Not unlike FM radio frequencies all falling within a fairly narrow band."

Chez spoke up again. "Give me some time, and I can create a program that would let the little man dish up a mess of signals. Sort of like a—like a rotating series of them."

"How long?" I asked.

"I'll get right on it."

Which meant he didn't know. But our teams were poised right now, 100 yards from Minor, Ure, and an unknown number of bionic devils. It wouldn't be long before they realized they'd lost contact with their sentries. And they'd come looking. Or shut everything down and evacuate everyone, including Ure.

And Beadle.

This is where it took every ounce of professional strength I could muster. My emotions were telling me to charge in there, root out that bastard, and put him down like the rabid dog he was. But a charge like that, against an advanced enemy like the NGS, could prove deadly to not only me, but to my team members. I couldn't get them killed just to satisfy my own blood-lust for Beadle.

And yet, it also couldn't be denied that we were pressed for time. We'd flipped the hourglass once we took down the guards inside the gate, and the sands were now racing through to the other side.

Sometimes all I wanted was a classic Old-West shoot-out. Just me and Beadle, standing in a dusty street outside the saloon, six-shooters hanging from our holsters, facing each other at 20 paces, waiting for the other to flinch so we could draw.

The fantasy would have to wait.

"Chez, get me a solution on that program. We'll wait 15 minutes. But after that, we can't risk getting discovered. We want surprise on our side."

"Will do," the drone master said.

"Fife," I said, "keep sifting through the files. Let me know if you spot anything else. Oberg, keep an eye on things for a few minutes."

"Where are you going?" the gum-chewer said.

"I'm gonna sneak in a little closer. We could use a little more intel from the inside. If I've got 15 minutes, I'm gonna use them to find Epperson."

Nobody spoke. I was sure they all thought it was a dangerous move. But the entire mission was dangerous as hell.

With my Glock at the ready, I pushed through the underbrush toward the camp. Whether I found Epperson or not, it couldn't hurt to see the enemy's position from ground level, rather than just the bird's-eye view we'd relied on to this point.

"Chez," I said in a low voice, "give me another quick check between the camp and my position. I don't want to stumble across anyone out taking a leak."

"Already done," he said. "All clear. I'll stay on this location and let you know if anything changes."

I reached the edge of the camp and knelt behind a large, fallen tree. Scanning the area, I saw a cluster of small cabins and, farther ahead, what looked like a lodge. This was probably where most of the business was transacted. I saw two people walking toward that lodge, engaged in conversation, but didn't recognize either of them. Then one of the cabin doors opened, and a woman stepped out. She was on her phone, carrying on a conversation in Spanish. She stayed on the front steps for a moment, talking and looking up through the trees at the sky.

"Yeah, yeah, wrap it up," I muttered to myself. She obliged, ending the call, then turned toward the lodge. It left me alone at this end of the camp. Keeping low, I scurried toward one of the cabins and pressed myself against the far side, remaining in the shadows. Everything was still and quiet. I assumed most people were indoors, perhaps having breakfast.

Each cabin had two windows on the side facing the woods. In two of the cabins, a small glow from the inside told me they might be occupied. But after scampering up to each and peeking in, I found them all deserted.

This surveillance from the shadows wasn't working. I needed to insert myself into the game a little more. Reckless, for sure, but I hated going into battle blind. Besides, Epperson was useless as a mole if I didn't get shit out of him.

"Nobody on the perimeter," I said to the team. "I'm gonna wander in and see what I can find."

"Uh—" Fife said, but then realized he was wasting his breath. "Try not to get killed. It'll slow down everything if we have to keep dragging your body along behind us."

I grinned and holstered the Glock inside my jacket. Best to look like just another face in the crowd if anyone saw me through a window. Maybe there were enough people around here that one more face wouldn't stand out. I just couldn't stumble into any of the assholes I actually knew.

I set a course for the lodge, then veered off to one side. A man came out of a small building and threw me a quick glance. I gave a wave, which must've been good enough for him. He returned a half-hearted wave and walked off. I'm telling you—just act like you know what you're doing.

Significant noise emanated from the lodge, confirming that it must be meal time. I imagined Minor, in his booming voice, holding court with Ure and everyone else within the room. Ure, meanwhile, was probably eager to get the whole thing over with and to acquire his new weapon. Which he undoubtedly would enjoy using first on his obnoxiously loud host.

Patience, I told myself. If something was going to happen, I couldn't force it. I made a leisurely stroll around the camp, noting the positions of the buildings, looking for anything unusual. On the far side from where I'd entered, a path led into the woods. I knew from the drone map that it led into the state park. And to the falls.

I casually walked behind one cabin and checked in. "Chez, anything?" I muttered.

"There are two guys near the north end of the camp. Pretty much where you entered. I think they're trying to reach the jerks we knocked out. Yeah. They're moving in that direction now."

I thought about this. "It could actually work to our advantage. Might break up the party early and get them outside." I peeked around the corner. Nobody was leaving the lodge yet. "All right. Oberg, you and Bolton filter in behind them and take them out. That'll be two fewer guns we have to worry about around here."

"Copy," he said. "On our way."

I needed a better vantage point of the lodge's front door, so I moved to my right. And that's when I caught the break of a lifetime. As I stepped past a window, I looked inside.

And there was Epperson. Sitting on a chair, talking on his phone. Hey, sometimes you *make* your luck.

I stopped long enough to consider my options. But there was only one. I went to the door, opened it, and stepped inside.

Epperson froze in mid-sentence. I held a finger up to my lips, pointed at the phone, then made the universal signal of cutting it short.

"Hey, let me call you back," he said and hung up. "What the hell are you doing? You're seriously just walking in here?"

"It was unlocked," I said. "Why aren't you at breakfast?"

"Get out of here!"

"Hey, keep your voice down." I sat down across from him. "What's the plan today?"

He looked exasperated. "Look, I don't need this shit. I gave you all the information you wanted. You don't need my help anymore. You'll just get me killed."

"What's the plan?" I repeated, enunciating each word.

Epperson kept the exasperated look on his face. "The demonstration was supposed to be at two o'clock, but Ure wants to leave by noon."

Just as I'd expected. Ure was no dummy.

"Where?" I asked.

He hesitated, and that really pissed me off. I couldn't understand why this little shit was being so difficult. So I did something that, in my opinion, needed to be done long ago. I stood up from my chair, walked over to him, and slapped him hard across the face. It knocked him out of his seat and onto the floor.

I reached down, picked him up by his shirt, and threw him back into his chair. Leaning into his face, I spoke in a growl.

"I've had it up to here with you, Jake. I can't for the life of me figure out how you sell out the lives of Americans to a known terrorist, and then put on these aggrieved airs with me. Now you can either get your shit together and start helping me, or I will teach you all about *real* pain. Am I clear?"

There was blood on his lip and fear mixed with anger in his eyes. Like many cowards, he could talk a good game right up until the time someone hit him in the face. It took everything I had to keep from slapping him again.

I sat back down. "Quit playing the victim with me, shithead. Where is the goddamned demonstration?"

He pawed at his lip, pulled back his hand, and saw the blood. That got his attention.

"It's—well, I don't know exactly." He saw my eyes narrow and held up his hand. "I mean it. Minor hasn't told us that. I think he's a little irked at having to change on the fly. So they didn't say where. But I think he has a sort of obstacle course set up."

It made sense. Covered by the forest canopy, his obstacle course could be almost anywhere on the property. And, in a natural setting, it wouldn't stand out like an urban training ground might.

I stood up again. "Then go rejoin the party. When things heat up, I'd recommend you keep your head down."

He tried his best to glare at me, but it fizzled. Without another word, I turned and walked out of the cabin.

"I hope you all caught that little chat," I said to my group through my mic.

"I don't like it," Fife said. "It's too disjointed. We don't know exactly where they'll be. We don't know how many NGS will be there. Too much seat-of-the-pants stuff."

After glancing around, I wandered into the trees to make my way back around the perimeter of the camp to where I'd started.

"Well, what do you recommend?" I said. "It's Minor's party. We're just crashing it." Before Fife could respond, I addressed my small team. "Oberg. Status?"

He responded immediately. "Just bushwhacked the two dipshits. They're bound and gagged and getting intimate with a tree trunk. Won't be going anywhere for a while."

"Hurry back," I said. "Shit's about to get real. Team two, work your way up to the edge of the camp on the south side and hold there. Team three, stay put for now. Fife?"

"Yeah."

"Let the big shots back home know what's happening, and tell them our out-of-town guest is planning on leaving in a matter of hours."

"Will do."

I met Kemp, who signaled all clear. A minute later, Oberg and Bolton joined us.

"Let's move toward that lodge," I said. "I'm assuming Minor and Ure are in there right now. We might be able to strike before things get started. I'd love it if everything went down peacefully and without a shot fired. But I don't think that's going to happen. Especially if Viktor Ure thinks he's about to be captured. So be on your toes."

They nodded, everyone did one more quick check of their gear, and we began circling through the woods toward the side of the camp where the lodge was situated. It had been about 15 minutes since I left Epperson, which meant Minor's little demonstration might begin soon.

We were dead quiet as we picked our way through the trees and underbrush. My mind began envisioning the upcoming confrontation with Ure, the NGS, and Beadle. It was impossible to specifically visualize the combat—but military battle was as much about mental preparation as it was tactical. It's what elevated a good soldier to an elite warrior.

My earpiece crackled.

"Whoa, hold on," I heard Chez say. "Stand by."

We instinctively dropped to a knee.

"Report," I said.

"Sudden movement. And I mean sudden. Moving—well, shit. Not just moving *fast*. Like, I can't keep up with them with just one drone. They've split up."

"How many?"

"Stand by."

"I *can't* stand by," I said, my voice gritty. "We're exposed out here. How many?"

There was frustration in Chez's voice. "A group of five just left that large building. But three were really fast-moving objects. They tore out of there. Like I said, the little man couldn't keep up with them."

It was the NGS. Three of them. It was possible they were just hurrying ahead to get into position for the demonstration. We were only 50 yards from the back of the lodge, which meant they might have already zoomed around us. I had to know.

"Chez—"

Before I could finish the sentence, a thundering voice crackled through the air. The same voice I'd heard booming across a dinner table more than once. Only this time it was amplified beyond its normal obnoxious levels.

"Mr. Swan," Ambrose Minor said over the loudspeaker system. "I understand you've shown up without an invitation. Would you be so kind as to step out and reveal yourself?"

CHAPTER THIRTY

Remember what I said about making your own luck?

Well, I'd made it all right. I'd made a big, stinking pile of poo by running into Jacob Epperson and losing my patience with him. He'd obviously not appreciated the slap. So the little asshole had weighed his options and decided he stood a better chance by ratting me out. And then watching me get killed.

I felt my team members staring at me, waiting for instructions. But I was in no hurry to rush into anything. Without looking at them, I used one hand to signal *calm*.

Fife had to have heard the announcement through our comm link, but he, too, was experienced enough to process the information. When Minor's announcement died away, I was left with the usual forest sounds of animals and insects, along with the nice, steady pounding of my heart.

There was no chance this was going to end peacefully. Minor had been caught with Viktor Ure as his guest. Whether he did prison time or not, it certainly meant his business career was kaput. His only option now was to flee the country. And, in order to do that, he'd have to get past me and the small band of agents. In his mind, he had nothing to lose. He wouldn't hesitate to use his fancy new toys to secure his getaway. As he'd once pointed out to me, he had more than enough money stashed around the world to live a life of luxury as an expat.

Or, he could use his vast legal resources to argue that he had no idea who was attacking his private property, and he'd simply defended himself against what might've been terrorist activity. He might say, "How could I have known they were government agents? I work in an industry rife with spies and mercenaries. I had to defend myself."

And while the struggle went on, Ure could casually slip away. Minor might claim he didn't know who this man was, other than a potential customer who'd given a fake name. "That was Viktor Ure?" he would say. "Oh, my. Thank goodness you caught him."

As for us, it was now a question of tactics. What steps would accomplish the plan?

Sitting on our asses in the woods wouldn't accomplish anything, but stepping out into a killing field was even worse. That meant we had to move, preferably into a battle zone a little more favorable to our small force. There was no real cover here in the woods, and we would be at a disadvantage to the enhanced NGS. We needed to get on relatively even ground, tactically.

That meant—as Miracle Max once put it—storming the castle. If the *hombres mecánicos* were swarming into the trees, we would occupy their buildings.

"Chez," I said in a low voice. "Where did those five people go?"

There was silence as I imagined him scanning his monitors. I knew every second gave Minor a chance to sniff us out, but Chez would not be rushed into making a bad call. He might've been a Mountain Dew-guzzling nerd, but he'd probably played enough video game simulations to offer solid feedback.

Finally, he answered. "Best I can tell, they've split up, some going clockwise around the outside of the camp, some going counter. They intend to flush you out."

"Teams Two and Three," I said. "We're going into the camp. Make your own way in until you can infiltrate buildings for some cover. Watch your backs."

It was like the old days, coordinating our movements against an enemy, often in a jungle setting. Except, in the old days, the enemy couldn't bolt like a bunny and use bionic eyes.

"All right," I said to my team. "Let's go."

We'd edged forward about 20 feet when a series of gunshots clipped the trees nearby. The bastards—with their high tech—had found us.

"Move," I said, and we picked up the pace. Silence was no longer necessary.

Another volley smacked into a branch near my head, flinging bark and debris into the air. This time, I'd caught the flash of muzzle fire, dropped to a shooting position, and squeezed off five rounds.

I saw Bolton standing to my right, about 10 yards away, his back to a tree. Oberg and Kemp had to be just beyond. Bolton looked over to see where I was. He never finished the maneuver. A burst of gunfire rang out, and he flew off his feet.

I rushed over to him, but it took me all of two seconds to realize he was dead. One round had sheared off part of his head. Cursing under my breath, I started toward the camp again. I saw Oberg and Kemp hesitating, either unsure where to go or simply waiting for me.

"To the right," I called out before I reached them. "Go for that nearest cabin. Move it!"

More shots split the air, one zipping just past my ear. That whine is a sound you never forget, forged through multiple battles over many years. I saw Oberg looking behind us.

"He's dead," I said. "Now let's go, or you will be, too."

We made it to the edge of the trees, spying a cabin just ahead. I knew we had to get out of sight as soon as possible; the NGS would be on top of us any second. But I wanted to get my team into solid cover, something more significant than a tree.

I heard gunfire from the far side of the camp.

"Team Two, Team Three, report," I said. There was no response. I waited a few seconds before trying again.

"Yeah," came a reply from Team Three. "We've got two soldiers down. Another injured. We couldn't make it inside the camp. They were waiting for us."

"How many?"

"Shit, as far as I can tell, just two. One of them is one of those specialty soldiers. The other, I think, is a regular mercenary. Stand by."

We heard two more shots. Then the voice came back. "Scratch the regular mercenary. That just leaves the NGS. He's—"

A flurry of more gunfire erupted.

"Team Three," I said. Silence. "Report." Still nothing.

"Shit," I muttered. Then: "Team Two. Report."

"We haven't seen anything yet. We just got into what appears to be a maintenance building on the side nearest the park. All clear so far."

I had to assume Team Three had been wiped out. That left my two remaining team members and the four who made up Team Two. Seven of us against three NGS.

Honestly, I didn't like the odds. And if I was going to die in this camp, I needed to take care of business first.

"Listen," I said to Oberg and Kemp. "I want you to make a beeline for that cabin. Get inside and take cover. If you get a free shot at any of them, take it. Take the bastards down."

"What about you?" Oberg said.

"I have business in that lodge. One man might make it there unseen. Not all of us. Get to cover."

He was pissed at the command. I could tell, because *I* would've been pissed, too. He was a soldier first, and an FBI special agent second. But he also had to follow orders. Before he could argue, I slipped to my right, circling back through the woods until I could get close enough to the lodge.

I heard shouts coming from a dense thicket of woods ahead. Those would be Minor's traditional guard detail. If there was anything I'd noted regarding the NGS, it was their creepy silence. They didn't have to intimidate anyone with words. I hunched down, hoping to conceal myself among a small thicket of goldenrods, and watched as two armed men raced by. I let them pass.

Then, just as I was about to get up and move again, I heard a sound I recognized. A slight metallic clank, faint but undeniable. Keeping my breathing as quiet as possible, I pushed aside some of the yellow plant and gazed through. Trailing the two guards who'd disappeared, an NGS made his way between the trees. Only he wasn't running. He was quietly stalking. Which, in all honesty, was much more frightening.

I slowly and deliberately switched off my headset. I couldn't take a chance of any voices bleeding out from my earpiece. The NGS might very well have bionic hearing to go along with its eyesight.

I considered my options. I could squeeze off a shot and hope to nail him in the head. But the shot would bring down a ration of hurt on top of me, and I had an appointment I wanted to make. The NGS stopped, staring ahead, then looking to its left, away from me. After what seemed an eternity, he started moving again, eventually picking up the pace and slicing into the trees, out of sight.

I let out a long breath and got to my feet. With an occasional glance back, I picked my way through the woods until I saw the steepled roof of the lodge. I noticed little movement, and it left me wondering where Minor, Ure, and Beadle might be holed up. Or had they already begun the process of evacuating?

It didn't seem likely. They'd come to watch a demonstration. What better way to gauge the effectiveness of the Next Gen Soldier than a live confrontation with government agents? Especially since Minor had doubtless told them our puny little force stood no chance.

And he may have been right.

I decided to focus my attention on the lodge, which seemed to be the nerve center. It was about 150 feet away, with little cover along the way. I'd have to—

A sudden sound from behind made me roll to my left and bring the Glock up to firing position.

"Whoa," a man whispered, holding up a hand. It was Oberg.

"Jesus," I hissed. "What the hell are you doing here? You're supposed to be—"

"Yeah, I know," he said, kneeling down beside me. "I'm supposed to be diverting attention from you while you raid the enemy's position. But you'll need help."

I shook my head. "There's an NGS nearby. You probably just led him back here."

"Nah," he said, shaking his head. "I was quiet. It couldn't have—"

The shot hit him in the fleshy part of his left arm. A spray of blood hit me in the chest, and Oberg cried out. Instinct kicked in for both of us, and we dove apart, rolling and searching for cover. That's when I heard the electronic whine.

The NGS had tracked Oberg right to me. Not to mention the fact that the gunshot had now also alerted everyone in the camp.

Well, first things first. I wouldn't have to worry about the armed forces around Minor and Ure if we didn't settle things with the freak of nature bearing down on us.

"You okay?" I called out to Oberg.

His voice came out strained. "Yeah. Tore off a chunk of my tricep. But I'm still in the game."

I nodded. As technically advanced as they were, the NGS were still human. Minor's team could give them an awful lot of fancy tools, but they still had to shoot. And if they were lousy shots in the first place, having bionic body parts wouldn't make them any better. I had to remind myself that these were still prototypes. Once the technology was paired with a sharpshooter, things would get really ugly.

The distinct sounds of additional gunfire pierced the air. These shots weren't coming from our friend nearby; a gun battle was going on near the park. I grimaced, realizing that Team Two had been discovered.

Which reminded me—Oberg and I were sitting ducks. Our own NGS was likely maneuvering into a better spot from which to pick us off.

As if on cue, I heard a faint sound moving from left to right. It had to be him. I made eye contact with Oberg and indicated the line. He gave one curt nod. I turned back to the woods and peered through the underbrush.

Then it hit me. I'd shut off my damned earpiece. Turning it back on, I said, "Chez, you with me?"

"Right here."

"Oberg and I are pinned down, just west of the compound, about 40 yards. Find the NGS for me."

It turned out I didn't need his assistance. Another volley of shots rang out, smacking the ground around me and the tree in front of me.

"I think you found him yourself," Chez said in my ear. "And I've got you. From your position, he's at two o'clock, about 70 feet. Not moving fast at all. He's got a support team of two. They're at one o'clock, 50 feet."

I didn't respond. I just leaned out and tried to spot the beast. Another shot hit the tree, but it allowed me to see his muzzle flash. I took aim and ripped off three rounds. Two must've missed entirely, but the third connected with something. There was a *twang* sound.

It was the armor plating on the chest of the damned thing.

I returned to my cover and heard him moving again. To make matters worse, sounds of movement from behind me—in the camp—filtered through the trees. Oberg and I were about to be bracketed.

"Gimme intel," I said to Chez.

"Three o'clock, moving in closer to you."

Good. I didn't say it out loud, but that's what I wanted. It would likely take a head shot to eliminate this monster. The closer he got, the better.

"Tell me the second he moves into an open space," I said. "Still three o'clock?"

"Yeah. Stand by. He's almost there."

Now the sound was obvious. The NGS, perhaps bolstered with a sense of superiority, hadn't focused on stealth. "Come on, you son of a bitch," I muttered, mostly to myself.

But then Oberg, perhaps hoping to make up for his blunder, moved from behind the tree where he'd been kneeling, and bolted toward a series of stumps. He fired as he ran, convinced he could take down the enemy. I saw the heads of the two traditional gunmen pop up from some underbrush. Oberg and I opened fire at the same time; he took down one, I the other.

That's when our luck ran out. Oberg was five feet from additional cover. He almost made it.

Almost.

Another rapid-fire series of shots from the NGS cut him down. I heard the FBI agent hit the ground. Without waiting, I leaned out and spied the hulk, 30 feet from me, apparently relishing his kill. I raised the Glock and squeezed off three more shots.

His head snapped back, and I distinctly saw gray matter spewing out.

Now, the sounds of voices from the camp grew clear. I grabbed my pack and ran over to Oberg. He was lying in a heap, his body and limbs twisted unnaturally, a wad of gum on the ground beside him.

"Dammit," I said. As I started running, I let the team know: "Oberg is down and out. So is one NGS."

I circled to my right, then made my way back toward the camp. "Chez, status."

"Three of them. Assault rifles. Approaching the area you just vacated. The path into the camp actually looks clear."

"They may think I'm running for my life," I said. "That could help. Have you made any progress with that electronic jamming?"

"Apparently not. I was trying it with the one you took down. Nothing."

"All right. Keep at it." I leaned against a tree and stole a glance toward the lodge. No one was in sight. "Kemp, report."

It took a moment, then I heard his voice. "I'm in one of the cabins. Do you need support?"

"No," I said. "Keep your head down for now. Have you seen any NGS?"

"No—"

The sound of gunfire cut him off. The NGS had found Kemp.

I grumbled a string of expletives, then said, "Team Two."

"Here."

"I'm entering the camp. Kemp needs help. Get over there and cut down that goddamned NGS and anyone with it. Head shots. Understood?"

"Understood."

Then Fife's voice came through.

"Swan, word from the boss. Pull out. Get back to the chopper and—"

"No," I said. "Sorry, Ah-nuld, I will not get to the choppah. We're not leaving here with nothing to show for the troops we've lost."

Fife didn't argue. He wouldn't, because he agreed with me. He'd done his job and passed along the order. But we both knew the order was bullshit.

I took one more look at the camp and sprinted to the far side of another cabin. All was still quiet. I hoped the crew that had been drawn to the noise of the shootout would take their time getting back.

The sun, which had temporarily been eclipsed by low clouds, spilled forth again, filtering through the trees. I mentally tapped into its power and moved from the shadows toward the lodge. Scanning left and right, I broke into a run. A man and woman emerged from one of the other cabins, guns drawn and pointed at me. I dove to the ground as they fired, then put them down with two shots.

Scrambling back to my feet, I got within 30 feet of the steps to the lodge and its wide, wraparound porch when the door burst open. A giant hulk of a man held an assault rifle. He also wore a sneer on his face, like he was just about the biggest badass in history. On the run, I lifted my gun and placed one shot in his chest, another in his forehead. Take that, badass.

I sprang up the steps and planted myself against the wall next to the open door. I looked back along the path I'd taken from the woods, but there was no one in sight. Minor's security people were deployed in the woods. Or it was possible a passel of them waited just inside this building, every barrel trained on the door, waiting for some idiot to just burst in.

I'd been that idiot in the past. Not today.

Instead of spinning into the doorway, I shuffled to my right, along the porch. At the edge of the building, I turned the corner, hugging the wall. Still no one. But there was a window ahead, and it was open. Fresh air fiends, apparently. Worked for me.

I reached into my pack and pulled out a pair of earplugs. After quickly inserting them, I switched off the transmit device on my radio and grabbed one of my favorite toys. Taking two deep breaths, I swiped off the safety clip, pulled the pin, and tossed the flash grenade through the window. I turned away and shoved both hands over my ears. Hey, never hurts to be extra mindful when it comes to these things.

Exactly one-point-five seconds later, a blinding flash of light accompanied a concussive bang, to the tune of 175 decibels. Pulling out the earplugs and tossing them aside, I spun around and dove through the window, rolled once, and came up with the Glock leveled.

A man and a woman were sprawled on the floor, unconscious, their weapons lying beside them. I picked up the pistols and tucked them into my pack. Flipping my radio back on, I said, "I'm in the lodge. Chez, anything to report?"

"Someone ran out the front door and stumbled to the ground. I'm not sure, but I think they're puking. Was that a flash-bang you used in there?"

Even in the midst of battle, I had to chuckle. "Roger that. Do me a favor. Focus your little man on Kemp's side of the camp. Help him and Team Two. There's not much more you can do for me here."

I moved toward the door and, after a slight pause, threw it open, prepared to fire.

The large, main room was empty. Tables had clearly been arranged for meals, and a whiteboard was covered with various labels and numbers. Minor must've been in the midst of a presentation when the good guys showed up and wrecked everything.

I crept through, keeping an eye on my flank while glancing ahead. Something felt off. Up ahead, there was a room with a door slightly ajar. That contributed to the feeling, but there was something else.

That's when I caught movement from the corner of my eye. Someone had rushed out from either a closet or another room. With no time to turn and fire, I fell quickly into a crouch.

The crouch wasn't enough. Something solid connected with the side of my head and I went flying. My headset fell in pieces onto the floor beside me and I felt the warmth of blood ooze down my cheek. My pack went skittering across the floor.

Rolling to one side, I brought up my gun—and stopped.

It was Epperson. He held a goddamned shovel like a baseball bat, cocked and ready to swing again. I think he was actually as stunned as I was that he'd managed to surprise me, and even more stunned that he'd knocked me down. But I wasn't out, and that was bad news for him.

Climbing to my feet, I growled, "Are you kidding me?" He snapped out of his trance and tried another swing. I wasn't having it. Leaning to one side, I let the heavy, metal end of the shovel swish by, then stepped forward and punched him as hard as I could.

His makeshift weapon clanged to the floor, and he dropped like a stone, his eyes rolled back into his head.

I dabbed at the wound on the side of my head and my hand came back smeared with blood. The son of a bitch had bashed me pretty good and destroyed my communications device. But he'd probably been an inch or two away from *really* hurting me. If he'd swung the shovel with the blade horizontal, like a sword, instead of flat, like a club, he might've even killed me.

Amateur.

"Screw you, Epperson," I said. Out of pure spite, I stomped down on his right hand. Even unconscious, he jerked in a spasm as the bones snapped. Totally unnecessary on my part, sure, but sometimes my inner monster could be a petulant and vindictive shit. Besides, the bastard more than had it coming.

I did a quick examination of the headset, but it was mangled. I tossed it aside. I reached behind me and pulled the radio itself off my belt. It had cracked when I hit the hard floor. It looked like a crushed cigar, with two wires poking out of the bottom. Its power light glowed red, gallantly trying to serve its purpose. But it was useless. I shoved it into a pocket, wondering if I might stumble across another headset. Otherwise, the rest of my adventure would be *incommunicado*.

Having survived the sneak attack, I approached the door hanging slightly ajar. I had a feeling this room was occupied, too. I took two deep breaths, steadying myself for a gunfight. And, if I was lucky, Ambrose Minor and Beadle would be waiting on the other side.

After another centering breath, I spun, kicked open the door, and crouched, my weapon raised.

Then I slowly lowered it to my side. Of all the things I could've expected, this would've been last on my list.

Ambrose Minor sat slumped in a chair, his head back, those wolf eyes staring at the ceiling.

With a nice, neat bullet hole centered in the middle of his forehead.

CHAPTER THIRTY-ONE

I don't know how long I stood there, gun at my side, looking at the corpse of the man who, until last week, had everything going his way. He'd bankrolled the research and development of a remarkable piece of military technology. He'd crafted relationships with powerful people, both in the legitimate world and the criminal side. He'd manipulated his chief competitor's son into betraying his family and his personal integrity, demolishing in months a small empire built over decades.

What had it earned him? A shameful, pathetic end. A cold, hard seat in a damp room, nestled within a small clearing of a dense forest, his brains oozing out the back of his head.

Who, exactly, had fired the shot? My mind weighed the options and delivered three possibilities.

Ure. Antoinette. Beadle.

I quickly rejected options A and C. Viktor Ure wouldn't make this kind of move. He was a guest, a potential client, unsure of how any of this was supposed to go, other than him observing a demonstration. He was probably pissing his pants at how things had blown up in a matter of minutes and regretting he'd ever left his rathole to sneak into the United States. I imagined him slinking away, not shooting his way out.

Beadle? I'd watched him kill people. Lots of people. He did it in the most callous ways imaginable, and he did it without a shred of remorse. But this time? This smacked of something a touch more sinister. I could see Beadle ordering the hit. In fact, as soon as I could sit down and connect all the dots, it would probably make all the sense in the world.

But Beadle didn't pull that trigger.

Antoinette pulled it. At Beadle's command. He enjoyed power. He especially enjoyed making others succumb to his power. Pointing at Minor, he would know that Antoinette wouldn't hesitate. She was one smart assassin, experienced enough in the ways of the underworld to know who her *real* boss was. She was intimately involved in Minor's business, but she knew Beadle pulled the strings. If he said "Shoot this man," Minor's brains would've been splattered before Beadle finished uttering the last syllable.

My nemesis was the kind of criminal mastermind who'd survived this long because he quickly assessed when things were going badly, then acted without hesitation. His NGS program, with him playing puppet master to Ambrose Minor, had come close to being the astonishing success he'd dreamed of. And then, in minutes, had collapsed.

He wouldn't go down with the ship. And his puppet paid the price for wasting so much of his time.

Now these last three—Ure, Beadle, and the Bulgarian killing machine—were on the loose. They'd jettisoned the useless dickhead named Epperson—he wasn't even worth wasting a single round—and made their escape. But no vehicles had left the compound. That meant they were on foot.

I knew where they were going. But before walking out of the lodge, I considered all the pieces on the board.

Kemp and hopefully members of Team Two were taking on the bulk of Minor's security detail. I'd taken out one NGS in the woods, but that meant two were still active. At least one would participate in the siege on Kemp and his unit. Maybe both.

Somehow I didn't believe that. If Beadle was escorting Ure out of the woods, protecting his last investment, he likely would call in the best troops for an escort. That meant both Antoinette and the last bionic soldier were at his service. The Bulgarian wasn't a full-fledged NGS, but I would never make the mistake of underestimating her skills.

There was nothing to be done about it. I couldn't reach Fife or Chez. Kemp and his unit had their hands full. Everyone else was dead.

I tore a strip of fabric from a tablecloth and tied it around my head, hoping to staunch the blood.

"Let's go, Rambo," I muttered to myself and opened the door.

The sun had now fully burned away any clouds or haze that might've lingered through the humid morning. I hustled toward the path leading into Amicalola Park.

Fife had mentioned that everyone had been escorted from the park. But a solitary SUV still sat there. You could argue it was someone who'd hiked out and would be coming back for it later. There was an approach trail from the park that led to the Appalachian Trail, which drew thousands of people. It was possible the SUV belonged to one of those people.

I knew better. It was Beadle's escape plan. The guy always had a plan. If Minor's property was bottled up, he could slip out through the state park with all the other citizens.

I ran. Branches whipped into me as I flew by, stinging my face and my forearms as I pushed them aside. Beadle's group wouldn't necessarily be sauntering along, but I didn't expect them to be racing ahead, either. As far as they knew, I had my hands full back in the camp. The park was a good 15 minutes away, and they had a five-minute head start. I could make up the difference if I hauled ass.

As I sped down the trail, I tried to contain the adrenaline rush that naturally bubbled up when I had a shot at Beadle. A good soldier channels that rush, funneling it into his or her performance, instead of allowing it to overwhelm them emotionally. Stories about ice-cold killers who behaved like automatons were pure myth; everyone feels something in these moments. It's how you use that energy that shapes and defines your competence under fire.

I'd been told I had nerves of steel. That was bullshit. Bullets flying around your head can either cause you to focus on survival or they can make you fall apart. Either way, your pulse is pounding. "Ice water in the veins" sounds great in a novel, but that's the only place it exists.

I was thankful the body I inhabited at the moment was in good, athletic shape. I needed that advantage, because my head throbbed where shithead had smacked me with the shovel. The makeshift bandana I'd tied around my melon was saturated with blood, some of which dripped onto my neck. I probably looked like the survivor of a plane crash. All I had to do was keep it together a little while longer.

Through a break in the trees, I glimpsed the trail rising about a quarter of a mile ahead. For a split second, I caught sight of people. Braking to a stop, I backed up so I could see that point on the trail again, but by then it was empty.

I was closing in.

A minute later, running full speed again, I heard the sound of rushing water. My time was running out. Once they reached that vehicle, they'd be gone. I had no way of warning Fife or anyone else.

And then, I broke into the open. Bright sunshine clearly lit up four people just 50 yards ahead, moving at a deliberate pace. I recognized three of them: Antoinette, Ure, and Beadle. The fourth person, tall and sculptured like a Greek god, had to be one of the NGS models.

They were making their way through a small parking lot. Ahead, a wooden walkway led to an observation platform above the falls. On the far side sat another parking lot. I saw a black SUV glinting in the sun.

Still moving at a good pace, I withdrew my Glock. But at that very moment, Antoinette looked back and saw me. She gave a short warning cry, and all of them stopped and turned.

I raised my gun and fired multiple shots on the run. One round hit Ure in his lower leg, and he crumpled. After the momentary hesitation, Beadle turned and ran quickly toward the platform and the path toward the far parking lot.

"Shit," I said. But there would be no chasing after him yet. The NGS and Antoinette had pulled their own weapons. I dove behind a landscaped berm as a multitude of rounds tore into the grass and dirt around me. After a pause, I reared up and got off four more shots before ducking back down. Crawling to my right, I peered around the edge of the mound and saw Beadle had reached the wooden platform above the falls. Antoinette was watching him, but not pursuing. Ure remained on the ground, curled up in agony.

The mechanical man hadn't gone anywhere. He took aim and let loose with another volley. I pulled my head back, cursing.

Then, things got even worse. I realized I'd left my pack on the floor of the lodge after getting clobbered by Epperson. The pack had my extra Glock magazines. Which meant I was down to just a few more rounds.

Idiot. By being in such a hurry to chase after Beadle, I'd royally screwed myself. I couldn't win a shootout without being able to reload.

No radio. No extra rounds. Facing two technological marvels. What did I have in my favor? Other than charm, of course.

Well, that would have to be enough. At least enough to get me within striking distance. Otherwise, what choice did I have?

"Hey," I shouted. "Antoinette. Will you and your Transformer friend hold your fire?"

There was no answer. But there were also no shots fired my way. I chanced a look over the top of the berm.

They stood 10 feet apart, just watching me, their weapons at their sides. Behind them, Beadle had reached the far side of the observation platform and was running up toward the other parking lot. I took a deep breath—hoping it wasn't my last—and got to my feet.

In a grand gesture, I held up my gun, then tossed it to the side. The NGS and the Bulgarian looked unimpressed. Even so, they didn't fire. So I walked toward them with my hands out at my sides, palms facing them. I was banking on the fact Antoinette would be curious to talk with me. Professional assassins were like an elite club; we often were paid to kill each other, but it didn't mean we weren't sympathetic. I've terminated many people who were actually quite interesting to talk with.

The NGS wasn't part of that club. He was purely a tool, but he answered to Antoinette, who called the shots here.

As I walked toward them, I glanced to my right. Beadle had reached the SUV. The engine started up. But instead of pulling out of the lot, he sat there. Waiting. Watching this new development.

He wasn't out of my reach yet. He, too, was curious.

I made a point of stepping directly over Ure, who seemed on the verge of passing out. When I got to within eight feet of her, Antoinette held up a hand. "That's close enough. What do you want?"

I lowered my hands. "I want to convince you that you're working for the wrong team."

A slow smile spread across her face. "Who determines which team is right and which is wrong? You?"

"I'm counting on you being smart enough to figure it out for yourself. The fact that you put a bullet in your boss's brain must mean you have doubts."

She shook her head. "That doesn't mean I want to change teams. My current team just needed a new coach."

I chuckled, then gave a nod toward the parking lot. "And you think that guy is the right coach? The one who scampered away when shots were fired? If you think that, I promise you'll be sorely disappointed, and soon. I know him. He's left a trail of dead former colleagues stretching back years. When the time comes, you won't mean anything special to him, Antoinette. Neither will your robot friend next to you. Your new coach would unplug him tomorrow if he needed parts to fix his toaster."

The NGS, who'd been staring at me hard from the moment I started talking, took two quick steps and backhanded me across the face. I was already bleeding from the side of my head. Now I had a bloodied lip to go along with it. But I stayed on my feet. Couldn't give the brass bastard the satisfaction.

Antoinette found it amusing. "I love being recruited. It gives one such a feeling of self-worth." She took a step toward me, her hands on her hips. "But if this is your pitch, Mr. Swan, I'm afraid you threw your gun away for nothing. Unless there's anything else you want to add that might sway me."

I had a mental flash of that hourglass, and the sand in the top half was nearly gone. I was down to my final grains. "Mostly, I just want to know a few things."

"Such as?" Her smile was still there.

I dabbed the blood away from my lip. "I'm pretty sure you killed Bryson Hedrick. That's right, isn't it?"

"One of my easier kills."

I studied her face. "So why didn't you kill me at the same time? You toyed with me, putting those shots into the couch. Why?"

She gave a shrug. "I didn't think you were much of a threat.

And if today is any indication, I was right. You're no threat. Besides, it was fun watching you scurry away."

"And the elder Hedrick? That was you, too? Knocking him off? Setting the fire?"

"All part of the plan."

I spit a mouthful of blood onto the wooden planks, then nodded toward the parking lot. "Whatever that guy told you his name is, it's a lie. His real name is Beadle. Do your own research on him. But remember this: If he was quick to order the hit on Ambrose today, what makes you think he won't do the same to you tomorrow?"

She gave a sad shake of her head. "I'm sorry, Mr. Swan. Right now, he seems like the better horse to bet on."

I had some witty response on the tip of my tongue, ready to hurl it at her, but was interrupted by the sound of a vehicle, approaching rapidly. We all turned to watch a small pickup, marked with Georgia State Parks emblems, roar into the lot.

Shit. No. Not now.

He was much too far away for me to cry a warning, especially with his engine running. I took one anxious step toward the parking lot, but the mechanical man caught my movement and stepped in front of me. Without a weapon, there would be no getting past him and Antoinette in time to do anything.

The truck screeched to a stop near the black SUV. I watched the driver's door open and an older man leap out. To him, he was doing his duty, finally getting an opportunity for some real excitement, apprehending real bad guys.

As soon as he was clear of his truck and walking toward the SUV, I yelled. "No! Get back in your truck. No!"

The man threw a glance my way, but I was sure all he heard was noise. The distance and the crashing of the falls cloaked my words.

It didn't matter. When the man was five feet from the SUV, Beadle rolled down his window. Two seconds later, a shot rang out. The ranger's head flew back, and his lifeless body tumbled to the ground.

My blood boiled. The guy might've been only two or three years away from retirement, just doing his duty in a state park. Beadle had executed him without a word.

I let out an animal cry and lunged at the NGS, slamming my forearm into his jaw. He staggered back, but recovered quickly. He raised his gun, but I kicked hard, knocking it away, then landed another blow to his face. With a roar, he was on me before I knew what was happening. He shoved me back, then followed up with his own punch. I ducked, but before I could retaliate he'd bolted to my left side and slammed a hard, metal-coated fist into the side of my head.

I collapsed, the bright sunlight dimming as fireworks popped across my vision. Through the bolts of pain, I heard laughter. Looking up from the wooden planks, I saw Antoinette, her arms crossed in absolute delight, enjoying the show. I needed to catch my breath and shake away the sparkles that still clouded my vision. The NGS could've easily retrieved his gun and pumped a dozen rounds into my body. But I'd made it personal. He wanted nothing more than to beat me to death with his metal fists. Thanks to my smart-ass mouth, I'd experienced the same thing with guys going all the way back to high school.

And at the moment, I at least had *that* going for me.

With a hard kick in the gut, he lifted me off the planks, banging me into the railing. I let out a loud grunt, which had to be intoxicating for the bully. But now, near my hands, there was a smooth rock, the size of a softball. I clutched it and rolled away, springing to my feet. As he moved toward me, I raised the rock— but the bastard was lightning fast. He slapped the rock away with one motion and backhanded me again with another. I fell onto my back, the pain now rocketing through my entire body.

A thought flitted through my head: *This beast is still just a proto-*

type. What would it be like when they perfected the damned thing?

Antoinette was still laughing, loving her front-row seat to the beating. But what really pissed me off was the fact that Beadle, fresh off his own kill, was drinking it in, too. Instead of me wringing his neck, he was watching me get throttled, getting a firsthand demonstration of how an NGS could operate in close-quarters combat.

As the soldier reached for me, I rolled again, escaping for the moment. As I pushed to my feet, I tried formulating some sort of plan. It would have to involve attacking, because there was no way I could win playing defense.

But just as I prepared to strike, psyching myself up for the pain that was sure to follow, something bizarre happened.

In mid-stride toward me, the NGS froze. A second later, his entire body went stiff and his head flew backward, his face arched toward the sky, displaying a look of utter agony. His mouth opened, but his cry of pain was cut short. He staggered a step back, his eyes now closed tight.

Chez to the rescue, I thought. The Mountain Dew freak had finally hacked the neuro-link.

I didn't let another moment pass. Reaching down, I grabbed the rock again and flew toward him, bringing the stone down on top of his forehead as hard as I could. He crumpled beneath me, blood gushing everywhere, mingling with my own.

There was no time for me to celebrate. Antoinette, unfazed by what had afflicted her partner in crime, was on me, one arm wrapped around my throat, pulling me away from the NGS.

All of my training with Quanta kicked in. I hammered an elbow back into her midsection, which created some distance. Twisting, I landed a punch that knocked her away. Now we were both bloodied. She pulled out her gun. With a kick, I sent it skittering away.

But she was an elite soldier for a reason. Antoinette could take a blow and strike back. She did. Again and again. I parried many of them, thankful I was once again fighting a mostly normal human being, someone without all the superpowers of an NGS, other than her vision. She landed her shots, but so did I. If I hadn't already been wounded multiple times, it would've been an even match.

I wanted to look to see if Beadle was still sitting in the SUV, taking in the show, but my hands were full with this Bulgarian nightmare. As we traded blows, I couldn't help but recall Fife's detailed report of Antoinette's violent background. Nothing he'd told me seemed exaggerated at the moment. She was cool and composed, but ferocious.

Around the fallen body of the mechanical man, we fought like two heavyweights in the ring. The problem was that I felt my strength draining away. I'd lost way too much blood, and the battle with the NGS had zapped most of my energy. One confrontation was enough for most people; taking on a tag team with a gaping wound on your head was asking too much.

We'd staggered down the wooden walkway and now found ourselves fighting on the overlook to the falls. The roar of the water was a backdrop to the blows we landed on each other. Blood-soaked, we kept it up, knowing this was a fight to the death.

She ducked a punch I threw, and, mostly a result of sheer exhaustion, I found myself off balance. With a kick to my chest, she sent me flying back against the railing overlooking the falls, and I slid down to the planks. She reached down to pull me back up—to finish me off, I was sure. But my hand grasped a small branch lying there, and, with a shout, I smashed it into her face.

Her grasp on me fell away, and she staggered back a few steps, pressing a hand to her face. More blood seeped between her fingers. When she pulled the hand away, it held the bionic eye. She looked back up at me and I stared into the damaged electronic socket. It was one of the most surrealistic images I'd ever seen: a bruised, bloodied warrior with a gaping hole in her face that winked a blue light at me before filling with more blood.

Antoinette actually laughed. She dropped the eye to the ground and launched another attack. Knocking the branch aside, she placed a forearm under my chin, pushing me back against the railing again. Now both of her hands, like vises, found their way around my throat. I reached up, trying to pry them away, but it was no good. She was shoving me hard against the railing, just feet above the water rushing to the edge of the cliff. The roar matched the sound of the blood pounding through my head as I grew weaker. It was all coming to an end. An inglorious ending in a state park, in front of the asshole I'd vowed to track down. Instead, he was watching me die.

With one last gasp effort, I reached for anything that might help me. I felt something in my front pocket. It was the remnants of my radio, the cigar-shaped device that had been cracked open by Epperson. I slipped my hand into the pocket and pulled it out. Then, just as everything began fading to black, I threw my last bit of strength into a hard stab. The cracked radio tube plunged into Antoinette's open eye socket.

There was an immediate spark and a small flame burst from her face. With a gasp, she moved her hands from my throat and reached up toward her eye, stumbling backward a step.

I caught my breath, then hauled off and punched her with my last bit of strength. Her head snapped back, but she wouldn't go down. She turned her face to me, and what I saw made me cringe. The eye socket was blackened by the electrical fire, and small tendrils of smoke rose through the bloody mess.

With a cry of anger, she rushed toward me, her arms outstretched, intent on killing me once and for all.

I quickly dropped to a knee and, as she came over the top of me, I lifted her up and used her momentum to throw her over the railing. She dropped into the small rapids and, in a flash, was carried over the drop-off. Even over the crashing roar, I heard the sharp crack as she struck the rocks below.

Struggling to breathe and feeling pain throughout every inch of my body, I slipped down to a sitting position against the railing, my back to the falls. More blood dripped onto my lap and I felt myself about to pass out. I noticed something lying beside me, and I reached out to pick it up.

It was Antoinette's eye. With a painful grunt of laughter, I closed my fist around it and, in one quick motion, threw it over my shoulder, into the roiling water of the falls.

"So, Antoinette," I said, gritting my teeth. "Think I'm much of a threat now?"

Then, forcing my gaze upward, I looked out to the parking lot.

The black SUV was gone.

CHAPTER THIRTY-TWO

It was unusual for me to be at Quanta's house without her kicking the shit out of me in a martial arts workout. But given that I'd just spent three days in the hospital, she granted me a hall pass. I sat at the round table in her kitchen, looking out a window onto the meticulously groomed garden in which she took so much pride. Since I normally viewed it as a battleground, it held less affection for me. But it *was* gorgeous.

Three days was longer than I might've expected to stay confined, but I'd dictated that timeline myself by opting to keep the body. Often, in cases where I'd been so badly damaged, I would upload, then vacate the old shell for a fresh, new body. It saved a lot of time, eliminating long, extensive rehab in exchange for a few hours of reorientation.

Something, however, prevented me from giving an okay for the standard routine. I felt this convict's stamina had earned the body its rehabilitation. It had served me well, accepting a brutal beating at the hands of both a freakish NGS and the Bulgarian nightmare, yet holding strong. I couldn't say that about all of my various incarnations through the years. Yes, this body deserved another round. Even with only nine and a half fingers.

That's what I told Quanta, anyway. And while it contained some elements of truth, it wasn't the real reason.

The real reason was that this particular assignment had been excessively bloody. Overall, nearly 20 people lost their lives in order to expose Ambrose Minor and to capture one of the world's most wanted terrorists. I don't generally feel too strongly about the whole "ends justifying the means" argument—but this time, the means struck me as much too expensive. If I could preserve one body out of this messy affair, it would be the one originally occupied by the convict who'd voluntarily forfeited it. To me, that was worth the pain of recovery.

My usual debriefing with Quanta was progressing slowly. With the death of two of America's most prominent businessmen—both of whom had forged relationships with other titans of industry over decades—and the capture of Viktor Ure, Quanta would need to tread carefully in front of some powerful government types. Many of them wouldn't even know about Q2, which added another layer of caution to her report. Getting everything straight with me was therefore crucial.

In a nutshell, it boiled down to this:

Ambrose Minor was dead. Antoinette Lazarov was dead. Oberg, Bolton, and six other FBI agents had lost their lives during the battle, all but one of them at the hands of NGS prototypes. That score could've been even worse, except that Kemp had led a successful counterassault that took out the second NGS. The rest of Minor's security detail were either killed or arrested.

An innocent older man, who'd arisen that fateful morning, thinking it would be just another routine day for a park ranger, was cut down. Brutally. Senselessly.

The body count also included Ty and Bryson Hedrick, along with Paige Walters.

Beadle, of course, got away. I didn't feel like talking with Quanta about that. It would have to wait for another debriefing on another day. Needless to say, though, it chafed me throughout my hospital stay. I was laid up while Beadle ran free.

His escape, along with the horrific death toll, prevented me from labeling this operation a success. How many times would I come this close, only to watch the bastard escape again? If you believed in a universe that keeps score on things like this, you'd begin to think the game was rigged. That Beadle—as we used to say growing up in Illinois—*knew a guy*.

Everyone had their own version of Beadle. The job promotion that never came. Ongoing misadventures in dating. Always one number off on the lottery ticket. Hitting the same red light every morning.

I wondered: Do constant failures at the same thing build character? Does being tantalizingly close—but coming up short—somehow make you stronger? Or does each close encounter, each near miss, each *tease* eventually wear you down until you become a bitter, angry lump?

It might depend on the person. But I lay in that hospital bed wondering just how many more times it would play out this way before the gods threw me a bone. Law of averages and all that happy horseshit. Hey, Bill Murray in *Groundhog Day* eventually saw the next sunrise.

It had been nothing but bad news for me every time I encountered the asshole. But the bad news for Beadle was that I would never give up.

Even without verbalizing all this, Quanta was a master at reading people. At least, at reading *me*. She gazed at me as if I were a bug under a microscope.

"I understand your state of mind," she said, careful to modulate an even tone. "Not everything went right during this assignment. But I hope you realize just how important it is that you captured Viktor Ure. There are countless notes of gratitude and congratulations pouring in from all over the world."

"Hoorah," I said, not bothering to hide my sarcasm.

"Jenna Macklin asked me to wish you well and to thank you."

I just gave a nod. Jenna was a solid contributor to the team, someone I envisioned as an important ally moving forward.

"And," Quanta said, "we've made additional progress in reverse engineering some of the accomplishments from Minor's developmental team."

I grunted. "You mean you're able to copy his work. Forgive me if I haven't warmed to the idea yet."

She studied my face, but before she could speak, I continued. "You never fooled me for a minute, Quanta. From the moment this case fell into your lap, you've been lusting to acquire the technology."

"I don't understand what you're implying. I haven't been coy. Why would I hide that desire? It could have very important implications for national defense."

"Of course it could. But you see it merely as a tool."

She raised an eyebrow. "And how do you see it?"

I leaned forward and looked her right in the eye. "I see it as sacrificing another chunk of our humanity. We've discovered the ability to transfer our consciousness from one body to another, and we ostensibly use it for good. But now we're going to redesign the bodies themselves. Throw in the neuro-link component, where we assimilate our brains with computers and AI, and I'm not sure that what comes out the other end of the conveyor belt will have much in common with a human being." I paused, sitting back. "It certainly won't have much of a soul, if any."

Quanta may have been surprised by the passion of my argument. But I knew my thoughts on the matter didn't surprise her at all. The loss of the soul—or whatever term you felt comfortable with—had always been my primary concern with the investment program. It had certainly been a personal fear from day one.

Her voice, when she spoke, was calm, but still conveyed her own passion. "I would like to think we'll inject wisdom into any project we attempt, Swan. We are not in the market for automatons."

I shook my head. "Easy to say now. But once we marry the two technologies, the bar will consistently be raised, again and again. Two or three generations of Next Gen *Anything* will instill a desire for bigger, better, faster, more complex. Once the genie is out of this bottle, it won't be long before we lose our sense of self. Or at least, a sense of *natural* self. We'll be prefabricated."

I sat back again. "Look, with just the improved body parts, I could see the potential benefit. I understand that argument. But combined with a sort of consciousness immortality and a neuro-hookup with AI? How can anyone argue that's a human being anymore?"

Quanta nodded. "Swan, I hear what you're saying. And you may be correct. But you also are smart enough to understand that it's coming, whether or not your fears are valid."

"So we just need to be first, right?"

She shrugged. "Ambrose Minor was first. And here's something else to consider. Like the investment program, this technology could stay hidden from the public. Research purposes only."

I gave a mirthless chuckle. "Quanta, you've done a remarkable job keeping my little secret under wraps. But I don't see how this —" I let the sentence hang there.

We sat in silence for a long time. When she spoke again, her tone took on a touch of tenderness.

"We can discuss all of this another time. I know you have other things on your mind right now." When I looked up at her, she said, "Christina. I know you're upset."

I was thankful I had a glass of water to hide behind for a moment. But after taking a long drink, I let out a sigh. "I let her down. I told her I'd be there when she went into labor, and instead I was sitting on the observation deck of a waterfall in Georgia."

"Practically unconscious," Quanta said. "You understand this was just bad timing. You couldn't know—"

"I *never* know," I said, with a little more force than I'd intended. "It's always something, isn't it? But this is more than just missing a dance recital or a parent-teacher conference. She gave birth."

"And you wouldn't have been in the delivery room, anyway. The new parents were there."

"You know a lot about this. Have you—"

"Talked to Christina? Of course I did. And I know she's not upset with you at all. The baby came early, after all."

I sat there, brooding. When I'd seen Christina just before everything went down, she couldn't have been more loving and understanding. I was the one who was bothered, not her.

Perhaps I just wanted something to be upset about.

"I'm not usually one to pat you on the head," Quanta said. "So while you're sulking over the timing of everything, let me just remind you that, in the first place, you're not even supposed to be married."

I stewed over that for a moment, staring down at my glass. When I finally looked up to make eye contact, Quanta had a half smile on her face. That finally broke through my hard shell. I chuckled.

"As soon as Christina is up for it, I'm going to take a vacation," I finally said. "But I'm sure you saw that coming."

"If you hadn't said it, I would've ordered it. The timing works, too. I have one quick assignment for you. Four or five days, max. Then go. Take Christina somewhere nice for her maternity leave. Spend three weeks. Go be a civilian for a while. Don't even think about being a spy."

I stood up. Quanta pointed a finger at me before I could walk away. "But go see Miller first."

She got up and headed toward the atrium where she meditated. Over her shoulder, she called back to me: "I have a hard time imagining you as an automaton, Swan. You're much too stubborn."

"I understand you'll be going away for a while."

It was late afternoon, and Miller sat in his usual seat. Clouds had turned Washington, DC, into a flat gray landscape, but, through the window, I could make out the Washington Monument in the distance. I'd once joked that every movie ever made with a scene in Paris *had* to include a shot of the Eiffel Tower. Like it was a law. I wondered now if Hollywood treated the Washington Monument the same way.

I let Miller's question sit there for a moment. It was a reminder that he and Quanta shared almost every bit of intel regarding my personal life and my thought patterns. I'd left her house only 90 minutes ago, but that was enough time for her to call and fill him in.

When I didn't answer, he added, "I don't recall you taking an actual vacation before. You've taken recovery time after injuries, but a vacation? That's new for you."

I turned back to look at him. "Well, it's finally time. Are you going to miss me?"

"I'm glad you're going."

"But you *have* to say that."

"You're probably right. Still, I'm curious what finally pushed you to the brink. I mean, I've seen you discouraged plenty of times. But your tonic has always been to keep working. What's different this time?"

It was a good question. I didn't have a good answer. I told him that.

"Okay," he said. "Let's talk about this last assignment. When you look back on it, tell me what you find yourself thinking about the most."

It was something Miller had asked me many times. So many

times, in fact, that these days I treated it like homework and came to his office with my answer.

"Here's what I was thinking about in the hospital. The fact that so many people are in the business of building death."

He narrowed his eyes. "Building?"

"Yeah. I even thought about it while I was lying on that platform in the park, nearly bleeding to death, and with bodies all around. How so many people had taken these remarkable and practical skills and used them to create killing machines."

I looked out the window again. "Even the so-called good guys, the Hedricks. What they and Ambrose Minor created could almost be called an art form. They use their minds and their hands to craft instruments of death. And then you have other people who use their hands to create things of beauty. Artwork. Architecture. Musical instruments. Similar skills, taking raw materials and shaping them—but as dissimilar in finished form as you could get."

Miller nodded slowly. "I see what you're saying. One pair of hands sculpts the David, another builds a gun."

"And I find that fascinating." I shook my head. "I'm not naïve. I understand different instincts drive both creators. But in the hospital, I wondered if there's just one incident in a person's life that pushes them down one path or the other."

"What do you think?"

I was quiet for a moment. "I think—well, I think I want to think more about it. Maybe that's how I'll spend my vacation."

"I hope not. Better if you put all of that on the shelf for a few weeks. It'll still be there when you get back."

"Not sure I can shut off my mind. It wants to solve these things."

"And yet it never does."

I wanted to argue, but of course he was right. "Yeah. I suppose I'll always be conflicted. Nature versus nurture. One inciting incident to change your path or a slow buildup over time."

"It's all right to be conflicted," Miller said. "We all are. It's part of our nature." He paused, then added, "Have you read Agatha Christie?"

"Read a ton of her stuff when I was younger."

"Well, she wrote a line for Hercule Poirot, her Belgian detective. At one point, he says, 'Each one of us is a dark mystery, a maze of conflicting passions and desires and attitudes.'"

I raised an eyebrow. "Look at you, quoting an entire passage."

"I think it's very insightful."

"'A maze of conflicting passions and desires,'" I said. "And you think that's me?"

"You're practically the poster child. You want to do the job. You feel like the world *needs* you to do the job. And yet, when you finish, you question whether or not you're a monster. It even has you wondering if one innocent thing in your life made you Eric Swan instead of Jackson Pollock. That sounds like a conflict to me."

"As you said, everybody is conflicted."

"That's right. A little internal conflict is healthy. If it's thoughtfully channeled and not always acted on in a compulsive manner. Reflection, Swan. You're good at reflecting."

I leaned back and stared at the ceiling. "God, sometimes you really sound like a therapist." After a pause, I said, "Quanta wants to not only keep uploading and downloading my mind, she now wants to make me bionic. What do you think of that?"

"What do *you* think of that? Are you opposed to the idea?"

"No. And yes." I stretched, raising my arms toward the ceiling, then sat up straight again and looked at Miller. "I'm already walking around in bodies that are alien to me. It doesn't really matter if the parts are skin and bone or gold and platinum, right?"

"But?"

"I thought about this, too, while I was laid up. Did a lot of thinking there, obviously. While they were sewing up some parts of me after putting in a small, metal plate, I wondered, how is that any different from a completely artificial foot or a new eye? Technology that can help catch bad guys has to be good right?"

Miller smiled. "I'm still waiting for the 'but.'"

"But every one of those NGS machines I encountered—they were different somehow."

"In what way?"

I squinted, trying to collect my thoughts. "They went beyond confidence. Beyond a sense of invulnerability. I know it's a small sample size, but they all seemed—detached."

It was Miller's turn to squint, deep in thought, but waiting for me to explain.

"It was as if the cyborg element, even if it was minor, was enough to make them feel like they were no longer constrained by normal, human emotions. Or feelings of decency. Like they—"

I thought about it a little more, trying to assemble the right words to express what I was thinking. Then a memory popped into my head. "Okay, this will sound like a stretch, but hear me out. Years ago, when I was in college, I insisted on hosting a Halloween party. Did it three years in a row. And I noticed something strange.

"When people came to that particular party, they would be in costume, and it made them act differently."

"Different how?"

"I mean, college kids are usually slobs, anyway. But at my Halloween parties, they'd spill shit on the carpet and just ignore it. At any other party, they'd run and get a towel. But not at these parties. Or they'd break shit and just laugh it off."

"Okay," Miller said. "I don't think I follow your thought process here."

"They were in costume," I said. "When people are in costume, they may not think it changes how they behave, but it totally does. It's like they become a different person. Not just that they look different; they *behave* like they're outside their body or something. That they're not responsible for anything. *They're* not doing it; the *character* is doing it." I paused. "Do you see where I'm going with this?"

Miller gave a nod. "Yes. But I want you to say it."

"The NGS—it's like they're in costume full-time. Once their bodies are enhanced, especially with the neuro-link, they not only will feel superior to the rest of us—they will have moved beyond any sense of common decency. They'll no longer be *responsible* for bad behavior."

I sighed. "I don't mind the technological innovations. Hell, nobody on the planet has experienced tech like I have. I'm wary of it all, but I'm not automatically resistant to it. But this? This melding of the investment process with a full-scale replacement of skin and bone? And, on top of that, assimilating my mind with enhanced computer connections?"

I left the questions unanswered. I knew that Miller knew what my answers might be.

Finally, he said, "So what do you recommend? How can we reduce this detachment? And most important: How do we explore changes and keep you rooted in the real Eric Swan?"

I stared at the ceiling again, pondering this.

When I left his office 10 minutes later, I still didn't have the answer.

Join the Swaniverse.
Get cool stuff.

With each new tale you'll learn a little more about Q2's super spy, Eric Swan.

You might also want to know how it all began. Join the Swaniverse and I'll send you Swan's **_Origin_** story as a thank you.

Plus, you'll be the first to learn of each new adventure *before* they're published. Just let me know where to find you.

Two ways to make it happen. Scan this QR code with your phone's camera and it'll take you to the Swaniverse page to sign up.

Or log on to EricSwan.com.

Thanks, and happy reading.
Dom Testa

More Eric Swan
from Dom Testa

Power Trip: Eric Swan Thriller #1

Swan takes on diabolical twins determined to bring down the power grid. If he fails, the country will slip into a dark age of chaos and anarchy.

Poison Control: Eric Swan Thriller #2

A treacherous madman is intent on poisoning the water supply. Swan must outsmart this rogue scholar before he can release his apocalyptic toxin.

God Maker: Eric Swan Thriller #3

Agent One has resurfaced, and he's kidnapped the mother of Q2's investment technology. Swan must not only battle this psychotic killer, but come to grips with his own fears.

Field Agent: Eric Swan Thriller #4

Swan's on the hunt for a tech billionaire who's out to control the world's food supply. But there's a sinister element to the plan with terrifying consequences.

Quiet War: Eric Swan Thriller #5

The world's most destructive hacker, a shadowy figure known only as *Ceti*, is on the brink of toppling the world's economy. How can Swan prevent international chaos when people see the madman as a hero?

Reviews matter.
They really do.

Reviews are critical for independent authors like me.

We don't have mega-publishers in New York or London pumping millions of dollars into promoting our work.

What we do have . . . is you. And you're very important to us.

One honest review from you can do so much to help an indie author. People *do* read them, and they *do* make decisions based on them.

So please, let other thriller fans know what you thought of Eric Swan. It's very appreciated.

Dom Testa

Made in the USA
Columbia, SC
21 July 2023

20686629R00224